She watched Leo straighten up as he **reached out** for the baby and felt a **pang of envy. What would it be like to have a little person so very pleased to see you?**

Wonderful. Amazing.

He slid the sunglasses up onto his head and held his arms out, and she could see the wonder in his eyes.

'She's wet,' Amy warned him, but he just shrugged.

'I don't care. I need a shower anyway. Come here, *mia bellissima bambina*,' Leo said, reaching for the baby, and his fingers brushed Amy's breast and she sucked in her breath. It was barely audible but he heard it, and their eyes clashed and held, his darkening to midnight.

For a moment they both froze. She couldn't breathe, the air jammed solid in her lungs, and then with a muttered apology he lifted Ella out of her arms and turned away, laughing and kissing her all over her face, making her giggle deliciously and freeing Amy from his spell.

After a second of paralysing immobility she grabbed a towel and wrapped it firmly round herself, then gathered up their things and headed for the steps, Leo falling in beside her at the top. They walked back together to their apartment, Ella perched on his shoulders with her little fists knotted in his hair, while he told her a little about his day, and they both pretended that the moment by the pool hadn't happened.

BEST FRIEND TO
WIFE AND MOTHER?

BY
CAROLINE ANDERSON

Published in Great Britain 2015
by Mills & Boon, an imprint of Harlequin (UK) Limited,
Eton House, 18-24 Paradise Road, Richmond, Surrey, TW9 1SR

© 2015 Caroline Anderson

ISBN: 978-0-263-25108-1

23-0215

Harlequin (UK) Limited's policy is to use papers that are natural, renewable and recyclable products and made from wood grown in sustainable forests. The logging and manufacturing processes conform to the legal environmental regulations of the country of origin.

Printed and bound in Spain
by CPI, Barcelona

Caroline Anderson describes herself: 'Mother, writer, armchair gardener, unofficial tearoom researcher and eater of lovely cakes. Not necessarily in that order. I love my family, my friends, reading, writing contemporary love stories, hearing from readers, walks by the sea with coffee/ice-cream/cake thrown in, torrential rain, sunshine in spring/autumn. What I hate: revising manuscripts, losing my pets, fighting with my family, cold weather, hot weather, computers, clothes-shopping. My plans? To keep smiling and writing!'

Huge thanks to Caroline and Adam, and Bryony and Owen, who inadvertently gave me wonderful wedding inspiration, and to Shirley and Roger, Mike and Trice, who invited us to share those days with them.
I love you all.

CHAPTER ONE

'ARE YOU READY?'

He eased a flyaway strand of hair from the corner of her eye, his touch as light as a butterfly's wing, his fingertips lingering for a moment as their eyes met and held. His voice, as familiar to her as her own, was steady and reassuring, but his words didn't reassure her. They sent her mind into free-fall.

They were such simple words, on the surface, but layered beneath were a million unasked and unanswered questions. Questions Leo probably didn't even know he'd asked her. Questions she'd needed to ask herself for months but somehow hadn't got round to.

Was she ready?

For the wedding, yes. The planning had been meticulous, nothing left to chance. Her mother, quietly and efficiently, had seen to that. But the marriage—the *lifetime*—with Nick?

Mingling with the birdsong and the voices of the people clustered outside the church gates were the familiar strains of the organ music.

The overture for her wedding.

No. Her *marriage*. Subtle difference, but hugely significant.

Amy glanced through the doorway of the church and caught the smiles on the row of faces in the back pew, all of them craning their necks to get a better look at her. The

Leabharlanna Poibli Chathair Baile Átha Cliath

villagers at the gate were mostly there for Leo, hoping to catch a glimpse of their favourite son, but these people in the church—her friends, Nick's—were here to see her marry Nick.

Today.

Right now.

Her heart skittered under the fitted bodice that suddenly seemed so tight she could hardly breathe.

I can't do this—!

No choice. Too late now for cold feet. If she'd been going to change her mind she should have done it ages ago, before the wheels of this massive train that was her wedding had been set in motion. Or later, at a push—but not now, so late it was about to hit the buffers.

The church was full, the food cooked, the champagne on ice. And Nick would be standing at the altar, waiting for her.

Dear, kind, lovely Nick, who'd been there for her when her life had been in chaos, who'd just—been there, for the last three years, her friend and companion and cheerleader. Her lover. And she did love him. She did…

Enough to marry him? Till death us do part, and all that? Or is it just the easiest thing to do?

You can *stop this,* the voice whispered in her head. *It's not too late.*

But it was. Way too late. She was marrying Nick.

Today.

A curious calm settled over her, as if a switch had been flicked, turning on the autopilot, steadying her fall into oblivion. The voice in her head didn't care.

Just because it's easy, because you know he'll be a good husband and father and he's safe? Is that enough?

Of course it was enough. It was just nerves unsettling her. That was all. Last-minute nerves. Nick was—fine.

Fine? Like safe, steady, reliable, predictable—that kind

of fine? No chemistry, no fireworks? And whatever happened to amazing?

She tuned the voice out. There were more important things than amazing. Trust, fidelity, respect—and chemistry was overrated—

How do you know that? You don't know that. You haven't got a clue, you've never felt it. And if you marry Nick, you never will...

She stifled the voice again, stuffing it firmly back in its box; then, easing her death grip on the bouquet, she straightened her shoulders, tilted up her chin and gave Leo her most convincing and dazzling smile.

'Yes,' she said firmly. 'I'm ready.'

Leo felt his breath catch at that smile.

When had she grown up? Turned into this stunningly lovely woman, instead of the slightly chubby, relentlessly accident-prone girl who'd dogged his footsteps for ever? He'd turned his back for what felt like five minutes, and she'd been transformed.

More like five years, though, give or take, and a lot of water under the bridge for both of them. Far too much, in his case, and so much of it tainted by regret.

He cradled her pale cheek in his hand, and felt her quiver. She was nervous. Of course she was. Who wouldn't be, on their wedding day? It was a hell of a commitment. Literally, in his case.

'You look beautiful, Amy,' he said gruffly, looking down into the wide grey eyes of this lovely young woman he'd known so well but now hardly knew at all. 'He's a lucky man.'

'Thank you.'

Her eyes searched his, a flicker of uncertainty in them echoing the tiny tremor in her cheek, the smile on her lush, pink lips a little hesitant now, and he felt himself frown.

Second thoughts? About time. There was nothing wrong with the man she was marrying, from what little he'd seen of him—in fact, he'd liked him, a lot—but they just didn't seem *right* for each other.

There was no chemistry between them, no zing that he could see. Maybe she didn't want that? Maybe she just wanted safe and comfortable? And maybe that was a really, really good idea.

Or maybe not, not for Amy...

He hesitated another second, then took her hand in his, his thumb slowly stroking the back of it in a subconscious gesture of comfort. Her fingers were cold, trembling slightly in his, reinforcing his concern. He squeezed them gently.

'Amy, I'm going to ask you something. It's only what your father would have done, so please don't take it the wrong way, but—are you sure you want to do this? Because if not, you can still turn around and walk away. It's your life, no one else's, and nobody else can decide this for you.'

His voice dropped, his frown deepening as he struggled to get the importance of this across to her before it was too late. If only someone had done this for him...

'Don't do it unless it's right, Amy, unless you really, truly love him. Take it from me, marrying the wrong person for the wrong reasons is a recipe for disaster. You have to be absolutely, completely and utterly sure that it's the right thing to do and for the right reasons.'

A shadow flitted across her eyes, her fingers tightening on his, and after an infinitesimal pause that seemed to last an eternity, she nodded. 'Yes. Yes, of course I'm sure.'

But she didn't look sure, and he certainly wasn't, but it was nothing to do with him, was it? Not his decision to make. And the shadows in her eyes could just as easily be sadness because her much-loved father wasn't here to give her away. Nothing to do with her choice of groom...

Not your business who she chooses to love. God knows, you're no expert. And he could be a lot, lot worse.

He hauled in a breath.

'OK. Ready to go, then?'

She nodded, but he saw her swallow again, and for a moment he wondered if she'd changed her mind.

And then she straightened up and took a breath, hooked her hand through his arm and flashed a smile over her shoulder at her bridesmaids. 'OK, girls? Good to go?'

They both nodded, and he felt her hand tighten on his arm.

'OK, then. Let's do this.' Her eyes flicked up and met Leo's, her fake smile pinned in place by sheer determination, but it didn't waver and anybody else might have been convinced.

Not your business. He nodded to the usher, who nodded to the organist, and after a moment's silence, broken only by the shuffling of the congregation getting to their feet and the clearing of a few throats, the evocative strains of Pachelbel's *Canon in D Major* filled the church.

He laid his hand over hers, squeezed her fingers and felt them grip his. He glanced down, into those liquid grey eyes that seemed flooded with doubt despite the brave smile, and his gut clenched.

He'd known her for ever, rescued her from a million scrapes, both literal and otherwise; dammit, she was his best friend, or had been before the craziness that was his life had got in the way, and he couldn't bear to see her make the mistake of her life.

Don't do it, Amy. Please, don't do it!

'It's still not too late,' he said gruffly, his voice muted, his head tilted towards her so only she could hear.

'Yes, it is,' she said, so softly he barely heard her, then

she dredged up that expected smile again and took the first step forward.

Damn.

He swallowed the lump in his throat and slowly, steadily, walked her down the aisle.

With every step, her legs felt heavier and more reluctant, her heart pounding, the sense of unease settling closer around her, chilling her to the bone.

What are you doing?

Nick was there, watching her thoughtfully. Warily?

It's still not too late.

She felt Leo ease his arm out from under her hand and step away, and she felt—abandoned?

It was her wedding day. She should feel a sense of joy, of completeness, of utter, bone-deep rightness—but she didn't.

Not at all.

And, as she glanced up at Nick, she realised that neither did he. Either that, or he was paralysed by nerves, which was unlikely. He wasn't remotely the nervous type.

He took her hand briefly, squeezed it in reassurance, but it felt wrong. So wrong...

She eased it away, using the excuse of handing her bouquet to the waiting bridesmaid, and then the vicar spoke, everyone started to sing 'Jerusalem', and she felt her mouth move automatically while her mind whirled. *Her mind*, this time, not the voice in her head giving her grief, or a moment of panic, stage fright, last-minute nerves or whatever. This time it was really her, finally asking all the questions Leo's 'Are you ready?' had prompted.

What are we doing? *And why? Who for?*

The last echoes of the hymn filtered away, and the vicar did the just cause or impediment bit. *Was* there a just cause? Was not loving him enough sufficient? And then she saw the vicar's lips move as he began to speak the words of the marriage service, drowned out by her thudding heart and the whirlwind in her head.

Until he said, 'Who gives this woman to be married to this man?' and Leo stepped forward, took her hand with a tiny, barely perceptible squeeze, and gave it—gave her—to Nick.

Dear Nick. Lovely, kind, dependable Nick, ready to make her his wife, give her the babies they both longed for, grow old with her...

But Nick hesitated. When the vicar asked if he would take this woman to be his wife, he hesitated. And then—was that a shrug?—his mouth twisted in a wry smile and he said, 'I will.'

The vicar turned, spoke to her, but she wasn't really listening any more. She was staring into Nick's eyes, searching them for the truth, and all she could see was duty.

Duty from him, and duty from her? Because they'd come this far before either of them had realised it was bound to be—what were Leo's words?—a disaster?

She gripped his hands. 'Will you? Will you *really*?' she asked under her breath. 'Because I'm not sure I can.'

Behind her she heard the slight suck of Leo's indrawn breath, the rustle from the congregation, the whispered undertone of someone asking what she'd said.

And then Nick smiled—the first time he'd really smiled at her in weeks, she realised—and put his arms around her, and hugged her against his broad, solid chest. It shook with what could have been a huff of laughter, and he squeezed her tight.

His breath brushed her cheek, his words soft in her ear. 'You cut that a bit fine, my love.'

She felt the tension flow out of her like air out of a punctured balloon, and if he hadn't been holding her she would have crumpled.

'I did, didn't I? I'm sorry, Nick, but I just can't do this,' she murmured.

'I know; it doesn't feel right, does it? I thought it would, but…it just doesn't. And better now than later.' She felt his arms slacken as he raised his head and looked over her shoulder.

'Time to go, sweetheart,' he murmured, his mouth tugging into a wistful smile. 'Leo's waiting for you. He'll make sure you're all right.' He kissed her gently on the cheek and stepped back, his smile a little unsteady now. 'Be happy, Amy.'

She searched his eyes, and saw regret and relief, and her eyes welled with tears. 'You, too,' she said silently, and took a step back, then another one, and collided with Leo's solid warmth.

His hands cupped her elbows, supporting her as everything slowly righted itself. She turned to him, met those steady golden eyes and whispered, 'Thank you.'

And then she picked up her skirts and ran.

She'd done it. She'd actually done it. Walked—no, sprinted, or as close to it as she could in those ridiculous shoes—away from disaster.

Leo watched her go, her mother and bridesmaids hurrying after her, watched Nick turn to his best man and sit down on the pew behind him as if his strings had been cut, and realised it was all down to him. Appropriate, really, since in a way he was the cause of it.

He hauled in a deep breath, turned to the stunned congregation and gave them his best media smile.

'Ladies and gentlemen, it seems there isn't going to be a wedding today after all. I'm not sure of the protocol for this kind of thing, but there's food ready and waiting for you in the marquee, and any of you who'd like to come back and enjoy it will be more than welcome to do so before you head off. I gather the chef comes highly recommended,' he added drily, and there was a ripple of laughter that broke the tension.

He nodded to his father, who nodded back, pulling his mobile phone out of his pocket to set the ball rolling with their catering team, and with a brief nod to the vicar, Leo strode swiftly down the aisle and out of the church after Amy.

The sun warmed him, the gentle rays bringing the life back into his limbs, and he realised he'd been stone cold at the prospect of watching her make a disastrous mistake. He flexed his fingers as he walked over to the vintage Bentley and peered inside.

She was in there, perched on the seat in a billowing cloud of tulle and lace, surrounded by her mother and bridesmaids all clucking like mother hens, and the villagers gathered around the gate were agog. As well they might be.

He ducked his head inside the car.

'Amy?' he murmured, and she stared blankly up at him. She looked lost, shocked and confused and just a little crazy, and he could read the desperate appeal in her eyes.

'Take her home, I'll follow,' he instructed the driver tersely, and as the car whisked her away one of the crowd at the gate yelled, 'What's going on, Leo?'

He didn't answer. They could see what was going on, they just didn't know why, and he had better things to do than stand around and tittle-tattle. He turned to scan the throng of puzzled guests spilling out of the church, milling aimlessly around, unsure of what to do next, and in the midst of them he found his parents heading towards him.

'Is she all right?' his mother asked worriedly, and he nodded.

'I think so. She will be. Let's get out of here. We've got things to do.'

* * *

She'd done it.

Stopped the train and run away—from Nick, from the certainty of her carefully planned and mapped-out future, from everything that made up her life, and she felt lost. Cast adrift, swamped by a million conflicting emotions, unsure of what to do or think or feel.

Actually, she couldn't feel anything much. Just numbness, a sort of strange hollowness deep in her chest as if there was nothing there any more.

Better than the ice-cold dread of doing the wrong thing, but not much.

She tugged off her veil, handing it to her bridesmaids. If she could she would have taken the dress off, too, there and then. She couldn't get out of it fast enough. Couldn't get out of all of it fast enough, the church, the dress, the car—the country?

She almost laughed, but the hysteria bubbling in her throat threatened to turn to tears so she clamped her teeth shut and crushed it ruthlessly down. Not now. Not yet.

'Are you all right, darling?' Her mother's face was troubled but calm, and Amy heaved a shaky sigh of relief. At least she wasn't going off the deep end. Not that her mother was a deep-end kind of person, but you never knew. And her daughter hadn't ever jilted anyone at the altar before, so the situation wasn't exactly tried and tested.

'Yes, I'm fine. I'm really sorry, Mum.'

'Don't be. It's the first sensible thing you've done for months.'

Amy stared at her, astonished. 'I thought you liked him?'

'I do like him! He's lovely. I just don't think he's right for you. You don't have that spark.'

Not her, too, joining in with her alter ego and reminding her she'd been about to do the wrong thing for the wrong reasons and should have pulled out much, much earlier.

Or he should. Both of them, for everyone's sake. Oh, what a mess!

The car door opened, and she realised they'd come to rest on the drive. Gathering up her skirts, she climbed awkwardly out and headed for the front door. Her mother unlocked it and pushed it open and Amy was swept inside on the tide of her redundant bridesmaids, into the hallway of the house she'd left such a short time before as a bride on the brink of a nice, safe, sensible marriage. Now she was—she didn't know what she was.

A runaway bride?

Such a cliché. She gave a smothered laugh and shook her head.

'I need to get out of this dress,' she muttered, kicking off her shoes and heading for the stairs and the sanctuary of her bedroom.

'I'll come,' her mother said, and they all fell in behind her, threatening to suffocate her with kindness.

She paused on the third stair and turned back. 'No, Mum. Actually, none of you. I think I'd like to be alone for a moment.'

They ground to a halt, three pairs of worried eyes studying her. Checking to see if she'd lost her marbles, probably. Wrong. She'd just found them, at the absolutely last minute. *Oh, Nick, I'm sorry...*

'Are you sure you're all right?' her mother asked, her face creased with concern.

'Yes,' she said, more firmly this time. 'Yes, I'm sure.' Sure about everything except what her future held. 'Don't worry, I'm not going to do anything stupid.' Or at least, nothing as stupid as marrying the wrong man would have been. Not that she knew who the right one was, or how she'd recognise him. She seemed to have a gift for getting it wrong.

They were all still standing there as if they didn't know

what to do now their carefully planned schedule had been thrown out the window, but it was no good asking her. She didn't have a clue. She turned back to the stairs, putting one foot in front of the other, skirts bunched in her quivering hands.

'Shall I bring you up a cup of tea?' her mother asked, breaking the silence.

Tea. Of course. The universal panacea. And it would give her mother something to do. 'That would be lovely, Mum. Whenever you're ready. Don't rush.'

'I'll put the kettle on.'

Her mother disappeared into the kitchen, the bridesmaids trailing in her wake as one after the other they came out of their trances, and she made it to the safety of her bedroom and shut the door before the bubble burst and the first tears fell.

Odd, that she was crying when she felt so little. It was just a release of tension, but without the tension there was nothing, just a yawning chasm opening up in front of her, and she thought she was going to fall apart. Pressing her hand to her mouth to stifle the sobs, she slid down the door, crumpling to the floor in a billowing cloud of lace and petticoats, and let the floodgates open.

He had to get to her.

He could only imagine what state she was in, but that look in her eyes when she'd glanced up in the car—

He pulled up on the driveway of his family home, and after checking that the baby was all right and the catering was under control he headed through the gate in the fence into Amy's garden and tapped on the kitchen door.

Amy's mother let him in, her face troubled. 'Oh, Leo, I'm so glad you're here,' she said, and hugged him briefly, her composure wobbling for a second.

'How is she?' he asked.

'I don't know. She's gone upstairs. She wouldn't let us go—said she needed to be alone. I've made her a cup of tea, I was just about to take it up.'

'Give it to me. I'll go and talk to her. This is my fault.'

'Your fault?'

He gave her a wry smile. 'I asked her if she was sure.'

Jill smiled back at him and kissed his cheek. 'Well, thank God you did, Leo. I haven't had the guts. Here, take it. And get her out of here, can you? She doesn't need all this hoopla.'

He nodded, took the tea and headed for the stairs. Her bedroom was over the kitchen, with a perfect view of the marquee on his parents' lawn and the steady stream of guests who were arriving for the wedding reception that wasn't.

Damn.

He crossed the landing and tapped on her bedroom door.

Someone was knocking.

Her mother, probably. She dropped her head back against the door and sucked in a breath. She wasn't ready to face her. Wasn't ready to face anyone—

'Amy? Can I come in?'

Leo. Her mother must have sent him up. She heard the knob turn, could feel the door gently pushing her in the back, but she couldn't move. Didn't want to move. She wanted to stay there for ever, hiding from everyone, until she'd worked out what had happened and what she was going to do with the rest of her life.

His voice came through the door again, low and gentle. 'Amy? Let me in, sweetheart. I've got a cup of tea for you.'

It was the tea that made her move. That, and the reassuring normality of his voice. She shuffled over, hauling her voluminous skirts with her, and he pushed the door gently inwards until he could squeeze past it and shut it behind him.

She sniffed hard, and she heard him tutting softly. He crouched down, his face coming into view, his eyes scanning the mess her face must be. She scrubbed her cheeks with her hands and he held out a wad of tissues.

He'd even come prepared, she thought, and the tears began again.

She heard the soft click of his tongue as he tutted again, the gentle touch of his hand on her hair. 'Oh, Amy.'

He put the tea down, sat on the floor next to her and hauled her into his arms. 'Come here, you silly thing. You'll be OK. It'll all work out in the end.'

'Will it? How? What am I going to do?' she mumbled into his shoulder, busily shredding the sodden tissues in her lap. 'I've given up my job, I'd already given up my flat—we were about to move out of his flat and buy a family house and have babies, and I was going to try going freelance with my photography, and now…I don't have a life any more, Leo. It's all gone, every part of it. I just walked away from it and I feel as if I've stepped off a cliff. I must be mad!'

Leo's heart contracted.

Poor Amy. She sounded utterly lost, and it tugged at something deep inside him, some part of him that had spent years protecting her from the fallout of her impulsive nature. He hugged her closer, rocking her gently against his chest. 'I don't think you're mad. I think it's the first sensible thing you've done in ages,' he told her gently, echoing her mother's words.

She shifted so she could see his face. 'How come everybody else knew this except me?' she said plaintively. 'Why am I so stupid?'

'You aren't stupid. He's a nice guy. He's just not the right man for you. If he was, you wouldn't have hesitated for a moment, and nor would he. And it didn't seem to me as if you'd broken his heart. Quite the opposite.'

'No.' There'd been nothing heartbroken, she thought, about the flash of relief in his eyes in that fleeting moment. Sadness, yes, but no heartbreak. 'I suppose he was just doing the decent thing.'

Leo's eyes clouded and he turned away. 'Yeah. Trust me, it doesn't work.'

'Was that what you did?' she asked him, momentarily distracted from her own self-induced catastrophe. 'The decent thing? When you married the wrong person for the wrong reasons?'

A muscle bunched in his jaw. 'Something like that. Are you going to drink this tea or not?'

She took the mug that he was holding out to her, cradled it in both hands and sighed shakily.

'You OK now?'

She nodded. She was, she realised. Just about, so long as she didn't have to make any more decisions, because clearly she was unqualified in that department. She sipped her tea, lifted her head and rested it back against the wall with another shaky little sigh. 'I will be. I don't know; I just feel—I can't explain—as if I can't trust myself any more. I don't know who I am, and I thought I knew. Does that make sense, Leo?'

'Absolutely. Been there, done that, worn out the T-shirt.'

She turned to him, searching his face and finding only kindness and concern. No reproach. No disappointment in her. Just Leo, doing what he always did, getting her out of the mess she'd got herself into.

Again.

'Leo, will you get me out of here?' she asked unevenly. 'I can't stay here, not with all this…'

'Of course I will. That's what I'm here for.'

'To rescue me? Poor you. I bet you thought you were done with all that at last.'

'What, me? Change the habits of a lifetime?' he teased, and she had to laugh, even though it wasn't really remotely funny.

She glanced down at herself, then at him. He'd abandoned the tailcoat, loosened the rose-pink cravat which showed off his olive skin to perfection, and turned back the cuffs on his immaculate white shirt to reveal strong wrists above hands criss-crossed with fine white scars. Chef's hands, he called them, but the scars didn't detract from his appeal, not in any way. He'd been fighting girls off with a stick since he'd hit puberty, and the scars hadn't put them off at all.

She managed a small smile. 'We might have to change first, before we go.'

His lips quirked. 'You think? I thought I looked rather good like this.'

So did she, but then she thought he looked good in anything.

'You do, but if the press catch a glimpse of us, they'll think the nation's favourite celebrity chef's secretly tied the knot again,' she said, her mouth on autopilot, and his face clouded.

'Yeah, well, it'll be a cold day in hell before that ever happens,' he said tightly, and she could have kicked herself for blundering all over such a sensitive area. She closed her eyes and let out an anguished sigh.

'Oh, God, Leo, I'm so sorry. I can't believe I said that—'

'It's OK, it doesn't matter, and you're quite right. I don't need that sort of publicity, and neither do you.' He smiled fleetingly, then looked away again. 'So, anywhere in particular you want to go?'

'I don't know. Got any ideas?'

He shrugged. 'Not really. My house is still crawling

with builders, and I have to fly to Tuscany tomorrow on business.'

'Oh.' Her heart sank at the thought of him going, and she felt her smile slip. 'I don't suppose you want to smuggle me out there in your luggage?' she joked weakly, and propped up her wavering smile. 'I promise not to be a nuisance.'

'How many times have I heard you say that?' he murmured drily, and she felt a wash of guilt flood over her.

He was right—she was always imposing on him, getting him to extract her from one mess or another. Or she had done, back in the days when they really had been best friends. And that was years ago.

She forced herself to ease away from him, to stop leaning on him, both metaphorically and physically. Time to get out her big girl pants and put their friendship on a more equal and adult footing.

She scraped up the last smile in the bottom of the bucket and plastered it on her face.

'I'm sorry, I was only joking. I know you can't. Don't worry about me, Leo, I'll be all right. It's my mess, I'll clear it up.'

Somehow...

CHAPTER TWO

HE COULDN'T DO IT.

He couldn't desert her when her life had just turned upside down—and anyway, it might well be the perfect solution for both of them.

He'd been worrying about leaving tomorrow and abandoning her with the repercussions of all this, worrying about how he was going to juggle his tiny daughter and business meetings, and here was the answer, on a plate. Unless...

He studied her thoughtfully, searching her face for clues. '*Were* you joking about coming with me? Because if not, it could be a great idea. Not the smuggling, obviously, but if you did it could solve both our problems.'

A tiny frown appeared. 'You've got a problem?'

He nodded. 'Sort of. I've got meetings to go to, and business and babies don't mix. Normally I'd leave Ella behind with my parents, but this is going to be for several days and it's not fair on them at their age, especially on top of the wedding—and don't say it,' he added, pressing a finger lightly on her lips to stifle the apology he knew was coming.

She took hold of his hand and moved it away. 'Why not, since it's true? It *is* my fault, and they've gone to so much trouble—'

He pulled his hand back and placed it firmly over her mouth to silence her before she got back onto that again.

'I don't want to argue, Amy. Hear me out. Please?'

She nodded, and he lowered his hand and carried on. 'I like to be there for Ella every day, even if it's only for part of it, even if it means dragging her around with me. It's the only way I've been able to look after her and my business, and it's a precarious balance that so far seems to be working. I don't want to upset that balance, abandon her for days and nights on end—and anyway, shortly after I get back I start filming the next TV series for eight weeks or so, and I'm going to need my parents' goodwill for that. If you would come to Italy with us and look after her just while I'm in the meetings, it would be amazingly helpful.'

Amy eyed him thoughtfully. 'Really? You mean it? I *was* only joking, really. I didn't expect you to say yes. I was just trying to—I don't know. Make light of it, really. I don't want to be a burden to you.'

'Absolutely I mean it, and you wouldn't be a burden. Not at all. You'd be a real help. I'm trying to set up a contract with a family there to supply our restaurants. I tasted some of their products at a trade fair, and I was really impressed. I want to see how they operate, taste the whole range, negotiate the price and see if we can strike a deal. And doing all that with Ella on my hip *really* won't work.'

She laughed a little wryly. 'No, I can see that. Not exactly professional, and not really fair on her, either.'

'No, it isn't, and she's my top priority. If necessary, I'd cut the trip short rather than compromise my relationship with her, but I don't want to have to do that, because this is a really great business opportunity and it could be important for her future as well as mine.

'So—will you come? You'll have lots of free time to take photos, and it's beautiful at this time of year. You can chill out away from all this, get some thinking time, clear your head, work out what you're going to do next.

Maybe work on a portfolio of images, if that's where you think you're going.'

It sounded tempting. Very tempting, and she could see that he quite genuinely needed her help. He wasn't just making it up—and anyway, even if he was, did she have a better choice? No. And to stay here another minute was unthinkable.

She could hear the sounds of people thronging outside in the garden—not their garden, but his parents' garden next door, where the marquee had been set up for the reception.

Her hand flew to her mouth, her eyes locked on his. 'Oh, Leo! All that food…!'

She was swamped with guilt, but he shook his head briskly, brushing it aside as if it was nothing. Which it wasn't, far from it.

'It's not wasted. There are lots of people there to eat it, it's fine.'

'Fine?' It wasn't fine. Nothing was fine, and all of a sudden she was overwhelmed again. 'It was supposed to be a *wedding* present from you, and I didn't even *have* the wedding.'

'Oh, Amy,' he sighed, and pulled her head back down against his shoulder, soothing her as the tears spilled down her cheeks yet again and the enormity of what she'd done, the chaos she'd caused, the things she'd walked away from, gradually sank in and left her breathless with guilt and remorse.

'I can't even pay you back,' she choked out, but he tutted softly and cradled her head against that solid, familiar shoulder that felt so good she could have stayed there for ever.

'Hush. You don't need to. Forget it, Amy, it's the least important thing in the world right now. Don't worry about it.'

She pushed herself up, swiping the tears off her cheeks

with her palms. 'But I *am* worried about it! At least let me pay you back for it when I get a job.'

If she ever did. Publishing was in a state of flux, and she'd just walked away from a great career in a really good publishing house because she'd thought she'd have financial security with Nick and could afford to try freelancing with her photography, and now she had nothing! No job, no home, no husband, no future—and all because of some vague sense of unease? She must have been mad—

'OK, so here's the deal,' he said, cutting off her tumbling thoughts with a brisk, no-nonsense tone. 'Come to Tuscany with me. Look after Ella while I'm in meetings, so I can work all day with a clear conscience and still put her to bed every night, and we'll call it quits.'

'*Quits*? Are you *crazy*? I know what your outside catering costs, Leo!'

He gave her a wry grin. 'There's a substantial mark-up. The true cost is nothing like the tariff. And you know how precious my daughter is to me. Nothing could be more important than leaving her with someone I can trust while I'm over there.'

He gripped her hands, his eyes fixed on hers. 'Come with us, look after her while I'm in meetings, have a holiday, some time out while you work out what to do next. And take photos for me—pictures of me cooking, of the produce, the region, the markets—all of it. Your photos are brilliant, and I can use them for my blog. That would be really valuable to me, so much more professional, and certainly something I'd pay good money for. I usually do it myself and blag people into taking photos of me with chefs and market traders and artisans, and if I'm really stuck I get reduced to taking selfies, and that's *so* not a good look!'

She laughed, a funny little sound between a chuckle and a sob that she quickly stifled, and he hugged her again.

'Come on. Do this for me—please? It would be so help-ful I can't tell you, and it'll get you away from all this. You're exhausted and you need to get away, have a total change of scene. And I need you, Amy. I'm not making it up. Not for the photos, they're just a valuable added bonus, but for Ella, and I can't put a price on her safety and happiness.'

She searched his eyes again, and saw behind the reas-suringly calm exterior that he was telling her the truth. He wasn't just being kind to her, he really was in a jam, and he'd never ever asked her for help, although God knows he'd given her enough over the years, bailing her out of umpteen scrapes.

Not to mention the catering.

No. She had no choice—and she realised she didn't want a choice. She wanted to be with Leo. His sound common sense was exactly what she needed to get her through this, and let's face it, she thought, he's had enough practice at dealing with me and my appalling life choices.

She nodded. 'OK. I'll come—of course I'll come, and I'll help you with Ella and take photos and do whatever else I can while you're there. It'll be a pleasure to help you, and it's high time I gave you something back. On one condition, though.'

'Which is?' he asked warily.

'I help you with her care when the filming starts—take some of the burden off your parents. Then I'll call it quits.'

'That's a big commitment.'

'I know that, but that's the deal. Take it or leave it.'

His shoulders dropped, relief written all over him, and she felt some of the tension leave her, too.

'I'll take it. And thank you, Amy. Thank you so much.' His brow furrowed. 'Do you have a case packed ready to go?'

'Yes. I've got smart-casual, beach, jeans—will that do?'

He nodded and got to his feet. 'Sounds fine. I'll get
Ella's stuff together and we'll go. I'm not sure, but we
might even be able to fly out today.'

'Today!'

'Is that a problem?'

She shook her head vehemently. 'No. Not at all. The
sooner the better. I was just surprised. I thought you said
you were going tomorrow.'

'I was, but today would be better and I seem to be unexpectedly free now,' he added, that wry grin tugging at
his mouth and making her want to hug him. 'I'll see what
I can do. How soon can you be ready?'

She shrugged. 'Half an hour? Twenty minutes, maybe?'

'OK. I'll call if there's a problem. Don't forget your
passport—and your camera.'

'In my bag. Just do one thing for me before you go. Get
me out of this dress? I'd forgotten all the stupid buttons.'

She scrambled to her feet and turned her back to him,
and he began undoing the million and one tiny satin buttons and loops that covered the zip underneath. And as he
worked, button by button, he became suddenly, intensely
aware of the smooth, creamy skin of her shoulders, the fine
line of her neck, the slender column of her throat. He could
see a pulse beating under the skin at the side, and feel the
tension coming off her. Off him, too, but for an entirely
different reason. Crazy. This was Amy, for goodness' sake!
She was his childhood best friend, virtually his sister!

He finally freed the last button and slid the concealed
zip down, and she caught the dress against her chest and
turned to face him, a peep of cleavage above some trans-
parent lacy undergarment taking him by surprise. He
hauled his eyes up away from it, shocked by the sudden
heat that flared through his body.

Really?

Amy?

He backed up a step. 'OK now?' he asked tersely, his throat tight.

'Yes. Thank you. I'll get changed and see you downstairs in a few minutes.'

'Good. Wear something comfortable for travelling.' Preferably something that covered her up. He backed away further, turning on his heel and reaching for the door handle, suddenly desperate to get out of there.

'Leo?'

Her voice checked him and he turned and looked at her over his shoulder, raising an eyebrow in question.

'I'm starving. Grab some food to take with us, would you?'

Food? He laughed, letting some of the tension go. Food was easy. Food he could do.

'Sure. See you in a bit.'

He called the catering manager on the way down the stairs, rang his mother to prime her and went into the kitchen.

Three pairs of eyes locked on him instantly. 'How is she?'

'She'll do. Jill, can you help her get ready? I'm taking her to Tuscany with me and we're leaving as soon as possible. I'm trying to get a flight this afternoon.'

'Tuscany? Brilliant, it's just what she needs.' She went up on tiptoe and kissed his cheek. 'Thank you, Leo. Bless you. She'll be ready.'

It was tight.

While he packed he rang the charter company he used from time to time, and found they had a small jet flying to Florence for a pick-up; he could hire the whole plane for the 'empty leg' rate, but it was leaving City Airport at three. And it was twelve forty already.

Tight, but doable, if she was ready to go. He rang to

warn her, loaded the car in no time flat and drove straight round there, reaching the front door as Amy opened it.

'I'm ready,' she said, her smile a little forced in her pale face, her eyes still red-rimmed, but there was life in them now, unlike the blank eyes of the woman he'd walked down the aisle less than an hour ago. Sure, she was hanging by a thread, but she'd make it, especially once he'd got her out of here, and he was suddenly fiercely glad that he'd managed to convince her to come with him.

'Got your passport?'

'Yes, I've got everything. What's the luggage limit?'

He smiled wryly. 'There isn't one. It's a private charter.'

Her jaw dropped slightly. 'Private—?'

He pushed her chin up gently with an index finger and smiled at her stunned expression. 'It's going on an empty leg to pick someone up—I'm only paying a fraction of the normal charge.' Which was still extortionate, but she didn't need to know that.

'Wow. Great. OK.' She turned to her mother, hugged her hard, hugged her bridesmaids and got in the car.

'Thank you, Leo,' Jill called, and he lifted a hand as he slid behind the wheel and closed the door.

'Did you get food?' Amy asked, and he leant over into the back and pulled out an insulated bag.

'Here. You can feed me en route.'

'Or I might just eat it all.'

'Piglet. Buckle up,' he instructed, but she was there already, her bottom lip caught between her teeth, the eyes that kept flicking to his filled with a welter of emotions that he couldn't begin to analyse. He didn't suppose she could, either, but there seemed to be a glimmer of something that could have been excitement.

He smiled at her, and she smiled back, but it was a fleeting parody of her usual open, happy smile, and he felt another sudden pang of guilt. What if it wasn't excitement?

What if it was hysteria? She was on a knife-edge, he knew that. Had he imposed his own feelings about marriage on her? Put doubts in her mind when they hadn't really been there at all? He hoped not—even if Nick hadn't been right for her, it wasn't his call to sabotage their wedding.

'You OK?'

She nodded. 'Yes—or I will be, just as soon as we get out of here.'

'Let's go, then,' he said, and starting the engine he pulled smoothly off the drive and headed for London.

Amy had never flown in such luxury.

From start to finish, boarding the little jet had been a breeze. They'd driven right up to the Jet Centre terminal, their luggage and the baby's car seat and buggy were handed over, and the car had been whisked away to secure parking. The security check-in was thorough but almost instant, and then they had a short walk to the plane.

At the top of the steps the pilot greeted them by name as he welcomed them aboard, gave them their ETA, a benign weather report and told them there was a car waiting for them at Florence. Then he disappeared through the galley area into the cockpit and closed the door, leaving them with the entire little jet to themselves, and for the first time she registered her surroundings.

'Wow.' She felt her jaw dropping slightly, and no wonder. It was like another world, a world she'd never entered before or even dreamed of.

There were no endless rows of seating, no central aisle barely wide enough to pass through, no hard-wearing gaudy seat fabric in a budget airline's colours. Instead, there were two small groups of pale leather seats, the ones at the rear bracketing tables large enough to set up a laptop, play games, eat a meal, or simply flick through a magazine and glance out of the window. And Ella's car seat was securely strapped in all ready for her.

Leo headed that way and she followed, the tight, dense pile of the carpet underfoot making her feel as if she was walking on air. Maybe she was? Maybe they'd already taken off and she just hadn't noticed? Or maybe it was all part of the weird, dreamlike state she'd been in ever since she'd turned her back on Nick and walked away.

A wave of dizziness washed over her, and she grabbed the back of one of the seats to steady herself and felt Leo's hand at her waist, steering her to a seat at the back of the plane across the aisle from Ella's.

'Sit. And don't argue,' he added firmly.

She didn't argue. She was beyond arguing. She just sat obediently like a well-trained Labrador, sinking into the butter-soft cream leather as her legs gave way, watching him while he strapped little Ella into her seat, his big hands gentle and competent as he assembled the buckle and clicked it firmly into place.

She hoped she never had to do it. It looked extraordinarily complicated for something so simple, and she was suddenly swamped with doubts about her ability to do this.

What on earth did she know about babies? Less than nothing. You could write it all in capitals on the head of a very small pin. He must be nuts to trust her with his child.

She heard voices as a man and woman in uniform came up the steps and into the plane, and moments later the door was shut and the woman was approaching them with a smile, her hand extended.

'Mr Zacharelli.'

Leo shook her hand and returned the smile. 'Julie, isn't it? We've flown together before.'

'We have, sir. It's a pleasure to welcome you and Ella on board again, and Miss Driver, I believe? I'm your cabin crew today, and if there's anything you need, don't hesitate to ask.'

She smiled at Amy as they shook hands, and turned her attention back to Leo.

'May I go through the pre-flight safety procedure with you?' she asked, and he delved into the baby's bag and handed Ella a crackly, brightly coloured dragonfly toy to distract her while Julie launched into the familiar spiel.

It took a few minutes, showing them the overhead oxygen, the emergency exit—all the usual things, but with the massive difference that she was talking only to them, and the smiles she gave were personal. Especially to Leo, Amy thought, and mentally rolled her eyes at yet another effortless conquest on his part. He probably wasn't even aware of it.

And then it was done, another smile flashed in his direction, and Julie took herself off and left them alone.

'Was that from me?' Amy asked, pointing at the dragonfly toy Ella was happily playing with.

Leo nodded, sending her a fleeting smile. 'You sent her it when she was born. She loves it. I have to take it everywhere with us.'

That made her smile. At least she'd done one thing right, then, in the last year or so. He zipped the bag up, stashed it in the baggage compartment, put her hand luggage in there, too, and sat down opposite Ella and across from Amy.

His tawny gold eyes searched hers thoughtfully.

'You OK now?'

If you don't count the butterflies stampeding around in my stomach like a herd of elephants, she thought, but she said nothing, just nodded, and he raised a brow a fraction but didn't comment.

'Do you always travel like this?' she asked, still slightly stunned by their surroundings but rapidly getting used to it.

He laughed softly. 'Only if I'm travelling with Ella or

if time's short. Usually I go business class. It's just much easier with a baby to travel somewhere private. I'm sure you've been in a plane when there's been a screaming baby—like this,' he added, as Ella caught sight of the bottle he'd tried to sneak out of his pocket so he could fasten his seat belt. She reached for it, little hands clenching and unclenching as she started to whimper, and Leo hid the bottle under the table.

'No, *mia bella,* not yet,' he said gently, and the whimper escalated to an indignant wail.

Amy laughed softly. 'Right on cue.'

She propped her elbows on the table and leant towards Ella, smiling at her and waggling her dragonfly in an attempt to distract her.

'Hi, sweet pea,' she crooned softly. 'You aren't really going to scream all the way there, are you? No, of course not!'

Finally distracted from the bottle, Ella beamed at her and squashed the toy. It made a lovely, satisfying noise, so she did it again, and Leo chuckled.

'Babies are refreshingly easy to please. Give them a toy and they're happy.'

'Like men, really. Fast car, big TV, fancy coffee maker... private jet—'

He gave a soft snort and shot her a look. 'Don't push it. And don't get lulled into a false sense of security because you managed to distract her this time. She can be a proper little tyrant if it suits her. You're a monster in disguise, aren't you, *mia bella*?'

He said it with such affection, and Amy's heart turned over. Poor little scrap, losing her mother so young and so tragically. Leo must have been devastated—although not for himself, from what he'd said. He'd told her that marrying the wrong person was a recipe for disaster and it would be a cold day in hell before he did it again, so it didn't sound as if his marriage had been a match made in heaven, by any means. But even so—

'I need to make a quick call to sort out where we're going to stay tonight. Can you entertain her, please, Amy? I won't be a moment.'

'Sure.' Amy shut the door on that avenue of thought and turned her attention to amusing Ella. She'd got enough mess of her own to deal with, without probing into Leo's.

But Ella didn't really need entertaining, not with her dragonfly to chew and crackle, so Amy was free to listen to what Leo was saying. Not that she could understand it, because he was talking in Italian, but it was lovely to listen to him anyway.

She always thought of him as English, like his mother, but then this amazing other side of him would come out, the Italian side that came from his father, and it did funny things to her insides.

Or maybe it was just the language doing that? That must be it. There was no way Leo talking Italian was sexy, that was just ridiculous. Not according to his numerous female fans, of course, but that didn't mean *she* had to fall under his spell. This was Leo, after all.

Yes, of course he was gorgeous, she knew that, and she'd had a serious case of hero-worship when she'd hit puberty, but she'd never felt whatever it was they all obviously felt—probably because she'd known him too long, knew all his weaknesses and irritating little habits as well as his strong points, like friendship and loyalty and generosity.

He was virtually a brother, a brother she loved to bits and would go to the end of the earth for. The best friend a girl could want. And no matter where she ended up, that would never change, but sexy? Nope—

'*Ciao. A dopo,*' he said in that delicious Italian of his, and her heart did a little back-flip to prove her wrong.

* * *

He put his phone away and smiled at Amy across the aisle.

'Well, that's our accommodation sorted,' he said with relief. 'I phoned Massimo Valtieri to tell him I'm bringing a friend to help with the baby so we'd make our own arrangements, but he wouldn't have any of it. He says there's plenty of room for you, too, and they're fine with us all staying at the *palazzo,* as from tonight. Problem solved.'

'*Palazzo*?' she squealed, and lowered her voice to a whisper. 'They live in a *palazzo?*'

Leo laughed softly at the awed expression on her face. 'Apparently. It's an old Medici villa. I've seen pictures of it, and it's very beautiful. It's been in the family for centuries, which is why I want to deal with them because it's not just a business, it's in their blood, it's who they are. The meetings will be there and they all live very close by, apparently, so it makes sense us being there, too, so if Ella kicks off and you can't cope, I won't be far away. And his wife's there, so you'll have company.'

'Oh, that's good,' she said, and a little worried crinkle in between her eyebrows smoothed away. She shook her head, her mouth kicking up in a wry smile. 'I still can't quite believe I'm going to be staying in a *palazzo.*'

She looked so flummoxed it made him chuckle. 'Well, you've got about four or five hours to get used to the idea,' he told her.

He was just relieved he'd be on hand; he didn't know what she knew about babies, but she knew almost nothing about Ella, so having a woman around who was a mother herself could only be a good thing, especially under the circumstances. He didn't want Amy feeling any more overwhelmed than she already was.

She was leaning over now and chatting to Ella, telling her what a lucky girl she was to stay in a *palazzo,* and he settled back in the seat and studied her. She was smiling,

the haunted look in her eyes retreating as she fell under
the spell of his tiny daughter, and for the briefest of fleeting seconds he wondered what life would have been like
for all of them if she'd been Ella's mother.

It took his breath away.

CHAPTER THREE

AMY GLANCED ACROSS at Leo and frowned.

He was staring at her with the strangest expression on his face. 'Have I got a smut on my nose or something?'

'What? No. Sorry, I was miles away. Ah, here's Julie, we might be in business,' he added, and he sounded relieved, for some reason.

'We're about to take off now,' Julie said. 'Is there anything you need to ask before we're airborne?'

'I'm fine. Amy?' Leo said, raising an eyebrow at her.

'No, I'm fine, thank you.'

Julie left them, took herself off to her seat behind the cockpit, and then the pilot's voice came over the loudspeaker and they were off.

Leo strapped himself in, reached across with Ella's bottle and began to feed her as they turned at the end of the runway.

'It helps her ears to adjust to the pressure change,' he explained, but Amy didn't care right then. She leant back, gripped the armrests and closed her eyes. She hated this bit—

'Oh!' She gasped as she was forced back into the seat and the plane tipped up and catapulted itself into the sky.

'Bit quicker off the ground than a heavy commercial jet,' Leo said with a grin as they levelled out and settled into a gentle climb, banking out over the Thames estuary and towards the coast.

She looked away from him, staring blindly out of the window at the slightly tilted horizon as the reality of what she'd done kicked in. They were still climbing—climbing up, up and away from England. Away from the wedding that hadn't been, the redundant marquee on the lawn next door, the dress lying in a crumpled heap on her bedroom floor.

And she was going to Italy. Not on her honeymoon, but with Leo and Ella. Without a husband, without a wedding ring, without the engagement ring that was sitting on her dressing table at home where she'd left it.

She looked down at her hand. Nope, no ring. Just a faint, pale line where it had been.

Just to check, she ran her finger lightly over the empty space on her finger, and Leo reached out to her across the aisle, squeezing her hand.

'You OK?' he murmured, as if he could read her mind.

She flashed him a smile but it felt false, forced, and she looked away again. 'Just checking it's not a dream. It feels like I'm on drugs. Some weird, hallucinogenic stuff.'

'No drugs. No dream. You're just taking time to get used to it. It's a bit of a shock, such a drastic change of course.'

Shock? Probably. Drastic, certainly. It felt like she was falling, and she wasn't sure if the parachute would work. She met his eyes, worrying her lip with her teeth. 'I wish I'd been able to get hold of Nick. He wasn't answering his phone.'

'Did you leave a message?'

She shook her head. 'I didn't really know what to say. "Sorry I dumped you at the altar in front of all our family and friends" seems a bit inadequate, somehow.'

'He didn't look upset, Amy,' Leo reminded her softly. 'He looked relieved.'

'Yes, he did,' she agreed. 'Well, I guess he would do, wouldn't he, not being stuck with me?'

Leo frowned. 'Why should he be relieved about that?'

'Because clearly I'm an idiot!'

Leo laughed softly, his eyes full of teasing affection. 'You're not an idiot,' he said warmly. 'Well, not much. You just got swept along by the momentum. It's easily done.'

It was. And he was right, she had. They both had. Was that what had happened to Leo and Lisa when he'd done the decent thing and married her for the wrong reasons?

The seatbelt light went off with a little ping, and Leo undid his lap strap and swung his seat round slightly as Julie approached them with a smile.

'Fancy a drink, Amy?' Leo asked her. 'Something to eat?'

Amy laughed. 'Eat? I couldn't eat another thing! That picnic was absolutely amazing. I'm still stuffed.'

'Well, let's just hope everyone enjoyed it. I'll have a cappuccino, Julie, please. Amy?'

'That would be lovely, thank you.'

Julie smiled and nodded, disappeared to the galley area behind the cockpit and left Amy to her thoughts. They weren't comfortable. All those people who'd travelled miles to see her married, and here she was running away with Leo and leaving them all in the lurch when she should have been there apologising to them.

'I wonder if they're all still there having a post-mortem on the death of my common sense?' she murmured absently. 'At least a lot of them turned up to eat the food. It would have been a shame to waste it.'

'I imagine most of them will have left by now—and your common sense didn't die, it just woke up a bit late in the day.'

'Maybe.' She sighed, and smiled at him ruefully. 'The food really was amazing, you know. I'm glad I got to try

it. Do you know how long it is since you cooked for me?'
she added wistfully, and he gave a soft huff of laughter.

'Years.'

'It is. At least four. Five, probably. You did it a lot when
my father died. I used to come and hang out in your restaurant while I was at uni and you'd throw something together for us when you'd finished, or test a recipe out on
me. I've missed that.'

'Me, too. I'm sorry. My life's been a bit chaotic since
the television series.'

Well, that was the understatement of the century. 'So I
gather,' she said mildly. 'And you've opened the new restaurant. That can't have been easy with a new wife and a
baby on the way.'

A shadow flitted through his eyes and he looked away,
his smile suddenly strained. 'No. It took a lot of my time.
Too much.'

So much that their marriage had fallen apart? If they'd
even had a marriage in the real sense. It didn't sound like
it, but she knew very little more than he'd just told her
and the rest was rumours in the gutter press. They'd had
a field day, but his parents didn't talk about it, and until
today she'd hardly seen Leo since before his marriage.

All she knew was what had been in the paper, that Lisa
had been knocked down by a car late one stormy night and
had died of her injuries, and the coroner had returned a verdict of accidental death. Ella had been tiny—two months
old? Maybe not even that. And Leo had been left with a
motherless baby, a new business venture that demanded
his attention and a television contract he'd had to put on
hold. Small wonder she hadn't seen him.

'Your cappuccino, Miss Driver.'

The drink was set down in front of her, and she flashed
a distracted smile at Julie and picked up her spoon, chasing
the sprinkled chocolate flakes around in the froth absently.

His hand came out and rested lightly on her arm, stilling it. 'It'll be all right, Amy,' he murmured, which made her smile. Trust Leo to be concerned for her when actually she was worrying about him.

'I'm fine,' she assured him. And she was, she realised. A little stunned, a little bemused almost at the turn of events, but Leo was whisking her away from it all so fast she didn't have time to dwell on it, and that could only be a good thing.

She pulled out her little pocket camera and pointed it at him. 'Smile for the birdie!'

'Make sure you get my good side.'

She lowered the camera and cocked an eyebrow at him. 'You *have* a good side?'

He rolled his eyes, that lazy grin kicking up his mouth and dimpling his right cheek, and her heart turned over. She clicked the button, turned to get an interior shot while her heart settled, and clicked again.

'Day one of your Tuscan tour blog,' she said lightly, and he laughed.

She caught it, grinned at him and put the camera away.

They landed shortly before five o'clock, and by five thirty they'd picked up the hire car and were on their way to the *palazzo*. Ella was whingeing a little, so he pulled over in a roadside *caffè* and ordered them coffee and pastries while he fed her from a pouch of pureed baby food.

It galled him to do it, but it wouldn't kill her. It was organic, nutritionally balanced, and had the massive advantage that it was easy. He had enough fish to fry at the moment without worrying about Ella.

He glanced up and met Amy's eyes. She was watching him, a strange expression on her face, and he tipped his head questioningly.

'What?'

'Nothing. Just—I've never really got used to the thought of you as a father, but you seem very comfortable with her.'

He looked back at Ella, his heart filling with love. 'I am. I didn't know what it would be like, but I love it—love her, more than I could ever have imagined loving anyone. She's the most precious thing that's ever happened to me.'

Amy's smile grew wistful. 'It shows,' she murmured, and he thought of all the plans she'd mentioned that she'd walked away from, all the things she'd sacrificed. Like starting a family. And if he hadn't interfered...

She might have ended up in the same mess as him, he reminded himself, bringing up a child on her own after the disastrous end of a doomed relationship.

'Amy, it'll happen for you, when the time's right,' he told her softly, and she gave a wry little smile that twisted his heart.

'I know. But I have to warn you, I don't know anything about babies so it won't hurt to practise on Ella so I can make my mistakes first with someone else's child.'

He chuckled, ruffling Ella's dark curls gently. 'You won't make mistakes, and even if you do, you won't break her. She's pretty resilient.'

Her wry smile turned to a grimace. 'That's probably just as well. She might need to be.'

'Chill, Amy. She's just a little person. She'll let you know what she needs.'

'Yeah, if you can mind-read a ten-month-old baby,' she said drily, but the smile reached her eyes now and he let his breath out on a quiet sigh of relief. She'd been hanging by a thread ever since she'd turned her back on Nick, and it had taken till now before he'd felt absolutely sure that she'd done the right thing. Having a baby with the wrong person was a disaster, and that's what she could have done if everything had gone to plan.

Which let him off the hook a bit on the guilt front.

'Here, you can start practising now. Give her the rest of this so I can drink my coffee, could you, please?' he asked, handing her the pouch and spoon and sitting back to watch. Amy took it cautiously, offered it to Ella, and the baby obediently sucked the gloop from the spoon, to Amy's delight and his relief. Contrary to her predictions, they seemed to be getting on fine. 'There—see?' he said lightly. 'Easy.'

She threw him a cheeky grin and put the empty pouch down. 'Well, this end was easy, but I think she'll need her daddy for the other one. I can only master one skill at a time and there'll be plenty of time to learn about that later.'

He laughed, put his cup down and scooped up Ella and the changing bag. 'I'm sure there'll be lots of opportunities.'

'I don't doubt it,' she said drily, but her wry, affectionate smile warmed his heart and he was suddenly fiercely glad that she'd come with them.

By the time the sun was getting low on the western horizon, they were turning onto the broad gravelled drive leading up to the Palazzo Valtieri.

The track dipped and wound along the valley floor, and then rose up the hill through an avenue of poplars to a group of stone buildings on the top, flushed rose by the setting sun.

'I think that's the *palazzo*,' he told her, and Amy felt her jaw drop.

'What, all of it? It's enormous! It looks as big as some of the little hilltop towns!'

He chuckled softly. 'There'll be all sorts of other buildings there clustered around it. It won't just be the house.'

But it was. Well, pretty much, she realised as they approached the imposing edifice with its soaring stone walls and windows that she just knew would have the most amazing views. She couldn't wait to get her proper camera out.

They drove under a huge stone archway in the wall and into a large gravelled courtyard, triggering lights that flooded the area with gold. There were several vehicles there, and Leo brought the car to rest beside a big people-carrier.

They were facing a broad flight of steps flanked by olive trees in huge terracotta pots, and at the top of the steps was a pair of heavily studded wooden doors, totally in proportion to the building.

She felt her jaw sag again. 'Oh. Wow. Just—wow,' she breathed.

Leo's grin was wry. 'Yeah. Makes my house look a bit modest, doesn't it?'

'I haven't seen your house yet,' she reminded him, 'but it would have to be ridiculously impressive to compete with this.'

'Then it's a good job I'm not a sore loser. Unless you count a sea view? That's probably the only thing they don't have.'

She cocked her head on one side and grinned at him. 'That might just do it. You know me—I always wanted to be a mermaid.'

'I'd forgotten that.' His cheek creased, the dimple appearing as he punched the air. 'Ace. My house trumps the seat of the Valtieri dynasty.'

'I did say "might",' she pointed out, but she couldn't quite stifle her smile, and he laughed softly and opened the car door.

'You haven't seen my view yet.'

She met his smile over the top of the car. 'I haven't seen theirs, either. Don't count your chickens.'

'Would I?' He grinned again, that dimple making another unscheduled appearance, and her heart lurched.

'I guess we'd better tell them we're here,' she said, but it seemed they didn't need to.

One of the great wooden doors swung open, and a tall man in jeans and a blinding white shirt ran down the steps, smiling broadly, hand extended as he reached Leo.

'Massimo Valtieri,' he said. 'And you're Leo Zacharelli. It's good to meet you. Welcome to Palazzo Valtieri.'

He spoke in perfect English, to Amy's relief, faintly accented but absolutely fluent, and he turned to her with a welcoming smile. 'And you must be Miss Driver.'

'Amy, please,' she said, and he smiled again and shook her hand, his fingers warm and firm and capable.

'Amy. Welcome. My wife Lydia's so looking forward to meeting you both. She's just putting the children to bed and the others are in the kitchen. Come on in, let me show you to your rooms so you can settle the baby and freshen up before you meet them.'

Leo took Ella out of the car seat and picked up the changing bag, Massimo picked up Leo's bag and removed hers firmly from her grip, and they followed him up the steps and in through the great heavy door into a cloistered courtyard. The sheltered walls were decorated with intricate, faded murals that looked incredibly old, and more olive trees in huge pots were stationed at the corners of the open central area.

It was beautiful. Simple, almost monastic, but exquisite. And she couldn't wait to start capturing the images. She was already framing the shots in her mind, and most of them had Leo in them. For his blog, of course.

Their host led them around the walkway under the cloisters and through a door into a spacious, airy sitting room, simply but comfortably furnished, with French doors opening out onto a terrace. The sun had dipped below the horizon now, blurring the detail in the valley stretched out below them, but Amy was fairly sure the view would be amazing. Everything else about the place seemed to be, and she just knew it would be crammed with wonderful photo opportunities.

Massimo pushed open a couple of doors to reveal two generous bedrooms, both of them opening out onto the same terrace and sharing a well-equipped bathroom. There was a small kitchen area off the sitting room, as well, and for their purposes it couldn't have been better.

'If there's anything else you want, please ask, and Lydia said she hopes you're hungry. She's been cooking up a storm ever since you rang and we'd love you to join us once you've got the baby settled.'

'That would be great, but she shouldn't have gone to any trouble. We don't want to impose,' Leo said, but Massimo was having none of it.

'No way! She's a chef, too, and not offering you food would be an unforgivable sin,' he said with a laugh. 'Just as soon as the baby's settled, give me a call on my mobile and I'll come and get you. Both of my brothers and their wives are here as well tonight. And we don't in any way dress for dinner, so don't feel you have to change. We'll be eating in the kitchen as usual.'

The door closed behind him, and Leo turned to her with a faintly bemused smile.

'Are you OK with this? Because I'm well aware you've had a hell of a day and I don't want to push it, but it does sound as if they want to meet us, or me, at least. If you don't feel up to company, just say so and I'll bring something over to you and you can have a quiet evening on your own. Up to you.'

Her stomach rumbled, answering the question, and she smiled ruefully. 'Honestly? Yes, I'm tired, but I'm absolutely starving, too, and I'm not sure I want to spend the evening on my own. And anyway, as you say, it's you they all want to meet. I won't understand what you're all saying anyway, so I'll just sit in the corner and stuff myself and watch you all.'

'I think you will understand, at least some of it. His wife's English.'

'Really?' Another knot of tension slid away, and this time her smile felt a bit more spontaneous. 'That's good news. I might have someone to talk to while you're in meetings.'

Leo chuckled. 'I'm sure you will. I'll just bath Ella quickly and give her a bottle and pop her into bed, and then we can go and meet the rest of the family.'

Ella! She hadn't even given her duties a thought, but now she did. 'Will it be all right to leave her, or do you want me to stay with her? It's you they want to meet.'

He picked something up off a side table and waggled it at her.

'Baby monitor,' he said, by way of explanation. 'They really have thought of everything.'

They had. Absolutely everything. There were posh toiletries in the bathroom, the fridge was stocked with milk, juice, butter and fresh fruit, there was a bowl of brown, speckled eggs and a loaf of delicious-looking crunchy bread on the side, and a new packet of ground coffee next to a cafetière. And teabags. Amy was glad to see the teabags. Real English ones.

While Leo heated the baby's bottle and gave it to her, she made them both a cup of tea and curled up on the sofa to wait for him. Ella fussed a little as he was trying to put her down, but it didn't take long before she went quiet, and she heard a door close softly and Leo appeared.

'Is that for me?' he asked, tilting his head towards the mug on the table in front of her.

She nodded. 'I didn't know how long you were going to be, so it might be a bit cold. Would you like me to make you a fresh one?'

'No, it's fine, I'll drink it now. Thanks. I ought to ring Massimo anyway. I don't want to keep them waiting and Ella's gone out like a light.'

'Before you call him—did you say anything to them? About me, I mean? About the wedding?'

A frown flashed across his face. 'No, Amy, of course not. I didn't think you'd want to talk about it and it just puts an elephant in the room.'

'So—no elephants waiting for me?'

He gave a quiet grunt of laughter, the frown morphing into a sympathetic smile. 'No elephants, I promise.'

'Good,' she said, smiling back as the last knot of tension drained away, 'because I'm really, really hungry now!'

'When aren't you?' he muttered with a teasing grin, pulling out his phone, and moments later Massimo appeared and led them across the courtyard and into a bustling kitchen filled with laughter.

There were five people in there, two men and three women, all seated at a huge table with the exception of a pregnant woman—Lydia?—who was standing at the stove, brandishing a wooden spoon as she spoke.

Everyone stopped talking and turned to look at them expectantly, the men getting to their feet to greet them as Massimo made a quick round of introductions, ending with his wife. She'd abandoned her cooking, the wooden spoon quickly dumped on the worktop as she came towards them, hands outstretched in welcome.

'Oh, I'm so glad you've both decided to come over and join us. I hope you're hungry?'

'Absolutely! It smells so amazing in here,' she said with a laugh, and then was astonished when Lydia hugged her.

'Oh, bless you, I love compliments. And you're Leo,' she said, letting go of Amy and hugging him, too. 'I can't tell you how pleased I am to meet you. You've been my hero for years!'

To Amy's surprise, Leo coloured slightly and gave a soft, self-effacing chuckle. 'Thank you. That's a real compliment, coming from another chef.'

'Yeah, well, there are chefs and chefs!' Lydia said with a laugh. 'Darling, get them a glass of wine. I'm sure they're ready for it. Travelling with a baby is a nightmare.'

'I'm on it. Red or white?'

Leo chuckled and glanced over at Lydia. 'Judging by the gorgeous smell, I'd say a nice robust red?'

'Perfect with it. And it's one of your recipes,' Lydia told him with a wry grin. 'I've adapted it to showcase some of our ingredients, so I hope I've done them justice.'

They launched into chef mode, and Amy found a glass of iced water put in her hand by one of the other two women. It appeared she was also English and her smile was friendly and welcoming.

'I don't know about you, but travelling always makes me thirsty,' she said. 'I'm Isabelle, and I'm married to Luca. He's a doctor, so more of a sleeping partner in the business, really. And this is Anita, the only native Valtieri wife. She's married to Giovanni. He's a lawyer and he keeps us all on the straight and narrow.'

'Well, he tries,' Anita said, her laughing words heavily accented, and Amy found herself hugged again. 'Welcome to Tuscany. Have you had a good day so far? I thought Leo was supposed to be at a wedding today, but obviously not.'

Well, how on earth was she supposed to answer that? Except she didn't have to, because Leo appeared at her side and answered for her, fielding the question neatly.

'We managed to get away early,' he said, and she only just stifled a laugh. 'The journey was great, though. Seamless. And our accommodation is perfect. Thank you all so much. It'll make it very much easier for all three of us.'

'You're welcome,' Massimo said, glasses and a bottle in hand, and he and his two brothers immediately engaged

Leo in a conversation about the wine, so Amy turned back to the women and found herself seated at the table while they poured her a glass of wine and chatted about the business and the area and their children, and asked about Leo.

'So, how long have you known him?' Lydia asked, perching on the chair next to Amy in a break in her cooking.

'Oh—for ever. Our families have been neighbours since before I was born.'

'Gosh. Literally for ever! Lucky you!'

She laughed. 'I don't know about that. He used to test recipes on me when we were kids, but I was a willing victim.'

'Victim?'

She wrinkled her nose. 'He was a little adventurous, so there were a few interesting disasters along the way. I think his palate's refined a little bit since then.'

They all laughed, even Leo, and she realised he'd been standing right behind her, listening to every word.

'Damned by faint praise,' he said wryly, and she swivelled round and looked up at him with a grin.

'Well, I wouldn't like to swell your head.'

'God forbid.'

His mouth twitched, and she laughed and turned back and found Lydia, Anita and Isabelle watching her thoughtfully. Why? They'd always behaved in this playful way, she just hadn't thought about it, but—were the three women reading something else into it? Something that wasn't there? She felt herself colour slightly and dunked a bit of olive ciabatta into the bowl of oil and balsamic vinegar on the table in front of her.

Good move. The flavour exploded on her tongue and suddenly she understood why they were there. 'Wow. This is lovely. Is it yours?' she asked, and to her relief the conversation moved on as the food was put on the table and they all piled in, and the slightly awkward moment passed.

Then as the last plate was cleared away and it looked as if they'd split up into two groups again, Ella cried out, the monitor flashing right in front of Leo, and Amy seized the opportunity to escape before the women could ask any more searching questions.

'I'll go,' she said hastily to Leo, scraping back her chair and snatching up the baby monitor. 'You stay and talk.'

'Are you sure?'

His eyes searched hers, concern etched in them, and she found a smile.

'Absolutely. We'll be fine, and if we aren't, we'll come and find you.' She turned to the others. 'I hope you'll excuse me. It's been quite a…long and complicated day.'

'Of course. We'll see you tomorrow. If there's anything you need, just ask,' Lydia said, and she nodded.

'Thanks.'

Leo reached out a hand and stopped her briefly. 'I'll be with you in a minute. I won't be long.'

She nodded back, dug out the smile again for the others, thanked Lydia for the meal and made her escape. Long and complicated didn't even begin to scratch the surface of her day, and she was only too ready to head across the beautiful courtyard to their suite of rooms, let herself in and close the door with a shaky sigh of relief.

For some reason she could feel tears threatening, and frankly she'd done enough crying this morning—no, this afternoon. Whenever. The wedding was supposed to have been at noon. So still less than twelve hours since she'd turned her back on Nick and run away.

And she would be spending her wedding night alone in an ancient medieval *palazzo* in Tuscany, instead of with Nick in the honeymoon suite of an old manor house prior to heading off to a sun-soaked beach in the Indian Ocean for her honeymoon.

She gave a tiny laugh that turned into a hiccupping sob, and ramming her hand over her mouth she headed towards the bedrooms.

And stopped, registering for the first time that the room with the travel cot in it had twin beds, and the other room had a huge double. Not that the twin beds were in any way small, but it seemed wrong for her to take the double instead of Leo and she was, after all, supposed to be here to look after the baby, even though Leo had said he'd share with Ella.

She pushed the door open a little further and peered into the travel cot. The baby was fast asleep and breathing quietly and evenly, whatever had disturbed her clearly not enough to wake her properly, and Amy turned away from the bedrooms and headed for the kitchen.

She was tired beyond belief, her brain worn out from going over and over the repercussions of her impulsive behaviour, but she couldn't go to bed until she'd discussed their sleeping arrangements with Leo, so she put the kettle on, made herself a cup of tea and settled down to wait for him.

CHAPTER FOUR

LEO STAYED IN the kitchen for a while longer, deep in conversation with the Valtieri brothers. They were fascinating men, with a passion for what they produced, for the land, for their family ties and history and also for their future—a future he realised he wanted to share.

Their business was a part of them, utterly fundamental, their enthusiasm burning so intensely that it was infectious. It was how he felt about his own chosen path, his constant striving for perfection, for excellence, and it was wonderful to meet people who produced the raw ingredients of his craft with the same passion.

He'd missed this—missed talking to people who understood what drove him and shared it, missed immersing himself in the thing he loved most in the world apart from his family. Especially his daughter—

His gut clenched. Oh, hell. Amy was looking after her, and he'd totally forgotten!

What was he thinking about? He'd let her take the baby monitor so he had no idea how long it had taken Ella to settle, and Amy had enough to deal with tonight, of all nights, without a tired and fractious baby.

He shouldn't have taken her for granted, but he'd been so wrapped up in his own agenda, so busy enjoying himself, that she'd completely slipped his mind.

How *could* he have let that happen? Especially when he was so worried about her. She'd been quiet all day, so unlike her usually bubbly self, and although she seemed to have enjoyed the evening there'd been a distracted look in her eyes—and when Ella had cried, she'd grabbed the opportunity to escape with both hands.

And he'd let her do it. What kind of a friend was he?

'Sorry, guys, I lost track of the time, I'm going to have to go,' he said a little abruptly. 'It's been a long day and I need to check on Ella.' And Amy. *Dio*, how *could* he—?

'Sure. We'll see you in the morning. Nine o'clock?'

He nodded. 'That's fine. I'll look forward to it.'

'Tell Amy we'll be around,' Lydia chipped in with a smile. 'She and Ella are more than welcome to join us.'

'Thank you. I'll pass it on. I'm sure she'll appreciate the company. And thank you for a lovely meal. It was delicious. I'll have to return the favour one evening.'

Lydia laughed. 'Feel free. I'd love you to cook for us. It would be amazing. You can give me a master class, if you like.'

He gave a soft chuckle. 'No pressure, then.'

'I'm sure you can handle it, Chef,' she said with a grin, and he chuckled again and got to his feet, shook hands with all the men, said goodnight to the ladies and crossed the courtyard swiftly, letting himself quietly into the guest suite.

Silence. No screaming baby, no sound from Amy desperately trying to pacify her, and the tension drained out of him. She must have gone to bed and left a lamp on in the sitting room for him.

He turned towards it, and then he saw her in the soft glow, curled up in the far corner of a sofa, her hands cradling a mug and her face in shadow.

'You're still up,' he said unnecessarily. 'I'm sorry, I didn't mean to be so long. I take it Ella's OK?'

'She's fine.'

He frowned. Her voice sounded—odd. Disconnected.

'Amy?' he said softly. She turned her head and looked up at him, and his gut clenched. She'd been crying. He could see the dried tracks of tears on her cheeks, her eyes red-rimmed and swollen, and guilt rose up and swamped him.

Damn.

She hadn't meant him to find her like this, and now there was guilt written all over his face. She closed her eyes, biting her lip and kicking herself for not just going to bed.

The sofa dipped as he sat down next to her, his thigh warm against her hip, his arm around her shoulders solid and comforting. She felt his breath ease out on a weary sigh.

'I'm so sorry. I got caught up in conversation and I should have been here for you, not abandoning you on your own to deal with Ella. Was she a nightmare?'

She shook her head. 'No. She was still asleep. It's not that. I spoke to Nick,' she said, and her voice clogged with tears. She swallowed and tried again. 'He rang to find out if I was OK.'

'And are you?' he asked, although she knew he could see quite clearly that she wasn't.

She shrugged. 'I suppose. I don't know. It's my wedding night, Leo. I should have been married—'

Her voice cracked, and he took the mug out of her hands and pulled her gently into his arms.

'Oh, Amy, I'm so sorry. This is all my fault.'

'What's your fault?' she asked, tilting her head back and searching his eyes. 'That I left it so long to realise it was a mistake? Hardly.'

'That you're not married. Not on your honeymoon. That you've thrown away all your carefully laid plans.'

She shook her head and cradled his cheek in her hand. It felt rough, the stubble growing out now at the end of the day, and there was something grounding about the feel of it against her palm. Something warm and real and alive that made it all make sense. Or complicated it all a whole lot more. She dropped her hand back in her lap.

'That I'm not married to the wrong man,' she corrected, her voice soft but emphatic, needing to convince him so he didn't carry this guilt around like a burden for ever. 'You did the *right thing*, Leo. It was me who didn't, me who ignored all the warnings going off in my head all the time. I thought I was just stressing about the wedding, but I wasn't, it was the marriage, the lifetime commitment to him that was worrying me. I just didn't realise it. So for goodness' sake don't beat yourself up over it, because it's *not your fault*, OK?'

'So why are you crying?'

She gave a little shrug. 'Because the pressure's off? Because I feel guilty because I'm glad I'm not married to him when he's actually a really nice guy? Take your pick.' She tried to smile, but it was a rubbish effort, so she sniffed and swiped the tears off her cheeks and tried again. 'There. Is that better?'

'Not much,' he said honestly, lifting a damp strand of hair away from her eyes with gentle fingers.

'Well, it's the best I can do,' she said, her voice choked again, and Leo closed his eyes and folded her close against his chest and rested his cheek against her hair. It felt a little stiff from the products she must have had put in it for the updo, not as soft and sleek as usual. Not his Amy.

His Amy? What was he thinking? She hadn't ever been *his* Amy, even in the old days. And now was not the time to reinvent their relationship, when both of them were an emotional mess. However appealing it might be. And where the hell had that come from?

With a quiet sigh he loosened his hold and sat up a little,

putting some much-needed distance between them before he did something stupid that he'd regret for ever.

'You'll feel better after you've had a good night's sleep. Why don't you have a shower and go to bed?' he murmured, and she looked up at him, her eyes lost.

'Where? Which bed? The room Ella's in has only got single beds and you can't possibly sleep in one of those, it seems all wrong. You should have the double.'

'Don't be daft. They're not small beds. You take the double, it's fine.'

'Are you sure?'

'Of course I'm sure, and I'm certainly not moving her tonight. I'll sort the luggage out, and then you go and have a shower and get off to bed. You'll feel better in the morning, honestly.'

'Is that a promise?'

She looked so forlorn that he laughed softly and hugged her. 'Yes, it's a promise. New day, new life.'

It sounded great. He just hoped it didn't turn out to be a false promise, because he was still waiting for that new life after copious new days. New weeks. New months. And there was no sign of it. He felt as if his life was on hold, in limbo, and every dawn was just as bleak as the one before...

Leo was right. She did feel better in the morning.

It shouldn't have surprised her; Leo was always right. Why hadn't she asked him about Nick before? Except of course it would have seemed disloyal, and even now it felt wrong talking to him about Nick because there was nothing *wrong* with Nick.

It wasn't about Nick. It was about her, and the fact that it had taken her such an unforgivably long time to realise she wasn't going to settle for sensible.

She sighed softly. She'd never been sensible. She only

had to look at the mess she'd made of her other relationships to know that, so she might have realised it was never going to work with Nick. Except that was the very reason she'd thought it *might* work, because for once it *was* sensible, and it had taken her far too long to realise she was wrong.

Well, at least she hadn't left it until after they were married. That would have been worse.

She threw back the covers and climbed out of the ridiculously enormous bed that Leo really should have had. She wished he *had* had it, because lying alone in the vast expanse of immaculate white linen had just underlined all the things she'd walked away from.

Still, as Leo had said, new day, new life. That was yesterday. Today was a new day, a fresh start, and she needed to get out there and embrace it.

'Bring it on,' she muttered, staring at herself in the mirror and digging out a smile. There. See? She could do it.

She could hear Leo and Ella in the little sitting room of their suite and they seemed to be having a lot of fun, babyish giggles interspersed with the deeper, soft rumble of Leo's voice. She'd go and join them, bask in the warmth of their love for each other and see if it could drive out this aching loneliness.

She delved in her suitcase for her dressing gown, and frowned. Damn. She'd completely forgotten that she hadn't brought the ratty old towelling thing that she'd had for a hundred years but a slippery little scrap of silk deliberately chosen because it was beautiful and elegant and undeniably sexy. To inject some fireworks into their honeymoon?

Maybe. It was what the garment was designed for, like the camisole nightdress she'd worn last night, and she hadn't even thought about it when she'd said that she was packed ready to go, but she should have done, she realised in dismay. Not that she'd exactly had a lot of time to think about it in the hurry to leave.

She contemplated getting dressed rather than going out into the sitting room what felt like half-naked, but she needed a cup of tea and a shower before she could put on her clothes, and it covered her from head to toe. She tugged the belt tighter and opened the door. There. Perfectly respectable, if a little on the thin side, and it was only Leo, after all.

Only?

Scratch that. He was dressed in a battered old T-shirt and jeans, his feet bare, and he was sitting cross-legged on the floor with Ella, playing peep-bo from behind a cushion and making her giggle hysterically. And for some ridiculous reason he looked as sexy as sin. It must be the bare feet, she thought, and dragged her eyes off them. Or the tug of the T-shirt across those broad, solid shoulders—

He's not sexy! She swallowed and wrapped her arms defensively around her waist. 'Hi, guys. Are you having fun?' she asked, smiling at Ella and trying to avoid Leo's eye as he turned to look at her over his shoulder.

'My daughter likes to see the sun rise,' he said drily, and she chuckled and risked another glance at him.

Mistake. His eyes were scanning her body and he looked quickly away, a touch of colour brushing the back of his neck, and she wished she'd just got dressed because now she'd embarrassed him. Oh, God. Did he think she was flaunting herself in front of him? Idiot! She should have dragged on her clothes and changed them after her shower—

'Tea?' he asked, in a perfectly normal voice that didn't for some reason sound quite normal because there was a tension vibrating in it that she'd never heard before.

'That'd be great. I'll make it.'

But he'd already uncoiled from the floor in one lithe movement and headed for the kitchen, as if he was suddenly desperate for some space between them. 'I've had two cups,' he said. 'I'll make yours, and you can sit and come round slowly and play with Ella while I have a shower, if that's OK. Deal?'

'Deal.'

He made it to the safety of the kitchen and let his breath out on a long, silent sigh of relief.

'Thank you,' she called after him.

'Don't mention it.'

He flicked the switch on the kettle, then stuck his head back round the corner while the kettle boiled, still managing to avoid her eyes by pretending to look at Ella. 'I've got a meeting at nine that'll probably go on all morning—will you be OK with her? She'll probably nap for a lot of it.'

'I'll be fine, I slept like a log. Were you OK in that single bed?' she asked.

Bed? Now she wanted to talk about the *bed*? He ducked back into the kitchen and busied himself with her mug, sending his unruly body a short, pithy reprimand. 'Fine, thanks,' he lied. 'I told you it would be.'

It hadn't been fine, but he wasn't telling her that. Oh, it had been perfectly comfortable, if he ignored the fact that he was used to sleeping in a huge bed all to himself. What wasn't fine was the fact that he'd been ridiculously conscious of her just on the other side of the wall, and swapping rooms wouldn't change that. It would also mean sleeping in her sheets, and he'd had enough trouble getting her out of his thoughts as it was, without lying there surrounded by the haunting scent of her.

He made her tea and went back through just as she was trying to rearrange the dressing gown over her legs on the floor, and he put the tea down out of Ella's reach and went on walking, keeping his eyes firmly off the slim, shapely thigh barely concealed by that slippery scrap of silk that wouldn't stay where it was put.

'Back in a minute. Don't forget to drink it while it's hot.'

He closed the bathroom door with a frustrated sigh and shook his head. Where the hell had this crazy attraction come from? Not that she was helping, flitting about in that insubstantial little silk thing, but why should that affect him now? It never had before, and Amy frankly wasn't his type.

He liked sophisticated women, and there had been plenty to choose from, especially since the first television series. But he'd used discretion, or so he'd liked to think, until Lisa. Nothing discreet or sophisticated about that. They'd brought out the worst in each other, and the only good thing to come of it was Ella. Their entire relationship had been a disaster of epic proportions, and Lisa had paid for it with her life. He'd never forgive himself for that, and there was no way he was ready for another relationship, especially not one with someone as vulnerable and emotionally fragile as Amy.

Sure, she was a woman now, a beautiful, warm, caring woman, and without a shadow of doubt if she'd been anybody else he wouldn't have hesitated. But she wasn't, she was Amy, and she trusted him. It had taken a huge amount of courage to call a halt to her wedding the way she had, and she'd turned to him for help. The last thing he'd do was betray that trust.

However tempting she'd looked in that revealing bit of nonsense. Oh, well. Maybe Ella would be sick on it and she'd have to wear something else and everything would get back to normal.

He could only hope…

By the time she emerged from the shower, he'd had breakfast and was ready to leave.

'I have to go, I'm supposed to be meeting up with them at nine,' he said, fiddling with his phone. 'Are you sure you'll be all right? Lydia said they'll be around. They all stayed over last night so you should have some company.'

'Fine. Great. And of course I'll be all right,' she said, crossing her fingers behind her back. 'Just go. We're fine, aren't we, Ella?'

He flicked her a quick glance, nodded, kissed Ella goodbye, handed her to Amy and left.

Not popular. The baby gave a little wail, and it took all the skill Amy hadn't known she had to distract her from the loss of her beloved father.

'He'll be back soon,' she promised, and retrieved the dragonfly and squished it, making it crackle. It worked, thankfully, and she ended up sharing her toast with Ella before they went to find the others.

They were in the kitchen, the women chatting at the table while the younger children played on the floor and the two oldest, both girls, sat quietly reading at the table.

'Amy, hi,' Lydia said with a smile. 'Have you had breakfast?'

'Yes, thanks, we're done. Leo said I should come and find you, if that's OK?'

'Of course it's OK. Would you like a coffee?'

'Oh, that would be lovely, if you're having one. Thanks.'

'I'm not, but it's no problem to make you one. We're all on fruit teas—caffeine and pregnancy doesn't go well together,' she said with a wry smile. 'Black, white, latte, cappuccino?'

They were *all* pregnant?

'Um—cappuccino would be lovely. Thanks.'

'I'm sorry, I'll see you outside,' Isabelle said, getting to her feet with a grimace. 'I can't stand the smell of it.'

'No, don't let me drive you out, I'll have tea!' she protested, but Isabelle laughed.

'You're fine. It'll be OK outside and we were just going out there anyway. Max, Annamaria, come on.'

They all went, leaving Amy alone with Lydia while she made the coffee, and Amy took it with a rueful grimace.

'I really wouldn't have had one if I'd known. I feel so guilty.'

'Oh, don't,' Lydia said with a laugh. 'We're used to it, and the men still drink coffee. They just do it elsewhere. One of us always seems to be pregnant and they're well trained.'

That made her smile. She couldn't imagine anything making Leo give up coffee. 'So, is this your fifth baby, or have I lost count?' she asked as they headed for the doors.

'Gosh, no! It's only my second. Massimo was widowed just after Antonino was born,' she explained, 'and I didn't know when we met if he'd want any more, but he just loves children, so this is our second, which will be his fifth, and Anita's on her second, and it's Isabelle's third—her husband's an obstetrician, which is quite handy.'

'Keeping it in the family?'

She chuckled. 'Something like that,' she said and led Amy outside onto the terrace. It seemed to wrap all around the outside of the house, giving stunning views over the surrounding countryside, and Amy was blown away by it.

They settled in the shade of a pergola draped with sweetly scented jasmine, and she cradled her cup and stared out over the beautiful valley below them, taking the time to soak up the scents and sounds that drifted around them on the air.

'Gosh, it's so beautiful here, I could take a lot of this,' she murmured. 'And the *palazzo* is absolutely fabulous.'

'Not when you have to clean it,' Lydia said with a laugh, 'but at least we have some help. And, yes, of course it's beautiful. We all feel very privileged to be guardians of it for future generations.'

'Well, there'll be no shortage of them,' she said with a smile. 'Would you mind if I took some photos of it? Leo's asked me to take some for his blog while we're in Italy, and this would be fantastic. We'd let you vet them first, of course.'

'Of course we wouldn't mind,' Lydia said. 'I'm sure the guys would be thrilled if it appeared in his blog. Just make sure he gives us a plug!'

'Oh, I'm sure he will. I haven't seen him look as fired up and enthusiastic as this in ages. Not that I'm surprised. It's just amazing here.'

'It is,' Isabelle agreed softly. 'It's a wonderful place to live, and it really doesn't take very long to fly home, which is great for keeping in touch with our families. Well, you know how long it takes, you've just done it.'

'Yes, but it doesn't really count. Our trip was ridiculously easy because Leo wangled a private charter from City Airport—'

'No!' Lydia said, laughing. 'Really? That's where I met Massimo! I was in a truly awful wedding dress, trying to blag a flight to Italy for a runaway bride competition—'

Amy sucked in her breath sharply, and Lydia stopped and frowned at her, her expression appalled. 'Amy—what did I say?'

She laughed. She had to laugh, there was nothing else to do really under the circumstances apart from cry, and she'd done enough of that. Time to introduce the elephant.

She gave them a brief précis of her impulsive actions, and Isabelle reached out and rested a hand lightly on her arm, her eyes searching. 'Oh, Amy. Are you sure you're all right?'

'Yes, of course I am,' she said lightly. 'Or I will be once the dust has settled.'

'Much more all right than if you'd married the wrong man,' Anita put in wryly. 'I wish more people had the sense to pull out instead of making each other miserable and putting their children through hell.'

Just as she and Nick might have done. She felt sick, thinking how close she'd come to it, how devastating it would have been for all of them.

Then Ella toppled over trying to pull herself up, which gave Amy the perfect excuse to leave the conversation for a moment and regroup. Not that the women had been anything other than kindness itself, but she just didn't want to talk about her not-quite wedding or their relentlessly burgeoning happy families. The full extent of what she'd turned her back on was still sinking in, but, although the shock was receding, in its place was a terrifying emptiness that she wasn't ready to explore.

Was Nick feeling the same sense of loss? Maybe. Or maybe not. He'd asked if she minded if he went on their honeymoon alone, and of course she'd said no, but she wondered now if it was a good idea for him or if it would just be making it worse.

Not that it could be much worse than her running full tilt down the aisle away from him. God, the humiliation!

She groaned quietly, and Lydia shot her a thoughtful look and got to her feet.

'I need to make lunch. Are you two staying or going?'

'We're going,' Isabelle said briskly, standing up too. 'Anita and I are going to plan a shopping trip for baby stuff.'

Anita frowned. 'We are?'

'Yes, you know we are. We talked about it the other day.'

Or not, Amy thought, because Anita looked confused for a micro-second and then collected herself, scooped up her baby and went, leaving Amy alone with Lydia.

Two down, one to go, she thought with relief, and Lydia had to make lunch, so she could excuse herself—

'Come and talk to me while I cook.'

'Ella could do with a nap,' she said hastily, using the

now grizzling baby as an excuse to escape, but Lydia just shrugged.

'Put her down, then, and come back. Bring the baby monitor. She'll be fine.'

Of course she would, and she went down like a dream, so Amy had no justification for not going back to the kitchen and facing what she felt was going to be an inquisition.

It wasn't, of course. Lydia was far too sensible and sensitive to do something so crass, and her smile of welcome was just that. There was a jug of what looked like home-made lemonade in the middle of the table, alongside two glasses, and Lydia was sitting there chopping vegetables while her children played outside the doors.

'That was quick. She's a good baby, isn't she?' she said as Amy sat down. 'Have you had much to do with her, or is she just good with people?'

'She must be. I haven't really been around recently and nor has Leo, so I haven't seen either of them much. I've been busy planning the wedding and working in London, and since Leo's wife died...' She gave a little shrug. 'Well, he hasn't had a lot of time for anything but work and Ella,' she trailed off awkwardly.

Lydia slid a glass of lemonade towards her. 'Yes, I can imagine. It must have been awful for him, and it must be a nightmare juggling his work with Ella. I know what it's like running one restaurant, never mind a group like theirs, and raising a baby is a full-time job on its own. I'm surprised he hasn't got a nanny.'

'I don't think he needs one at the moment. His parents are close by and they've helped him a lot, but he likes to be hands on. Even so, I think it's been a real struggle.'

'It was good of you to offer to help him.'

She gave a little laugh that hitched in the middle. 'Well, I didn't have anything else to do, did I? And he didn't have to try hard to convince me. I love Italy, and I owe him big time. He's done a lot for me over the years.'

Lydia's eyes searched her face for a second before she turned her attention back to the vegetables. 'Like making sure you didn't marry the wrong man?

Her smile felt a little twisted. 'Absolutely. That's probably the biggest single thing he's ever done for me. He was giving me away—or not,' she said, trying to laugh it off, but the laugh turned into a sigh. 'My father died eight years ago, just after I went to uni, and I suppose I could have asked my uncle or his father or someone, but I wanted Leo, because he knows me better than anyone else on the planet. So I'm really rather glad I did or I might have ended up married to Nick and it would have been a disaster. Not that there's anything wrong with Nick, he's a lovely guy, it's just...'

'You weren't right for each other?' Lydia said wryly, meeting her eyes again.

She returned the understanding smile. 'Pretty much. Although why it took me so long to work out I have no idea. Probably because there *is* nothing wrong with him!' She gave a wry chuckle.

'And it's nothing to do with you and Leo?' 'No! Absolutely not!' she protested. 'I've known him all my life. It would be like marrying my brother.' Except it hadn't felt like that this morning, seeing him on the floor with Ella, when he hadn't been able to look at her, or her at him...

Lydia shrugged and gave a rueful smile. 'Sorry. It's not really any of my business, but—there just seems to be something, almost like some invisible connection, a natural rapport between you,' she said gently. 'Like with Anita and Gio. It took them years to work out what we could all see. And you seem to be so good together.'

Amy shrugged. 'He's just a really great friend. Or he was, but then Nick came along just after Leo's career took off, and then of course he got married, and Nick and I got engaged—and you know the rest. As I say, we've hardly seen each other recently, but he's still just Leo and I know if I ever need him I only have to ask. He's always got time for me, and he's still a really good friend. The sort you can lean on.'

Lydia nodded slowly. 'Well, I'm glad for you that you've got him. Going through something like this, you need a good friend to lean on. There's nothing like being with someone you don't have to explain yourself to, someone who knows you inside out and loves you anyway. I couldn't want a better friend than Massimo by my side.'

She threw the chopped vegetables in the pot, gave them a quick stir, put the lid on and turned back with a smile.

'So, tell me, what do you do when you're not running away from bridegrooms and being Leo's guinea pig?'

Amy laughed, as she was meant to, and the conversation moved on to safer, less turbulent waters, but Lydia's words echoed in Amy's head for the rest of the day.

Sure, she and Leo were the best of friends, but did that have to mean they couldn't be anything else to each other? Not now, of course. She was an emotional mess, and he was still dealing with the fallout of Lisa's death, but maybe, some time in the future…

…*someone who knows you inside out and loves you anyway*…

Like Leo?

And it suddenly occurred to her that for all these years, like Gio and Anita, they could have been missing something blindingly obvious that was right under their noses.

CHAPTER FIVE

THE MEN CAME back at lunchtime, and she found herself looking at Leo in a new light.

She could see just from the look on his face how much he'd enjoyed the morning, and their discussions continued for a few minutes, standing outside the kitchen door on the terrace with long, cold drinks in their hands, and they were all talking Italian.

It was the first time she'd heard them together like that, and it dawned on her with blinding clarity that, yes, it was a musical language but, no, they didn't *all* sound sexy. It wasn't the language, it was *Leo* talking the language.

Which changed everything.

They switched back to English as they came into the kitchen, but his voice still did things to her that no one else's did, and when he scooped Ella up in his arms and smiled the smile he reserved for her, Amy's heart melted all over again.

The conversation over lunch was very animated, but that didn't stop him juggling little Ella on his lap while he ate, and after lunch he handed her back to Amy reluctantly.

'I'm sorry. We're going out again to look at the olive oil processing plant this afternoon, if that's OK? Has she been all right?'

He looked a little worried, but Amy just smiled and shook her head slowly. 'She's been fine, Leo. Just go and do what you want to do. We're OK here. Lydia's been looking after us, haven't you, Lydia?'

Lydia smiled reassuringly. 'Leo, don't worry about us. Amy and I are getting on like a house on fire, and Ella seems perfectly happy. Just go. Shoo. We're fine.'

He frowned fleetingly, then gave a brisk nod, kissed the baby and left with the others, and to her relief the baby didn't cry this time.

'Have you got swimming things with you?' Lydia asked as the door closed behind them. 'We've got a heated pool, just in case you were wondering.'

Amy frowned. 'Yes, I have, but I don't know if Ella has.'

Lydia flapped a hand. 'She doesn't need one. I've got loads of swim nappies and arm bands and things. She'll be fine, and it'll only be us and the kids,' she said with a smile, and Amy felt herself relax.

'It sounds lovely. Really inviting.'

Lydia laughed. 'Oh, it is. I think we'd die without it when it gets really hot. At the end of a scorching day in the summer, it's just gorgeous to sink under that water in the evening when the kids are in bed and the stars are glittering overhead. So romantic.' She grinned mischievously. 'You and Leo should try it one night.'

She laughed awkwardly. 'I think the romance might be rather lost on us,' she said, trying not to picture herself and Leo alone under the stars.

Lydia found her a swim nappy, and they all changed and made their way to the pool set down below the terrace at a lower level. The water felt blissful on her hot skin, and Ella seemed to love it, so they spent hours playing in the pool, and it was lovely.

Ella, finally exhausted by all the fun, got a little grizzly, so Amy gave her a bottle and put her down to sleep in a travel cot strategically situated in the shade. She went out like a light, leaving nothing for Amy to do except chill out.

She should have brought a book with her, but she hadn't thought of it, so she settled herself on a sun lounger, arms wrapped round her knees, basking in the late afternoon sun and watching Lydia and the children playing in the water under the shade of a huge hanging parasol. Their squeals of delight washed over her as she gazed out over the beautiful valley below and soaked up the sun, and for the first time since the wedding that hadn't happened she felt herself relaxing.

Till the men appeared.

'The girls must be swimming,' Massimo said, and led Leo across the terrace to the railings. He could hear splashing and shrieking, and he leant on the railings beside Massimo and looked down at them.

Lydia was on the side with the youngest, wrapping him in a towel, and the other children were still in the water, but Amy was sitting on a sun lounger and he could see Ella sleeping in a travel cot in the shade just below them.

'Well, hi, there,' he said, and she looked up, her eyes shielded from him by her sunglasses.

'Hi,' she said, and wrapped her arms around her knees a little self-consciously. Not surprising. He could tell from here that her bikini was pretty insubstantial, and he felt himself willing her to unfurl her body so he could see it.

She smiled up at them, but it looked a little forced. Because of the bikini? Another honeymoon special, he thought, and his body cheered.

'Had a good time?' she asked, and he nodded.

'Great. Really interesting, but quite hot. That water looks very tempting.'

'Feel free, Leo. We've just finished,' Lydia said, gathering up the children's things and heading up the steps with the baby, the older children trailing in her wake, 'but help yourself. You're more than welcome to use it any time you like.'

'Yes, do,' Massimo agreed. 'I'd love to join you but I need to make a few calls before I can escape.' And taking the baby from her arms, he went inside with Lydia and the children, leaving Leo alone with Amy.

She didn't look any too thrilled. Because of the bikini? She would have worn it in public with Nick, he felt sure, so why did the fact that she was alone with him make any difference? Except of course it did. It certainly made a difference to him.

He went down the steps and crossed over to her, sitting on the edge of the sun lounger beside hers and pushing his sunglasses up onto his head so he could study her better. 'You've caught the sun,' he said with a slow smile. 'Just here.'

And because he couldn't resist it, he trailed a finger over her shoulder, and the heat that shot through him should have blistered his skin. Hers, too.

Why? It wasn't as if her skin was that hot. 'Mind if I join you for a swim?' he asked, and she shifted, straightening up so her shoulder was out of reach and giving him a perfect view of her cleavage.

'Actually, I'm going to go in, if you don't mind. I've been out here quite long enough,' she said, and swung away from him, getting to her feet on the other side of the sun lounger and wrapping the towel round herself quickly—but not before he'd been treated to the sight of her smoothly rounded bottom scarcely covered by a triangle of fabric, and his body reacted instantly.

She gathered up her things with indecent haste and turned to him, not quite meeting his eyes.

'Do you mind watching Ella till she wakes up? I could do with a shower.'

He swallowed. 'No, that's fine. How long's she been asleep?'

'I don't know. Half an hour? Bit more, maybe. She was pooped after the swimming. She's had a bottle.'

He nodded. 'OK. You go ahead, I'll take care of her.'

She walked slowly up the steps and across the terrace, resisting the urge to run away. She had been doing a lot of that recently, and look where it had got her, but the heat in his eyes had stirred something inside her that she couldn't trust herself not to act on, and she couldn't get away from him quick enough.

Because it echoed what she felt for him? Or because she feared it was just the knee-jerk reaction of a healthy adult male to a woman in about three square inches of fabric? In which case doing anything other than retreating could just embarrass them both.

She went in through the kitchen, across the courtyard and into their suite, closing the door behind her with relief. She didn't know how long he'd be before he followed her, but she wasn't going to hang around.

She showered quickly, opened her suitcase to look for some after-sun lotion and found the sheet of contraceptive pills that were part of her morning routine. She lifted them out slowly, staring at them without seeing while all thoughts of Leo drained away.

It was to have been her last course before she and Nick started trying for a baby, and she felt an aching sense of loss that had nothing to do with Nick and everything to do with the unfulfilled promise of motherhood.

Ironic that she'd never had much to do with babies before, and yet here she was now, surrounded by pregnant women and small children, so that just when it was suddenly out of reach she saw exactly what she'd be missing.

She hesitated for a moment, then popped the now purposeless pill out of the sheet and swallowed it, simply because she didn't want her cycle messed up.

She found the after-sun lotion, smeared it on her shoulders where she could still feel the tingle of Leo's fingertip, pulled on clean clothes and emerged from the bedroom just as he appeared, Ella grizzling unhappily and arching backwards in his arms.

'She's a bit grumpy, aren't you, sweetheart?' Leo murmured gently, his voice rich with the warmth of his love. He looked up from the baby and smiled at Amy, and the vague sense of loss she'd been feeling was overlaid with another, much more complex emotion that was much more troubling.

'I don't suppose you fancy putting the kettle on, do you?' he suggested. 'I could murder a cup of tea.'

'It was my next job,' she said lightly, and walked past them into the kitchen, wondering how on earth, when her world was steadily imploding, the scent of Leo's skin warmed by the sun could possibly be so intoxicating...

The next morning Lydia dropped the children off at school and ran a few errands, so Amy followed her suggestion and spent a while exploring the grounds with the baby in the buggy, taking photos either for Leo or possibly her own portfolio. Assuming she could find an outlet for them, which was by no means certain. Still, just to be on the safe side, she kept clicking, and she took lots of photos of Ella for Leo.

He checked in on his mobile from time to time, just to make sure that everything was OK, and then Lydia collected the children from school and the men came home for lunch, and after that they all went in the pool to cool off before the men went back to work.

It was stiflingly hot, so Amy joined them, but it didn't take very many minutes to realise that frolicking about in

the water in her skimpy little honeymoon bikini in front
of Leo wasn't clever. It had been bad enough yesterday
when she'd just had to stand up and wrap herself in a towel,
but in the water everything seemed to take on a life of its
own and she'd had an embarrassing wardrobe malfunc-
tion when Ella had grabbed her bikini top. It was only by
a miracle that no one else had noticed, but Leo had, and
she vowed never to do it again, no matter how tempting
the water was.

Then Ella started to fuss, so she grabbed the opportunity and climbed out of the pool, swathed herself in her
towel and took the baby from Leo in the water, towelling
her gently dry and putting a nappy on her before giving her
a drink and settling her in the travel cot for a nap.

Leo swam to the side and folded his arms on the edge
of the pool. 'Coming back in?'

'No, I don't think so,' she said without looking at him.
'I thought I could take some photos of you all for the blog.'

'Sure?'

'Sure.'

She forced herself to meet his searching gaze, then he
shrugged and sank back under the water, leaving her to it.

She stayed resolutely on the side, wrapped in her towel
and perched on a sun lounger, and spent the next hour
capturing images of them all playing in the water with
the children—ostensibly for Leo, since a disproportionate
number of the photos were of him, but mostly so she didn't
have to frolic about feeling hopelessly under-dressed.

Then Ella woke, so Leo swam to the side and vaulted
out, water streaming off his lean, muscular frame and plas-
tering his shorts to strong, straight thighs, and her heart
somersaulted in her chest. She clicked the shutter, capturing the image for posterity, then put the camera away in its
case, giving him time to grab a towel and knot it loosely
round his hips.

'Your turn to swim, I'll look after Ella,' he said, but she shook her head and glanced back at him.

Not better. Not better at all. To her all too vivid imagination it just looked as if he had nothing on under the towel, and it was too much for her.

'I'm going to shower and get dressed, and then I'll download the photos,' she said, getting hastily to her feet, and with a smile and a wave to the others, she picked up her camera and headed for the sanctuary of the house.

She hardly saw him on Tuesday because the men didn't come back for lunch and then had a meeting after dinner, but then on Wednesday afternoon Massimo and Gio had a prior commitment and the women and children were at a birthday party, so they were left to their own devices.

'How about playing tourists?' Leo suggested, so they went out in the car with the baby and explored a nearby hill town Lydia had recommended for its food shops, and while he investigated them she clicked away on her camera, recording the day for Leo's blog.

It made her smile, watching him interacting with the shopkeepers. He went all Italian, of course, smiling and laughing and waving his hands all over the place, and she realised that he was always like that when he was fired up about something, and she just hadn't registered it until now, when it was slightly more exaggerated.

He'd always been just Leo, and she'd never really analysed him before, but she was doing it now, constantly, with every click of the shutter. Every move, every smile, every frown, every gesture, all logged and recorded in a little part of her brain labelled 'Leo', and her feelings were getting utterly confused.

Inappropriate? No, maybe not that, but certainly different, threatening the platonic status quo that she'd just realised was so fragile, and because of that, and because she wasn't going to repeat the fiasco with her bikini, when she spotted a likely-looking shop she took the opportunity to check it out.

'Can I have five minutes?' she asked him. 'I need another swimming costume if we're going to swim every day.'

A muscle twitched in his jaw and he nodded. 'Sure. I'll wait here for you.'

The shop was perfect, and she found a ludicrously expensive but utterly plain black one-piece swimsuit. She didn't bother to try it on. Whatever it was like, it had to be better than the bikini, and there was a limit to how many photos even she could take of Leo in and around the water. And anyway she wanted to swim; she just wasn't going to risk another disaster.

She picked up a pretty little pink swimsuit for Ella, as well, because it was irresistible, and she didn't even look at the price. She'd hardly given the baby anything, only the crackly dragonfly that was her constant companion, so she could easily justify it to herself.

She managed to pay without flinching, put her purse away, scooped up her shopping and went out into the sunshine to find Leo and Ella.

He wondered what she was looking for. Hopefully something that covered her up a little more successfully than that bikini, which had already given him two sleepless nights since Ella had grabbed it.

He was trying to keep an eye on the shop door, but an elderly matron who should have known better had cornered him and was flirting outrageously, so he was relieved to see Amy emerge.

'Got what you wanted?' he asked, and she nodded and waggled the bag at him.

'Yup. Are you done?'

'Definitely. We need to make a move.'

He turned to the woman to excuse himself, and she caught him by the shoulders and kissed his cheeks, laughing as she let him go with an outrageous parting shot and a cheeky pat on his behind.

He felt the colour run up his neck and walked hastily away, shaking his head in despair.

'What did she say to you?' Amy asked, eyeing him curiously as she struggled to keep up.

'Nothing,' he mumbled. 'Just goodbye.'

'I don't believe you. She was flirting—and she groped you.'

'No, she didn't. It was just a little pat. She recognised me, that's all.'

Amy rolled her eyes. 'I wasn't born yesterday, Leo. Most people don't pat you on the behind, and even I can tell a starstruck old biddy when I see one. She was hitting on you.'

He fought the rising tide of colour, and lost. 'OK, OK. She said if she was twenty years younger, she'd give you a run for your money. I didn't think it'd be wise to point out that we're not together. She might have dragged me off on her broomstick.'

Her chuckle was delicious, and he couldn't help but join in.

'You're such a babe magnet, Zacharelli,' she teased. 'They all hurl themselves at you, it doesn't matter how old they are.'

All except Amy.

The thought popped into his head without warning, but it was true. If he was such a babe magnet, how come she'd never even noticed him in that way? Well, not since she was fourteen and had come down with a serious case of hero-worship, and that didn't really count. Although God only knows he'd noticed *her* recently. Like Monday, with the bikini top that Ella had so helpfully dragged out of the way and that she'd now seen fit to replace. He'd certainly noticed that.

'Can we change the subject, please?' he muttered, to himself as much as Amy, and headed back to the car with Ella, leaving Amy to follow, still chuckling, in his wake.

The next day the men were out again, visiting the cousin who made the gorgeous balsamic vinegar that appeared with oil and bread at every delicious meal, and she and the three wives were left to their own devices for the whole day.

It seemed odd now, not seeing him at all for such a long time, and she seemed to miss him more than the baby did, which was a bit telling. They went to Isabelle's for lunch, for a change, and then retreated to the pool in the afternoon, and then at five, as they were just getting the children out of the water, Massimo, Gio and Leo reappeared, making her profoundly glad she'd bought the new one-piece.

Leo walked towards her, his eyes shielded by sunglasses, and she turned, the baby on her hip, to point him out.

'Hey, look, baby, it's your daddy!' she cooed to Ella, and Ella held her arms out to him, little starfish hands opening and closing as she jiggled with excitement.

Amy could identify with that. She watched Leo's face light up as he reached out for the baby, and felt a pang of envy. What would it be like, to have a little person so very pleased to see you?

Wonderful. Amazing.

He slid the sunglasses up onto his head and held his arms out, and she could see the wonder in his eyes.

'She's wet,' Amy warned him, but he just shrugged.

'I don't care. I need a shower anyway. Come here, *mia*

bellissima bambina,' Leo said, reaching for the baby, but his fingers brushed Amy's breast and she sucked in her breath. It was barely audible, but he heard it, and their eyes clashed and held, his darkening to midnight.

For a moment they both froze. She couldn't breathe, the air jammed solid in her lungs, and then with a muttered apology he lifted Ella out of her arms and turned away, laughing and kissing her all over her face, making her giggle deliciously and freeing Amy from his spell.

After a second of paralysing immobility, she grabbed a towel and wrapped it firmly round herself, then gathered up their things and headed for the steps, Leo falling in beside her at the top. They walked back together to their apartment, Ella perched on his shoulders with her little fists knotted in his hair, while he told her a little about his day and they both pretended that the moment by the pool hadn't happened.

'Sounds like it was worth going,' she said lightly as they went in and closed the door behind them, and he nodded.

'It was,' he said, prising the baby's fingers out of his hair and swinging her down into his arms. 'We had a lot to talk about, and we still have. And they're all off to visit their parents tomorrow. It's their mother's birthday and they can't reschedule, there isn't another time they're all available, which means we can't finalise the deal until after they're back on Sunday. Will that be a problem for you?'

A whole weekend alone with Leo? She felt a flicker of trepidation—anticipation? She didn't know. All she knew was that she couldn't refuse him and she didn't want to. 'No—why should it?'

He shrugged. 'I don't know. I said maybe a week, but we won't leave now until at least Monday or Tuesday and I don't know if you can give me that long or if there's something you need to get back for.'

She stared at him blankly. 'Leo, I can give you as long

as it takes. That's why I'm here. I owe you so much, for so many things—really, don't give it another thought. Do what you need to do. It's fine. I have nowhere else to be.'

'Sure?' he asked, but she could see the relief in his eyes and she wondered if he'd expected her to refuse.

She rolled her eyes. 'Of course I'm sure. Anyway, I'm having fun,' she said, keeping it light. 'So I'm going to be forced to spend a few more days in a medieval Medici palace with a beautiful swimming pool and a view to die for, playing with a cute baby and being fed by a celebrity chef. What a tragedy!'

He laughed softly, shrugged acknowledgement and put Ella on the floor on her towel, crouching down to peel off her costume. 'This is lovely, by the way. Really cute. Where did it come from? Did you borrow it?'

'No, I bought it yesterday in the shop while you were being chatted up by Methuselah's mother—and before you say anything, it's a present. So, are we going to be completely on our own, then, while they're away?' she asked, striving for casual while her hormones were having a field day.

'I believe so. They're going to give us keys and we'll have the run of the place till Sunday lunchtime, so we'll be able to just chill out, which is lovely. I really need that. It'll be like being on holiday, and I'll have a chance to try out some recipes using their ingredients. I'm actually really looking forward to it. I'm cooking for them all on Sunday so they don't have to do it when they get back, and I want to play around with some ideas for that.'

'Can I be your guinea pig?' she asked hopefully, latching onto the safe and familiar, and he tilted his head to look at her and grinned, suddenly looking like the old Leo.

'I'm relying on it. You have a terrifying gift for honesty where my food's concerned. And I'll try not to poison you.'

'You do that,' she said, secretly flattered by his back-

handed compliment and relieved that the conversation had
steered them seamlessly into safer waters.

'So how was your day?' he asked, straightening up with
the naked baby in his arms. 'I felt I'd abandoned you. Were
you both OK?'

'Leo, we were fine, and we've had a lovely day together.
She's gorgeous. I didn't realise what fun a baby could be.'

His smile softened his features. 'Nor did I,' he murmured, brushing Ella's head with a gentle kiss, and the
tender gesture turned her heart to mush.

Oh, Leo...

She showered and changed, then took herself outside, sitting on the bench in the cool shade of their east-facing
terrace and leaving him to deal with Ella while she took
advantage of a few moments to herself when she didn't
have to pretend anything.

She'd tipped her head back and closed her eyes, but then
she heard the gravel crunch, then the slight creak of the
bench as he sat down beside her.

'Here. I've brought you a drink.'

She opened her eyes and sat up, taking the glass of sparkling water with a slice of lime floating in it, the outside
beaded with moisture.

'Just what I wanted. Thank you. Is she asleep?'

'Yes, she's gone out like a light. The swimming must
have tired her out. Look, I wanted to talk to you about this
weekend. Are you OK with me doing all this cooking?'

Amy looked at him in astonishment, puzzled that he
would even ask. 'Why wouldn't I be? You're the one doing
all the work and it's not as if I won't get to eat it. It's not
down to me.'

'It is in a way,' he pointed out. 'If I'm cooking, you'll
need to look after Ella, and it's not really why you're here.
I should have checked with you instead of just assuming.'

'Of course I don't mind,' she said, puzzled that he would even ask her. 'You know I don't. Ella's lovely, and, anyway, I am here to look after her.'

'Only when I'm in meetings. That was the deal.'

'Leo, it's fine, and, as you said, you need to play around with their produce, try out some recipes, and I'm more than happy to help you in any way I can. I owe you so much—'

'You owe me nothing,' he said softly, his eyes curiously intent. 'I've told you that.'

She shook her head briefly to free her from the magnetic hold of those mesmerising eyes. 'I do. Not just the catering. I'm OK with that now. That's just money, really, but—well, without you I would have married Nick, and it would have been a disaster. If you hadn't said what you did...'

His sigh sounded weary and dredged up from his boots. 'I had to, Amy. You just didn't seem happy enough for it to be right, and there was no way I could let you sleepwalk into a doomed marriage.'

'Like you did into yours?' she asked rashly, and then bit her lip and waited for his reply.

It was quiet on the shady terrace, the valley stretched out below them, the doors to his bedroom open so he could hear Ella if she woke. A light breeze whispered over Amy's skin, welcome after the heat of the day, and she pressed the cold glass to her face to cool it.

He glanced at her, then looked away. 'I didn't sleepwalk into it,' he said at last. 'Lisa did, to a certain extent, but I was railroaded into it by my own sense of decency. Lisa was pregnant, I was the father, I was responsible for her and the baby. I did, as they say, the decent thing. End of. Except that wasn't the end of it,' he added bleakly, 'and I don't know if it ever will be.'

He was staring out over the rolling hills, his eyes remote and shuttered, and she reached out and laid a hand on his shoulder.

'Oh, Leo, I'm so sorry,' she said softly. 'Want to talk about it?'

He glanced briefly back at her, then away again. 'Not really. Why would I? What's the point? It won't change anything.'

It was a less than subtle hint to drop the subject, but somehow she couldn't, so she pressed on. 'I know that, but you always used to talk to me, get things off your chest. I thought it might help you. You must be so sad, for Ella if not for yourself.'

'Sad?' He gave a bitter little laugh that made her wince. 'I don't think sad even scratches the surface. Gutted? Wracked with guilt? Ashamed?'

Ashamed...?

He turned his head to look at her, and in the depths of those beautiful amber eyes she could see an unfathomable despair. And then the shutters came down and he looked away, glancing pointedly at his watch.

'It's time we went over for dinner,' he said, changing the subject so emphatically now that there was no way she was about to argue with him. And that was that—the end of anything deep and meaningful, at least for now.

Just as well. She was getting altogether too interested in Leo and his thoughts and feelings, and it was time she remembered that it was none of her business, and that he was just a friend.

It's not wrong to take an interest in your friends. You were only asking because you care.

No, she wasn't. She was being nosy, delving into parts of his psyche that were absolutely none of her business, friend or not. If he wanted to tell her about his disastrous marriage, no doubt he'd do it in his own time, but it wasn't down to her to ask.

He got up and went inside, leaving her sitting alone on the terrace. She closed her eyes, tilted her head back against the worn old stone and sighed softly.

There had been a time, not all that long ago, when he'd told her everything. He'd poured his heart out to her on numerous occasions; break-ups with his girlfriends, rows with his parents—all manner of things. She'd done the same with him, and there'd never been anything they couldn't talk about.

And there'd been the good things, too, like the time he'd won the TV cookery competition when he was only nineteen, and his first job as a head chef when he'd scarcely finished his training, and his meteoric rise to success as a TV celebrity chef.

That was when his ageing father had handed over the reins of the company restaurant business, and he'd raised his game and gone from strength to strength.

But all the time he'd talked to her. She'd been part of all his ups and downs, but not any more, apparently. Not since Lisa, and the marriage that had left him, of all things, ashamed.

Why? Why *ashamed*? Of his choice of bride? His behaviour towards her? Because she'd died in such tragic circumstances? Hardly his fault—unless there was something about her death that she didn't know. And she wasn't likely to now, because apparently he wasn't prepared to share anything more intimate than a menu, and she couldn't believe how much it hurt.

CHAPTER SIX

As THEY WERE seeing the others off the following morning, Massimo apologised for abandoning them.

'Don't worry about it, we'll be fine,' Leo said. 'Can I raid your vegetable garden, Lydia?'

'Oh, feel free, you don't have to ask,' she said whole-heartedly. 'Use anything you want, there or in the kitchen. Are you sure you don't mind doing lunch for us all? I don't want you to feel you have to.'

He laughed. 'Don't be silly, it'll be a pleasure and I love a family party. It'll be fun. And don't worry about us, we'll be fine, won't we, Amy?'

'Of course we will,' Amy said, but the butterflies were at it again at the thought of forty-eight hours alone with him. His accidental touch yesterday by the pool was still fresh in her mind, and they'd been surrounded then. What would have happened if they'd been alone?

Nothing, probably, and if there was another awkward moment like that she'd only have to mention Lisa and he'd back off at the speed of light. She let out a quiet sigh and waved goodbye to the family.

'Right,' he said, watching the dust trail thrown up by their car as they drove away. 'I need to do some food shopping. There's a market on where we went the other day. Want to come?'

'Sure.' She flashed him a cheeky smile. 'I can defend you from all the old women who want to grope you.'

He chuckled and rolled his eyes. 'Oh, Amy, how would I cope without you?' he said softly.

'Well, aren't you lucky you don't have to?' she quipped straight back at him, and turned away so he didn't see the yearning in her eyes.

Ella fell asleep in the car, so he put her carefully in the buggy and plundered the produce stalls while Amy followed with Ella and captured the atmosphere on her ever-present camera. He found the butcher Lydia had recommended and got into an earnest conversation, which as usual brought out his lovely Italian side that was so irresistibly sexy.

He bought a shoulder of mutton, not something readily available in England, and three racks of lamb. 'I'm going to do lamb two ways for Sunday lunch,' he told her when he finally got away. 'Easy for the numbers, and tender enough for the kids to eat.'

'Yummy.'

'It will be. Even though you have no faith in me.'

She laughed. 'I never said that.'

His mouth twitched but he said nothing, just hung the bag on the back of the buggy and carried on, wandering along the stalls, chatting to people and picking up this and that as they went, and she strolled along behind him with Ella in the buggy, taking photos and pretended to herself that they were a couple.

'Right, I'm done here. Anything else you want to do before we go back?'

She shook her head, so they walked back to the car, him laden with bags, her pushing the buggy with that surreal sensation that somehow it was her place to do it. If only...

'It's getting hot,' he said, tilting his head back and looking up at the sun. 'It'll be a scorcher later.'

'It's hot enough now,' she said, happy to walk in the

shade and wondering if everyone was looking at them and speculating, because everywhere they went he was recognised, and not just by women old enough to be his grandmother. She hadn't realised his fame was so widespread in Italy, but apparently it was.

And mostly he tolerated it with good grace, but she could tell that for once he would have liked to be able to walk around without people saying something to him, or nudging each other and staring. At him, or them together? Would it spark a whole lot of media speculation about his private life? She hoped not, for his sake, and she was glad to get back to the car and away from prying eyes.

He stashed everything in the boot, strapped Ella into her seat and drove home.

No. Not home. They didn't have a home, and there was no 'they', either. Just him and Ella, and her.

'I fancy a dip,' he announced, putting the last things away in the kitchen. 'Want to swim, baby?'

She opened her mouth to answer and then realised he was talking to Ella. Well, of course he was! Why wouldn't he be? He'd never called her baby. Never called her anything except Amy. And brat, on occasions, when she had been, which had been quite often all those years ago.

'Going to join us?'

Was she? She turned her head and met his eyes. They told her nothing. 'Do you want me to?'

He shrugged. 'Only if you want to. It's easier with Ella if there are two of us, but it's not strictly necessary if you'd rather not.'

Of course. He just wanted help with the baby, and put like that it was hard to refuse. Besides, she couldn't think of anything she'd rather do than dive into the cool, refreshing water, so they changed and went over to the pool, and he rigged up the tilting parasol so it hung across the water and they played in the shade with Ella until it was time for her lunch.

'Stay here a bit longer if you like. I'll get her dressed and feed her and then I might put her down for a bit,' he said, handing the baby to her for a moment while he vaulted out of the water, rubbed himself down roughly with a towel and then bent and took Ella from her and walked away.

She let out a long, slow, silent sigh of relief as he went up the steps and disappeared from sight onto the terrace. She'd put on the one-piece again that she'd bought on Wednesday, but she'd felt every bit as naked and as aware of him in that as she had in the bikini.

Because his hand had brushed her breast yesterday afternoon? It meant nothing, she told herself, just an accidental touch.

So why couldn't she forget it, and why couldn't he look at her straight in the eye any more? Or, at least, he hadn't in the past hour or so, since she'd been wearing it.

Stupid. So, so stupid. And it was changing the dynamics of their relationship.

She kicked away from the end of the pool, gliding under the surface with her arms stretched out in front of her until her fingertips hit the other end, and then she tumble-turned and swam back again, up and down, up and down, pushing herself harder and harder until her arms and legs were shaking with the effort.

Even Leo hadn't worked her that hard the summer he'd coached her to swim for the school relay team. And she was thinking about him *again!*

She swam two more lengths to get him out of her mind, then gave up and rolled onto her back and kicked lazily into the centre of the pool, floating with her face turned up to the sun and her arms and legs outstretched like a star.

It was gorgeous. The heat of the sun warmed her where the water had cooled her skin, and she felt all the tension of the last few days soaking out of her body and drifting away across the surface of the pool.

Bliss. Utter, utter bliss—

Something cold splashed onto her face, and she gave a startled shriek and jack-knifed up, frantically treading water while she looked up into Leo's laughing eyes.

'How long have you been there?' she asked indignantly, righting herself and glowering at him.

'Only a moment or two. You looked so peaceful it seemed a shame to disturb you, but I've brought you a nice cold drink.'

'Yes, I rather got the *cold* when you tipped it on me.'

'Drizzled. Not tipped.'

'Semantics,' she muttered. She stood up, cupping a handful of water and hurling it at him. It hit him right in the middle of his chest, and he folded in half and backed away, laughing as he tugged the wet material away from his midriff.

Oh, for the camera...

'I've only just put this shirt on!'

'You should have thought of that before you tipped my drink all over my face. At least I threw warm water at you.' She folded her arms on the side of the pool and grinned up at him cheekily. 'Well, come on, then, let me have it.'

He gave a soft huff of laughter and dangled the glass just out of reach. She stretched up, and just too late she caught the mischief in his eyes.

She should have seen it coming. She knew Leo well enough to know he wouldn't let her get away with soaking him. Even so, the icy flood down her arm and over her chest caught her by surprise, and she gave a strangled shriek and ducked back under the warm water for a second, coming up further away, out of reach.

She swiped the wet hair back off her face and tried to glare at him. 'That was so mean!'

Leo just smiled, set the glass down on the edge of the pool and retreated to a sun lounger a safe distance away. Wise. She swam over to the half empty glass and sipped cautiously.

Gorgeous. Ice-cold sparkling water with a dash of lime. Pity it was only half a glass now, but she wasn't going to pick a fight with him over it. She knew she'd never win. Leo always, always had the last word. She drained the glass and set it down.

'Where's Ella?'

'Napping. She was pooped after the swimming so I stuck her in the travel cot the second she'd finished eating and she went out like a light.' He tipped his head on one side and eyed her thoughtfully. 'Your shoulders have caught the sun again. Are you going to stay in there until you look like a fried prune?' he asked mildly.

It was tempting. The alternative was to get out of the pool in front of him, and she felt curiously, ridiculously naked, even in the one-piece, but she couldn't stay in there for ever, so she swam over to the steps where her towel was waiting, climbed out and wrapped herself in it before she turned round to face him.

'Happy now?'

'I was quite happy before,' he said deadpan. 'It was you I was worried about.'

'You don't need to worry about me, Leo. I'm a big girl now. I can take care of myself. And don't worry about Ella. I'll look after her, if you want to play in the kitchen. I could do with downloading today's photos and sorting through them.'

Anything to keep herself out of his way.

Picking up her empty glass and the baby monitor, she headed up the stone steps to the top of the terrace and left him sitting there alone, hopefully oblivious of the trembling in her legs and her pounding heart and this crazy, absurd awareness of him, which seemed to have sprung out of nowhere in the last few days...

Leo let her go.

Not that there was anything else he could do, short of grabbing her and hanging on, and that didn't seem like an immensely good idea right now. So he settled for watching the slight sway of her hips as she went up the steps, the beads of water on her shoulders sparkling in the sun.

His eyes tracked down to linger on those slender ankles below the smooth, gleaming curve of her calves. Her legs were browner. Even in the last few days she'd acquired a delicate tan from the glorious Tuscan weather. It was early June, hot yet still bearable, and Amy was flourishing, like a flower turning its face up to the sun.

And he was getting obsessed. He had ingredients to experiment with, the Sunday lunch menu to finalise, and he was wasting the precious time he had while Ella was asleep. He should be using that time wisely, not staring at Amy's legs as they disappeared up the steps and behind the parapet wall and imagining them wrapped around him.

And he should *so* not be thinking about her like that!

He groaned. He wasn't interested in Amy.

At all.

So why was he still watching her?

She vanished from sight and he closed his eyes and dragged his hand down over his face as if he could wipe away the image from his mind.

Not a chance. With a sigh dredged up from his boots, he picked up his glass, got to his feet and took her advice. Time to go and have a look at the vegetable garden, and then do something useful in the kitchen, instead of fantasising the day away. And from now on he was going to keep his distance and hope that also meant he could keep his sanity.

* * *

'So, my little guinea pig, are you ready for this?' Leo asked.

He was lolling against the kitchen cupboards, lean hips propped on the edge of the worktop, arms folded, a slight smile playing around the sides of his mouth, and he looked good enough to eat. He also looked more like the old Leo, to her relief, so she played along, trying hard not to be distracted by how downright gorgeous he looked.

Not your business! Nothing about him is your business, especially not that. Only Ella, and her care, and taking photos for his blog. Nothing else. He couldn't have made it clearer if he'd tattooed 'Back Off' all over himself...

'Are you ready for my honesty?' she said drily.

His warm chuckle filled the kitchen and made her insides melt. 'Oh, ye of little faith,' he teased, eyes crinkling at the corners and making her heart turn over. 'I just fancied playing around with some ideas and I didn't know if you were up for it.'

She shook her head slowly. 'Leo!' she said reproachfully, trying not to think about playing around with him or what she might be up for. 'When have I ever said no to you?'

'Oh, now, let me think—when I tried to kiss you?'

A distant memory stirred, and she laughed. 'I was eight!'

'I think you were nine, actually, and I was nearly thirteen—and as I recall, you told me not to be gross.'

She bit her lips to stop the smile. 'I remember. I also remember when I was fourteen and wanted you to try again, but you never did.'

His eyes changed, becoming curiously intent. 'You were a child, Amy, a minor, and I was an adult by then, so, no, I never did,' he said.

'I'm not a child now,' she said, her mouth on autopilot.

The soft caramel of his eyes darkened, the pupils flaring as he gave her a slow, slightly wry smile.

'I had noticed,' he murmured slowly, and pushed himself away from the worktop, heading towards the fridge. 'So—are you up for this, then? I promise not to poison you.'

She let her breath ease out on a sigh. 'You've tried before.'

'I have not!' he said indignantly, but it didn't work because she could hear the laughter underlying it and her lips twitched.

His laughter was so infectious she gave up the struggle and joined in, the sensual moment pushed into the background as their old banter resumed. 'Oh, all right, if you insist,' she relented.

'Ah, see? You still love me, really.'

Her heart crashed against her ribs. Love him? *Really?* She *loved* him? *Like that?*

'In your dreams,' she said drily, and wondered if he could see her heart pounding in her chest.

She couldn't—could she?

Still grinning, he wandered over to her and hugged her briefly, swamping her in that brief moment with a welter of scents and sensations that sent her emotions into a tailspin, before letting go all too soon to open the fridge and examine the contents.

'Do you fancy a glass of fizz while I cook?'

'Now you're trying to get me drunk and kill my taste buds,' she said, her heart still jiggling after the hug, the word *love* echoing in her head like the aftermath of a thunderclap.

He just rolled his eyes and plonked a bottle down on the table. 'Some people are never satisfied,' he said, then set two flutes down in front of her. A quick twist, a soft pop and he filled the glasses with pale, delicately foaming Prosecco, put the bottle back in the fridge and starting pulling out ingredients.

She sat back in her chair, twiddling the glass, watching condensation bead on the outside as the bubbles rose and popped on the surface.

Did she love him? As in, *in love* with him?

Well, at last! You've taken your time to work that one out.

She ignored her inner voice, took a slurp of the Prosecco and tried not to sneeze when the bubbles went up her nose, then swivelled round to look at him, camera in hand.

'So, what exactly are you planning to experiment with?'

He shrugged, his broad shoulders rising and falling and grabbing her attention. How had she never noticed them before this week? Had she been utterly blind? Evidently. But not any more. She clicked the shutter for posterity. Or her private collection, which was growing at an embarrassing rate.

'I'm not really sure. I haven't come up with anything concrete yet.'

'Concrete? How about your rock buns?' she added to get a rise out of him.

He rolled his eyes. 'They were fine.'

'They were rocks, and you know it.'

He sighed softly, but his eyes were brimming with laughter. 'So they were a little over-baked. I was—what? Nine? And you've never let me forget it.'

'You must have been more than that.'

'Not much. Ten at the most. And you had trouble biting into them because you didn't have any front teeth, I remember that.'

'Yes, and you teased me constantly about it.'

'And you rose to the bait without fail. You always did. Still do.' He stopped teasing her and shook his head *slowly,* a soft smile playing around his mouth. 'That was a long time ago.'

'It was. It feels like another lifetime.'

'Maybe it was.' The smile faded, a fleeting sadness in his eyes, and he turned his attention back to the fridge, effectively changing the subject.

'So, what are you going to kill me with tonight, then?' she asked lightly, swirling her Prosecco in the flute and following his lead.

He shrugged away from the worktop and shoved his hands into the back pockets of his jeans, drawing her attention in a way that did nothing for her peace of mind. She captured the image. Not that she needed to. It was burned onto her brain, alongside all the others.

'I don't know. I just want to play around and get a feel for their oil and cheese, amongst other things. I've had a look at Lydia's vegetable garden, which has given me some ideas. I think tonight's going to be pretty tame, though, so you're safe.'

She didn't feel safe. She felt—confused. As if her world had slipped on its axis, even though, in reality, nothing had changed.

Nothing? You ran away from your bridegroom at the altar! This is not nothing!

But it was nothing to do with Leo.

Or was it? Was that why she hadn't married Nick? Because of Leo?

The thought held her transfixed, and she watched him blindly while her thoughts cartwheeled in the background.

He diced an onion at the speed of light, pulled cupboards open, inspected spices and herbs, chose some, rejected others. She could almost hear him thinking on his feet. A slab of bacon appeared out of the fridge, and he cut a thick slice and diced it rapidly into lardons and tossed them into a sizzling pan with the onion.

The aroma of frying bacon began to fill the kitchen, and her mouth was watering. Rice appeared, a glug of wine, some stock—

'Are we having risotto?' she asked hopefully.

'Looks like it,' he said with a grin.

Her stomach grumbled. 'Sorry. Smells good.'

'Twenty minutes,' he said, and while he stirred and added a glug of this and a drop of that, he pressed thin slices of ciabatta onto a griddle and stirred something else in another little pan that he piled onto the crispy bread.

'Here, try this,' he said, sliding a plate across to her. 'Tell me what you think. I've used their oil and olives.'

'Gorgeous,' she mumbled, and had to say it again because he didn't understand her first attempt.

'Didn't your mother ever tell you it's rude to speak with your mouth full?' he said, laughing at her, and she poked her tongue out at him.

'Is this all for me?' she asked, and he leant over and snatched the plate back.

'No, it's not!'

'Pity,' she said, watching as his almost perfect white teeth bit through a slice of the delicious *bruschetta* topped with some gorgeous sundried tomato and olive concoction topped with anchovies. She didn't know what she wanted more, the *bruschetta* or the man.

She stifled a laugh and picked up the camera again. If she had the *bruschetta*, she'd eat it this once and that would be the end of it. If she had the man, she could have the *bruschetta* any time she asked for it. And not just the *bruschetta*—

Heat shot through her, stealing her breath and leaving her gasping.

There was a squeak from Ella over the baby monitor, and she shot back her chair and got to her feet. 'I'll go, you're busy,' she said, and left the kitchen hastily, glad of an excuse to get away from him while she reassembled her jumbled thoughts.

Closing the door of their apartment softly behind her, she leant back against it with a quiet sigh.

Whatever the change in direction of her feelings, and probably his, it was perfectly obvious that Leo wasn't in the slightest bit interested in a relationship with her other than the one they already had, a friend helping him out by looking after his daughter. That was all she was here for, and she had to remember it and keep her overactive imagination under control before it got them both into a whole heap of trouble and embarrassment.

Or her, at least, because for all the banter Leo wouldn't even talk to her any longer about anything personal, far less take advantage of her shaky emotional state. Which, she was beginning to realise, was more to do with Leo than it was with Nick and the abandoned wedding.

She pushed away from the door and crept over to the bedroom, but all was quiet. Ella was lying on her front with her bottom stuck up in the air, and she was fast asleep.

And Leo would know this, because the monitor had gone silent. She closed her eyes briefly, sucked in a deep breath and made herself go back to the kitchen. Nothing had changed, nothing was any different, and it wouldn't be if she kept a lid on it. Yes, she loved him, but just in the way she always had. Nothing more, nothing less, and certainly not like *that*—

Liar!

'Gosh, that smells lovely,' she said brightly, walking back into the kitchen and ignoring the nagging voice that had far too much to say for itself. 'Really yummy.'

'Is she okay?'

'Yes, she's fine. Fast asleep.' She picked up her glass and peered at the dribble in the bottom. 'Any more Prosecco in the fridge?'

He glanced over his shoulder. 'There should be, unless you've already drunk it all. You can top me up while you're at it. I've been working hard.'

She arched a brow at him and chuckled. 'Don't give me that. You could make that risotto in your sleep.'

His lips twitched, drawing her attention to their soft, ripe fullness, and she had an overwhelming urge to get up and walk over to him and kiss them.

No! What was she *thinking* about?

She did get up, and she did walk over to him, but only so she could top up their glasses. Then she retreated back to the table, sat herself down and concentrated on the power of mind over matter. Or head over heart, more likely. The last thing she needed was to allow herself to fantasise about being in love with Leo. Not that she was even thinking about love. Nothing so ethereal. Just at the moment, she was quite preoccupied enough with thinking about kissing him senseless.

She stifled a groan of frustration and impatience at herself, chewed her way thoughtfully through another slice of the delicious *bruschetta* and tried not to down the wine so fast that she fell off her chair. Getting drunk would *not* be an asset to the situation!

In the nick of time a wide, flat bowl appeared in front of her, heaped with risotto drizzled with green-gold oil and scattered with torn basil leaves, and Leo leant across her and shaved some slender curls of a wonderful hard pecorino cheese over it. She sniffed appreciatively, and got a touch of Leo in the fragrant mix.

'Wow, that smells amazing,' she said, bending down to hide the sudden flush of colour that swept her cheeks. 'Utterly gorgeous.'

Leo, sitting down opposite her in front of his own plate, couldn't agree more. She was. Utterly gorgeous, and he'd never really noticed it before the last few days. When it had happened, he couldn't work out, but it had, and he was finding it quite difficult to ignore—especially since the incident with her bikini top earlier in the week.

He frowned, picked up his fork and plunged it into the steaming pile of creamy rice and tried to blank the image of the pale swell of her breast out of his mind, but the delicate rose pink of her nipple, puckered with the cold, was seared on his retina, and he could still feel the soft jut of it on the back of his hand when he'd brushed against her yesterday, taking Ella from her.

Spending time with her was awakening something that had been dormant for months—years, maybe. Something hungry and a little wild and beyond his control that was flaring to life between them. Maybe he didn't need to ignore it. Maybe he needed to talk to her about it?

But not now, if ever. She was a friend, a good friend, helping him out when he was in a bad place and so was she. The last thing either of them needed was him muddying the waters at this point in their lives, but his body had gone stone deaf to the pleading from his mind.

'So what do you think of it?' he asked, watching her demolish the risotto. 'I like the pea and mint with the bacon, and I think their oil and cheese really lend something interesting.'

'Mmm. Not going to argue,' she said, scraping the bowl. 'Is there any more?'

CHAPTER SEVEN

WELL, HE'D MANAGED to keep the conversation on track, he thought with relief as the door closed behind her.

They'd finished their meal, and then he'd told her he needed more time to play with the flavours so she'd gone to do some more work with the photos, which didn't surprise him because every time he'd looked up for the past few days she'd had that wretched camera in her hands.

But at least she was taking his request seriously, he thought as he worked. She must have recorded every last breath he'd taken, but he wasn't going to complain because the results that he'd seen so far were far better than anything he'd ever managed.

He fiddled around in the kitchen for another hour or two before it dawned on him that he was just keeping out of the way until he was sure she was asleep. Then he cleared up the kitchen, which meant there was nothing else for him to do tonight apart from test every type of wine they produced.

Which would be a waste, he thought morosely, staring at the opened bottle on the table in front of him. It was far too good to use as anaesthetic, and the last thing he needed was a hangover in the morning. He folded his arms on the table, dropped his head down and growled with frustration.

He should have been tired—not tired as in just finished a nineteen-hour shift in one of his restaurants, but tired enough to sleep, at least. Instead, he felt restless. Edgy.

He glanced at the baby monitor. She'd left it behind when she'd gone, and he'd heard her go in to check Ella, heard the gentle murmur of her voice when Ella had cried out once, but now there was nothing. He could let himself back in there, pick up his shorts and a towel and have a swim without disturbing them. That was what he needed. A long, hard swim, to burn off that excess restless energy. And maybe then he'd be able to sleep.

Something had woken her. She wasn't sure what, but she realised she was hot and thirsty. Maybe it had just been that?

But her bedroom door was still wide open. She'd left it open so she'd hear Ella, as Leo had the baby monitor in the kitchen, but she would have expected him to close it, or at least pull it to.

She lay for a while and listened, but there was nothing, no creaks or snores, not a sound even from Ella. She slid her legs over the edge of the bed and picked up her phone, checking the time. Twelve thirty-four. He must be back, she just hadn't heard him.

She tiptoed out into the hall and peered into Ella's room, but his bed was undisturbed, and there were no lights on anywhere except the dim glow of Ella's nightlight and the slanting moonlight through the French windows. The baby was sleeping peacefully, bottom in the air as usual, one little arm flung out to the side, and otherwise the apartment was deserted.

Surely he wasn't still cooking?

Tugging on her robe, Amy walked barefoot across the moonlit courtyard to the kitchen and found it empty, the room in darkness. She switched the light on and looked around.

It was spotlessly clean, everything cleared away, the

fridge humming quietly in the background. And the doors to the terrace were open.

She stood in the open doorway and listened. There. A rhythmic splash, barely a whisper, but continuous.

He was swimming.

And suddenly there was nothing in the world she wanted more than a swim. She went back to her room and realised the more modest black costume was still wet, so she put the bikini on, grabbed her towel and the baby monitor, and crossed the terrace.

She could see him now in the moonlight, every stroke leaving a sparkling trail of ripples on the surface, and she picked her way carefully down the steps, dropped her towel on a sun lounger and slipped silently into the water.

It was cool, the air around sweetly scented with jasmine, and she let her breath out on a quiet sigh of pleasure. There was something magical about it, about swimming in the moonlight with Leo, the soft water lapping gently around her, the drift of jasmine in the air. Beautiful.

Romantic.

That was what Lydia had said to her. *'It's just gorgeous to sink under that water in the evening when the kids are in bed and the stars are glittering overhead. So romantic...you and Leo should try it.'*

Her heart hitched a little in her throat. It wasn't meant to be romantic. She'd just wanted to join him for a swim, but suddenly it didn't feel like that, with the moonlight and the silence. She was playing with fire, crossing a boundary into dangerous territory, and she had to go. Once he'd turned and was swimming away from her, she'd make her escape and he need never know she'd been there.

Except, of course, he didn't turn.

The best-laid plans and all that, she thought as he slowed his pace and coasted in right beside her, standing up as he reached the end, sluicing water off his face and hair and knuckling the water out of his eyes.

The water streamed off his shoulders, turning to ribbons of silver in the moonlight, and she wanted to reach out and touch them.

Touch him.

No! Why hadn't she stayed inside, left him alone, kept out of his way, instead of surrendering to this magnetic attraction that had sprung out of nowhere in the last few days and taken her completely by surprise?

She must have moved or taken a breath, done something, because he turned his head towards her, his eyes black in the moonlight, a frown creasing his brow.

'Amy?'

'Hi,' she said awkwardly, the word a little breathless and utterly inadequate somehow in these odd circumstances.

His head tilted slightly. 'What's the matter?'

'Nothing. Ella's fine, she's fast asleep. I came to find you,' she explained, hoping it sounded more plausible than it felt at that moment. 'It was late, and I woke up and wondered where you were, but then I realised you were swimming and I thought it seemed like a good idea. You know, as it's a hot night...'

She floundered to a halt, trying to bluff it out when all she wanted to do was run away. Or throw herself into his arms. Neither exactly brilliant options. Oh, why on earth had she been so stupid?

Leo let out a quiet sigh and sank back into the water, stretching his arms out to grasp the edges of the pool as he faced her from his position in the corner.

What sneaky twist of fate had made her wake and come down here to torment him? His fault, most likely, going in there to pick up his shorts and towel. Damn. Well, thank God he'd got the shorts on and hadn't decided to skinny-dip. At least this way he could hide his reaction.

'Sorry, I didn't mean to disturb you. I just didn't feel tired enough to sleep, and I was hot and sticky, and the thought of the water just tempted me.'

That, and the fact that he hadn't trusted himself to go back into their apartment until he was too tired to act on the physical ache that had lingered long after she'd left the kitchen. And he'd just about done it, and now here she was to undo it all over again.

'It's the middle of the night, Leo,' she said, her voice troubled. 'You must be exhausted.'

Apparently not. Not nearly exhausted enough if his body's reaction was anything to go by. 'And you're not? Why are you here, Amy?' he asked, a trifle desperately. It was a rhetorical question, since she'd already told him, but she answered it anyway and perhaps a bit more truthfully.

'I was concerned about you. You just seemed—I don't know. Not you. Sometimes it's fine and then all of a sudden there's this great gulf that opens up between us and it's as if I don't know you at all.'

She gave a soft, disbelieving laugh. 'And I don't know why. All the time I feel as if I'm walking on eggshells with you, as if anything I say can upset you, and you just won't talk to me. It's like you're avoiding me or something and I don't know why.'

Because I want you. Because it's inappropriate, messy, and I'm not going there—

'I'm not,' he lied. 'I do talk to you. I've been talking to you all day.'

'Not about anything that matters. And that's not like you. You've always told me what's wrong, and now you won't. So what is it? Is it me? And if so, why? What have I done to hurt or upset you, Leo? Just tell me.'

He sighed softly. 'You haven't done anything, Amy. It's nothing to do with you.'

'So why won't you talk to me? You always used to; you

said it helped you sort through things, cleared your mind. I only want to help you…'

Her hand reached out and rested on his arm, her cool fingers burning him with a river of fire that scorched through his veins and threatened all his hard-won control. His eyes closed, shutting out the image of her fingers pale on his skin. 'You can't help me, Amy. You're just adding another complication.'

She whisked her hand away, her voice puzzled. 'I'm a *complication*?'

'That wasn't what I meant—'

'So what did you mean? What's going on, Leo? What's changed? Because it's not just me, is it?'

He let his breath out, a long, silent exhalation, and dragged a hand through his hair.

'No. No, Amy, it's not just you, and I don't know where it's come from or why, but I can't let it happen. I *won't* let it. You're emotionally fragile at the moment, and I'm a complete mess, but we're both adults, we've got needs, and what we're feeling is just a knee-jerk response. We feel safe with each other, we can trust each other, but it isn't safe, not for either of us.'

He gentled his voice, not sure how to handle this situation and desperate not to make it any worse. 'I'm sorry it's all gone wrong for you, and I know it should have been your honeymoon, but I'm not the guy you need to choose for your rebound affair, Amy, so don't humiliate either of us by asking me, please.'

Rebound affair? For a moment she was so shocked she could hardly reply. 'I don't want—'

'No? So why are you *really* here now, then?' He shook his head, his harsh sigh slicing through the air. 'I'm not doing this, Amy. There's no way I'm adding you to the list of things in my life that I'm ashamed of.'

Pain ripped through her, making her gasp. *He was* ashamed *of her?*

Like he'd been ashamed of Lisa?

He turned and vaulted lightly out of the pool, the water streaming off him in ribbons as he picked up his towel and the baby monitor and walked away towards the steps, leaving her standing there, her lips pressed tightly together, her eyes stinging with tears as she watched him walk away.

They scalded her cheeks, searing their way down, and she closed her eyes, turning away from him and holding her breath until the heavy silence told her he'd gone. Then she folded her arms on the side of the pool, rested her head on them and sobbed her heart out.

It was a good hour—no, scratch that, a lousy hour—before he heard her enter the apartment.

He'd towelled himself roughly dry and pulled on his boxers and a T-shirt, then gone out onto the terrace, sitting on the bench against the wall and staring out over the moonlit landscape while he drank the wine he'd picked up on the way over. Not a wise move, but he didn't care any more. He was over being wise. It didn't seem to be working, not for either of them.

The valley was flooded with a cold, eerie light, and he felt oddly chilled. Not that it was cold, it was just that the moon drained all colour from the surroundings and turned it into a mass of stark white, interspersed with menacing black shadows.

Under other circumstances, it would have been romantic. Not tonight, when he was sitting here waiting for Amy and wondering how long he could leave it before he went to find her. Because he would have to, he knew that.

Oh, Amy. What a mess.

What was she doing? What was she thinking? He

shouldn't have left her like that, but he hadn't trusted himself to get closer to her, to reach out to her, because if he
once let himself touch her, that one touch would never be
enough and there was no way—*no way*—that he was going
there. Not with Amy. He was a mess, his life in tatters, the
last thing she needed when she was so emotionally fragile.
Not even he with his appalling track record could betray
her trust to that extent.

He heard a door creak slightly, the click of a latch, water
running, the muffled sound of her bedclothes as she got
into bed a few moments later. The doors of her room were
open to the terrace, as were his, and he listened for any
further sound.

Nothing. Then a soft, shaky sigh, followed by a dull
thump—punching her pillow into shape?

He put his glass down, got up and crossed the gravel,
standing silently in the open doorway. She was lying on
her side, facing him. Her eyes were open, watching him,
waiting for him to move or speak, to do something, but
he couldn't. He had no idea what to say to her in these circumstances, so he just stood there and ached with regret.
He couldn't bear to lose her friendship, and he was horri-
bly afraid that was the way it was heading.

'What have I ever done to make you ashamed of me?'

Her voice was soft, barely a whisper, but it shocked
him to the core.

'I'm not ashamed of you,' he said, appalled that that
was what she'd been thinking. 'Amy, no! Don't ever think
that! I'm not ashamed of you, not in the slightest, and I
never have been.'

'But—you said…'

She trailed off, sitting up in the bed, arms wrapped
around her knees defensively, and in the good old days he
would have thought nothing of climbing on the bed and
hugging her. Not now. Not with this demon of desire stalk-

ing them both. He rammed his hands through his hair and gave a ragged sigh.

'I didn't mean it like that. Really. Believe me. I'm sorry—I'm really so sorry—if you misunderstood, but it isn't, and it never has been, and it never will be you that I'm ashamed of. It's me, the things I've done, the people I've hurt.' He sighed wearily. 'I need to tell you about Lisa, don't I?'

'Yes, you do,' she said, her voice stronger now, making his guilt twinge, 'because I don't know who you are any more and I can't help you like this. Not really. Sometimes I think I understand you, but then you say something, and—it just confuses me, Leo. Tell me what it is that's happened that's destroying you,' she pleaded, her eyes dark holes, featureless in the faint light, unreadable. 'Help me to understand what's hurting you.'

He hesitated for a moment, then gave another quiet sigh. 'OK. But not here, like this. Come outside. Have some wine with me. I picked up a bottle from the kitchen on the way back and I need help drinking it or I'm going to have a killer hangover. I'll get you a glass.'

He checked Ella as he passed, fetched another glass from the kitchen and went back out to the terrace and found her waiting for him.

She was curled into one corner of the bench, her arms wrapped round her legs. He recognised it, that defensive posture, shielding herself from hurt, the wide, wary eyes and wounded mouth making her look like a child again. A hurt and frightened child, but she wasn't a child. Not any more. And that just made it all the more complicated.

He sat down at the other end of the bench at a nice, safe distance, put the wine glass down between them next to his and filled them both.

'Here.'

She reached out and took it from him, her fingers brushing his, and he felt them tremble. 'So—Lisa,' she said, re-treating back into the corner with her wine glass. 'What happened between you that's changed you so much, Leo?'

'It hasn't changed me.'

'It has. Of course it has. It's taken the life out of you. Most of the time you're fine, and then, bang, the shutters come down and you retreat. The only time you really relax is when you're with Ella, and even then there's something wrong. I thought at first it was grief, but it isn't, is it? It's regret, but why? What happened that you regret so much, that you're so ashamed of?'

How had he thought she looked like a child? She was looking at him now with the eyes of a sage, coaxing him to unburden himself, and once he started, he found he couldn't stop.

'I didn't love her,' he began. 'It was just a casual fling. She was part of the team on the last TV series. I'd never spoken to her, but she must have decided she'd like a piece of me as a trophy so she engineered an invitation to the party to celebrate finishing the filming, cosied up to me and—well, she got pregnant. I thought I'd taken care of that, but she told me much later she'd sabotaged it, and she didn't show a shred of remorse. And at the time she didn't seem shocked or upset by the surprise pregnancy. Far from it. Not until the whole situation became much more of a reality, and then she just went into meltdown.'

'So you didn't love her? You married her just because she was pregnant?'

He gave her a wintry smile. *'Just because?'*

Amy found herself smiling back, but she wanted to cry for him, for what she'd heard in his voice. 'You could have said no to her instead of doing the decent thing.'

'Except that it was my fault. She'd had too much to drink, I shouldn't have done it.'

'Was she very drunk?' she probed.

'I thought so, but she might have been acting. But then, to be fair, I wasn't exactly sober so it's hard to tell. It was quite a party, and I suspect my drink was being well and truly spiked by her. And that was only the first time. She stayed all weekend—'

'You took her back to yours?' To his flat over the restaurant? The place they'd sat and talked long into the night, over and over again? She knew it was ridiculous, knew he must have taken countless women there, but still she felt betrayed.

'The party was at the London restaurant. I lived above it. Where else would I take her?'

'Anywhere in the world?' she suggested, and he gave a rueful laugh.

'Yeah. Hindsight's a wonderful thing. But after the weekend I told her I wasn't interested in a relationship. I had the new restaurant opening coming up in Yoxburgh in a few months, so much to do to prepare for that, and I was trying to consolidate the business so I could afford to abandon it for a while to get the new restaurant up and running smoothly before the next TV series kicked off, and a relationship was the last thing I needed.'

'So—she left you alone?'

'Yes, she left me alone, sort of, for a few weeks, anyway. And then she turned up at the restaurant late one night and said she needed to speak to me, and she told me she was pregnant. I didn't believe her at first, but she had a scan six weeks later and the dates fitted, and she was adamant it was mine. And she was delighted. Of course.'

'What did your family say?'

He snorted softly. 'Have you never met my grandmother?' he asked unnecessarily, and Amy smiled wryly.

'Nonna told you to marry her?'

'She didn't need to. She listened to my side of the story, told me I'd been a fool to let it happen, but that I owed my child the right to have its father in its life. And she was right, of course. I already knew that. I also knew that the business didn't need the media circus that would follow if I walked away from a pregnant woman, and I knew she wouldn't keep it quiet. So we had a quiet wedding and moved up to Suffolk, into a rented house, so I could concentrate on the new restaurant.'

'Don't tell me. She didn't like it?'

'She didn't like it one bit. She'd thought we'd have a glamorous life in London, and she didn't take kindly to being imprisoned in a tinpot little backwater like Yoxburgh. Her words, not mine. And then Ella was born, and she was even more trapped, and she started drinking.'

'Drinking? As in—?'

'Heavy drinking. Getting utterly bat-faced. Night after night. I told her to stop, promised her a new house, said we could go back to London, split our time between the two, but that wasn't enough. To be honest, I think the reality of the whole thing—the pregnancy and birth, the move, the amount of time I was giving to the restaurant—it was all too much. It would have been too much for anyone, but she was so far out of her comfort zone that it was just impossible. And then...'

He broke off, the words choking him, and Amy shifted, moving the glasses out of the way and snuggling up against his side, one hand lying lightly over his heart. He wondered if she could feel it pounding as he relived that hideous night.

'Go on,' she said softly, and he let his arm curl round her shoulders and draw her closer against him, her warmth reassuring.

'She came to the restaurant. She'd left Ella at home, six weeks old, and she'd driven down to the restaurant to tell me she was leaving me. It was a filthy night, sheeting down with rain, the waves crashing over the prom, and she'd been drinking. I took the car keys off her and told her to go home and wait for me, but she started swearing and screaming in front of the customers. I called her a taxi, told her to wait, but she walked out of the restaurant into the lashing rain and straight into the path of a car. The driver didn't stand a chance, and nor did she. She died later that night in hospital, and all I felt was relief.'

Amy's arms tightened round his waist, hugging him gently, and he turned his head and rested his cheek against her hair. 'I didn't love her, Amy, but I didn't want her to die. I just wanted the whole situation to go away, but not like that.'

'Is that why you're ashamed? Because you wanted her gone, and when she was you were secretly relieved? Do you think you're to blame in some crazy way?'

'I *am* to blame,' he told her emphatically, pulling away slightly. 'I should have made it clearer to her what our life was going to be like, but I knew she'd got pregnant deliberately, knew that she'd set a trap for me that weekend, so I suppose I felt she'd got what she deserved. But she didn't deserve to die, and I didn't deserve to have to go through all that, and Ella certainly had done nothing to deserve anything that either of us had done. Nor had my family, and the media had a field day with it. Don't tell me you didn't know that because I don't believe it.'

'Oh, Leo. I read things, of course I did, and I was worried about you. I tried to call you several times, but you weren't taking any calls, and your parents were really protective so I couldn't get through to you and I gave up. I shouldn't have done. I should have come and seen you.'

Her voice was soft, filled with anguish for him, and she turned her head and lifted her face to his, touching her lips gently to his cheek. 'I'm so sorry. It must have been dreadful for all of you.'

Her lips were inches away. Less. All he had to do was

turn his head a fraction, and they'd be there, against his mouth. He fought it for seconds, then with a shuddering sigh he turned his head and moved away from danger. Not far. Just enough that he could still rest his head against hers but with his lips firmly out of the way of trouble.

'Leo?'

'Mmm?'

'I wasn't trying to seduce you earlier,' she said, her voice a fractured whisper. 'I really wasn't. I was just concerned about you.'

He sighed, his breath ruffling her hair, and his arm tightened around her. 'I know. But things are changing between us, and I don't want them to. I love you, Amy. I love you to bits, but I'm not going to have an affair with you, no matter how tempted either of us might be—'

She pushed away, tilting her head to stare up at him, her eyes wide with something that could have been indignation. Or desperation? 'When have I asked you to do that? *Ever?* When have I *ever* suggested that we—?'

'You haven't. Not in so many words. But it's there in your eyes, and it's in my head, and I'm not doing it, I'm not going to be drawn in by it, no matter how tempting it is to turn to each other for comfort. Because that's all it is, Amy. Comfort. And it would change everything. We've been friends for ever, and I don't want to change that. I need it, I treasure it, and I can't bear to think I could do something stupid one day to screw it up, because I will. I'll let you down—'

She moved abruptly, shifting so she was facing him, holding his face in her hands and staring intently into his eyes.

'No, you won't,' she said slowly and clearly. 'You've never let me down, Leo. I've let myself down, plenty of times, and I expect you've done the same, but you'll never let me down. You've just stopped me making the biggest mistake of my life—'

'Yes, I have, and I'm not going to let you—or either of us—make another one when your emotions are in chaos and you're clutching at the familiar because your life's suddenly going to be so different from what you'd planned.'

He took her hands in his, easing them away from his face and closing his fingers over them, pressing them to his lips before he let them go. He tucked a damp strand of hair behind her ear and gave her a rueful smile. 'You just need time, Amy. Time to let the dust settle and work out what you want from life. And it isn't me. It really isn't. I'm no good for you—not in that way. You don't really want me, you just want what I represent—the familiar, the safe, but I'm not safe, and I can't replace what you've lost by not marrying Nick. I know what you want, what you've lost, but I'm not it.'

She nodded, shifting away a little, turning her head to stare out over the valley. After a moment she gave a shaky sigh.

'I know that—and I know I'm not ready for another relationship, especially not with you. I mean, how would that work?' she said, her voice lightly teasing now, but he could still hear the hurt and confusion underlying it. 'I wouldn't have my sounding board any more, would I? How would I know it wasn't another awful mistake? I made the last mistake because I didn't talk to you. I don't want to do that again.'

She turned back to him, throwing him a sweet, wry smile. 'Thank you for telling me about Lisa. And don't blame yourself. It wasn't your fault.'

'It was. I should have driven her home instead of calling a taxi—handed the restaurant over to the team and left, taken care of her, but I didn't, I didn't realise she was that fragile, that unstable, and because of that she died.'

'No, Leo. She died because she got drunk and did something reckless, with far-reaching consequences. Everything else stemmed from that. You were her husband, not her keeper. She was an adult woman, and she made bad decisions. And on the last occasion it killed her. End of.'

'Except it's not the end, is it? I've got a motherless child and a career I've neglected for the past nine months—more, really. And there's nothing I can do about it. What's done is done. All any of us have to do is take care of the future, and I have no idea how. All I can do is survive from day to day and hope it gets better.'

'It will.'

'Will it? I hope so, because I can't go on like this.'

He stood up, tugging her to her feet and wrapping her in his arms and holding her tight, his face pressed into her hair. 'Thanks for listening to me. And thanks for being you. I don't know what I'd do without you.'

'You aren't without me. You won't be without me.'

'Promise?'

'I promise. Just keep talking to me.'

He nodded, then eased away. 'I will. Now go to bed. You need some sleep and so do I. I'll be up at the crack of dawn with Ella.'

'Well, good luck with that,' she said ruefully. 'Look at the sky.'

They stared out across the network of fields and hills, still leached of colour by the moon, but on the horizon there was the faintest streak of light appearing in the sky.

'It's a new day, Leo. It *will* get better.'

He looked down at her, her eyes shining with sincerity, the one person he could truly trust with all his hopes and fears. He bent his head, touched his lips to her cheek and then, as he breathed in and drew the scent of her into his body, he felt his resolve disintegrate.

He let his breath out on a shuddering sigh and turned his head, as she turned hers, and their lips touched.

They clung, held, and with a ragged sigh of defeat he pulled her closer, feeling her taut limbs, the softness of her breasts, the warmth of her mouth opening like a flower under his, and he was lost.

He couldn't get enough of her. One hand slid round and found her breast through the slippery silk of that tormenting gown, and he felt her nipple peak hard against his hand.

She moaned softly, arching against him, her tongue duelling with his as he delved and tasted, savouring her, learning her, aching for her.

Her hands were on him, learning him, too, their movements desperate as she clung to his arms, his back, cradling his head as he was cradling hers, her fingers spearing through his hair and pulling him down to her.

He groaned, rocking his hips against hers, needing her for so much more than this, and she whimpered as his hands slid down and cupped her bottom, lifting her against him.

Amy...

Amy! No, no, no, no!

He had to stop. She had to stop. One of them had to stop. He uncurled his fingers and slid his hands up her back, but he didn't let go. He couldn't. He needed her. Wanted her. He had to...

His hands cradled her face, the kiss gentling as he fought with his warring emotions. And then she eased away and took a step back, out of reach, and he felt bereft.

Their eyes met and locked, and after an agonising second he dragged a hand down over his face and tried to step back, to put more space between them while he still could, but his feet were rooted to the spot, his chest heaving with the need that still screamed through him, and he

tilted his head back and stared blindly at the pale streak
of sky that promised a new tomorrow.

Could he trust it? Could he trust her?

She reached out, her hand finding his, their fingers tan-
gling, and he lowered his head and met her eyes again, and
saw nothing in them but honesty.

'Make love to me, Leo,' she murmured, and the last ves-
tige of his crumbling self-control turned to dust.

CHAPTER EIGHT

AMY LAY ON her side, one leg draped over his, her head pillowed on his chest, her lips tilting into a smile of utter contentment and wonder as his hand stroked idly over her back.

So that's what the fireworks were like. The chemistry she'd dismissed. The 'amazing' that she'd never, ever found before.

His lips brushed her hair, his breath warm against her scalp, and she turned her head so she could reach his mouth.

He kissed her slowly, lazily, shifting so he was facing her, his hand sliding round her ribcage and settling on her breast, and she snuggled closer, feeling the jut of his erection against her body as her leg curled over his hip and drew him up against her.

He groaned, deep in his chest, the vibrations resonating through his breath and into her like the faint tremors of an earthquake. 'I want you,' he breathed raggedly. 'I need you—so much. Oh, Amy—'

He rolled her onto her back, their bodies coming together instinctively, surely, and she felt the first quivers of another shattering climax ripple through her body. 'Leo...'

'I'm here. I've got you...'

His head fell forward into the curve of her neck, his mouth open, his breath hot against her skin as he said her name over and over again while she fell, spiralling down and down, reaching out, clinging to him as his body caught up with hers and took them both over the edge.

Their muted cries tangled in the soft light of dawn, their bodies blurring into one, and as their hearts slowed and their breathing quietened, he rolled to the side, taking her with him into sleep.

Leo lay beside her, staring at the ceiling and trying to make sense of his tangled emotions.

All these years, he'd been so careful to preserve their friendship, to keep it platonic, to treasure the bond they had without crossing the invisible line between them. It had been so vitally important to him, his respect for Amy's friendship so deeply ingrained that it hadn't ever occurred to him to muddy the waters by sleeping with her. Other women had fulfilled that need for him, women who didn't trust him or depend on him or need him, women who wanted from him only what he wanted from them. Women who weren't Amy, or anything like Amy, because Amy was sacrosanct, untouchable.

Well, he'd certainly touched her now, the line well and truly crossed, and there was no going back. What he didn't know was what lay ahead, because he had nothing to offer her except the few scraps of himself that were left over from work and from caring for his daughter. And it hadn't been enough for Lisa, so why on earth did he imagine it could be enough for Amy?

He groaned silently.

He should never have kissed her, never have let her lead him into her bedroom, never peeled away the flimsy barriers of their clothing and with them the protective layers of their friendship, exposing the raw need and desperate hunger that lurked beneath.

He'd made a catastrophic mistake by doing that, but what an incredible, beautiful, exquisite mistake it had been.

Because he loved her, in every way, without reservation, and what they'd done had felt so right, so good, so pure and simple and innocent and—just *right*.

Oh, Amy. His lips moved silently on the words, his eyes drifting shut against the tears of joy and regret that welled in them. *Don't let me hurt you. Please, don't let me hurt you.*

But he knew he would. Somehow, some time, sooner or later it would happen. And it would break his heart, as well as hers.

Ella woke her, the baby's wail cutting through her dream and dragging her back to reality, and she stretched out to Leo but he was gone.

Oh.

She stretched and yawned and lay there for a moment waiting, sure he must have gone to her, but there was no sound from him and the baby was still crying, so she threw back the covers, found her nightdress and went to investigate.

'Hello, sweetheart. Where's your daddy?' she murmured, lifting the baby out of the cot and cuddling her close.

'I'm here. Sorry, I was in the other kitchen but there was something I couldn't just drop. Come here, poppet.'

He took her out of Amy's arms, his eyes brushing hers fleetingly, warm and gentle but troubled, and she gave an inward sigh.

'I know what you're thinking,' she said, sitting down on the bed while he put Ella down on the changing mat at her feet and knelt down. 'But don't.'

He shot her a sideways glance. 'How do you know what I'm thinking?'

'Because I know you inside out, Leo. You might have changed a little, grown older and wiser—'

His snort cut her off, but she just smiled and carried on, 'But you're still the same over-protective person you always were, and you're beating yourself up at the moment, taking all the blame, wishing you hadn't done it—'

'No.' He sat back on his heels and looked up at her, his eyes burning. 'No, Amy, you're wrong. I'm not wishing I hadn't done it. I just wish I could give you more, wish I could offer you a future—'

'Shh.' She leant forward and pressed a finger to his lips, silencing him. He kissed her finger, drew it into his mouth, suckled it briefly before he pulled away, and she nearly whimpered.

'You were saying?'

'I can't remember.'

His eyes were laughing. '*Shh* was the last thing.'

'So it was.' She smiled, and carried on. 'Forget about the future, Leo. It's far too soon to think about that. Forget everything except the here and now. We've got a few more days. Let's just enjoy them, get to know each other better, the people we are now, and have some fun with Ella. Have a holiday—'

'I have to cook.'

'You have to cook one meal.'

'And try out their stuff.'

'You're making excuses. I thought it was supposed to be a simple lunch?'

He smiled crookedly. 'I don't do simple, apparently. I want to do something that tastes amazing.'

'All your food tastes amazing.'

He arched an eyebrow. 'What happened to my critic?'

'Oh, she's still here, she'll come out when necessary,' she said with a laugh, and then sighed and threw up her hands. 'OK. I concede. Cook, play in the kitchen, and Ella and I'll play with you when we can, and you'll play with us when you can, and I know when they get back you'll be in meetings, but we'll still have the nights.'

She heard the suck of his indrawn breath, saw the flaring of his pupils as he straightened to look at her again, the jump of a muscle in his jaw. 'And then?'

She shrugged. She didn't know. And maybe it was better that way. 'What happens in Tuscany stays in Tuscany?' she said softly, and their eyes held.

'OK. I'll buy that for now.'

'Good. Oh, and by the way, you were amazing last night,' she said casually, and stood up to walk past him.

'So were you. Incredible.' His arm snaked out, his hand sliding up under the short hem of her nightdress and curving round her naked bottom, drawing her in against him. He rested his head briefly against her, his breath hot on her body through the fine silk, and then he let her go, his hand sliding down her leg and leaving fire in its wake. She sat down again abruptly.

'So, what are you doing today?' she asked when she could speak, but her voice was breathy and he tilted his head back and speared her with his eyes.

'I don't know. I know what I'm doing tonight. That's as far as my thoughts have gone for now.' A lazy, sexy smile lit up his face, and she felt heat shiver through her.

'OK,' she said slowly. 'So—assuming we're going to do something a little more practical in the meantime, shall I shower first, or do you want to?'

'I've showered. You were sleeping the sleep of the dead,' he told her, that lazy smile still lingering on his delectable and clever, clever mouth. 'If you could shower now and take Ella from me so I can get on, that would be great. I'll make us all breakfast if you like.'

'I like. I definitely like. I'm starving.'

He rolled his eyes and got to his feet, Ella cradled in one

arm, and he turned Amy and pushed her gently towards the bathroom door. 'Shoo. I've got a lot to do.'

'So, little Ella, what are we going to do while Daddy's busy this morning?' she asked. 'A walk? That sounds like a great idea. Where shall we go? The olive groves? OK.'

Ella grinned at her, a toothy little grin with a gurgle of laughter that made her heart swell in her chest until she thought it'd burst.

'Was that funny?' she asked, and Ella laughed again, so that by the time she was strapped in her buggy they both had the giggles.

'What's the joke?'

He'd stuck his head out of the kitchen door, and she turned her head and grinned at him. 'No joke. She just started laughing, and it's really infectious.'

'Tell me about it. Are you off for a walk now?'

'Mmm. Ella thought we might like to go down to the olive groves.'

'Did she now?' he asked, coming over to them and crouching in front of Ella.

'She did.'

He chuckled softly, bent and kissed the baby and then, as he straightened and drew level with her, he kissed Amy. It caught her by surprise, the sure, gentle touch of his lips, the promise of heat in his eyes, the lingering warmth of his hand against her cheek.

'Have fun. I'll see you later,' he murmured, and waggling his fingers at Ella he headed back to the kitchen to carry on.

They had a lovely walk, the air full of the buzzing of bees and the scent of the olive blossom as they strolled along beneath the trees, and predictably the rocking motion of the buggy sent Ella to sleep, so Amy's mind was free to wander.

And of course it wandered straight to Leo, and stayed there.

Not surprising, really, after last night. She'd never felt like she had then, but it wasn't because of anything in particular that he'd done, it was just because it had been him—his touch, his kiss, his body. It had just felt—right, as if everything in the universe had fallen neatly into place when she had been in his arms.

And today the sun was brighter, the grass greener, the birdsong louder. A smile on her face, she turned the buggy round and headed back up the hill to Leo. It was time she went back, anyway. She'd been out in the sun too long and her shoulders were burning.

She left the buggy with Leo and went to put after-sun lotion on, and when she got back Ella was awake, so they played outside the kitchen until Leo called them in for lunch, then Amy took her back in the garden under the shade of the pergola until she yawned again.

'I'm going to put her down in her cot,' she told Leo. 'Do you need any help?'

He shot her a warm but distracted smile. 'No, not really.'

'I'll sort some more photos, then,' she said, and going up on tiptoe she kissed his cheek and left him to it.

She couldn't quite believe how many pictures she'd taken of Leo.

Leo cooking, Leo swimming, Leo laughing, frowning, smiling, winking at her cheekily—hundreds. Hundreds and hundreds. Lots of Ella, too, and the two of them to-gether. They brought a lump to her throat.

There were others, of the family, of the *palazzo* and its grounds, the olive groves, the vineyards, the chestnut woods—anywhere he'd gone and she'd been with him, she'd taken photos. And she'd lent him the camera so he could take some when she wasn't there, and she scrolled through those with interest.

He'd certainly have plenty to choose from for his blog, she thought with relief, so she didn't need to feel she owed him anything, not by the time she'd added in the babysitting this week and for the eight weeks of the filming.

Eight weeks in which they'd do—what? She'd said what happens in Tuscany stays in Tuscany, but if they were together, at home, would that still apply? Or would it be awkward?

Was their relationship going to end when they left Italy? She didn't know, and she didn't want to ask him, because she wasn't sure she'd want to hear the answer.

Then Ella cried, and she shut down her laptop and went to get her. She was sitting up in her little cot, rubbing her eyes and wailing sleepily, and she held her arms up to Amy.

'Hello, baby,' she murmured. 'It's all right, I'm here.'

She scooped her up gently and hugged her, and Ella's little arms snaked round her neck, chubby fingers splayed against her sunburnt shoulders. The tousled little head snuggled down into the crook of Amy's neck, and she squeezed the baby tight, deeply touched by the little one's affection. She'd formed a real bond with her in this short time, and it would be such a wrench not to see her again every day, not to be part of her life when this was done.

She was such a sweet child, and it was so sad that she would grow up without her mother. How would that feel? For all her gentle interference, Amy's mother was a huge part of her life. How would it have been never to have known the security and warmth that came with being so deeply, unreservedly and unconditionally loved by the woman who'd given you life? Even the thought of it made Amy ache inside for her.

Could she take that woman's place? In a heartbeat.

Would she be invited to? As his wife?

'It'll be a cold day in hell before that happens.'

Oh, Leo…

She gave a quiet sigh and changed Ella's nappy, put her back in the little sun dress she'd been wearing in the morning, picked up her pretty, frilly sun hat and went to find him.

There was no sign of him in the kitchen, but there was a bit of paper propped up on the table with 'In veg garden' scrawled on it in Leo's bold hand.

She plonked the sun hat on the baby's head, went out through the open French doors onto the terrace and followed it around until she spotted him on the level below, in a sheltered spot amongst the orderly rows of vegetables.

She went down the steps and walked towards him. He was crouched down, balancing on the balls of his feet as he studied the lush mounds of greenery all around him, and he turned and squinted up at her in the sun. It would have made a brilliant photo, but for once she didn't have her camera.

'Hi, there. Everything okay?'

'Yes, fine. We just wondered what you were doing.'

Ella lunged towards him, right on cue, and said, 'Dadadad,' her little face beaming, and of course he couldn't resist that.

'Ciao, mia bellisima,' he said, his face lighting up with a smile for his little daughter. He straightened up, his hands full, and bent his head to kiss Ella, his eyes softening with a love that made Amy's heart turn over.

He was standing close enough that she could smell him, her nose tantalised by a slight, lingering trace of aftershave overlaid by the heady scent of warm male skin, and he turned his head and captured her mouth with a slow, lingering kiss. Then he lifted his head, and she took a step back and pointed in the direction of his hands.

'What are those?'

He glanced down. 'Zucchini flowers—courgettes. They're so pretty, and they're delicious stuffed. I thought I might do them as a vegetable. Heaven knows, Lydia's going to have enough of them,' he said, waving a hand at the rows of rampant plants he'd been inspecting.

'I'm sure she'll think it's worth the sacrifice. So what are you going to stuff them with?' she asked, trying to focus on something other than the scent of his skin in the warm sunshine, and the lingering taste of him on her lips.

'I don't know. I've got a few ideas. I'll try them out on you this evening.'

He picked up a basket overflowing with the things he'd raided from the garden, plucked the baby off her hip, settled her on his and headed back to the kitchen, nuzzling Ella and blowing raspberries on her neck and making her giggle.

He was so good with her. Good enough that the loss of her mother wouldn't matter? And what about when they got back to England and *she* wasn't around any more? Would that matter to Ella? Would she even notice?

Don't borrow trouble.

Amy followed them, the taut muscles of Leo's tanned calves in easy reach as he walked up the steps in front of her. His long shorts clung to his lean hips, giving her a tantalising view of muscles that bunched and stretched with every step, and she wanted to reach out her hand and touch them, feel their warmth and solidity, test the texture of rough hair over smooth tanned skin. Taste the salt on his skin—

Later...

He crossed over to the kitchen, dumping the basket of vegetables on the big table. 'Tea or coffee?' he asked, turning his head to look at Amy over his shoulder.

'Something cold?' she said, and he pulled open the

fridge and took out the spring water. 'So what's the plan for the rest of the afternoon?'

He shrugged, those broad, lean shoulders shifting under the soft pale blue cotton of his shirt, the cuffs turned back to reveal strong, tanned forearms. He'd always tanned really easily, she remembered, part of his Latin heritage.

'I don't know,' he said, jiggling Ella on his hip. 'It rather depends on madam here and what she'd like to do.'

'I'm happy to look after her, if you want,' Amy volunteered, but he shook his head.

'No, it's okay, I haven't seen her all day and I'm going to need you tomorrow morning so I'm keeping you sweet for that,' he said with a grin. He unscrewed the bottle and poured two glasses of fizzy water, added a slice of lime to each and handed her one. 'Has she had her bottle?' he asked, and Amy shook her head.

'No, but it's in the fridge there. I thought I'd come and find you first, see what you're doing.'

'This and that.' He took the bottle out, hooked out a chair with his foot and sat down with the baby. 'So how have you been getting on?' he asked as he gave Ella her bottle. 'Did you look at the photos?'

'Yes. There are some really good ones that'll be great for your blog. They're on my laptop. There's a ton of dross as well, of course, but you can have a look later.'

'I'd love to, but probably not until after tomorrow. I've got enough on at the moment.' He gave her a wry grin. 'I hate to ask, but would you be able to keep an eye on Ella for a while later on so I can do some more prep? You can stay in here so she can see me, but I could just do with an hour or two to make up a marinade and get some risotto under way. I'll put her to bed.'

'It's why I'm here, Leo.'

His mouth softened into a smile. 'So you keep saying. I tell you what, how about a swim first?'

* * *

She wore the bikini, and when Ella grabbed the top again, he just smiled and gently disentangled the baby's fingers, which of course involved his own getting nicely into the mix.

He eased Ella away, met Amy's eyes and winked at her, and she blushed, which made him laugh softly.

'Later,' he promised, and her mouth opened a fraction and then curved into a smile that could have threatened his sanity if he hadn't already lost it.

And before he knew what she was doing, she slipped beneath the surface and swam towards him, nudging his legs apart with her hands before twisting through them like a mermaid. She'd done it before, hundreds of times when they were growing up, but not now, when he was so aware of the brush of her body against his.

'Boo!' she said, surfacing right behind him, and Ella squealed with laughter, so she did it again, and again, and again, and every time her body slid past his, grazing intimately against him until he called a halt.

'Right, enough. I need to get on.'

'We'll come out, too.'

She went first, reaching down to take Ella from his arms and treating him to the soft, lush swell of her breasts threatening to escape from the bikini that was proving so rewarding.

Never mind mermaid. She was a siren, luring him onto the rocks, and tonight was so far away...

'Are you sure you don't mind?'

'Positive,' she said patiently. 'Leave her with me and go and make a start, and I'll change her nappy and then we'll follow you. I can take photos of you cooking, and give you the benefit of my considerable expertise as a guinea pig while I play with her. And at least that way

I'll get something to eat, because I know what you're like when you start something like this. You get totally focussed and forget everything else, and supper will just go out of the window.'

He smiled, as he was meant to, and went.

'So what's that you're doing now?' she asked, carrying Ella into the kitchen a few minutes later and peering over Leo's shoulder.

'Broad bean, mint and pecorino risotto—it's the stuffing for the zucchini flowers, a variation on what we had last night.' He stuck his finger into the pan, scooped out a dollop and held it out to her lips. 'Here. Try it.'

He'd done it so many times before, and yet this time seemed so different. She opened her mouth, drew his finger into it and curled her tongue around the tip, sucking the delicious, creamy risotto from it without ever losing eye contact.

'Mmm. Yummy. You've put more mint in it. So are they going to be cold or hot?' she asked.

Leo hauled in a slow, quiet breath and tried to concentrate on anything other than the sweet warmth of Amy's mouth, the curl of her tongue against his finger, the gentle suction as she'd drawn the risotto into her mouth all too quickly. He turned away to check the seasoning of the risotto and gave his body a moment to calm down.

'Warm. Things taste better that way, often, and they need to be deep fried in tempura batter and served pretty much immediately, which rather dictates it.'

'They'd go well with the lamb,' she suggested, and he nodded.

'They would. And I could cook them at the last moment when everything else was ready to go. Here, try this. I've been playing with the topping for the bruschetta.'

He handed her a dollop—on a spoon, this time, since

he really couldn't afford to get that distracted, but it was nearly as bad. 'OK?'

'Lovely. Really tasty. So what do you want me to photograph?'

He shrugged, his shoulders shifting under the shirt, drawing her attention yet again to his body. 'Anything you like. You tell me, you're the photographer.'

'I don't know. What are you doing now?' she asked, casting around for something to take her mind off his body, because even framing the shots for the camera wasn't helping. If anything, it was making it worse because it meant focussing on him and she was having trouble focussing on anything else.

'Marinade for the mutton.' He'd set the vegetables on one side and was pounding something with a pestle and mortar, grinding garlic and herbs together with a slosh of olive oil and a crunch of salt and pepper, his muscles flexing as he worked. 'I'll smoosh it all over the meat, leave it till later and put it in the oven overnight so I can shred it and shape it first thing in the morning.'

He stopped pounding, to her relief, pulled out the shoulder of mutton from the fridge, stabbed it all over with a knife and smeared—no, *smooshed*, whatever kind of a word that was—the contents of the bowl all over the outside of the meat, dropped it back into the oven tray on top of the chopped vegetables, wrapped it in foil and stuck it back in the fridge.

'Right. Mint jelly.'

She watched him while Ella was playing contentedly with some stacking blocks, clicking away on the camera to record it all for his blog. Most of the shots were probably underexposed, but she didn't have any lights or reflectors so she was relying on the natural light spilling in through the open French doors to the terrace, and the under-cup-board lights that flooded the work area with a soft, golden light that worked wonders with his olive skin.

And as a perk, of course, she got to study him in excruciatingly minute detail.

The mint jelly setting in the fridge, he moved on, pulling together the ingredients for a dessert that made her drool just watching him.

'Tell me it's going to be your panna cotta?'

He threw her a grin over his shoulder. 'Was there a choice?'

Of course not. It was one of his signature dishes, and she'd never eaten a better one anywhere. Technically difficult to produce reliably—or for her to produce reliably, at any rate; she doubted Leo had any problems with it— he was making it with the ease of long practice, talking as he worked, and he was a joy to watch. But then, he was always a joy to watch...

'I'm going to turn them out and serve them with a compote of freshly sliced home-grown strawberries in their cousin's balsamic vinegar. I'm hoping I can talk them into letting me have a few bottles a year. It's amazing. It's almost a syrup, and it's—oh, it's just lovely with fruit. Beautiful. Works perfectly with it. I'll make a few spares. If you're really good, I'll give you one later.'

'I'll be really, really good,' she vowed, and he turned, holding her eyes for a second or two.

'Is that a promise?' he murmured, and it turned her legs to mush.

He finished the panna cotta, poured it carefully into the moulds and slipped the tray into the fridge.

'This kitchen's a joy to work in,' he said, and turned back to her with a grin that wiped the promise of dessert right off the menu and made her think of something much, much sweeter, powerful enough to blow her composure right apart.

And his, if the look in his eyes was anything to go by.
Which was not a good idea when he was busy.

'I'll take Ella out in the garden in the shade. She's bored,
and she loves the little sandpit.'

And scooping up the baby, she headed for the French
doors to give him space.

Leo watched her go, let his breath out on a long sigh and
braced his arms on the worktop. Why was he suddenly so
intensely aware of her, after so many years? What was it
that had changed for them? She wasn't a child any more,
not by a long shot, but she'd been a woman for some considerable time, and it had taken this long for the change
to register on his Richter scale.

And how.

But it wasn't for long. They only had a few more days
here in Tuscany, by which time he would have sealed the
deal with the Valtieri brothers.

Because he was going to. He'd decided that on the first
evening, but he'd needed to know more about them and
what they produced. And now he did, they could sort out
the small print and he could go home.

He just had no idea where that would leave him and
Amy.

CHAPTER NINE

'So I was right, then,' she said, trying to keep it light. 'No supper.'

'Don't worry, you won't starve.'

'I didn't think I would for a moment, but I have no doubt I'll have to sing for it.'

He gave a soft huff of laughter and carried on fiddling at the stove. 'Did she settle all right?'

'Yes, she's fine.'

'Good. Thanks. Here, try this.'

He put some things on a plate and set it on the table in front of her. Several slices of bruschetta—with the new topping, she guessed—and a couple of the stuffed zucchini flowers, dipped in the most delicate batter and briskly deep fried, then drained and drizzled in more of the heavenly olive oil.

'Try the *bruschetta*. I think this topping works better.'

She picked it up and sank her teeth into it, and sighed as the flavours exploded on her tongue. 'Gorgeous,' she mumbled, and looked up and caught his cocky grin.

'Did you expect anything less?' he said, with a lazy smile that dimpled his right cheek and an oh-so-Italian shrug that nearly unravelled her brain. 'Try the zucchini flowers. I tweaked the risotto filling again. Here—rinse your mouth first.'

She obediently drank some of the sparkling water he

passed her, then bit the end off one of the little golden parcels and groaned. 'Mmm. Yummy. Mintier?'

He nodded. 'I thought it might work with the main course as you suggested, instead of potatoes.'

'I don't suppose you've cooked any of the meat yet, have you, so we can try them together?' she said hopefully, and he chuckled.

'Not a prayer. It's going to take hours.'

He picked up the second zucchini flower and bit into it, and a little ooze of the risotto filling caught on his lip and she leant over, hooked her hand around the back of his neck to hold him still and captured it with her tongue.

He swore softly in Italian and shook his head at her.

'How am I supposed to concentrate now?' he grumbled, putting the rest of it in his mouth, but he was smiling as he took the plate and slid it into the dishwasher.

'I don't suppose the panna cotta's set yet?'

'You want some, I take it?'

'Absolutely. With the strawberries. And the balsamic. I want the whole deal. A girl has to eat. And you wanted my terrifying honesty, anyway.'

He sighed and rolled his eyes, muttering something about demanding women, and she smiled. It was just like old times, but not, because now there was something new to add to the mix, and it just made it even better.

She propped her elbows on the table and watched as he dipped the mould briefly in hot water, tipped the panna cotta out, spooned some sliced strawberries in dark syrup over the edge and decorated it with a mint leaf and a dust of vanilla icing sugar, and then shoved the plate in front of her, his spoon poised.

'I have to share it?' she joked, and then nearly whimpered as he scooped some up and held it to her lips.

It quivered gently, soft and luscious, the strawberries smelling of summer. She let it melt on her tongue—the sweet, the sour, the sharp, the…fiery?—and let her breath out slowly. 'Oh, wow. That's different. What's it got in it?'

'Pink peppercorns. Just a touch, to give it depth and warmth, and mint again for freshness. So what do you think of their balsamic? Good, isn't it?'

'Lovely. Beautiful. The whole thing's gorgeous.' She took the spoon from him and scooped up another dollop and felt it slide down her throat, cool and creamy and delicious, with a touch of lingering warmth from the pink peppercorns and the fresh richness of the ripe strawberries soaked in the glorious balsamic vinegar waking up every one of her taste buds. She groaned softly, opened her eyes again and met Leo's eyes.

And something happened. Some subtle shift, a hitch of breath, a flare of his pupils, and she felt as if she'd been struck by lightning.

For long seconds they froze, trapped in the moment, as if the clocks had stopped and everything was suspended in time. And then he leant in and kissed her, his mouth cool and sweet from the panna cotta, a touch of heat that lingered until he eased away and broke the contact.

'OK, I'm happy with that. Happy with all of it, so that's it for the testing,' he said, backing away, his voice a little rough and matter-of-fact, and if it hadn't been for the heat in his eyes she would have thought she'd done something wrong

'Can I give you a hand to clear up?'

'No, you're fine. I'll do it. I've got more mess to make before I'm done.'

'Shall I wait up for you?'

He shook his head, and a slow smile burned in his eyes. 'No. You go to bed. I'll come and find you.'

She hadn't even made it to the bedroom before he followed her in. 'I thought you had more to do?' she said softly.

'It'll keep. I have more pressing concerns right now,' he murmured, and tugged her gently into his arms.

She heard him get up, long before the sun rose, when the sky was streaked with pink and the air was filled with birdsong. She propped herself up on one elbow and groped for her phone, checking the time.

Five thirty.

He must be mad. Or driven. This meal was important to him, a chance to showcase his skills to the Valtieri team, and of course he was driven. There was a lot riding on it, and he wasn't going to derail it just because they'd fallen into an unscheduled affair. Even if it was amazing.

At least she didn't have to get up yet. She could sneak another hour, at a pinch, before Ella woke up. She flopped back onto the pillow and closed her eyes again, and the next thing she was aware of was the sound of knocking, then something being put down on her bedside table. She prised her eyes open and Leo's face swam into view.

'Tea,' he said economically, his voice gruff with lack of sleep. 'Ella's up and I need to get on. Can I drag you out of bed?'

She blinked to clear her eyes. 'Time?'

'Nearly seven.'

Rats. 'Give me five minutes,' she mumbled, and closed her eyes again. Mistake. She felt a wet trail across her forehead and opened them again to see Leo dipping his finger in her water glass again.

'Noooo,' she moaned, and forced herself to sit up. 'You're such a bully.'

His smile was strained, his eyes tired. 'Sorry,' he said, sounding utterly unrepentant. 'I really need you. Five minutes,' he repeated firmly, and went out, closing the door softly behind himself.

She looked longingly at the pillows, then sighed, shoved

them up against the headboard and shuffled up the bed. Five minutes, indeed. She groped for the mug, took a sip, then a swallow, and gradually the fog cleared from her brain. She had to get up. Now. Before temptation overwhelmed her and she slithered back down under the covers.

With Leo?

'Don't distract him,' she growled, and dumped the empty mug down and threw off the covers, just as Leo came back in.

His eyes flicked to her legs, then up again, and he zoomed in for a hot, quick kiss. 'Just checking you weren't asleep again.'

'I'm not,' she said unnecessarily, trying not to smile. 'Shut the door on your way out and go back to work.'

He backed out, pulling it to as he went. 'I'm taking Ella to the kitchen to give her breakfast while I carry on. That should give you time for a shower.'

The latch clicked, and she sighed and went over to the French doors and stared out at the valley.

Today was a big day for him, but it was also nearly the end of their stay. She knew Leo needed far more from her than a random fumble when he was too tired to think straight, but if she was going to be there for him for the next few weeks at least, to help him through the disastrous fallout from his doomed marriage, then her feelings and his had to remain on an even keel, which meant playing it light and not letting herself take it too seriously.

And certainly not distracting him when he needed to work, even if it killed her.

She showered rapidly and pulled her clothes on before heading for the kitchen. It was still only half past seven. How on earth was he functioning on so little sleep?

She found them in the kitchen, Ella mashing a soldier of toast all over the tray of the high chair, Leo doing something fast and dextrous with a knife and a rack of lamb.

There was a pile of zucchini flowers in the middle of the table, and the air was rich with promise.

'Smells good in here,' she said.

'That's the mutton,' he said tersely. 'I got up at three and put it in the oven, and I've shredded it and rolled it up into sausages in cling film and it's chilling, and I'm just prepping the racks. She could do with a drink and a handful of blueberries. They're in the fridge.'

She opened the door and was greeted by shelves crammed with goodies of all sorts, including the lovely, lovely panna cotta. 'Which shelf?'

He turned and pointed, then went back to his prepping, and she gave Ella the blueberries and put a slice of bread in the toaster for herself.

'Do you want a coffee?'

'I've had three,' he said. 'Not that it's helping. I'll have another one.'

'Or I could give you a glass of spring water with lemon in it and you could detox a bit for half an hour?'

'Just give me a coffee,' he growled, and gave an enormous yawn. 'My body's finally decided I'm tired. Talk about picking its moments.'

She laughed a little guiltily and handed him a coffee, weaker than he would have made it, longer, with a good slug of milk, and he gave her a look but took it anyway.

'Thanks.'

'You're welcome.'

He took a gulp and carried on, and she sat down with Ella, leaving him to it while she ate her breakfast and tried to stop the blueberries escaping to the floor.

'Tell me if there's anything you need me to help with,' she said, and he nodded.

'I'm fine. You're doing the most useful thing already.'

'I've brought my camera.'

'To catch me at my worst?'

She turned her head and studied him. His hair was tousled and spiky, his eyes were bleary and he had on yesterday's shirt and ancient jeans cut off at the knee, showing off those lean muscular calves that she'd recently realised were irresistible. His feet were bare, too, the toes splayed slightly as he leaned over, strong and straight and curiously sexy. Why had she never noticed them before?

She dragged her eyes off them.

'I think your fans will be able to cope,' she said drily, and pulled out her camera. One for her personal folder…

The family arrived back at eleven thirty, and Lydia came straight into the kitchen to ask if he needed help.

'No, I'm fine,' he said. 'All under control.' Unlike his emotions. 'What time do you want to eat?'

'Twelve thirty?'

He nodded. 'I thought we should eat in the garden under the pergola, unless you'd rather be in here?'

'The garden would be lovely. So, can I ask what's on the menu?'

He told her, and her eyes lit up. 'Fabulous,' she said. 'Bring it on—I'm starving! And I *will* be picking your brains later.'

He couldn't help but laugh. 'Feel free. Now leave me alone so I can concentrate.'

Not a chance. The kitchen became party central, but it didn't matter. He was used to working in chaos, and Lydia made sure they all stayed out of his way and she helped him unobtrusively, taking over the stuffing of the zucchini flowers while he checked on the other things.

Which was fine, except of course Amy was there, and his eyes kept straying to her, distracting his attention from the core business.

He forced himself to focus. The last thing he needed was the lamb rack overcooked or the zucchini flowers burnt in the hot oil when he started to cook them in a few minutes.

But it seemed that although she was pretty much ignoring him, Amy was very much aware of what he was doing, and with twenty minutes to go she chivvied them all outside into the garden to leave him in peace. He stopped her as she was following them.

'Amy?'

'Do you need me?'

What a choice of words, after all that had happened last night. He held out a serving plate piled high with bruschetta.

'Could you give them these—and try and make sure you don't eat them all yourself,' he added, grinning.

She took the plate from him with an unladylike snort and a toss of her head, and he chuckled. Still the same old Amy. 'Thank you,' he called after her, and she relented and threw him a smile over her shoulder as she went out of the door.

She checked her watch. Any minute now, she thought, and leaving Ella in Lydia's care she slipped back into the kitchen.

'Anything I can do?'

'Take the plates out and make sure they're all sitting down ready and then help me ferry stuff in a couple of minutes? I'm just frying the last of the zucchini flowers and everything else is done. The lamb's resting, the mutton's keeping warm and the veg are steaming.'

He was working as he talked and she glanced at the clock on the kitchen wall. Twelve twenty six. Bang on time. She felt her mouth tug in a wry smile. He'd never been on time for anything in his life until he'd started cooking professionally.

'OK. Nothing you want me to do except ferry?'

'No, I'll be fine. And, Amy?'

She turned and met his eyes.

'Thank you. For everything. I couldn't have done it without you. You've been amazing.'

She felt his warmth flood through her.

'You're welcome. And I know you'll be fine. They'll love it. You have some serious fans out here. Just don't burn the zucchini flowers.'

He *was* fine.

Everything was fine. More than fine, and he was in his element.

The food was amazing, and everyone from the babies upwards loved it. The zucchini flowers he'd finally chosen as the starter were beautiful and utterly delicious, and once the lamb two ways—*agnello in due modi* as Leo called it for the benefit of their Italian hosts—was on the table, he looked utterly relaxed. And by the time he brought out the panna cotta and strawberries, he was Leo at his best.

This was his dish, the thing he'd made his own, and Lydia, who by now was muttering things about how on earth she was expected to feed the family after this, was begging him for a master class or at the very least a recipe.

'Any time. It's so easy.'

'Easy to make, but not easy to make taste like *that*,' Lydia pointed out, and he laughed

'But it's nothing without the right ingredients.' His eyes swung to Massimo.

He was leaning back in his chair, wine in hand, his eyes on Leo, and he nodded slowly. 'We need to talk. Heaven knows my wife's an excellent chef, and I'm used to amazing food on a daily basis, but you've taken our ingredients and lifted them into something incredible. We have to do a deal. I want our produce on the table in your restaurants.'

For a moment Leo said nothing, but then a slow smile

started in his eyes and lit up his whole face. 'Thank you. I was going to say the same thing. I don't know what it is about your produce—maybe the care you take, the land, the generations of expertise, but I've been able to find a depth of flavour that I've never found before, and I really want to work with you. And I want that *balsamico* on the list,' he added with a wink.

They all laughed. 'I'm sure that can be arranged. Nine o'clock tomorrow. We'll sort out the fine print,' Massimo said, and drained his glass.

She was sitting on the terrace nursing a cup of tea and watching the swallows when he appeared. Ella was in bed and the families had all gone their separate ways, and they were alone.

He dropped onto the other end of the bench and let out a satisfied sigh. 'Well, that went OK.'

She laughed softly. 'Did you ever doubt it would?'

'Absolutely. There are always doubts, but it looks as if I've achieved what I'd come for.'

'With bells on. They really like you, Leo. And if they hadn't, it wouldn't happen.'

'I know. Tell me about it. And I really like them, too. I trust them, and I couldn't have wanted more from this trip.' He turned his head, his eyes seeking hers. 'And I couldn't have done it without you.'

She looked away, suddenly awkward. 'I haven't done that much—'

'Yes, you have,' he said sincerely. 'I needed to know that Ella was all right, and she was, which left me free to see everything there was to see and take my time getting to know them. It's an important deal, and I wanted to be clear about what I was getting.'

'And are you?'

'Oh, yes. I imagine they'll want to tie up the loose ends

tomorrow, but we're pretty much done. Time to go home. I've neglected my business long enough.'

Home.

Whatever that meant.

Amy stared out over the rolling hills and felt a stab of apprehension mingled with regret. She'd always known this was just for a short time, but it had been a wonderful time, cocooned in a dream world of sunshine and laughter and playing happy families. And now it was almost over. Eight weeks with Leo and Ella, and then she had to find something to do, some way of earning a living until her photography took off, and she had no idea where to start.

Whatever, it meant an end to her time with them in this magical place, and the thought left a hollow ache in the centre of her chest. Things had changed now for ever and, whatever the outcome of their affair, it would never go back to that easy, loving friendship it had been.

'So, what's next for you?' he asked, as if he could read her mind, and she gave a little shrug and dredged up a smile.

'Oh, you know. This and that. I'm sure something'll crop up. I imagine there'll be wedding stuff that still needs dealing with, and I've got a lot of work to do on the photos for your blog, and pulling a portfolio together. I'll need to do some studio shots, clever things with lighting, that sort of thing. Arty stuff. Maybe I can do that while they're filming and the lights are there. And then I'll have to market it. Or myself.'

He nodded thoughtfully. 'I just wondered—I've been thinking I ought to do some cookery books ever since you first nagged me about it, but it's never seemed like the right time before.'

'And it does now?'

'Yes, I think it does. It will be a lot of work, but it might tie in well with Ella. And if I do, of course, I'll need a photographer.'

'You will. And you're right. I told you years ago you should do it but it just wasn't right for you at the time.'

'I don't suppose you want to take it on?'

'Being the photographer?'

Would she? It would mean seeing him again. Over and over again. Which would be fine if they were still together, but torture if they weren't. 'Mind if I think about it? I don't know where I'll be or what I'll be doing.'

'No, I understand that, but bear it in mind. I'd be really grateful. Your photos are amazing.' He gave a huff of laughter. 'There's just the small matter of a publisher, of course.'

'Now there I can definitely help you. I've got contacts, remember?'

'Great. Sound them out, by all means.'

He smiled at her, and her heart flipped over. Could it work? It would mean working with him again, spending time with him, helping him move on with his life. And moving on with hers. She knew a cookery book by him would fly off the shelves, and it would ensure her success, too, but more than that it would give them a better chance to find out if they could forge a future together.

'I'll see what I can do. I'd have a vested interest, of course, in getting this off the ground,' she reminded him. 'Always assuming I'm free.'

'I know. There's no rush. I've got the TV contract outstanding, and that'll have to come first.'

'They might want to tie them together—launch the book of the series, as it were. They do that a lot. Ask them.'

'I will. I'll sound them out, but they're getting impatient. The producer wants to see me like yesterday. I've told him I should be back by Tuesday and I can't deal with it until then.'

'Assuming tomorrow goes to plan.'

'That's right. So we need to fly out on Tuesday morning at the latest. Earlier if we can. I'd rather go tomorrow.'

'Another posh plane?' she asked drily, ignoring the sinking feeling in her gut, and he laughed.

'Probably. It's less stressful than killing time at an airport with Ella, and we need to pick the car up. It's easier. But we'll get whatever we can whenever we can.'

'See how it goes,' she said. 'I'll make sure all our stuff's packed ready first thing in the morning.'

'OK.' He reached out, threading his fingers through hers. 'I think we ought to turn in now. It's been a busy day and I need my business brain working for the morning.'

'Don't you trust them?'

He laughed, his eyes creasing up at the sides, that fascinating dimple flirting with her near the corner of his mouth. 'Of course I trust them, but they'll want the best deal and so do I. I need to be able to think clearly. I'm not going to sign my life away without realising it.'

He got up.

'Come to bed,' he said softly, and she nodded.

'Just give me a couple of minutes. You go first in the bathroom. I want to say goodbye to the valley.'

'Crazy girl,' he murmured, but his voice was full of affection, and he crunched softly over the gravel and went in through the French doors.

She let her breath out slowly. Less than forty-eight hours ago, they'd sat there together while he'd poured his heart out. And then he'd kissed her. Or had she kissed him? She wasn't sure, but she knew that from that moment on everything had changed.

Could she work with him on a cookery book? Maybe, maybe not.

She sat there a little longer, knowing they'd most likely be leaving in the early afternoon and this would be her last chance to soak up the time between day and night, that wonderful time when the swallows went to bed and the bats woke and took over the aerial display in a carefully orchestrated shift change.

She'd miss this. Miss all of it, but most especially the family, Lydia in particular. The warmth of their welcome had been amazing, and she knew it wasn't just because Leo was a celebrity. It was because they were lovely, decent people with a strong sense of family and loyalty, and she'd miss them all.

But most of all she'd miss being with Leo and Ella in this stolen moment in time. The little girl had crept into her heart when she'd least expected it, and Leo...

She sighed softly. Leo had always been massively important to her, but this holiday had changed things, shifted the delicate balance of their friendship from platonic to something she'd never anticipated.

She had no idea what the future would bring, but she knew it would be a long time before she'd be looking for any other man. Her emotions were a mess, her judgement was flawed, and it was far too soon for her to be thinking about another relationship, even with Leo.

Not that he was in any better shape than her emotionally, and probably a whole lot worse. The pair of them were a lost cause. Could they save each other and build a future together?

She desperately hoped so, but she had a feeling the answer would be no, once reality intruded.

She watched the swallows depart, watched the bats dart in to take their place, and when her eyes could hardly make them out in the darkness, she got to her feet and went inside to Leo.

Tomorrow would be here all too soon. It was time to go back to the future.

CHAPTER TEN

'SOON BE HOME.'

She glanced across at him and found a smile. 'Yes. Not long now.'

Not long enough. He'd booked another charter, not getting the benefit of the empty leg rate this time but there were bigger fish to fry, she guessed, like the meeting with the TV series producer tomorrow.

She wasn't complaining, though. This flight, like the last, had been seamless, the car ready and waiting when they arrived, and they were cruising steadily towards Suffolk as the light faded, Ella fast asleep in her car seat behind them.

She glanced over her shoulder at the little girl she'd somehow fallen in love with, and felt a sudden pang of loss at the thought of parting from her. From both of them.

Leo's face was expressionless, his hands relaxed on the wheel, his eyes on the road. He flicked a glance at her and smiled. 'You'll get a lie-in in the morning,' he said, with something like envy in his voice, but she'd swap her lie-in for a cuddle with Ella any day.

'Yes, I will,' she said evenly, trying not to dwell on how much she'd miss those special moments. She'd be going back home to her mother and he to his parents, at least until his house was finished, so at the very least their affair was on hold for now.

'So, when do you want to look at the photos?' she asked, clutching at straws. 'Shall I download them onto a memory stick for you? Obviously they'll need some work before you can put them in your blog, but you'll want to choose some initially for me to work with.'

'Yeah, that would be good. Maybe we could go over them one evening this week? I need to write it, too. I made some notes while we were over there, but to be honest I've had so much to think about my mind hasn't been on it at all. Not to mention certain other distractions,' he added, and she could hear the smile in his voice.

'Going through the photos will help,' she said. 'Will you be staying with your parents?'

'Initially, which'll make life easy when I go to London tomorrow and have to leave Ella behind. I guess you'll be with your mother?'

She would, at least for a little while, and they'd be next door. Her heart gave a little leap of joy. 'Where else?' she said, trying to keep it light. 'In case it's slipped your mind, I no longer have a home.' Or a job, after the next eight weeks. Or Leo?

'It hasn't slipped my mind.'

His hand reached out and found hers, his fingers curling around it as it lay on her lap. 'It'll be all right, Amy. Everything'll work out, one way or the other.'

Would it? She desperately hoped so, but she didn't like the sound of 'other'. The uncertainty of her future was thrown into sharp focus by the raw reminder of her homelessness. And joblessness. Not to mention the touch of his hand.

'Does that apply to you, too, or is it only me you've sprinkled fairy dust on?'

He gave a short huff that could just have been laughter, and put his hand back on the steering-wheel. 'I'm a lost cause,' he said, which was just what she'd thought last night, oddly, but hearing him say it gave her a hideous sinking feeling.

'You're not,' she argued gently, her own situation forgotten because his was far, far worse. 'You've just been in a bad place, Leo, but that'll change. It's already changing. You need to start working again, doing more at the restaurant, getting back into the filming, focussing on your USP.'

'Which is what, exactly?'

She shifted in the seat so she could study him. He hadn't shaved today—or yesterday, probably, either—and the stubble darkening his jaw gave him a sexy, slightly rakish air. How on earth had she never noticed before this week just how gorgeous he was?

'You have great media presence,' she said truthfully, avoiding the obvious fact of his sex appeal in the interest of their mutual sanity. 'Everyone loved your first two television series. Another one will raise your profile, and you can cash in on that with the cookery book. You're a great communicator, so communicate with your public, charm the punters in your restaurant, flirt with the camera, sell yourself.'

His brow crunched up in a frown. 'But I'm not the product. My food's the product.'

How could he really be so dense? 'No. You're inseparable. You, and your enthusiasm for food, your quirky take on things, your energy—that's what people love.'

What she loved. What she'd loved about him since she'd been old enough to be able to spell 'hormone'. She just hadn't realised it until now.

'Well, how on earth would I market that?' he asked, and she laughed. He really didn't get it.

'You don't have to market it! You just have to be you, and the rest will follow. The TV, the cookery book idea, your blog—all of it showcases you. The food is secondary, in a way. You were doing all the right things already. Just keep doing them and you'll be fine.'

He grunted, checked over his shoulder and pulled out to overtake. 'Right now I'm more worried about where we're going to do the filming. The plan was to do it in my new house, in my own kitchen, but it's not ready and time's running out. I won't do London again, and they want more of a lifestyle thing, which will fit round Ella, but that's no good without the house.'

'So how long will it be before it's done?'

'I have no idea,' he said, and he sounded exasperated. 'The builder's running out of time, even though there's a penalty clause in the contract, but of course I've been away over a week so I haven't been on his case and I don't know how well they've got on.'

'What's left to do?'

'It's mostly done, it's just the finishing off. They were fitting the kitchen, which is the most important thing as far as filming's concerned, and it should be straightforward, but every time I think that it all goes wrong, so who knows?'

'Could you use the restaurant kitchen in Yoxburgh?'

'Not without disrupting the business, and it's going well now, it's getting a name for itself and it's busy. I don't want to turn people away; I have to live in the town, it's where I'll be working, so it's the flagship restaurant, and that makes it hugely important to the brand. It would be career suicide and I'm doing pretty well on that already.'

'So push him.'

'I will. I'll call him in the morning, on my way to London, see how far off finishing he is.'

He turned off the main road, and she realised they were nearly home—if family homes counted, and at the moment they both seemed to be homeless, so she guessed they did count. He drove slowly through the village, turned into her mother's drive and pulled up at the door.

He didn't cut the engine, presumably so he didn't wake Ella, but he got out and by the time she'd picked up her bag and found her key he was there, holding the car door open for her.

'I'll get your stuff. I won't stop, I need to settle Ella and I've got a million and one emails to check tonight. I've just been ignoring them.'

He opened the back of the car and pulled out her bag, carrying it to the door for her. She put her key in the lock and turned to thank him, but he got there before her, reaching out a hand and cupping her face, his thumb sweeping a caress across her cheek.

Her eyes locked with his, and held.

'I don't know what I would have done without you, Amy,' he said softly, his voice a little gruff. 'You've been amazing, and I'm so grateful.'

Her heart thumped, her face turning slightly as she looked away, her cheek nestling into his hand so his thumb was almost touching her mouth.

'Don't be,' she murmured. 'You saved my life, getting me out of here. I don't know quite what I would have done if you hadn't.'

'You would have been fine. Your mother would have seen to that.'

She felt her mouth tip in a smile, and she turned her head again and met his eyes. 'Yes, she would, but it wouldn't have been the same. Thank you for rescuing me for the umpteenth time. I'll try not to let it happen again.'

And without checking in with her common sense meter, she went up on tiptoe and kissed him. The designer stubble grazed her skin lightly, setting her nerve endings on fire and making her ache for more, but before either of them could do anything stupid, she rocked back onto her heels and stepped away.

'Good luck tomorrow. Let me know how it goes.'

'I will. Enjoy your lie-in and think of me up at the crack of dawn with my little treasure.'

Think of him? She'd thought of very little else for the past week or more. 'You know you love it.' She turned the key in the door, pushed it open and picked up her bag. 'Goodnight, Leo.'

''Night, Amy. Sleep tight.'

It was what he said to Ella every night, his voice a soft, reassuring rumble. *'Goodnight, my little one. Sleep tight.'*

She swallowed the lump in her throat, walked into the house and closed the door behind her.

Time to start sorting out her life.

Her mother was pleased to see her.

She was in the sitting room watching the television, and she switched it off instantly. 'Darling! I didn't hear the car, I'm sorry. Is Leo with you?'

'No, he's got to get Ella to bed and he's got an early start in the morning.'

'Oh. OK. Good journey?'

'Yes, fine. It seems odd to be home.'

Odd, but good, she thought as her mother hugged her tight and then headed for the kitchen. 'Tea? Coffee? Wine?'

She laughed and followed her. 'Tea would be great. I've had a lot of wine this week. Wine, and food, and—'

Leo. Leo, in almost every waking moment, one way or another.

'So how was Tuscany? Tell me all about the *palazzo*. It sounds amazing.'

'Oh, it is. I've got a million photos I've got to go through.

I'll show them to you when I've had time to sort them out a bit. So how's it been here?' she asked, changing the subject. 'I'm so sorry I ran away and left you to clear up the chaos, but I just couldn't face it.'

'No, of course you couldn't, and it's been fine. Everyone was lovely about it. I went next door and spoke to them all, and the family came back here and it was lovely, really. We had quite a good time, considering, and Roberto made sure we had plenty to eat, so it was fine.'

'What about the presents?' she asked.

'No problem. I spoke to the store, and they agreed to refund everyone. They just want to hear from you personally before they press the buttons, and people will need to contact them individually, but it'll be fine. Nothing to worry about.'

That was a weight off her mind. There was still Leo's gift, of course, but she'd done what she could about that, and there was more to come. Looking after Ella for a week had been a joy, and photographing Leo had been a guilty pleasure, but she'd promised her help for eight weeks to help during the filming, and if that didn't come off, for any reason, she could give him those photos, edit them until they were perfect for what he needed, so even if she couldn't help him with a cookery book, he shouldn't come off too badly from their deal.

'Mum, are you OK with me staying here for a while?' she asked, before she got too carried away with the planning. 'Just until I get my life sorted out?'

Her mother tutted and hugged her. 'Darling, it's your home. Of course you can stay here. You're always welcome, and you always will be. And don't worry. Things will sort themselves out. I just want you to be happy.'

Happy? She felt her eyes fill, and turned away.

'I don't suppose there's anything to eat?'

'Of course there is! I knew you were coming home so I made curry. I'll put the rice on now.'

Ella wouldn't settle.

He couldn't blame her. She'd been trapped in her baby seat for a long time today, one way and another, and she'd slept for a lot of it. Not surprisingly, she wanted to play.

With him.

Again, he couldn't blame her. She hadn't seen nearly as much of him as usual in the past week, and she'd been in a strange place, with a strange carer. Not that she'd seemed to mind. She adored Amy.

His daughter had good taste. Excellent taste.

He covered his eyes and wondered how long it would take to get her out of his system. A week? A month?

A lifetime?

'Boo!'

Ella giggled and crawled up to him, pulling his hands off his face again and prising his eyes open. He winced, lifted her out of range and opened them, to her great delight. Another giggle, another bounce up and down on his lap, another launch at his face. She was so easily pleased, the reward of her smile out of all proportion to the effort he was putting in.

He reeled her in and hugged her, pushing her T-shirt up and blowing a raspberry on her bare tummy and making her shriek with laughter.

His email was squatting in his inbox like a malevolent toad, and he had phone calls to make and things to do, but he didn't care. The most important thing was checking in with the restaurant, but they were shut on Monday nights so that wasn't a problem for today.

She pulled up her little T-shirt again and shoved her tummy in the air, and he surrendered. Ella wanted her father and, dammit, he wanted her, too. The rest would keep.

* * *

She stood at her bedroom window, staring across at Leo's family home. The light was on in his bedroom, and through the open window she could hear Ella's little shriek of laughter and Leo's answering growl.

They were playing. That wouldn't please him, with all he had to do, but they sounded as if they were having fun, or at least Ella was.

She couldn't help smiling, but it was a bitter-sweet smile. She already missed them so much. Watching him playing with Ella, focussing all that charismatic charm on his little girl, not caring at all that he was making an idiot of himself.

Oh, Leo.

It was warm, but she closed the window anyway. She didn't need to torture herself by listening to them. It was bad enough without that.

She turned and scanned the room.

Her wedding dress was gone, of course, hung up in another room, she imagined, together with the veil and shoes. And her ring? She'd left it on the dressing table, and that was where she found it. Her mother had put it back in the box, but left it out for her to deal with.

She'd send it back to Nick, of course. It was the least she could do, it must have cost him a fortune. Not that he was exactly strapped for cash, but that wasn't the point.

She got out her laptop, plugged in the memory card from the camera and propped herself on the bed against a pile of pillows. She'd have a quick look through the photos before she went to bed, but she wasn't even going to attempt her emails. No doubt her inbox was full of sympathetic or slightly sarky comments about the wedding fiasco, and she might just delete the lot. Tomorrow.

Tonight, she was looking at photos.

* * *

'Are you busy?'

Busy? Why should she be busy? All she'd had to do today was draft a letter to all the guests, hand-write them and take them to the post office. Preferably not in the village so she didn't have to stand in the queue and answer questions or endure sympathetic glances. And sort through the photos.

So far, she hadn't even got past first base.

'No, I'm not busy. Why?'

'I just wondered. I'm back, I've put Ella to bed and I've got a site meeting with the builder in half an hour, but then I thought we could go through the photos.'

Ah. She hadn't got far last night. About five minutes in she'd been reduced to tears, and she'd had to shut her laptop. 'I haven't had time to go through them yet and delete the dross.' Or extract the ones that were for her eyes only. There were a lot of those. And it had been nothing to do with time.

'That's fine. We can do it together.'

'Here, or yours?'

'How about the new house? The builder said it was habitable, pretty much, so we could take the laptop over there.'

She could always say no—tell him she was tired or something. Except that so far today she'd done almost nothing. A bit of laundry, a lot of wallowing in self-pity and kicking herself for being stupid didn't count. And at least it would deal with the photos.

'Fine,' she agreed, dying to get a look at his house and too weak to say no.

'Great. Come round when you're ready, and we'll go from here.'

That meant seeing his parents, and they'd been the ones with the marquee in the garden, the catering team crawling all over the place, the mess left behind afterwards. And all for nothing.

She'd been going to take them something by way of apology, but now he'd short-circuited her plans and she wouldn't have a chance.

She shook her head in defeat.

'OK. I'll be round in a minute.'

'We're in the kitchen. Come through the fence.'

So she did. Through the gate in the fence that their fathers had made together years ago, and into their back garden where just over a week ago there had been a marquee for her wedding. You couldn't tell. The garden was immaculate, a riot of colour and scent. The perfect setting for a wedding.

She turned her back on it, walked in through the kitchen door and straight into Mrs Zacharelli's arms.

'Welcome home, Amy,' she said, and hugged her hard.

Amy's eyes welled, and she swallowed hard and tried not to cry. 'I'm so sorry—' she began, but then the tears got the better of her and Mrs Zach hugged her again before she was elbowed out of the way by her husband. He hauled Amy into a bear hug and cradled her head like a child.

'Enough of that,' he said. 'No tears. It was the right thing to do.'

'But you did so much for me,' she protested.

'It was nothing. Sit. Drink. We're celebrating.'

He let her go, pushed her into a chair and thrust a glass into her hand. Prosecco? 'Celebrating what?'

'Leo hasn't told you? They're starting filming the new television series next week.'

She turned her head and met his eyes. 'Really? So quick? What about your house?'

'We'll see. The builder says it'll be ready. Drink up, or we're going to be late.'

* * *

It was beautiful.

Stunning. She vaguely remembered seeing the cliff-top house in the past, but it had been nothing to get excited about. Now—well, now it was amazing.

While Leo poked and prodded and asked the builder questions about things she didn't know anything about, she drifted from room to room, her eyes drawn constantly to the sea, wondering how on earth she'd thought that Palazzo Valtieri could trump this. Oh, it was hugely impressive, steeped in history and lovingly cared for, but there was none of the light and space and freedom that she felt in this house, and she knew where she'd rather live.

He found her upstairs in one of the bedrooms. 'So, what do you think?'

'I think you need to give me a guided tour before I can possibly judge.'

His mouth kicked up in a smile, and he shook his head slowly. 'Going to make me wait? I might have known it. You always were a tease. So…' He waved his arm. 'This is my bedroom.'

'I see you chose the one with the lousy sea view.'

He chuckled and moved on. 'Bathroom through there, walk-in wardrobe, then this is the principal guest room—'

'Another dreadful view,' she said drily, and followed him through to Ella's bedroom.

'Oh! Who painted the mural? It's lovely!'

He rubbed his hand over the back of his neck and gave a soft laugh. 'I did. I wanted her room to be special, and I thought it was something I could do for her, something personal. I'm sure I could have paid a professional to do it much better, but somehow that didn't seem right.'

Her eyes filled, and she ran her fingertips lightly over the intertwining branches of a magical tree that scrambled up the wall and across the ceiling, sheltering the corner where she imagined the cot would go.

'It's wonderful,' she said, her voice choked. 'She's a lucky little girl.'

'I wouldn't go that far, but I do my best under the circumstances.'

He turned away, walking out of the room and down the stairs, and she followed him—through the hall, a sitting room with a sea view, a study fitted out with desk and shelves and storage facing the front garden and the drive this time, a cloakroom with coat storage and somewhere to park Ella's buggy—and then back across the hall into the main event, a huge room that opened out to the deck and the garden beyond.

Literally. The far wall was entirely glass, panels that would slide away to let the outside in, and right in the centre of the room was the kitchen.

And what a kitchen! Matte dark grey units, pale wood worktops, sleek integrated ovens, in the plural—and maybe a coffee maker, a steam oven, a microwave—she had no idea, but a bank of them, anyway, set into tall units at one side that no doubt would house all manner of pots and pans and ingredients as well. There was a huge American-style fridge freezer, still wrapped but standing by the slot designed to take it, and he told her it was to be plumbed in tomorrow.

'So—the verdict?'

She gave an indifferent shrug, and then relented, her smile refusing to hide. 'Stunning. It's absolutely stunning, Leo. Really, really lovely.'

'So who wins?'

She laughed softly and turned to face him. 'It grieves me to admit it, but you do. By a mile.'

His eyes creased into a smile, and he let out a quiet huff of laughter. 'Don't ever tell them that.'

'Oh, I wouldn't be so rude, and it's very beautiful, but this...'

'Yeah. I love it, too. I wasn't sure I would, because of the circumstances, but I do. I started planning it before Lisa died, but she had no interest in it, no input—nothing. And it's changed out of all recognition.'

'So she's not here.'

'No. And she's never been here. Not once. She wouldn't set foot in it. And now I'm glad, because it isn't—'

He broke off, but the word 'tainted' hovered in the air between them.

She took a breath, moved the conversation on, away from the past. 'So, will it be ready for filming on Monday?'

He shrugged, that wonderful Latin shrug that unravelled her every time, and his mouth quirked into a smile. 'He tells me it's done, all bar the fridge-freezer plumbing and the carpets, which are booked for tomorrow. I've gone over everything with him this evening to make sure it's OK, and I can move in whenever I want.'

'Oh. Wow. That was quick,' she said, and was appalled at the sense of loss. She'd thought they'd be next door with his parents, but now they wouldn't. He and Ella would move into their wonderful new house a few miles up the road, and she'd hardly see them.

Oh, well. It had to happen sooner or later.

'It had to be. The series team liked the Tuscany idea, by the way, and it's a brilliant opportunity to showcase the Valtieri produce, so they won't be unhappy with that. I just need to knock up some recipes, bearing in mind the schedule's pretty tight.'

'So you're going to be really busy setting it all up this week. Do you want me to look after Ella from now on?'

He ran his hand round the back of his neck. 'Yeah, I need to talk to you about that. We'll be filming all day from Monday, and I need to spend some time in the restaurant in the evenings, and I can't do that and look after her. She loves you, she's happy with you—but I don't know how you'd feel about moving in.'

'Moving in? Here? With you?'

He shrugged. 'Not—with me. Not in that way. I just think it would be easier all round if you were here, but you don't have to do it. You don't have to do any of it. It was never part of the deal.'

'I changed the deal. And you agreed it.'

'And then we moved the goalposts into another galaxy. You have every right to refuse, if you want to.' His face softened into a wry smile. 'I'm hoping you won't because my parents need a holiday and I'd like to cut them some slack. They've been incredible for the past nine months, and I'm very conscious that I've taken advantage, but I know that moving in with me is a huge step for you, and I'm very conscious of what you said about what happened in Tuscany—'

'Stays in Tuscany?' she finished for him. 'That's not set in stone.'

'But we could still do that. Keep our distance, get to know each other better before we invest too much in this relationship, because we're not the people we were.'

'So what do you want to know about me?'

'Whether or not you can live with me would be a good start.'

'We seem to have done a pretty good job of it this week.'

'We haven't shared the toothpaste yet,' he said, his mouth wry.

'We've done everything else.'

'No, we haven't. We haven't been together while I've been running the business, which takes a hell of a lot of my time, and what's left belongs to Ella. And that's not negotiable.'

'I know that, Leo, and I can handle your schedule. I've

already proved that. I'm not a needy child, and I'm not Lisa. I haven't been transplanted into an alien environment. I've got friends and family in the area, a life of my own. Don't worry, I'll find plenty to do.'

'I still think we need to try it. And to do that, I'd need you living here, at least while my parents are away, and preferably for the whole time we're filming. If you could.'

She hesitated, part of her aching to be there helping him and spending time with Ella, making sure she was safe and happy, the other part wary of exposing herself to hurt.

No contest.

'So how long is it? Is it eight weeks, as you thought?'

'I don't know. They're talking about eight episodes. Probably a couple of days for each, plus prep and downtime for me while they cut and fiddle about with it. I reckon a week an episode. That's what it was last time. Or maybe six, at a push. It's a serious commitment. And it's a lot to ask—too much for my mother and father, even if they weren't going on holiday.'

Eight weeks of working with him, keeping Ella out of the way yet close enough at hand that he could see her whenever he had a chance. Eight weeks of sleeping with him every night? Maybe. Which meant eight more weeks to get to know him better, and fall deeper and deeper in love with both of them.

And at the end—what then?

She hesitated for so long that he let out a long, slow sigh and raked his hands through his hair.

'Amy, if you really can't, then I'll find another way,' he said softly. 'I don't want to put you under pressure or take advantage of you and it doesn't change things between us at all. I still want to get to know you better, but if you aren't sure you want to do it, I'll get a nanny—a childminder. Something. A nursery.'

'Not at such short notice,' she told him. 'Even I know

that. Anyone who's any good won't be able to do it, not with the restaurant hours as well.' She sighed, closed her eyes briefly and then opened them to find him watching her intently.

'So where does that leave us?' he asked.

'With me?'

'So—is that a yes?'

She tried to smile, but it slipped a little, the fear of making yet another catastrophic mistake so soon after the last one looming in her mind. 'Yes, it's a yes. Just remind me again—why it is that you *always* get your own way?' she murmured, and he laughed and pulled her into his arms and gave her a brief but heartfelt hug.

'Thank you. Now all I have to do is get the furniture delivered and we can move in and get on with our lives.'

Well, he could. Hers, yet again, was being put on hold, but she owed him so much for so many years of selfless support that another eight weeks of her life was nothing— especially since it would give them a chance to see if their relationship would survive the craziness that was his life.

She'd just have to hope she could survive it. Not the eight weeks, that would be fine. But the aftermath, the fallout when the series was filmed, the crew had left and he'd decided he couldn't live with her?

What on earth had she let herself in for?

CHAPTER ELEVEN

THEY WERE IN.

He looked around at his home—their home, his and Ella's and maybe Amy's—and let out a long, quiet sigh of relief. It had been a long time coming, but at last they were here.

Ella was safely tucked up in her cot in her new room, his parents had stayed long enough to toast the move, and now it was all his.

He poured himself a glass of wine, walked out onto the deck and sat down on the steps, staring out over the sea. He was shattered. Everything had been delivered, unpacked and put in place, and all he'd had to do was point.

In theory.

And tomorrow the contents of the store cupboards in the kitchen were being delivered and he could start working on some recipes.

But tonight he had to draft his Tuscan tour blog. Starting with the photos, because they hadn't got round to them on Tuesday night and he hadn't had a spare second since. Amy was coming round shortly with her laptop, and they were going through them together. Assuming he could keep his eyes open.

The doorbell rang, and he put his glass down and let her in. He wanted to pull her into his arms and kiss her, but with what had happened in Tuscany and all that, he really wanted to give their relationship a chance.

'Did she go down all right?'

He smiled wryly. Typical Amy, to worry about Ella first. 'Fine. She was pooped. I don't know what you did with her all day, but she was out of it.'

She laughed, and the sound rippled through him like clear spring water. 'We just played in the garden, and then we went for a walk by the beach, and she puggled about in the sand for a bit. We had a lovely day. How did you get on?'

'Oh, you know what moving's like. I'll spend the next six months trying to find things and groping for light switches in the dark. Come on through, I'm having a glass of wine on the deck.'

'Can we do it in the kitchen, looking at the photos? There are an awful lot. And can I have water, please? I'm driving, remember.'

'Sure.' He retrieved his glass, poured her water from the chiller in the fridge and sat next to her at the breakfast bar overlooking the sea. 'So, what have we got?'

'Lots.'

There *were* lots, she wasn't exaggerating. And there were gaps in the numbers, all over the place.

'What happened to the others? There are loads missing.'

'I deleted them.'

He blinked. 'Really? That's not like you. You never throw anything out.'

'Maybe you don't know me as well as you think,' she said.

Or maybe you do, she thought, scrolling down through the thumbnails and registering just how many she'd removed and saved elsewhere.

'Just start at the top,' he suggested, so they did.

Him laughing on the plane. She loved that one. Others in their suite, in the pool—still too many of them, although she'd taken bucket-loads out for what she'd called her private collection.

Self-indulgent fantasy, more like.

She knew what she was doing. She was building a memory bank, filling it with images to sustain her if it all went wrong.

There were some of her, too, ones he'd taken of her shot against the backdrop of the valley behind their terrace, or with Ella, playing. She'd nearly taken them out, too, but because nearly all of them had Ella in, she hadn't. He could have them for his own use.

'Right, so which ones do you want me to work on?'

He didn't hold back. She got a running commentary on the ones he liked, the ones he couldn't place, the ones he'd have to check with the Valtieri family before they were used.

'How about a *short*list for the blog?' she suggested drily, when he'd selected about two hundred.

He laughed. 'Sorry. These are just the ones I really like. I'll go through them again and be a bit more selective. I was just getting an overview. Why don't you just leave them with me so I'm not wasting your time? Did you copy them?'

She handed him the memory stick with the carefully edited photos that she'd deemed fit to give him. 'Here. Don't lose it. Just make a note and let me know.'

'I will. Thanks. Want the guided tour?'

'Of your furniture? I think I'll pass, if you don't mind. I still have stuff to do—like writing to all my wedding guests.'

'Sorry. Of course you do. And I've taken your whole day already. Go, and don't rush back in the morning. I should be fine until ten, at least.'

She moved in on Sunday, and the film crew arrived on Monday and brought chaos to the house—lights, reflectors, a million people apparently needed to co-ordinate the shoot, and Ella took one look at it all and started to cry.

Amy ended up taking her home for the day more than once, which would have been fine if they'd stopped filming at her bedtime, but sometimes it dragged on, and then she'd be unsettled, and he'd have to break off and read her a story and sing to her before she'd go back to sleep.

'I'm sorry, this is really tough for you both,' Leo said after a particularly late shoot. 'I didn't know it would disrupt her life so much. I should have thought it through.'

'It's fine, Leo,' she assured him. 'We're coping.'

And they were, just about, but it was like being back in Tuscany, tripping over each other in the kitchen in the morning, having breakfast together with Ella, doing all the happy families stuff that was tearing her apart, with the added bonus of doing it under the eyes of the film crew.

And because of the 'what happened in Tuscany' thing, the enforced intimacy was making it harder and harder to be around each other without touching and she was seriously regretting suggesting it.

Then one night Ella cried and she got up to her, but Leo got there first. 'It's fine. I'll deal with her, you go back to bed,' he said, but the fourth time she woke there was a tap on her door and Leo came in.

'Amy, I think she needs the doctor. She must have an ear infection or something. I have to take her to the hospital. They have an out of hours service there, apparently.'

'Want me to come?'

The relief on his face should have been comical, but it was born of worry, so she threw her clothes on and went with him. It took what felt like hours, of course, before they came home armed with antibiotics and some pain relief, and Leo looked like hell.

'I feel sorry for the make-up lady who's going to have to deal with the bags under your eyes in the morning,' she said ruefully when the baby was finally settled.

'Don't you mean later in the morning?' he sighed,

yawning hugely and reaching for a glass. 'Water? Tea? I've given up on sleep. Decided it's an overrated pastime.'

She laughed softly and joined him. 'Tea,' she said.

'Good idea. We'll watch the sun come up.'

Which wasn't a good idea at all. Tuscany again, and sitting on the terrace overlooking the valley with the swallows swooping. Except here it was the gulls, their mournful cries haunting in the pale light of dawn.

'Thank you for coming with me to the hospital,' he said quietly.

'You don't have to thank me, Leo. I was happy to do it. I was worried about her.'

She stared out over the sea, watching it flood with colour as the sun crept over the horizon. It was beautiful, and it would have been perfect had she been able to do what she wanted to do and rest her head on his shoulder, but of course she couldn't.

'How's the filming going?' she asked, and he sighed.

'OK, I think, but I'm neglecting the restaurant, and I haven't even touched the Tuscany blog. On the plus side, we're nearly two weeks in.'

Really? Only six more weeks to go? And when it ended, they'd have no more excuse to be together, so it would be crunch time, and she was in no way ready to let him go. She drained her tea and stood up.

'I might go back to bed and see if I can sleep for a few more minutes,' she said, and left him sitting there, silhouetted against the sunrise. It would have made a good photo. Another one to join the many in her private collection.

She turned her back on him and walked away.

The filming was better after that, the next day not as long, and Leo had a chance to catch up with the restaurant over the weekend. Ella was fine, her ear infection settling quickly, but she'd slept a lot to catch up so Amy had helped him with the blog over the weekend, edited the photos, pulled it all together, and she showed it to him on Monday night after Ella was in bed.

'Oh, it looks fantastic, Amy,' he said, sitting back and sighing with relief. 'Thank you so much. The photos are amazing.'

'Better than your selfies?' she teased lightly, and he laughed.

'So much better!' He leant over and kissed her fleetingly, then pulled away, grabbing her by the hand and towing her into the kitchen. 'Come on, I'm cooking you dinner.'

'Is that my reward?'

'You'd better believe it. I have something amazing for you.'

'That poor lobster that's been crawling around your sink?'

'That was for filming. This is for us. Sit.'

She sat, propped up at the breakfast bar watching him work. She could spend her life doing it. What was she thinking? She *was* spending her life doing it, and it was amazing. Or would be, if only she dared to believe in it.

'The producer was talking about a cookery book,' he told her while he worked. 'Well, more a lifestyle-type book. Like the blog, but more so, linking it to the series. It would make sense, and of course they've got stills they've taken while I've been working so it should be quite easy.'

So he wouldn't need her. She stifled her disappointment, because she was pleased for him anyway. 'That sounds good.'

'I thought so, too.'

He was still chopping and fiddling. 'Is it going to be long? I'm starving,' she said plaintively.

'Five minutes, tops. Here, eat these. New amuse-bouche ideas for the restaurant. Tell me what you think.'

'Yummy,' she said, and had another, watching him as she ate the delicious little morsels. The steak was flash-fried, left to rest in the marinade while he blanched fresh green beans, and then he crushed the new potatoes, criss-crossed them with beans, thinly sliced the steak and piled it on before drizzling the marinade over the top.

'There. Never let it be said that I don't feed you properly. Wine?'

He handed her a glass without waiting for her reply, and she sipped it and frowned.

'Is this one of the Valtieri wines?'

'Yes. It goes well, doesn't it?'

'Mmm. It's gorgeous. So's the steak. It's like butter it's so tender.'

'What can I say? I'm just a genius,' he said, grinning, and hitched up on the stool next to her, and it would have been so natural, so easy to lean towards him and kiss that wicked smile.

She turned her attention back to her food, and ignored her clamouring body. Let it clamour. They had to play it his way, and if that meant she couldn't push him, so be it. He was turning his life around, getting it back on track, and she wasn't going to do anything to derail his rehabilitation. Or her own.

And Leo was definitely derailing material.

'Coffee?' he asked when she'd finished the crème brûlée he'd had left over from filming today.

'Please.'

And just because they could, just because it was Leo's favourite thing in the world to do at that time of day, they took it outside on the deck and sat side by side on the steps to drink it.

He'd turned the lights down in the kitchen, so they were sitting staring out across the darkened garden at the moonlit sea. Lights twinkled on it here and there, as the lights had twinkled in Tuscany, only here they were on the sea, and the smell of salt was in the air, the ebbing waves tugging on the shingle the only sound to break the silence.

She leant against him, resting her shoulder against his, knowing it was foolish, tired of fighting it, and with a shaky sigh he set his cup down, turned his head towards her and searched her eyes, his arm drawing her closer.

'Are we going to be OK, Amy?' he asked, as if he'd read her mind. His voice was soft, a little gruff. Perhaps a little afraid. She could understand that.

'I don't know. I want us to be, but all the time there's this threat hanging over us, the possibility that it won't, that it's just another mistake for both of us. And I don't want that. I want to be able to sit with you in the dark and talk, like we've done before a million times, and not feel this…crazy fear stalking me that it could be the last time.'

She took a sip of her coffee, but it tasted awful so she put it down.

'I'm going to bed,' she said. 'I'm tired and I can't do this any more. Pretend there's nothing going on, nothing between us except an outgrown friendship that neither of us can let go of. It's more than that, so much more than that, but I don't know if I can dare believe in it, and I don't think you can, either.'

She got to her feet, and he stood up and pulled her gently into his arms, cradling her against his chest. 'I'm sorry. Go on, go to bed. I'll see you in the morning.'

He bent and brushed his lips against her cheek, the stubble teasing her skin and making her body ache for more, and then he let her go.

She heard him come upstairs a few minutes later. He hesitated at her door and she willed him to come in, but he didn't, and she rolled to her side and shut her eyes firmly and willed herself to sleep instead.

* * *

The film crew interrupted their breakfast the next morning, but she didn't mind. The place stank of coffee, and she couldn't get Ella out of the house fast enough.

She strapped her into the car seat, pulled off the drive and went into town. They were running short of her follow-on milk formula, so she popped into the supermarket and picked up some up, and then she headed for the seafront. They could go to the beach, she thought, and then they passed a café and the smell of coffee hit her like a brick.

She pressed her hand to her mouth and walked on, her footsteps slowing to a halt as soon as they were out of range. No. She couldn't be. But she could see Isabelle's face so clearly, hear her saying that she couldn't stand the smell of coffee, and last night it had tasted vile.

But—how? She was on the Pill. She'd taken it religiously.

Except for the first day in Tuscany, the Sunday morning. She'd forgotten it then, taken it in the afternoon, about four. Nine hours late. And it was only the mini-pill, because she and Nick had planned to start a family anyway, and a month or so earlier wouldn't have mattered. And she'd hardly seen Nick for weeks before the wedding. Which meant if she was pregnant, it was definitely Leo's baby.

She turned the buggy round, crossed the road and went to the chemist's, bought a pregnancy test with a gestation indicator and went to another café that didn't smell so much and had decent loos. She took Ella with her into the cubicle which doubled as disabled and baby changing, so there was room for the buggy, and she did the test, put the lid back on the wand and propped it up, and watched her world change for ever.

He hadn't seen them all day.

The filming had gone well and the crew had packed up early, but Amy and Ella still weren't home.

Perhaps she'd taken Ella to her mother's, or to a friend's house? Probably. It was nearly time for Ella to eat, so he knew they wouldn't be long, but he was impatient.

He'd been thinking about what Amy had said last night, about their lives being on hold while they gave themselves time, and he'd decided he didn't want more time. He wanted Amy, at home with him, with Ella, in his bed, in his life. For ever.

Finally the gravel crunched. He heard her key in the door, and felt the fizz of anticipation in his veins, warring with an undercurrent of dread, just in case. What would she say? Would it be yes? Please, God, not no—

'Hi. Have you had a good day?' he asked, taking Ella from her with a smile and snuggling her close.

'Busy,' she said, heading into the kitchen with a shopping bag. 'Where are the film crew?'

'We finished early. So what did you do all day?'

'Oh, this and that. We went to town and picked up some formula, but it was a bit hot so we went to Mum's and had lunch in the garden and stayed there the rest of the day.'

'I thought you might have been there. I was about to ring you. Has she eaten?'

'Not recently. She had a snack at three. Are you OK to take over? I've got a few things I need to do.'

He frowned. He couldn't really put his finger on it, but she didn't sound quite right. 'Sure, you go ahead. Supper at seven?'

'If you like. Call me when you're done, OK? I might have a shower, it's been a hot day.'

She ran upstairs, and he took Ella through to the kitchen, put her in her high chair and gave her her supper. She fed herself and made an appalling mess, but he didn't care. All he could think about was Amy, and what was wrong with her, because something was and he was desperately hoping it wasn't a continuation of what she'd said last night.

What if she turned him down? Walked away and left him?

On autopilot, he wiped Ella's hands and took her up to bath her.

'Amy?'
    'Yes?'

He opened her bedroom door and found her sitting up on her bed, the laptop open on her lap. She shut it and looked up at him. 'Is supper ready?'

'It won't take long. Can you come down? I want to talk to you.'

'Sure,' she said, but she looked tense and he wondered why.

'Can I go first?' she said, and he hesitated for a moment then nodded.

'Sure. Do you want a drink?'

'Just water.'

He filled a tumbler from the fridge and handed it to her, and she headed outside to the garden, perching on the step in what had become her usual place, and he crossed the deck and sat down beside her.

She drew her breath in as if she was going to speak, then let it out again and bit her lip.

'Amy? What is it?'

She sucked in another shaky breath, turned to look at him and said, 'I'm pregnant.'

He felt the blood drain from his head, and propped his elbows on shaking knees, the world slowing so abruptly that thoughts and feelings crashed into each other and slid away again before he could grasp them.

'How?' he asked her, his voice taut. He raised his head

and stared at her. 'How, Amy? You're on the Pill—I know that, I watched you take it every morning.'

'Not every morning,' she said heavily. 'The first day, I forgot. I didn't take it until the afternoon.'

'And that's enough?'

'Apparently. I didn't even think about it, because it didn't matter any more. I wasn't on my honeymoon, and we weren't—'

He was trying to assimilate that, and then another thought, much harder to take, brought bile to his throat.

'How do you know it's mine?' he asked, and his voice sounded cold to his ears, harsh, uncompromising. 'How do you know it isn't...?' He couldn't even bring himself to say Nick's name out loud, but it echoed between them in the silence.

'Because it's the only time I've taken it late, and because of this.'

She pulled something out of her pocket and handed it to him. A plastic thing, pen-sized or a little more, with a window on one side. And in the window was the word 'pregnant' and beneath it '2-3'.

A pregnancy test, he realised. And 2-3?

'What does this mean?' he asked, pointing to it with a finger that wasn't quite steady.

'Two to three weeks since conception.'

The weekend they'd been alone in the *palazzo*. So it *was* his baby. Then another hideous thought occurred to him.

'When did you do this test?'

'This morning,' she told him, her voice drained and lifeless.

'Are you sure? Are you sure you didn't do it a week or two ago?'

Her eyes widened, and the colour drained from her face.

'You think I'd lie to you about something as fundamental as this?'

'You wouldn't be the first.'

She stared at him for what seemed like for ever, and then she got to her feet.

'Where are you going?'

'Home. To my mother.'

'Not to Nick?'

She turned back to him, her eyes flashing with fury. 'Why would I go running to Nick to tell him I've been stupid enough to let you get me pregnant?' she asked him bluntly. 'If you could really think that then you don't know me at all. It's none of Nick's business. It's my business, and it could have been yours, but if you really think I could lie to you about something so precious, so amazing, so beautiful as our child, then I don't think we have anything left to say to each other. You wanted my terrifying honesty. Well, this is it. I'm sorry you don't like it, but *I am not Lisa*!'

He heard her footsteps across the decking, the vibrations going through him like an earthquake, then the sound of the front door slamming and the gravel crunching under her tyres as she drove off.

He stared blindly after her as the sound of her car faded into the evening, drowned out by the cries of gulls and the soft crash of the waves on the shore below, and then like a bolt of lightning the pain hit him squarely in the chest.

Her mother was wonderful and didn't say a thing, just heard her out, hugged her while she cried and made them both tea.

'Do you know how wonderful you are?' she asked, and her mother's face crumpled briefly.

'Don't be silly. I'm just your mother. You'll know what I mean, soon enough. It'll make sense.'

Her eyes filled with tears. 'I already know. I'm not going to see Ella again, Mum. Never.'

'Of course you will.'

'No, I won't. Or Leo.' Her voice cracked on his name, and she bit her lips until she could taste blood.

'That's a little difficult. He has a right to see his child, you know.'

'Except he doesn't believe it is his child.'

'Are you absolutely certain that it is?'

'Yes,' she said, sighing heavily. 'Nick was away, wasn't he, for five weeks before the wedding. I only saw him a couple of times, and we didn't...'

She couldn't finish that, not to her mother, which was ridiculous under the circumstances, but she didn't need to say any more.

'You ought to eat, darling.'

'I couldn't. I just feel sick.'

'Carbs,' her mother said, and produced a packet of plain rich tea biscuits. 'Here,' she said, thrusting one in her hand. 'Dunk it in your tea.'

Was it really his? Could this really be happening to him again?

He'd sat outside for hours until the shock wore off and was replaced by a sickening emptiness.

The pregnancy test, he thought. Check it out. He went up to her room and opened her laptop, and was confronted by a page of images of him. Images he'd never seen. Ones she'd lied about deleting. Why? Because she loved him? And he loved her. He could see it clearly in the pictures, and he knew it in his heart.

He searched for the pregnancy test and came up with it. As accurate as an ultrasound.

Which meant if she *had* just done it, the baby was his— and he'd accused her of lying, of trying to pass another man's baby off as his.

And he knew then, with shocking certainty, that she hadn't lied to him. Not about that. As she'd pointed out at several thousand decibels, she wasn't Lisa. Not in any way. And he owed her an apology.

A lifetime of apologies, starting now.

But he couldn't leave Ella behind, so he lifted her out of her cot, put her in the car and drove to Jill's. Amy's car was on the drive, and he went to the front door and rang the bell.

'Leo.'

'I'm an idiot,' he said, and he felt his eyes filling and blinked hard. 'Can I see her?'

'Where's Ella?'

'In the car, asleep.'

'Put her in the sitting room. Amy's in her room.'

He laid her on the sofa next to Jill, went upstairs to Amy's room and took a deep breath.

'Go away, Leo,' she said, before he even knocked, but he wasn't going anywhere.

He opened the door, ducked to avoid the flying missile she hurled at him and walked towards her, heart pounding.

'Get out.'

'No. I've come to apologise. I've been an idiot. I know you're not Lisa, and I know you wouldn't lie to me about anything important. You've never really lied to me, not even when you knew the truth was going to hurt me. And I know you're not lying now.' He took another step towards her. 'Can we talk?'

'What is there to say?'

'What I wanted to say to you when you got home. That I love you. That I don't want to wait any longer, because I do know you, Amy, I know you through and through, and you know me. We haven't changed that much, not deep down where it matters, and I know we've got what it takes. I was just hiding from it because I was afraid, because I've screwed up one marriage, but I'm not going to screw up another.'

'Marriage?' She stared at him blankly. 'I hate to point this out to you, but we aren't exactly married. We aren't exactly anything.'

'No. But we should be. We haven't lost our friendship, Amy, but it has changed. Maybe the word is evolved. Evolved into something stronger. Something that will stay the course. We were both just afraid to try again, afraid to trust what was under our noses all the time. We should have had more faith in each other and in ourselves.'

He took her hand and wrapped it in his, hanging on for dear life, because he couldn't let her go. Let them go.

'I love you, Amy. I'll always love you. Marry me. Me and Ella, and you and our baby. We can be a proper family.'

Amy sat down on the edge of her bed, her knees shaking.

'Are you serious? Leo, you were horrible to me!'

'I know, and I can't tell you how sorry I am. I was just shocked, and there was a bit of déjà vu going on, but I should have listened to you.'

'You should. But I knew you wouldn't, because of Lisa—'

'Shh,' he said, touching a finger to her lips. 'Lisa's gone, Amy. This is between you and me now, you and me and our baby.'

'And Ella,' she said.

'And Ella. Of course and Ella. She won't be an only child any more. I was so worried about that.'

'You said it would be a cold day in hell before you got married again,' she reminded him, and his eyes filled with sadness.

'I was wrong. It felt like a cold day in hell when you walked out of my life. Come back to me, Amy? Please? I need you. I can't live without you, without your friendship, your support, your understanding. Your atrocious sense of humour. Your untidiness. The fact that you do lie to me, just a little, on occasions.'

'When?' she asked, scrolling back desperately.

'The photos,' he said with a wry smile on the mouth she just wanted to kiss now. You told me you'd deleted them, but you haven't. They're still on your laptop. I saw them just now. I opened your laptop to check up on pregnancy tests and I found them. Photos of me. Why?'

She closed her eyes. 'It doesn't matter why.'

'It does to me, because I know why I would want photos of you. Why I took them. So I can look at the images when you're gone, and still, in some small way, have you with me. Amy, I'm scared,' he went on, and she opened her eyes and looked up at him again, seeing the truth of it in his eyes.

'I'm scared I'll fail you, let you down like I let Lisa down. My lifestyle is chaotic, and it's not conducive to a happy marriage. How many celebrity chefs—forget celebrity, just normal chefs—are happily married? Not many. So many of their marriages fall apart, and I don't want that to happen to us, but I need you in my life, and I'll have to trust your faith in me, your belief that we can make it work. That I won't let you down.'

'You already have, today. You didn't listen.'

He closed his eyes, shaking his head slowly, and then he looked up, his eyes locking with hers, holding them firm.

'I know. And I'm sorry, but I'll never do it again. I love you, Amy, and I need you, and I've never been more serious about anything in my life. Please marry me.'

He meant it. He really, truly meant it.

She closed her eyes, opened them again and smiled at him. She thought he smiled back, but she couldn't really see any more. 'Yes,' she said softly. 'Oh, yes, please.'

He laughed, but it turned into a ragged groan, and he hauled her into his arms and cradled her against his heart.

'You won't let me down,' she told him. 'I won't let you. Just one more thing—will you please kiss me? I've forgotten what it feels like.'

'I've got a better idea. Ella's downstairs with your mother, and she needs to be back in bed in her own home, and so do I. Come home with us, Amy. It doesn't feel right without you.'

It didn't feel right without him, either. Nothing felt right. And home sounded wonderful.

'Kiss me first?' she said with a smile, and he laughed softly.

'Well, it's tough but I'll see if I can remember how,' he murmured, and she could feel the smile on his lips…

EPILOGUE

'ARE YOU READY?'

Such simple words, but they'd had the power to change the whole course of her life.

Was she ready?

For the marriage—the *lifetime*—with Leo?

Mingling with the birdsong and the voices of the people clustered outside the church gates were the familiar strains of the organ music.

The overture for their wedding.

No. Their *marriage*. Subtle difference, but hugely significant.

Amy glanced through the doorway of the church and caught the smiles on the row of faces in the back pew, and she smiled back, her heart skittering under the fitted bodice that suddenly seemed so tight she could hardly breathe.

The church was full, the food cooked, the champagne on ice. And Leo was waiting for her answer.

Her dearest friend, the love of her life, who'd been there for her when she'd scraped her knees, had her heart broken for the first time, when her father had died, who'd just—been there, her whole life, her friend and companion and cheerleader. Her lover. And she did love him.

Enough to marry him? Till death us do part, and all that?

Oh, yes. And she was ready. Ready for the chemistry, the fireworks, the amazingness that was her life with Leo.

Bring it on.

She straightened her shoulders, tilted up her chin and gave Leo her most dazzling smile.

'Yes,' she said firmly. 'I'm ready. How about you? Because I don't want you feeling pressured into this for the wrong reason. You can still walk away. I'll understand.'

'No way,' he said, just as firmly. 'It's taken me far too long to realise how much I love you, and I can't think of a better reason to marry you, or a better time to do it than now.'

His smile was tender, his eyes blazing with love, and she let out the breath she'd been holding.

'Well, that's a relief,' she said with a little laugh, and he smiled and shook his head.

'Silly girl. Amy, are you sure you don't want my father to walk you down the aisle? He's quite happy to.'

'No. I don't need anyone to give me away, Leo, and you're the only man I want by my side.'

'Good.You look beautiful, Amy,' he added gruffly, looking down into her eyes. 'More beautiful than I've ever seen you.'

'Thank you,' she said softly 'You don't look so bad yourself.'

She kissed his cheek and flashed a smile over her shoulder at her bridesmaids. 'OK, girls? Good to go?'

They nodded, and she turned back to Leo. 'OK, then. Let's do this,' she said, and she could feel the smile in her heart reflected in his eyes.

'I love you, Amy,' he murmured, and then slowly, steadily, he walked her down the aisle.

And when they reached the chancel steps he stopped, those beautiful golden eyes filled with love and pride, and he turned her into his arms and kissed her.

The congregation went wild, and he let her go and stood back a little, his smile wry.

'That was just in case you'd forgotten what it's like,' he teased, but his eyes weren't laughing, because marrying Amy was the single most important thing he would ever do in his life, and he was going to make sure they did it right.

* * * * *

"I don't know why I just told you all that…" Mackenzie said to fill the silence.

While Mackenzie was telling her story, it reminded Dylan of the girl she had once been. The girl he remembered so vividly from his childhood—the chubby bookworm with thick glasses. All the boys in the neighborhood ignored her, but he never had. He had never thought to analyze why. He had always just liked Mackenzie.

"Because we used to be friends," Dylan said.

"Were we?" Mackenzie asked.

"I always thought so." Dylan caught her gaze and held it. "And I tell you this, Mackenzie. If I had known that you were pregnant…if you had just trusted me enough to give me a chance, I never would've let you or Hope go through any of this stuff alone. I would have been there for you…both of you…every step of the way."

MARRY ME, MACKENZIE!

BY
JOANNA SIMS

MILLS
BOON®

Published in Great Britain 2015
by Mills & Boon, an imprint of Harlequin (UK) Limited,
Eton House, 18-24 Paradise Road, Richmond, Surrey, TW9 1SR

© 2015 Joanna Sims

ISBN: 978-0-263-25108-1

23-0215

Harlequin (UK) Limited's policy is to use papers that are natural, renewable and recyclable products and made from wood grown in sustainable forests. The logging and manufacturing processes conform to the legal environmental regulations of the country of origin.

Printed and bound in Spain
by CPI, Barcelona

Joanna Sims lives in Florida with her awesome husband, Cory, and their three fabulous felines, Sebastian, Chester (aka Tubby) and Ranger. By day, Joanna works as a speech-language pathologist, and by night, she writes contemporary romance for Mills & Boon® Cherish™. Joanna loves to hear from readers and invites you to stop by her website for a visit: joannasimsromance.com.

Dedicated to Aunt Gerri and Uncle Bill
You are loved more than words can say!

Chapter One

Mackenzie Brand parallel parked her 1960 Chevy sedan and shut off the engine. She leaned against the steering wheel and looked through the windshield at the swanky condos that lined Mission Beach, California. She checked the address that her cousin, Jordan, had given her and matched it with the address on the white, trilevel condo on the left. With a sigh, she unbuckled her seat belt and slipped the key out of the ignition.

"All right. Not exactly your crowd. But a job's a job and a favor's a favor." Mackenzie got out of her car, locked the door and dropped the keys into her Go Green recycling tote bag. She could hear a mixture of classic rock, loud talking and laughing as she walked quickly to the front door. It sounded like the Valentine's Day party that Jordan was throwing with her fiancé, Ian, was already in full swing.

Mackenzie rang the doorbell twice and then knocked on the door. While she waited, she stared down at her holey black Converse sneakers. They had passed shabby chic several months ago—definitely time to get a new pair. After a few minutes spent contemplating her pitiful tennis shoes, Mackenzie pressed the doorbell again. When no one opened the door, Mackenzie turned around to head to the beach side of the condo. She was about to step down the first step when she heard the door open.

"Hey!" Dylan Axel swung the front door open wide. "Where're you going?"

Dylan's voice, a voice Mackenzie hadn't heard in a very long time, reverberated up her spine like an old forgotten song. Mackenzie simultaneously twisted her torso toward Dylan while taking a surprised step back. Her eyes locked with his for a split second before she lost her balance and began to fall backward.

"Hey…" Dylan saw the pretty brunette at his door begin to fall. He sprang forward and grabbed one of her flailing arms. "Careful!"

Silent and wide-eyed, Mackenzie clutched the front of Dylan's shirt to steady herself. Dylan pulled her body toward his and for a second or two, she was acutely aware of everything about the man: the soapy scent of his skin, the strong, controlled grasp of his fingers on her arm, the dark chest hair visible just above the top button of his designer shirt.

"Are you okay?" Dylan asked. He didn't know who she was, but she smelled like a sugar cookie and had beautiful Elizabeth Taylor eyes.

If he hadn't caught her, she would have fallen for sure. Could have seriously injured herself. And Mackenzie's body knew it. Her heart was pounding in her chest, her skin felt prickly and hot, and her equilibrium was off-kilter. Mackenzie closed her eyes for a moment, took in a steadying breath, before she slowly released the death grip she had on his shirt.

"I'm fine," Mackenzie said stiffly. "Thank you."

"Are you sure?"

Mackenzie nodded. She forced herself to focus her eyes straight ahead on the single silver hair on Dylan's chest instead of looking up into his face.

"You can let go now." Mackenzie tugged her arm away from Dylan's hand.

Dylan immediately released her arm, hands up slightly as if he were being held up at gunpoint. "Sorry about that."

Mackenzie self-consciously tugged on the front of her oversize Nothin' But Cupcakes T-shirt. "No, *I'm* sorry."

Dylan smiled at her. "Let's just call it even, okay?"

That was classic Dylan; always trying to smooth things over with a smile. He wasn't as lanky as he had been in his early twenties. His body had filled out, but he was fit and had the lean body of an avid California surfer. And he still had that boyish, easygoing smile and all-American good looks. Even back in middle school, Dylan had been popular with absolutely everyone. Male or female, it didn't matter. He had always been effortlessly charming and approachable. Right then, on Dylan's porch, the last ten years melted away for Mackenzie, but she knew that he obviously hadn't recognized her.

Still smiling, Dylan stuck out his hand to her. "I'm Dylan. And you are?"

Instead of taking his offered hand or responding, Mackenzie stared at him mindlessly. It felt as if all of her blood had drained out of her head and rushed straight to her toes.

I'm not ready for this...

Dylan's smile faded slightly. He gave her a curious look and withdrew his hand. "You must be one of Jordan's friends. Why don't you come in so we can track 'er down."

Mackenzie was screaming in her mind, demanding that her stubborn legs take a step forward as she plastered a forced smile on her face.

"Thank you." She squeaked out the platitude as she skirted by Dylan and into the condo.

"Mackenzie!" Jordan wound her way through the crowd of people gathered in the living room and threw her arms around her cousin. "Thank *God* you could come! You're the *best*, do you know that?"

"Jordan!" Relieved, Mackenzie hugged her cousin. "Okay—first things first—I have to see this ring in person."

Jordan held out her hand and wiggled her finger so her large cushion-cut blue diamond engagement ring caught the light.

"Jordan, it's beautiful." Mackenzie held Jordan's left hand loosely while she admired the large blue diamond.

"I know, right? It's ridiculous." Jordan beamed. "It's way too extravagant. Ian really shouldn't have…but I'm glad he did."

"Dylan." Jordan draped her arm across Mackenzie's shoulders. "*This* is my *awesome* cousin, Mackenzie. She owns Nothin' But Cupcakes, home of the famous giant cupcakes. Look it up." To Mackenzie she said, "Thank you again for bringing us emergency cupcakes."

"Of course." Mackenzie kept her eyes trained on her cousin in order to avoid making eye contact with Dylan. For the first time in a long time, she wished she still had her thick tortoiseshell glasses to hide behind.

"Mackenzie—this's Dylan Axel… Dylan is the *Axel* in Sterling and Axel Photography. He's also a certified investment planner. He totally has the Midas touch with money, so if you ever need financial advice for your business, he's your man."

Mackenzie had to make a concerted effort to breathe normally and braced herself for Dylan to recognize her. But when she did finally shift her eyes to his, Dylan still didn't show even a *flicker* of recognition. He didn't seem to have the *first clue* that he was being introduced to a woman he had known in the *biblical* sense of the word. Instead, he looked between them with a slightly perplexed expression on his good-looking face. No doubt, he was wondering how she had managed to sneak into gorgeous Jordan's gene pool.

"Now I know your name." Dylan held out his hand to her once more. "Mackenzie."

The way Dylan lingered on her name sent her heart palpitating again. He was looking at her in the way a man looks at a woman he finds attractive. Dylan had never looked at her this way before. It was...*unsettling*. And yet, *validating*. It was undeniable proof that she had truly managed to eradicate the obese preteen with Coke-bottle glasses and tangled, mousy hair that she had once been.

Mackenzie forced herself to maintain the appearance of calm when she slipped her hand into his. She quickly shook his hand and then tucked her hand away in her pocket. Inside her pocket, where no one could see, Mackenzie balled up her fingers into a tight fist.

Oblivious to her cousin's discomfort, Jordan rested her arm across Mackenzie's shoulders. "Do you need help bringing in the cupcakes?"

Mackenzie nodded. "You wanted a ton. You got a ton."

Jordan walked with Mackenzie through the still-open front door. She tossed over her shoulder, "Give us a hand, Dylan, will you?"

"We can manage," Mackenzie protested immediately.

"I'm not about to let you ladies do all the heavy lifting by yourselves," Dylan said as he trailed behind them.

As they approached her car, Dylan whistled appreciatively. It was no surprise; men always commented on her car.

"The 1960 Chevrolet Biscayne Delivery Sedan painted with the original factory turquoise from back in the day. *Nice.*" Dylan ran his hand lovingly over the hood of her car. "She's yours?"

Mackenzie nodded quickly before she walked to the back of the delivery sedan; she unlocked, and then lifted up, the heavy back hatch of the vehicle.

"Who did this restoration?" Dylan asked as he leaned down and looked at the interior of the Chevy.

"A place up near Sacramento." Mackenzie wanted to be vague. Her brother, Jett, who had restored her Chevy at his hot-rod shop, had been friends with Dylan back in middle school. In fact, the last time Mackenzie had seen Dylan Axel was *at* Jett's wedding nearly eleven years ago.

"Well—they did an insane job. This car is *beautiful.* I'd really like to take a look under her hood."

"Hey!" Jordan poked her head around the back of the car. "Are you gonna help us out here, Axel, or what?"

"I'm helping." Dylan laughed as he strolled to the back of the vehicle. "But you can't blame a guy for looking, now, can you?"

"Here. Make yourself useful, will ya?" Jordan rolled her eyes at him as she handed him a large box of cupcakes. "And, no, I don't get the obsession with cars that went out of production *decades* ago. They don't make them anymore for a *reason.* Now, if you want to get excited about a motorcycle, I can totally relate to that!"

Dylan took the box from Jordan but smiled at Mackenzie. "Well—your cousin gets it, don't you?"

Mackenzie looked directly into Dylan's oh-so-familiar crystal-clear green eyes for a split second. "I get it."

"See!" Dy[...]
[...]s it."
[...]ll—sur[...]
fe[...]garag[...] B[...]
"None" [...]
box in the cro[...]
heavy hatch door. [...]
with her hip to shut it comp[...]n. "She

"Okay," Mackenzie said, want[...]zie
"Let's get the troops out of the sun." [...]

Dylan kept pace with her as they walked [...]
condo. "I haven't heard someone say that since I was a
kid."

"Really?" Mackenzie pretended to be fascinated with
the neighbor's house. "I hear it all the time."

That was one of her father's favorite phrases; no doubt,
Dylan had heard him use it a zillion times before he moved
away from the neighborhood. Her father had restored vintage cars as a hobby in the garage behind her childhood
home, and all of the neighborhood boys, including Dylan,
had loved to hang out with him.

"This works." Jordan put her box down on the large
marble slab island that separated the kitchen from the great
room.

Mackenzie put her box down next to Jordan's and
started to formulate an exit strategy. Dylan opened the
top of his box and reached for a cupcake. Jordan slapped
his hand playfully and put the box lid back down.

"Get your sticky paws off the cupcakes, mister! Ian isn't
even here yet! I can't believe he's late for his own party."

"I'm still surprised he agreed to this at all," Dylan said.
"You know Ian hates crowds."

"No. You're right. He does. But I'm determined to pull

...g and screaming if I have
...e out of the back pocket of her
...To Mackenzie she said, "Giv...
...o see what's holding him u...
...en met each other yet." ...ne to the other
...ged one ear and held ...
...ned outside to call ...nancé. Even though there
...large group of people milling around in the great
...m, using it as a pass-through to the bathrooms or the
...eck outside, at the moment, Mackenzie and Dylan were
the only two people in the kitchen. Dylan sent her a conspiratorial wink as he lifted the box top and snagged one
of her giant cupcakes.

Dylan devoured the devil's food cupcake in three bites.
"These are incredible. Did you make these?"

Mackenzie nodded. "There's another cupcake designer
who works for me, but these are mine."

Dylan grabbed a second cupcake and sent Mackenzie
a questioning look. "I can count on you not to tell Jordan, right?"

"She *is* my cousin," Mackenzie said as she scratched
her arm under her long-sleeved shirt. Being around Dylan
again was making her skin feel itchy and hot.

"Good call," Dylan said before he bit into the second
cupcake. "You gotta pick family over some random guy
you just met. I understand."

Before she could respond, a statuesque Cameron Diaz
look-alike in a tiny bikini breezed into the kitchen like
she owned it.

"Babe," Jenna said as she dropped a quick kiss on
Dylan's cheek, "we're running out of ice out there *already*."

"Okay. I'll run down to the store and grab some more,"
Dylan said before he took another bite.

Jenna opened the refrigerator and pulled out a can of

I want to be is all *puffy* and *bloated*. I don't know how you can put that poison into your body anyway."

"Happily." Dylan winked at Mackenzie.

"Whatever." Jenna walked to the door. She paused in the doorway and yelled, "Ice!"

"Got it." Dylan didn't look at Jenna as he wolfed down the final bite of the cupcake.

Instead of leaving to get ice, Dylan stayed with her in the kitchen. "So—did you grow up in Montana, too?"

Mackenzie looked up at Dylan—one part of her wanted to exit stage left without saying a word, but the other part wanted to rip off the Band-Aid and get the inevitable out of the way. It wasn't a matter of *if* she would confront Dylan about their past—it was a matter of *when*. She was impatient by nature, so perhaps, *when* she should bring up their past was *right now*.

Gripping the side of the kitchen counter to hold her body steady, Mackenzie asked quietly, "You don't recognize me, do you?"

Dylan's brow dropped and a question mark came into

"I really...

"What a drag.

ness first. Ian's *exactly* the same way.

"I'll text you," Mackenzie promised. "We'll figure—
when we can sync our calendars."

"Okay. It's a plan," Jordan agreed as she hugged her cousin one last time. "Give Hope a kiss for me."

"I will." Mackenzie glanced nervously at Dylan, who hadn't stopped staring at her. Jordan's phone rang. She checked the number. "It's the caterer. Let me grab this first and then I'll walk you out."

"Don't worry about it." Dylan, still staring hard at Mackenzie's face, said to Jordan, "I'll walk her out."

"You're all right, Dylan—I don't care what they say about you." Jordan punched Dylan lightly on the arm, and then gave Mackenzie one last parting hug before she answered the call.

Mackenzie could feel Dylan's intent gaze on her as they walked the short distance to the front door. Dylan opened the door for her.

"You say we've met?" Dylan asked curiously after he shut the front door behind him.

Dylan studied the petite, curvy woman walking beside

"See!" Dylan smiled triumphantly at Jordan. "She gets it."

"Well—sure. Her dad and brother raised Mackenzie in a garage. Basically, she's been brainwashed. No offense, cuz."

"None taken." Mackenzie balanced the large cupcake box in the crook of her arm while she pulled down the heavy hatch door. Mackenzie gave the hatch door a bump with her hip to shut it completely.

"Okay," Mackenzie said, wanting to speed things along. "Let's get the troops out of the sun."

Dylan kept pace with her as they walked back to the condo. "I haven't heard someone say that since I was a kid."

"Really?" Mackenzie pretended to be fascinated with the neighbor's house. "I hear it all the time."

That was one of her father's favorite phrases; no doubt, Dylan had heard him use it a zillion times before he moved away from the neighborhood. Her father had restored vintage cars as a hobby in the garage behind her childhood home, and all of the neighborhood boys, including Dylan, had loved to hang out with him.

"This works." Jordan put her box down on the large marble slab island that separated the kitchen from the great room.

Mackenzie put her box down next to Jordan's and started to formulate an exit strategy. Dylan opened the top of his box and reached for a cupcake. Jordan slapped his hand playfully and put the box lid back down.

"Get your sticky paws off the cupcakes, mister! Ian isn't even here yet! I can't believe he's late for his own party."

"I'm still surprised he agreed to this at all," Dylan said. "You know Ian hates crowds."

"No. You're right. He does. But I'm determined to pull

that man out of his shell kicking and screaming if I have to." Jordan pulled her phone out of the back pocket of her dark-wash skinny jeans. To Mackenzie she said, "Give me a sec, okay? I want to see what's holding him up. The two of you haven't even met each other yet."

Jordan plugged one ear and held the phone to the other as she headed outside to call her fiancé. Even though there was a large group of people milling around in the great room, using it as a pass-through to the bathrooms or the deck outside, at the moment, Mackenzie and Dylan were the only two people in the kitchen. Dylan sent her a conspiratorial wink as he lifted the box top and snagged one of her giant cupcakes.

Dylan devoured the devil's food cupcake in three bites. "These are incredible. Did you make these?"

Mackenzie nodded. "There's another cupcake designer who works for me, but these are mine."

Dylan grabbed a second cupcake and sent Mackenzie a questioning look. "I can count on you not to tell Jordan, right?"

"She *is* my cousin," Mackenzie said as she scratched her arm under her long-sleeved shirt. Being around Dylan again was making her skin feel itchy and hot.

"Good call," Dylan said before he bit into the second cupcake. "You gotta pick family over some random guy you just met. I understand."

Before she could respond, a statuesque Cameron Diaz look-alike in a tiny bikini breezed into the kitchen like she owned it.

"Babe," Jenna said as she dropped a quick kiss on Dylan's cheek, "we're running out of ice out there *already*."

"Okay. I'll run down to the store and grab some more," Dylan said before he took another bite.

Jenna opened the refrigerator and pulled out a can of

diet cola. She popped the top, took a sip and put the can on the counter.

"Hi," she said to Mackenzie and then moved on.

Dylan gave his girlfriend a "look" and handed her a coaster to put under the can. Jenna rolled her eyes, but put the coaster beneath the can. Then she crossed her arms over her chest, her pretty face registering a combination of disbelief and disgust.

"Babe—*what* are you *eating*?" Jenna frowned at him.

"Cupcakes." Dylan took another bite of the giant cupcake and pushed a box toward his girlfriend. "Want one?"

"Are you *insane*?" Jenna asked, horrified. "Carbs, Dylan! I've got an audition tomorrow in LA—the last thing I want to be is all *puffy* and *bloated*. I don't know how you can put that poison into your body anyway."

"Happily." Dylan winked at Mackenzie.

"Whatever." Jenna walked to the door. She paused in the doorway and yelled, "Ice!"

"Got it." Dylan didn't look at Jenna as he wolfed down the final bite of the cupcake.

Instead of leaving to get ice, Dylan stayed with her in the kitchen. "So—did you grow up in Montana, too?"

Mackenzie looked up at Dylan   one part of her wanted to exit stage left without saying a word, but the other part wanted to rip off the Band-Aid and get the inevitable out of the way. It wasn't a matter of *if* she would confront Dylan about their past—it was a matter of *when*. She was impatient by nature, so perhaps, *when* she should bring up their past was *right now*.

Gripping the side of the kitchen counter to hold her body steady, Mackenzie asked quietly, "You don't recognize me, do you?"

Dylan's brow dropped and a question mark came into

his eyes. He stared at her face hard, and she could almost see the wheels in his brain turning, trying to place her.

"You're not going to believe this, you guys." Jordan threw her hands up into the air as she walked into the kitchen. "He's stuck at the studio—his editor needs him to do something for the new book. He won't be here for *at least* another hour." Jordan's shoulders sagged as she asked Mackenzie, "You can hang out that long, can't you? I've been so busy with my gallery show that I've hardly spent any time with you—"

"I really can't stay." Mackenzie shook her head. "I have to get back to the bakery."

"What a drag." Jordan sighed. "I know, I know…business first. Ian's *exactly* the same way."

"I'll text you," Mackenzie promised. "We'll figure out when we can sync our calendars."

"Okay. It's a plan," Jordan agreed as she hugged her cousin one last time. "Give Hope a kiss for me."

"I will." Mackenzie glanced nervously at Dylan, who hadn't stopped staring at her. Jordan's phone rang. She checked the number. "It's the caterer. Let me grab this first and then I'll walk you out."

"Don't worry about it." Dylan, still staring hard at Mackenzie's face, said to Jordan, "I'll walk her out."

"You're all right, Dylan—I don't care what they say about you." Jordan punched Dylan lightly on the arm, and then gave Mackenzie one last parting hug before she answered the call.

Mackenzie could feel Dylan's intent gaze on her as they walked the short distance to the front door. Dylan opened the door for her.

"You say we've met?" Dylan asked curiously after he shut the front door behind him.

Dylan studied the petite, curvy woman walking beside

him and he tried to figure out who she was before she had to tell him. He had had a lot of drunken hookups when he was in college and he hoped that she wasn't one of them.

It seemed to Mackenzie that her heart was pumping way too much blood, too quickly, through her veins. She was light-headed and for a split second, as she was coming down the front steps, it felt as if she might just pass out.

This is happening. After all these years. This is really happening.

"Yes. We've met," Mackenzie said as she walked quickly to her car, unlocked the door and then opened it so she would have something to lean on.

"You were good friends with my brother, Jett, back in middle school." Mackenzie gripped the frame of the open car door so hard that her fingers started to hurt.

"Jett...?" Dylan shook his head slightly as if he didn't connect with the name, but then recognition slowly started to dawn as a smile started to move across his face.

"Wait a minute!" Dylan exclaimed. "*Big Mac*? Is that you?"

Mackenzie blanched. No one had called her that horrible nickname since high school.

"I don't like to be called that," she said. When she was growing up, no one called her "Mackenzie." Jett and her friends always called her "Mac." Cruel kids at school had added the "Big" to it and the horrible nickname had followed her like a black cloud until she graduated from high school.

"Hey—I'm sorry. I didn't mean anything by it." He couldn't stop staring at her face. This was not the Mackenzie he remembered. The thick, old-lady glasses were gone, her hair was darker and longer, and she had slimmed down. She wasn't skinny; she was curvy, which was a pretty rare occurrence in California. The word *voluptuous* popped into his head to describe her now.

"Just don't call me that anymore, okay?"

"Yeah. Sure. Never again, I promise," Dylan promised, his eyes smiling at her. "Man. I can't believe it…Jett's little sister! You look great."

"Thanks," Mackenzie said.

"Man…" Dylan crossed his arms loosely in front of his body and shook his head. "How long has it been? Five, six years?"

"Ten," Mackenzie said too quickly and then added more nonchalantly, "Give or take."

"Ten years." Dylan nodded as he tried to remember the last time he had seen her. When it hit him, he snapped his fingers. "Jett's wedding, right? I can't believe I didn't recognize you right away—but, in my defense, Mackenzie, you've changed."

"Yeah, well…losing a hundred pounds will do that to a person," Mackenzie said. She was watching him closely; it still didn't seem to be registering with him that they had slept together after Jett's reception.

"A hundred pounds?" he repeated, surprised. "I don't remember you needing to lose that much."

"You'd be one of the few." Mackenzie heard that old defensiveness creep into her tone.

Several seconds of silence slipped by before Dylan asked, "So—how's Jett doing nowadays? Still married?"

"Uh-uh." Mackenzie shook her head. "The marriage didn't work out. But he's got custody of both kids, so that's the upside of that situation."

"Does he live around here, too?"

"No. He owns a hot-rod shop up in Paradise, California. He wanted to be closer to Dad and he thought a small town would be better for the girls."

"A hot-rod shop, huh? So wait a minute—did Jett do this restoration?" Dylan asked with a nod toward her car.

"Yep." Mackenzie nodded proudly. Her older brother had managed to build a lucrative career out of a passion he shared with their dad.

"Man—I'm telling you what, he did a *fantastic* job on this Chevy. I really respect that he kept it true to the original design. I've gotta tell you, this's pretty amazing timing running into you like this because I've been looking for someone to restore my Charger. I gotta get her out of storage and back out on the road."

"You should check out his website—High-Octane Hot Rods."

"High-Octane Hot Rods. I'll do that." Dylan hadn't stopped smiling at her since he'd realized she was Jett's little sister. "So, tell me about you, Mackenzie. Are you married? Got any kids?"

Instead of answering his question, Mackenzie slipped behind the wheel of the car. "Listen—I wish I could spend more time catching up, but I've really gotta go."

"No problem," Dylan said easily, his hands resting on the door frame so he could close the door for her. "We're bound to run into each other again."

Mackenzie sent him a fleeting smile while she cranked the engine and shifted into gear. Fate had unexpectedly forced her hand and now she was just going to have to figure out how to deal with it.

Chapter Two

Once out of Dylan's neighborhood, Mackenzie drove to the nearest public parking lot. She pulled into an empty space away from the other cars, fished her cell phone out of her pocket and dialed her best friend's number with shaky fingers.

"Rayna…?"

"Mackenzie? What's wrong? Why do you sound like that? Did something happen to Hope?"

"No." Mackenzie slouched against the door. "She's fine."

"Then what's wrong? You sound like something's wrong."

"I just ran into Dylan." There was a tremor in her voice.

"Dylan who?"

"What do you mean, Dylan *who*?" Mackenzie asked, irritated. "Dylan *Axel*."

"What?" Now she had Rayna's attention. "You're kidding!"

"No." Mackenzie rubbed her temple. She could feel a migraine coming on. "I'm *not* kidding."

"Where in the world did you run into him?"

"At his condo. In Mission Beach."

"He lives in Mission Beach?"

"Apparently so."

"What were you doing there?"

"Delivering cupcakes to Jordan's fiancé's birthday party," Mackenzie said as she tilted her head back and closed her eyes. "Dylan is *Ian's* best friend."

Rayna didn't respond immediately. After a few silent seconds, her friend said, "Oh. Wow. Are you okay?"

"I feel like I'm suffocating."

"Anxiety," Rayna surmised.

"Probably." Mackenzie put her free hand over her rapidly beating heart.

"Just close your eyes and take in long, deep breaths. You'll feel better in a minute."

"Okay…"

"Where are you now?"

"I'm parked. I didn't feel…stable enough to drive."

"That was smart," Rayna said. "Look—just take your time, pull yourself together and then come over. We'll figure this out. Hope's still at the barn?"

"Yeah. I pick her up at seven, after they bed down the horses."

"Charlie'll be home by the time you get here—we'll commiserate over pasta," Rayna said in her typical take-charge tone.

"Thank you." Comfort food with friends sounded like a great idea.

"And, Mackenzie?"

"Yeah?"

"It's going to be okay," Rayna said. "God is answering our prayers."

Rayna was one of the pastors for her nondenominational church of like-minded hippies and saw all life's events through the lens of a true believer.

"Hope's prayers," Mackenzie clarified. "Hope's prayers."

"Hope's prayers *are* our prayers. Aren't they?" Rayna countered gently. "Listen—I'll put on a pot of coffee and I'll see you when you get here. Be safe."

Mackenzie hung up the phone but didn't crank the engine immediately. Her mind was racing but her body was motionless. After ten minutes of taking long, deep breaths, Mackenzie finally felt calm enough to drive and set off for her friend's Balboa Park bungalow. Rayna was right. Her daughter's prayers *were* her prayers. She just hadn't been prepared for *this* prayer to be answered so quickly.

"Little one!" Molita Jean-Baptiste, the bakery manager, poked her head into the kitchen. "There's a young man out here who wants to talk to you."

"Okay," Mackenzie said as she slid a large pan of carrot-cake cupcakes into the oven. "I'll be right there."

Mackenzie closed the door of the industrial baking oven and then wiped her hands on a towel before she headed for the front of the bakery. She put a welcoming, professional smile on her face as she pushed the swinging doors apart and walked through. But her smile dropped for a split second when she saw Dylan standing next to one of the display counters.

"Hi," Dylan greeted her with his friendly, boyish smile. "Nice place."

"Thank you." Mackenzie glanced over at Molita who was restocking the cases and pretending to mind her own business. "Are you here to order cupcakes?"

"No." Dylan laughed. "I'm here to see you."

"Oh." Mackenzie frowned. "Okay."

For the last week, she had lost countless hours of sleep trying to figure out what to do about Dylan. And after so many sleepless nights, she *still* hadn't figured out how to blindside the man with a ten-year-old daughter.

"Would you like something to eat, young man?" Molita asked. Haitian-born and in her sixties now, Molita was as round as she was tall. Whether Molita was having a day of aches and pains or not, she always greeted the customers like family. She was the backbone of Nothin' But Cupcakes, and Mackenzie often joked that customers came to see Molita as much as they came for the cupcakes.

"No, thank you." Dylan put his hand on his flat stomach. "I'm trying to watch my girlish figure."

"Well…" Molita smiled warmly at Dylan. "You'll let me know if you change your mind. I just put on a fresh pot of coffee."

Dylan thanked Molita for the offer and then asked in a lowered voice, "Is there someplace we can talk?"

"Um…yeah. We can talk in my office, I suppose. But I only have a minute."

"This won't take too long," Dylan said.

"I'll be right back, Moll. I'm just going to step into my office for a minute or two."

"You know I'll call ya if I need'ja," Molita called out from behind the counter.

Dylan followed her to the office. She didn't typically take anyone to the office, and it struck her, when she opened the door, just how tiny and cluttered it really was.

"Sorry about the mess." Mackenzie shuffled some papers around in a halfhearted attempt to straighten up. "Believe it or not, I have a system in here…"

"I'm not worried about it." Dylan closed the door behind

him. If Jenna didn't use a coaster under a glass, it bugged him. But, for whatever reason, Mackenzie's untidy office didn't bother him so much.

Dylan squeezed himself into the small chair wedged in the corner on the other side of Mackenzie's desk.

"It smells really good in here." Dylan shifted uncomfortably, his knees pressed against the back of the desk.

Mackenzie hastily shoved some papers in a drawer. "Does it?"

"It does." Dylan looked around the office. "Now I know why you smell like a sugar cookie."

Surprised, Mackenzie slammed the drawer shut and stopped avoiding the inevitable eye contact with Dylan.

When Mackenzie looked at him with those unusual lavender-blue eyes, Dylan felt an unfamiliar tingling sensation in the pit of his stomach. There was something about Mackenzie's eyes that captivated him. He hadn't been able to get those eyes out of his head since the party.

"So…" Mackenzie said after an awkward lull. "What can I do for you, Dylan?"

Out of the corner of her eye, she could see the framed picture of her daughter, Hope, and resisted the urge to turn it away from Dylan.

"Actually…" Dylan tried to cross one leg over the other in the tight space and failed. "I wanted to do something for you."

Mackenzie pushed her long sleeves up to her elbows. "What's that?"

Dylan took the picture of Hope off the desk. "Cute kid. Yours?"

"Yes." Mackenzie's pulse jumped. "That's my daughter, Hope, at her fourth birthday party."

Mackenzie waited, anxiety twisting her gut, and wondered if Dylan would recognize his own flesh and blood in that picture. When he didn't, part of her was relieved and the other part was disappointed. Dylan put the picture back on the shelf without ever realizing that Hope was his. Mackenzie moved the frame to her side of the desk and turned it away from Dylan.

"Is Brand your married name? I remember you as Bronson." Dylan glanced down at the ring finger of her left hand.

"No." Mackenzie shook her head. "I decided to take my mom's maiden name when Hope was born. I wanted Hope to truly be her namesake."

Dylan's gaze was direct as he asked, "So, you're not married…?"

"No." Mackenzie wasn't subtle about looking up at the clock on the wall. As much as she knew that she needed to talk to Dylan about Hope, this wasn't the right time. They had three catering gigs set for the evening, and the afternoon lunch crowd would be lining up soon. She was already struggling to make payroll; she couldn't afford to lose one sale.

"Dylan…look, I don't mean to be rude…" Mackenzie started to say.

Dylan held up his hands and smiled sheepishly. "Okay… okay. I'll admit it. I'm stalling. It's just that, what I wanted to say to you seemed like a good idea this morning, but now…"

Mackenzie leaned forward on her arms and waited for Dylan to continue. Whatever it was that he wanted to say was making him turn red in the face and shift nervously in his chair. He had turned out to be a nice-looking man, with his dark brown hair and vivid green eyes. But Dylan wasn't classically handsome. He wasn't a pretty boy. Dylan's nose had been broken when they were kids and it hadn't healed back completely straight. There was a Y-shaped scar directly under his left eye from the time he'd caught a baseball with his face during a Little League game. These little imperfections didn't detract from his good looks for Mackenzie; they enhanced them.

"All right." Dylan rubbed the back of his neck. "I'm just going to say what I came here to say. I owe you an apology, Mackenzie."

Mackenzie's chair squeaked loudly when she sat back. "Why in the world would you need to apologize to *me*?"

"Because…" Dylan looked at her directly in the eyes. "I remember what happened between us the night of Jett's wedding."

Mackenzie ran her hand over her leg beneath the desk and gripped her knee hard with her fingers. "Oh."

"Obviously that wasn't the sort of thing that I wanted to bring up while we were standing on the street."

"No." Mackenzie shook her head first and then nodded in agreement. "I'm glad you didn't."

"But…I didn't want you to think that I had forgotten about…*after* the reception…"

"We both had a lot to drink that night…" Mackenzie said faintly.

"Yes—we did. But, I still think I owe you an apology…" Dylan leaned forward. "You were Jett's little sister, and no matter how much I had to drink that night, I shouldn't have…taken advantage of you."

"Taken *advantage* of me?" Mackenzie asked incredulously. "You didn't take advantage of me, Dylan. I knew exactly what I was doing."

"You had just broken up with your boyfriend…" Dylan said.

"And you had just broken off your engagement…" Mackenzie countered. "I think we both need to just give each other a break about that night, okay?"

Dylan took a deep breath in as he thought about her words. Then he said, his expression pensive, "I should've called you, Mackenzie. After that night, I should've called you."

"And said what?"

"I don't know..." Dylan shrugged his shoulders. "I could've checked on you, made sure you were okay." He looked down at his hands for a second before he looked back up at her. "I should've let you know that I'd gotten back with Christa. I look back and I think maybe I used to be kind of an insensitive jerk...I know I can't apologize to everyone, but at least I have a chance to apologize to you."

"Well..." Mackenzie crossed her arms in front of her body. "I appreciate the apology, Dylan. I do. But, I never thought that you'd *wronged* me in any way. And I don't ever remember you being a jerk, at least not to me. You were the only one of my brother's friends who never ignored me. You never treated me like the weird *fat* girl."

"I never saw you that way," Dylan said, surprised. "And it'd make me feel better if you'd accept my apology..."

"Then I accept." It felt as if she just might be laying the groundwork for him to accept *her* apology later. "Of course I accept."

"Good." Dylan smiled at her. "Thank you."

"You're welcome." Mackenzie stood up. "Listen—I'm sorry that it seems like I'm always cutting things short, but..."

"No. No. That's okay." Dylan's chair knocked into the wall when he stood up. "I'm holding you up from work. But before I take off, I really want to show you something outside. It'll only take a second, I promise. And, trust me. You're gonna want to see what I have to show you."

"Okay. But then I really need to get back to work. I have a ton of special orders to fill." Mackenzie walked through the door that Dylan held open for her. "And let me tell you, there's a seedy underbelly of sugar addicts in San Diego and they all start to line up for a lunchtime fix." Mackenzie stopped at the counter and checked on Molita. "Are you doing okay, Moll?"

"Don't you worry about me, now. I've got everything under control." Molita sprayed glass cleaner on the front of the display case. "You go handle your business."

"I'll be right back," Mackenzie said.

"I wanted to show you my baby." Dylan held open the bakery door for her. "My girlfriend doesn't understand old school, but I knew you'd appreciate her."

Mackenzie stepped onto the sidewalk, but halted in her tracks just outside the door. "Is that what I *think* it is?"

Dylan smiled triumphantly at her as he walked over to his car. "Didn't I tell you you'd want to see her?"

Mackenzie couldn't take her eyes off Dylan's rare, vintage car. This car could easily sell for one hundred and fifty *thousand* dollars. "You do know that this is the stuff of legends, right?"

"You know I do," Dylan said. "And *you* know exactly what you're looking at, don't you?"

"Of course I do. I took Old School 101 with Dad and Jett...which I aced, by the way," Mackenzie bragged as she walked over to his car. "This sweet girl is a 1963 split-back Chevy Corvette. Super rare because the split window went out of production in 1964."

"You got it." Dylan's smile broadened.

"Basically, the Holy Grail." Mackenzie ran her hand along the curved hood of the car.

"That's right." Dylan nodded his head, his arms crossed loosely in front of him. "See? I *knew* you'd be excited to see her."

"You have no idea." Mackenzie walked around to the

back of the car. "Dylan—this's all original. Jett would die to get his hands on this car. She's not for sale, is she?"

"Not a chance." Dylan shook his head as he walked up to stand beside her. "But I really want Jett to restore my Charger."

Mackenzie found herself smiling at Dylan. "That would mean a lot to Jett, Dylan. It really would."

"I was thinking about giving the Charger this same silver-flake paint job with flat black accents. What do you think?"

Mackenzie's phone rang. "Hold that thought."

"Sure." Dylan leaned casually against his car.

"Hi, Aggie." Mackenzie leaned her head down and plugged one ear. "Wait a minute—what happened?" Mackenzie's face turned pale. "Tell Hope I'm on my way."

"Everything okay?" Dylan asked.

"No." Mackenzie headed back to the bakery. "My daughter got hurt at the barn."

"I hope she's okay," Dylan called after her.

"Thanks." Mackenzie pulled the bakery door open. Inside the bakery now, she stopped and threw up her hands in the air. "Tamara has my car! Molly—did you drive today?"

"My granddaughter dropped me off." Molita put a cupcake in a box for a customer.

Mackenzie made a quick U-turn and pushed the bakery door back open. "Molly—I have to go get Hope. Hold down the fort, okay?"

"What happened?" Molly asked, concerned.

"She hit her head at the barn." Mackenzie pushed the door open. "I'll call you later with an update as soon as I have one!"

Dylan had his blinker on and he was about to ease out onto the street when he saw Mackenzie bolt out of the cupcake shop and run toward his car. He braked and rolled down the passenger window.

Mackenzie bent down so she could see Dylan. "Can you give me a ride? My car is out with the deliveries."

Dylan reached over, unlocked the door and opened it for Mackenzie. "Hop in."

The thirty-minute ride out to the barn was a quiet one. Mackenzie's entire body was tense, her brow wrinkled with worry; seemingly lost in her own internal dialogue, she only spoke to give him directions. And he didn't press her for conversation. He imagined that if he were in her shoes, he wouldn't be in the mood for small talk, either.

"Turn left right here." Mackenzie pointed to a dirt side road up ahead. "You'll have to go slow in this car—with all the rain lately, there are potholes galore on the way to the barn. Not many Corvettes brave this road."

"I can see why not." Dylan slowed way down as he turned onto the muddy dirt road. He looked at the large sign at the entrance of the road.

"Pegasus Therapeutic Riding—is that where we're heading?"

"Yes." Mackenzie unbuckled her seat belt.

Dylan glanced over at Mackenzie. "What's wrong with your daughter?"

"There's *nothing* wrong with Hope. She's perfect," Mackenzie snapped. After a second, she added in a tempered tone, "Hope loves horses and she loves helping people. Volunteering here is what she wants to do with her free time."

"She must take after you." Dylan drove up onto the grassy berm in order to avoid a large pothole. "I remember you were always busy with a cause…collecting canned goods and clothing for the homeless, volunteering at the animal shelter…you were never satisfied with playing video games and hanging out at the beach like the rest of us…"

Mackenzie's shoulders stiffened. She had been picked on mercilessly when she was a kid about her causes. "There's nothing wrong with caring about your community."

Dylan jerked the wheel to the left to avoid another pothole. He glanced quickly at Mackenzie; her arms were crossed, her jaw was clenched. He'd managed to put her on the defensive in record time. Usually he was pretty good at navigating his way around women.

"I meant it as a compliment," Dylan clarified. "And Hope sounds like a really good kid."

"She is." Mackenzie stared straight ahead. "She's the best kind of kid."

"How old did you say she was?"

"I didn't say." Mackenzie spotted the weathered brown barn up ahead. "You can pull in right there between the van and the truck…"

As Dylan eased the car to a stop, Mackenzie already had her hand on the door handle. With her free hand, she touched his arm briefly. "Thank you, Dylan. You've managed to rescue me twice in one week."

"Do you want me to wait here for you?" Dylan shifted into park.

"No!" Mackenzie pushed the door open and climbed out of the low-slung car. "I mean…no. That's okay. You've already done enough."

Dylan leaned down so he could see her face. "Are you sure?"

"Yes. Really. We'll be fine." Mackenzie closed the car door and hoped that she had also closed the subject of Dylan sticking around. Now that she was at the barn, she couldn't imagine what she had been thinking. This was *not* the time or place for Dylan to meet his daughter. Something that life-altering took planning. And she didn't have a plan. Not for this.

Dylan shut off the engine, pulled the keys out of the ignition and jumped out of the car. He wanted to follow Mackenzie, but she was sending out some pretty obvious back-off signals.

"I could just hang right here…."

Mackenzie spun around and walked backward a couple of steps. "I'll catch a ride from someone here. Really. I'm sure you have a day."

Dylan stared after Mackenzie. It didn't seem right just to drop her off and then leave, no matter what she said. But, on the other hand, she hadn't exactly been diplomatic about telling him to shove off. Reluctantly, Dylan climbed back into his car and shut the door. He rolled down the window, slipped the key in the ignition and turned the engine over. Mackenzie had been right about one thing. He did have a day. And he needed to get back to it.

Chapter Three

Dylan shifted into Reverse, but he just couldn't bring himself to back out. Instead, he shifted back into Park, shut off the engine and got out of the car. Whether or not Mackenzie wanted him to make certain she was okay before he took off, it was something he felt he needed to do. Dylan set off toward the barn entrance; he carefully picked his way through long grass, weeds and sun-dried horse manure.

"You need some help?" Dylan was greeted by a young man in his early twenties leading a dark brown mare to one of the pastures. The young man appeared to have cerebral palsy and walked with a jerky, unsteady gate.

"I'm looking for Hope and her mom," Dylan said.

"They're in the office." The young man pointed behind him.

"Thanks," Dylan said just before he felt his left shoe sink into a fresh pile of manure. "Crap!"

"Yes, sir." The young man laughed as he turned the mare loose in the pasture. "That's exactly what it is."

Dylan shook his head as he tried to wipe the manure off his shoe in the grass. Today of all days he had to put on his Testoni lace-ups; he had spent some time this morning, polishing and buffing them to just the right amount of shine. Once he managed to semiclean his pricey leather shoes, he got himself back on track and found his way to the office. Dylan quietly stepped inside the disheveled hub of Pegasus. Dirt and hay were strewn across the floor and a large, rusty fan was kicking up more dust than circulating air. Mackenzie, a girl who must have been her daughter and a tall woman with cropped snow-white hair were gathered near a gray metal desk at the back of the rectangular office.

"Mom—I'm okay. When I bent down to grab a currycomb, I hit my head on the shelf. It's no big deal," Dylan heard Hope say.

Mackenzie brushed the girl's bangs out of the way to look at the bump on Hope's forehead. "Well—you've got a pretty good knot up there, kiddo."

"Here." The older woman held out a Ziploc baggy full of ice. "This'll hold her till you can get her checked out."

"But we still have more riders coming," Hope protested.

Mackenzie took the bag of ice. "Thanks, Aggie."

"They need my help, Mom! I'm *fine*. Really. I don't need to go to the doctor." Hope tried once again to reverse her fortune.

"Honey—I'm sorry." Mackenzie held her daughter's hand in hers. "We've gotta get this checked out. If the doctor gives you the green light, I promise, you'll be right back here tomorrow."

Hope sighed dramatically and pressed the ice to the lump on her forehead. "Fine."

Not wanting to interrupt the mother-daughter negotiation, Dylan hung back.

"Can I help you?" Aggie was suddenly in his face and confronting him like a protective mama bear with a cub.

Dylan slipped off his sunglasses and hooked them into the collar of his shirt. "I'm just checking on Mackenzie."

Mackenzie jerked her head around when she heard his voice. She swayed slightly and heard ringing in her ears as sheer panic sent her blood pressure soaring. "Dylan... why are you still here?"

"I'm just making sure you're okay before I leave." Dylan couldn't figure out why Mackenzie was freaked out about him looking out for her. Her overreaction struck him as odd.

Trapped, Mackenzie turned to face Dylan and blocked his view of Hope with her body. "That's my ride, Aggie."

"Oh!" Aggie wiped the sweat from the deep wrinkles etched into her brow. "If I'd known that, I would've made it a point to more cordial. I thought you might be one of them developers the Cook family's been sending around here lately...."

"Developers?" Mackenzie asked, temporarily distracted from her immediate problem.

Aggie waved her hand back and forth impatiently. "I don't want to borrow trouble talkin' about it right now.

"Agnes Abbot." Agnes stuck out her hand to Dylan. "You can call me Aggie or Mrs. Abbot—take your pick. But if you call me Agnes, don't expect an answer."

"Nice to meet you, Mrs. Abbot." Aggie's hand was damp and gritty. "Dylan Axel."

"And when I said that you could take your pick, I meant for you to pick Aggie."

"Aggie," Dylan repeated with a nod.

"Who's that, Mom?" Hope peeked around Mackenzie's body.

Realizing that there was no way out of this trap except forward, Mackenzie suddenly felt completely, abnormally, calm. This *was* going to happen. This meeting between father and daughter was unfolding organically, out of her control. Wasn't Rayna always preaching about life providing the right experiences at the right time? Maybe she was right. Perhaps she just needed to get out of life's way. So she did. She took a small step to the side and let Hope see her father for the first time.

"Hope—this is my friend Dylan." Her voice was surprisingly steady. "Dylan—I'd like you to meet my daughter, Hope."

Mackenzie zoomed in on Dylan's face first, and then Hope's, as they spoke to each other for the first time. If she had expected them to recognize each other instantly, like a made-for-TV movie, they didn't.

"Hi, Hope. How's your head?" Dylan had walked over to where Hope was sitting. For Mackenzie, it was so easy to see Dylan in Hope—the way she walked, the way she held her shoulders. Her smile.

"It doesn't even hurt," Hope explained to him.

Hope had Mackenzie's curly russet hair, cut into a bob just below her chin, as well as her mother's violet-blue eyes. But, that's where the resemblance ended. Her face was round instead of heart-shaped like her mother's; her skin was fairer and she had freckles on her arms and her face. The thought popped into his head that Hope must take strongly after her father's side of the family.

To Aggie, Hope said, "I think I should stay here. Don't you think I should stay?"

"No, ma'am." Aggie shook her head while she riffled around in one of the desk's drawers. "Your mom's got the right idea. They'll be just fine without us while we get you checked out."

"Nice try, kiddo." Mackenzie held out her hand to Hope. "You're going."

"Man…" Hope's mouth drooped in disappointment. But she put her hand into Mackenzie's hand and stood up slowly.

"Come on, kiddo…cheer up." Mackenzie wrapped her arm tightly around Hope's shoulders and kissed the top of her head. "We've been through worse, right?"

"Right." Hope gave her mom a halfhearted smile and returned the hug.

"Found one." Aggie pulled a pamphlet out of the pencil drawer and tromped over to Dylan in her knee-high rubber boots.

"Here." Aggie pressed the pamphlet into Dylan's hand, then she tapped on the front of it. "Here's the 411 on this place. We're always looking for volunteers. Do you have any horse experience?"

Dylan looked at the pamphlet. "Actually, I do."

"Perfect! We can always use another volunteer with some horse sense," Aggie said to him, hands resting on her squared hips. Then to Mackenzie, she said, "Well— let's get."

While Dylan skimmed the pamphlet quickly, it occurred to Mackenzie that she had just survived a moment that she had dreaded, and worried herself sick about, for years. Dylan and Hope had met and the world hadn't fallen off its axis. It gave her reason to believe that when the truth about their relationship came out, things would be okay for all of them.

Dylan folded the pamphlet and tucked it into his front pocket.

"Are you going to volunteer?" Hope asked him.

Mackenzie and Hope were standing directly in front of him now, arm in arm, the close bond between mother and daughter on display. It didn't surprise him that Mackenzie had turned out to be a dedicated and attentive mother. The way she had always taken care of every living thing around her when they were young, he didn't doubt it had been an easy transition into motherhood.

"I don't know." Dylan shifted his eyes between mother and daughter. "Maybe."

"You should." Hope tucked some of her hair behind her ear. "It's really fun."

From the doorway, Aggie rattled her keys. "We're burning daylight here! Let's go!"

"We're coming," Mackenzie said to Aggie, then to Dylan, "Thank you, Dylan. I'm sure you had a lot of things to do today. I hope this didn't put you behind schedule too much…"

"I was glad I could help." Dylan found himself intrigued, once again, by Mackenzie's unique lavender-blue eyes.

"Well…thank you again." Mackenzie sent him a brief smile. "Come on, kiddo. Aggie's already got the truck running."

"Nice to meet you, Hope," Dylan said.

"Bye." Hope lifted her hand up and gave a short wave.

Dylan waited for Mackenzie and Hope to turn and head toward the door. As Hope turned, something on the very top of her left ear caught his eye. Instead of following directly behind them, Dylan was too distracted to move. Dylan's eyes narrowed and latched on to Hope as he reached up to touch a similar small bump at the top of his own left ear.

"Are you coming, Dylan?" Mackenzie had paused in the doorway.

"What?" Dylan asked, distracted.

"Are you coming?" Mackenzie repeated.

Dylan swallowed hard several times. He couldn't seem to get his mouth to move, so he just nodded his response and forced himself to remain calm. Hands jammed into his front pockets, Dylan followed them out. He watched as Mackenzie and Hope piled into Aggie's blue long-bed dual-tire truck. Aggie backed out, Mackenzie waved good-bye and Dylan's jumbled thoughts managed to land on one very disturbing truth: the only other time he had ever seen a small bump like Hope's was when he was looking at himself in the mirror.

Instead of heading to the studio, which was his original plan, Dylan drove home on autopilot from the barn. His mind was churning like a hamster on a hamster wheel, just going around and around in the same circle. No matter how hard he tried, he couldn't remember if he'd used a condom when he'd slept with Mackenzie. He had always been religious about it, but he hadn't expected to sleep with anyone at the wedding. He had still been licking his wounds from his breakup with Christa, and ending up in Mackenzie's hotel room that night had been a completely unplanned event. And, unless Mackenzie was in the habit of carrying condoms, which seemed out of character, there was a real good chance they'd had unprotected sex that night. In that case, it was possible, *highly* possible that Mackenzie's daughter was his child.

Dylan pulled into the garage and parked next to his black Viper. He jumped out of his car and headed inside. He walked straight into the downstairs bathroom, flipped on the light and leaned in toward the mirror. He touched the tiny bump on his ear with his finger. He hadn't been imagining it—Hope's bump matched his. What were the odds that another man, the one who'd fathered Hope, would have the same genetic mark?

"I wouldn't bet on it," Dylan said as he left the bathroom. He went into the living room and pulled open the doors of the custom-built bookcases. He knelt down and started to search through the books on the bottom shelf. He found what he was looking for and pulled it off the shelf. His heart started to thud heavily in his chest as he sat down in his recliner and opened the old family photo album. On the way home, an odd thought had taken root in his mind. There was something so familiar about Hope and he couldn't get a particular family photo, one of his favorites, out of his mind.

Dylan flipped through the pages of the album until he found the photo he'd been looking for. He turned on the light beside the recliner and held the photo under the light.

"No…" Dylan leaned over and studied the photo of his mother and his aunt Gerri sitting together on the porch. His mom had to be around twelve and Aunt Gerri looked to be near eight or nine. Hope was the spitting image of Aunt Gerri. Yes, she had Mackenzie's coloring, but those features belonged to *his* family. That bump on Hope's ear came directly from *his* genes. He'd stake his life on it.

"No…" Dylan closed his eyes. A rush of heat crashed over his body, followed by a wave of nausea. He had a daughter. He was a father. Hope was *his* child.

What the hell is going on here?

"Babe!" Jenna came through the front door carrying an empty tote bag over her shoulder. "Where are you?"

"In the den." Dylan leaned forward and dropped his head down.

"There you are…" Jenna dropped her bag on the floor. She climbed into his lap and kissed him passionately on the mouth.

"I've missed you, babe." Jenna curled her long legs up; rested her head on his shoulder.

"I've missed you, too," Dylan said in a monotone.

"Whatcha lookin' at?" Jenna asked.

Dylan reached over with his free hand and shut the album. "I was just checking something out for Aunt Gerri."

"Be honest." Jenna unbuttoned the top button of his shirt. "Are you upset with me?"

"Why would I be upset with you?" Dylan felt suffocated and wished Jenna wasn't sitting on him, but he didn't have the heart to push her away.

"Because I'm going to be staying with Denise in LA… didn't you get my message?"

Dylan tried to focus on what Jenna was saying. "When are you leaving?"

"Tomorrow. Remember the audition I had this week? I got the pilot!" Jenna squealed loudly as she hugged him tightly. "Can you believe it?!"

"Congratulations, Jenna. I'm really happy for you."

"And not mad?"

"No." Dylan rubbed his hand over her arm. "Of course not."

"I mean—we can still probably see each other on weekends."

"Sure."

"And…" Jenna kissed the side of his neck. "I think the sex'll be even hotter when we *do* see each other, don't you think?"

Dylan tried to muster a smile in response, but he just wanted her to get off his lap.

"Do you want to go upstairs for a quickie before I grab my stuff?" Jenna slipped her hand into his shirt so she could run her hand over his bare chest. "I only have, like, an hour because I have to finish packing over at my place, but...we still have time. If you want..."

Dylan patted her leg. "Not now, Jenna. I'm...beat."

Jenna shrugged nonchalantly. "That's okay. But at least come up and keep me company while I pack."

Jenna uncurled herself from his lap, held out her hand and wiggled her fingers so he'd take her hand. Dylan followed Jenna up the stairs. He sat on the edge of the soaker tub while Jenna cleaned out the drawer he had cleared out for her. He listened while she chattered excitedly about her new job, but he couldn't focus on her words. His mind was fixated on one thing and one thing only: Hope. Usually he enjoyed hanging out with low-demand Jenna. But today she was grating on his nerves, and he had never been so happy to see her go. He had gone through the motions of carrying her bag out to her BMW and then kissing her as if he meant it before she drove away. There was an unspoken goodbye in that kiss; he had the feeling that it was only a matter of time before their relationship fizzled under the pressure of distance. They had both always known that neither one of them was playing a long game.

After seeing the last of her taillights, Dylan closed the front door and went outside on the balcony so he could look at the ocean waves. He needed to clear his head, figure out his next move. The best way he knew to clear his head was to get on his surfboard. The waves were small, but he didn't care. He just needed to blow off some steam and get his head screwed back on straight. After he spent several hours pounding the waves, Dylan jumped into the shower with clarity of mind—he knew exactly what he needed to do. He wasn't about to let this thing fester overnight. He was going to have to confront Mackenzie. He was going to ask her point-blank if Hope was his child. *Direct* was the only way he knew how to do business. Dylan dried off quickly, pulled on some casual clothes and then dialed a familiar number.

"Jordan. I'm glad I caught you." Dylan held a pen in his hand poised above a pad of paper. "Listen—I think I may have a job for your cousin Mackenzie. Can I grab her number from you real quick?"

Mackenzie put all of Hope's medicine bottles back in the cabinet. Even though Hope had fought it valiantly, getting injured at the barn, however minor, had worn her out. After she ate and took her medicine, Hope had gone to bed early.

"So tell me what happened," Rayna said over the phone. "They actually met today?"

Mackenzie pushed some recipe boxes out of the way and sat down on the love seat. "I needed a ride. He was there. It just happened."

"Well…you know I don't believe in coincidences…"

"I know…"

"So…what are you going to do?"

Mackenzie slumped down farther into the cushion and rubbed her eyes. "I'm going to get myself through this week, and then I'm going to call him. Ask to meet."

"I think you're doing the right thing. Do you know what you're going to say?"

"No. Not a clue." Mackenzie stared up at the ceiling. "I have a couple of days to think about it. What's the etiquette on something like this?"

"I don't know. We could look it up online."

Mackenzie kicked off her shoes and pulled off her socks. "I was joking, Ray."

"I know. But I bet there's a ton of stuff out there about how you tell your baby daddy that he *is* your baby daddy…"

Mackenzie curled into the fetal position on the love seat. "Ugh. I hate that term. *Baby daddy*."

"Sorry. But you know what I mean. You know someone had to write a 'how to' manual. There's probably a *DNA for Dummies* out there…"

Mackenzie's phone chirped in her ear, signaling call waiting. "Hold on, Ray. Someone's calling."

Mackenzie took the phone away from her ear and looked at the incoming call.

Dylan Axel was the name that flashed across the screen.

"Dylan's on the other line," Mackenzie told Ray.

"I'm hanging up," Rayna said quickly. "Call me back!"

Dylan couldn't sit still while he waited for Mackenzie to answer. He had been staring at Mackenzie's number for nearly an hour. Before he dialed her number, he began to question his own logic. Yet, after nearly an hour of careful consideration, his gut just wouldn't stop prodding him to place the call. If Hope *was* his daughter, then he had a right to know.

"Hello?" Mackenzie picked up the line.

"It's Dylan, Mackenzie." It was work to control his tone. "How's Hope?"

"She's worn out, but doing fine. The doctor cleared her to return to the barn tomorrow…"

"I'm glad to hear it." Dylan was pacing in a circular pattern.

After an uncomfortable silence, Mackenzie asked, "Um…did Jordan give you my private number?"

"Yes." Dylan needed to get to the point. "She did. Look—there's something that I need to ask you, Mackenzie."

There was a razor-sharp edge in Dylan's tone that brought her to the edge of the love seat.

"What's that?" Her attempt to sound casual failed.

JOANNA SIMS 45

"And I need you to give me an honest answer…"
Dylan stopped pacing, closed his eyes and tried to control his out-of-control heartbeat, as he posed his simple, straightforward question:
"Is Hope my child?"

Chapter Four

Mackenzie sat like a statue on the edge of the love seat, but bit her lip so hard that she could taste blood on her tongue. Once again, fate had snatched control away from her grasp. She had wanted to broach the subject with Dylan gently, calmly, at the right moment and in the right setting. This wasn't how she wanted it to go at all.

Dylan waited impatiently at the other end of the line. But he had heard Mackenzie suck in her breath when he asked the question, followed by silence. For him, he already had his answer. Hope was his daughter.

"Mackenzie." Dylan repeated the question, "Is Hope my child?"

Mackenzie stared in the direction of Hope's room, grateful that she had gone to bed early. "I…" She whispered into the phone, "I don't think that we should discuss this over the phone."

"You're probably right," Dylan agreed. "You pick the place and time and I'll be there."

"I can meet after work tomorrow." Mackenzie pushed herself to a stand. "But I don't know where we should meet."

"Let's meet at my place." Dylan's forehead was in his hand, his eyes squeezed tightly shut.

Mackenzie pressed her back against the wall and crossed one arm tightly over her midsection. "I'll get my friends to watch Hope. I can be at your place around six-fifteen, six-thirty."

"I'll see you then." Dylan opened his eyes. "Good night, Mackenzie."

"Good night." Mackenzie touched the end button and slowly slid down the wall until she was sitting on the floor. She wrapped her arms tightly around her legs and rested her forehead on her knees. From the moment she had held Hope in her arms at the hospital, she had *felt*, like a splinter under her skin, this day would eventually come. And now that it had, she felt undeniably shell-shocked and strangely...*relieved*.

But with the relief came another strain of uncertainty. She prayed for Hope's sake that Dylan wouldn't reject her. But what if Dylan decided that he wanted to play a larger role in Hope's life? She had raised Hope on her own for ten years. It had always been Mackenzie and Hope against the world. And she knew she was being selfish, but she *liked it* that way.

When Dylan ended the call, he started to straighten up the condo to keep his body busy and his mind occupied. He moved restlessly from room to room, cleaning surfaces and pounding pillows into submission. He wound up back in the kitchen and began to unload the dishwasher even though the housekeeper would be there in the morning. One by one, he put the glasses in the cabinet, setting them down hard and then shutting the cabinet doors a little bit more firmly than he normally would. Finished with the chore, Dylan tried to push the dishwasher drawer back in, but it caught.

"Dammit!" Dylan rattled it back into place and then with a hard shove, slammed it forward. He lifted up the dishwasher door and shut it, hard. Stony faced, he leaned back against the counter, arms crossed over his chest. Still frustrated and restless, Dylan headed down to the beach and once his feet hit the sand, he started to run. He was grateful for the cover of the night. He was grateful that there were only a few souls on the beach with him. He started to run faster, his feet pounding on the hard-packed sand. Pushing his body harder, pushing himself to go faster and farther than he had ever gone before. His lungs burned, but he didn't let up. His leg muscles burned, but he didn't let up. He didn't let up until his leg muscles gave way and he stumbled. His hands took the brunt of his body weight as he fell forward into the sand. Fighting to catch his breath, he sat back, and dropped his head down to his knees. He pressed his sandy fingers into his eyes and then pinched the side of his nose to stop tears from forming.

He'd never wanted to be a father and he'd worked damn hard to make sure it never happened. That he never had a slipup. He had been *vigilant* all of his sexual life to make sure that he never got anyone pregnant. Even if he had been dating someone for a while, even if he saw them take the pill every day, he *always* wore a condom. But the one time he didn't—the *one* time he *didn't*—he'd gotten caught. And now, he had to face the one fear he had never intended to face: Was being a bad father genetic?

"I'm here." Mackenzie pulled into a parking spot a couple of doors down from Dylan's condo. She was on speakerphone with Rayna and Charlie.

"Mackenzie—you've got this," Charlie said.

"And don't forget—" Rayna began.

"Rayna," Mackenzie interrupted her. "Please, please, *please* don't give me another spiritual affirmation. I just can't take it right now."

After a pause, Rayna said in her "let's meditate" voice, "I was just going to say—don't forget that we're always here for you, anytime, no matter what."

"Oh. Sorry. Thank you," Mackenzie said. "I'll be by to pick up Hope after I'm done."

Mackenzie hung up with her friends and then got out of the car. She stood by her car for several minutes, staring at Dylan's condo, before she forced herself to get the show on the road. Stalling wouldn't help. She needed to face this conversation with Dylan head-on and get it out of the way.

Mackenzie took a deep breath in and knocked on the door. This time, unlike the last time she stood in this spot, Dylan opened the door seconds after she knocked.

"Come on in." Dylan stepped back and opened the door wider.

Mackenzie walked, with crossed arms, through the door and into Dylan's world. She noticed, more so than she had the first time she was here, how neat and organized Dylan's home was. His home was sleek, expensive and masculine: the ultimate bachelor pad. It was a sharp contrast to her 1930s Spanish-style Balboa Park rental with an interior decor that was cobbled together with flea-market finds and garage-sale bargains. The lives they lived, the lives they had built for themselves, couldn't be more different.

"Can I get you something to drink?" Dylan stood several feet away from her, hands hidden in his front pockets. He looked different today. The boyish spark was gone from his eyes. The features of his face were hardened, his mouth unsmiling. Today, he seemed more like a man to her than he ever had before.

"No. Thank you." Mackenzie shook her head, wishing she were already on the back end of this conversation.

"Let's talk in the den." Dylan slipped his left hand out of his pocket and gestured for her to walk in front of him. "After you."

Mackenzie waited for Dylan to sit down before she said, "I'm not sure where to begin..."

"Why don't we start with an answer to my question." Dylan was determined not to let this conversation spiral out of control. He had always been known for his cool head and he wanted to keep it that way.

"I think you've already figured out the answer to your question, Dylan. But if you need to hear me say it, then I'll say it," Mackenzie said in a measured, even voice. "Hope is your daughter."

Instead of responding right away, Dylan stood up and walked over to the large window that overlooked the ocean. He stared out at the waves and rubbed his hand hard over his freshly shaven jawline. With a shake of his head, he turned his back to the window.

"I'm just trying to wrap my mind around this, Mackenzie. It's not every day that my friend's sister turns up with my kid."

"I understand." Mackenzie wished that she could stop the sick feeling of nerves brewing in her stomach.

"How long have you known that she's mine, Mackenzie?" Dylan asked pointedly. "Have you always known... or did you think that she was your ex-boyfriend's child?"

Mackenzie's stomach gurgled loudly. Embarrassed, she pressed her hands tightly into her belly. "I've always known."

"How?" Dylan asked quietly, his face pale. "How did you know?"

"You were the only one I'd slept with in months, Dylan. It couldn't've been anyone else *but* you."

Dylan leaned back against the window; he felt off balance. "That's not what I expected you to say."

"It's the truth…." Mackenzie said.

Dylan didn't respond; he didn't move. He didn't trust himself to speak, so he didn't.

"I have a question for you." Mackenzie turned her body toward him. "What made you think she was yours?"

"The bump…on her ear. It matches mine."

"Oh…" Mackenzie said faintly. Dylan had always worn his hair long when they were kids—she never noticed that birthmark before.

"And then there was this." Dylan retrieved the photo album, opened it and held it out for Mackenzie to take.

"Look familiar?" Dylan pointed to the picture of his aunt Gerri.

Mackenzie nodded, stared closely at the picture.

"Who needs a DNA test, right?" Dylan nodded toward the picture.

Mackenzie stared at the old black-and-white photograph. "This little girl…she's the spitting image of Hope." Mackenzie looked up. "Who is she?"

"That's my aunt Gerri when she was nine."

"I remember your aunt Gerri. We went to their horse farm a couple of times. She played the organ for us."

Dylan's jaw set. "Hope should be able to remember my aunt Gerri, too. Uncle Bill's the closest thing to a father I've ever had. He *deserved* the chance to know my daughter."

Dylan's well-crafted barb hit its intended mark. And it hurt. Because Mackenzie knew that he was right. Silently, she carefully closed the photo album and handed it back to Dylan.

Dylan put the photo album on the coffee table and sunk down on the couch a cushion away from Mackenzie. He leaned forward, rested his elbows on his legs and cradled his head in his hands.

"So…" Dylan said quietly. "We both know she's mine. The next question I'd like answered is…why did you know ten years ago and I'm only finding out *now*?"

Mackenzie leaned away from Dylan. "I found out I was pregnant really early on. I'm regular…like clockwork. So when I didn't get my period after the wedding…I knew."

"And you didn't think it was important to share this information with me, because…?"

"I was going to tell you. It never occurred to me *not* to tell you."

"But you didn't…" Dylan lifted his head, looked at her. "Why not?"

"Jett told me that you were back with Christa…"

"Jett knew?"

"No. Not back then. And not until long after the two of you had already lost touch."

Dylan nodded and Mackenzie continued her story.

"After I found out that your engagement was back on, I thought it was the best thing for both of us if I didn't tell you…"

"No." Dylan shook his head. "You should have told me. I had the *right* to know."

"You forget, Dylan. I knew how much you loved Christa. That's all you talked about the night Jett got married. And you and I both know what would've happened if she found out you'd gotten someone *pregnant* at the wedding! She would've broken off the engagement and you would have lost the love of your life because of me!

I couldn't see any *reason* to screw up your life, Dylan... not when *I* didn't even know if I wanted to keep the baby."

"I didn't *marry* Christa," Dylan challenged her. "But, you *did* keep the baby."

"Yes. I did. I thought about adoption. I thought about... abortion. In the end, I decided to keep her."

Dylan stabbed his leg with his finger. "That's a decision we should have made *together*."

"I admit that I may have called it wrong..."

"Called it wrong...?" he repeated incredulously.

"But I was young and I thought I was doing the right thing for all of us." Mackenzie touched her finger to her chest. "I got Hope and you got to marry the woman you loved."

"I didn't even know what love was back then..." Dylan shook his head. "At least now I know why you were so anxious to get rid of me at the barn the other day. You didn't want me to meet my own daughter."

"Not like that I didn't." Mackenzie set the record straight. "I didn't want that for Hope...and I didn't want that for you."

In a rough voice, Dylan asked, "Were you ever going to tell me, Mackenzie? Or were you just going to let me go the rest of my life not knowing?"

"No." Mackenzie clasped her hands together. "I was going to tell you. I had decided to start looking for you this year..."

Dylan's eyes were glassy with emotion. "You're telling me...that if we hadn't run into each other at Ian's party, you were going to track me down? Why? Why now?"

Mackenzie took a deep breath in and when she let it out, her shoulders sagged.

"It's what Hope wanted. When we were filling out her

Make-A-Wish application, she wrote—I wish I could meet my dad."

"Wait a minute…" What she had just said didn't sink into his head right away. "Make-A-Wish? Isn't that for sick kids?"

"Yes." Mackenzie waited for Dylan to ask the next logical question.

"Are you trying to tell me that Hope is sick?"

"Hope has been battling leukemia for the last two years." Mackenzie managed to say those words without tearing up.

As Dylan often did, he went silent. He stared at her for a long time with puzzled, narrowed eyes.

"Do you need a drink?" he finally asked. "I need a drink."

Dylan stood up suddenly and walked toward the kitchen. He stopped when he realized that she was still sitting on the couch. "Are you coming?"

Wordlessly, Mackenzie stood up on shaky legs and followed Dylan into the kitchen.

"Can I interest you in a cold malt beverage?" Dylan pulled a bottle of beer from the side door.

"Sure. Why not?"

"Why not, indeed," Dylan said cryptically as he popped the tops off the beers and handed her one. "We're both consenting adults here."

"Thank you," Mackenzie said. She brought the bottle up to her mouth but Dylan stopped her.

"What should we toast to?" He held out his bottle to her.

"Anything you'd like," Mackenzie said tiredly. She was exhausted. She was exhausted all the time, and had been for years. The stress of Hope's illness and the stress of trying to run a business had been catching up with her for a long time. And now she had a sinking feeling that dealing with Dylan was only going to add to her exhaustion.

Dylan tapped her bottle with his. "To Hope."

"To Hope," Mackenzie seconded.

"Could you go for some fresh air?" Dylan asked.

Mackenzie nodded and Dylan opened the French door leading out to the deck. "After you."

Mackenzie stepped onto the large deck and was immediately drawn to the edge of the railing that overlooked the beach. She stared at the sun setting over the small, rolling waves and tried to relax her shoulders. Dylan, who used to be so simple to read, wasn't so easy for her to read tonight. She had no idea what type of emotional shift she might encounter. Next to her, but not too close, Dylan rested his forearms on the railing, bottle loosely held in one hand.

"So…" Dylan said in a calm, almost contemplative tone. "Hope has cancer."

"Yes…" Mackenzie nodded. "She has acute lymphoblastic leukemia. ALL. She was diagnosed when she was eight."

"Leukemia. What is that? Blood cancer?"

Mackenzie nodded. "At first I just thought that she was pushing herself too hard between school and the barn. She was tired all the time, losing weight. She just wasn't herself. When she started to complain about an ache in her bones and a sore throat…" Mackenzie lifted one shoulder. "I thought she was coming down with the flu. I mean… who would immediately jump to cancer?"

Dylan sat down in one of the chairs encircling a fire pit. Mackenzie joined him.

"I remember being really stressed out that day…the day we found out. I had to rearrange my entire morning so I could get Hope to the doctor. Traffic was ridiculous, I was on the phone with the bakery…on the phone with clients…I remember thinking that it was the worst possible time for Hope to be catching something on top of everything else." Mackenzie pushed strands of hair out of her face. "And all I could do was start adding things to do to my already gigantic to-do list—stop by the pharmacy, arrange for someone to stay with Hope…blah, blah, blah…"

Mackenzie stopped to take a swig from her beer. She shook her head as she swallowed the liquid down. "I had no idea how frivolous *everything* I'd just been obsessing over was about to become."

Dylan listened intently, while Mackenzie talked. "The doctor sent us to the hospital, tests were run and she was diagnosed that day. And just like that…literally in what seemed like the blink of an eye…our world imploded. No parent is ever prepared to hear the words *your child has cancer.*" Mackenzie rubbed fresh tears out of her eyes. "But even more than that, I'll never forget the look on Hope's face when she asked me—'Did she just say that I have cancer?' I've never been that scared in my life. Hope was admitted to the hospital, and ever since then, our lives just became this never-ending revolving door of chemo and steroids and tests and checkups and hospital stays…"

When Mackenzie realized that she was the only one talking *and* that she had said much more than she had ever intended, she stopped herself from blurting out more by taking a swig of her now-tepid beer. She picked at the label on the bottle, wishing that Dylan would do something other than sit in his designer lounge chair and stare at her.

"I don't know why I just told you all of that," Mackenzie said to fill the silence.

At first, Dylan really didn't know what to say. He had been dragged from one emotional spectrum to the next in the span of an hour. At the beginning of their meeting, all he felt for Mackenzie was anger. But while Mackenzie was telling her story, and with the ocean wind blowing the wispy tendrils of her hair across her pretty face, she reminded him of the girl she had once been. The girl he remembered so vividly from his childhood—the chubby bookworm with thick glasses who used to read her books in the backseat of one of her father's vintage cars. All the boys in the neighborhood ignored Jett's sister, but he never did. Maybe it was because he liked how different she was than the rest of the girls. Or maybe it was because he had only seen her smile once after her mom died. He had never thought to analyze it. He had always just *liked* Mackenzie.

"Because we used to be friends," Dylan said.

"Were we?" Mackenzie asked.

"I always thought so." Dylan caught her gaze and held it. "And I tell you this, Mackenzie. If I had known that you were pregnant…if you had just trusted me enough to give me a chance, I never would've let you or Hope go through any of this stuff alone. I would have been there for you… both of you…every step of the way."

Chapter Five

It took Dylan a couple of weeks to make a decision about Hope. He had gone about his daily life trying to focus on business. He hadn't told anyone about Hope, not his girlfriend, his aunt or his best friend. He needed to get right with it in his own head before he could open up to other people. And after many distracted days and restless nights, he had an epiphany of sorts: Didn't he have a moral obligation to Hope? Yes, the idea of becoming an "instant parent" terrified him. But if he was brutally honest with himself, the idea of repeating his father's mistakes scared him even more. Once he came to a decision, he took the only next logical step: he called Mackenzie.

"Hello?" Mackenzie answered the phone.

"Hi, Mackenzie. It's Dylan. How are you?"

"I'm fine. Busy. But fine," Mackenzie said. "Hope's doing really well. Her recent blood tests came back clear. She's still in remission."

"That's good to hear."

When he didn't add anything more, Mackenzie asked, "How are you doing, Dylan?"

"I'm okay. Still sorting through this thing, I think." Dylan rested his forehead in his hand. "Look, Mackenzie, I've been thinking a lot about Hope…are you sure that getting to know me is what your daughter wants?"

Mackenzie hated that she hesitated before she said, "I'm sure."

"Then, let's set it up." Dylan stared out the window at the calm ocean in the distance. His tone was steady but his heart was pounding.

"Um…" Mackenzie rubbed her temples to prevent a migraine from flaring up. "I haven't told Hope that I found you yet. I was waiting to hear from you. I didn't want to get her excited and then…well, you know…"

"Understood." Dylan sounded as if he was arranging a business meeting rather than a meeting with his newly discovered daughter. It was his comfort zone and it helped him stay sane. "When can you get that done?"

"Not tonight," Mackenzie said distractedly. "She has chemo tomorrow and she'll be sick all weekend…but maybe next week sometime when she's feeling better…"

"That's fine." Dylan nodded his head. "Once that's done, give me a call and we'll figure out the next step. Does that work for you?"

"Yes," Mackenzie said after she cleared her throat. "I'll call you once I've spoken with my daughter."

After they ended the call, Mackenzie stared at the phone for several seconds.

"Well?" Rayna was staring at her like a cat gearing up to pounce on a catnip toy. "That had to be Dylan, right? What did he *say*?"

"He wants to meet Hope."

Rayna turned the burner on the stove down. "See? Look at that! Prayers in action! This is *great* news!"

"What's great news?" Charlie walked through the front door wearing mint-green scrubs. She hung her keys on the hook just inside the door.

"Hi, honey." Rayna smiled at her wife, Charlotte. "Dylan finally came to his senses and called. He's agreed to meet Hope!"

Rayna was the yin to Charlotte's yang. Rayna had shoulder-length wispy blond hair, pretty, Slavic features and alabaster skin. Charlotte, who preferred to be called Charlie, was an attractive mix of Irish and Mexican heritage with light brown eyes, golden-chestnut skin and thick black wavy hair worn loose and long. At first, Rayna and Charlie were just her landlords, but they had become family after Hope was diagnosed. Rayna and Charlie had been in the trenches with them right from the start—cooking meals, running errands and pulling all-nighters watching Hope while Mackenzie caught a few hours of sleep. And Rayna's church had held fundraisers to help raise money to help pay for Hope's burgeoning medical bills. It was hard to imagine how she would have gotten through the first year of Hope's treatment without them.

"Huh…" Charlie kissed Rayna on the lips. "How come you're happy and Mackenzie's not?"

"You know Mackenzie resists change." Ray held out a wooden spoon to Charlie. "Here. Taste this."

Charlie tasted the sauce. "That's really good."

"I don't think I *resist* change," Mackenzie said.

A sleepy-eyed, rotund gray tabby cat named Max appeared. Charlie scooped him up, kissed him on the head. "I thought this was the call you've been waiting for all week…?"

"It's not that I'm *not* glad that he called. I am. It's just a lot to take in, that's all. It's always just been Hope and me." Mackenzie rested her chin on her hand. "I like how things are between us now…"

"Resistant to change," Rayna said in a singsong voice.

Charlie got some water and then joined Mackenzie at the kitchen table. "But maybe this will turn out to be a great thing. You yourself already said that he's a good guy. What could it hurt to have another person share the load? Between the bakery and managing Hope's leukemia treatments, let's face it…you've got your hands full."

At Mackenzie's feet, Max was preparing for a leap onto her lap. Mackenzie patted her legs for encouragement.

"Oh, my dear lord, what have you been feeding this cat, Ray?" Max landed on her leg with a grunt. "I thought he was on a diet."

Charlie sent Rayna an "I told you so" look. Rayna was immediately defensive. "He *is* on a diet! Don't listen to them, Max-a-million. You're just big boned!" Rayna pointed a spatula at her. "And don't change the subject. What's really scaring you?"

Rayna could read her like a book. "I don't know. I suppose I am, a little scared. I mean…what if…

"What if…" Mackenzie hadn't admitted this private thought aloud. "What if Dylan ends up wanting custody of Hope? What if Hope decides that she wants to live with him down the road?"

Charlie and Rayna both shook their heads in unison.

"Nope. Not gonna happen." Charlie twisted her thick wavy hair into a bun.

Rayna came to the table. "Not a chance."

"I feel stupid admitting that out loud…" Mackenzie scratched behind Max's chops.

"It's not stupid," Rayna said. "It's human."

"I suppose so…" Mackenzie helped Max to the floor

safely. "You know what, guys? If it's all the same to you, I think I'm just gonna skip dinner."

"Are you sure?" Rayna asked, disappointed. "I was going to try out a new recipe on you! And I have wine..."

"Yeah. I'm sure." She stood up, glad that she lived next door. "I just need some time to...decompress before Hope gets back from the movies."

"Bath salts, candles and a hot bath." Rayna hugged her tightly at the door. "Everything always looks better after a bath."

Dylan drove slowly up the winding, tree-lined private driveway that led to his aunt's farm. When he was growing up, and Uncle Bill was still alive, the farm had been bustling with activity. Now the place felt lifeless. The horses were gone, the stable hands and horse trainers were gone. The only thing left were empty pastures, empty stables and Aunt Gerri's sprawling two-story 1900s farmhouse with its wraparound porch and old tin roof. At one time, Forrest Hanoverians claimed over a hundred acres and were renowned for the quality of their Hanoverian breeding program. Over the years, Aunt Gerri had sold off much of the farm's land until only the central twenty acres of the farm remained.

Dylan parked his car in the circle driveway in front of the house. Aunt Gerri swung open the front door and waved at him.

"I was just getting ready to play the organ, when I saw you coming up the driveway!" Aunt Gerri called to him from the door. Just shy of her eighty-third birthday, Geraldine Forrest was a petite woman with intelligent bright blue eyes, a steel-trap memory and a kind-hearted disposition. Dylan always marveled at her energy; she kept herself busy going to garage sales, playing the organ at her church and socializing with her long list of friends.

"How are you, Aunt Gerri?" Dylan walked up the porch steps.

"Well…I'll tell you…I'm fit as a fiddle." Aunt Gerri held out her arms to him. "Oh! I'm so happy to see you!"

"I'm glad to see you, too, Aunt Gerri." Dylan hugged her and kissed her on the cheek.

"Okay…so let's go inside." Aunt Gerri turned to head back into the house. "You'll have to shut the door real hard—it's been sticking lately."

Dylan ran his hand up the edge of the door. "I'll fix it for you before I leave."

"Oh! Would you?" Aunt Gerri beamed. "That would be such a big help. I was finally going to break down and call someone about it tomorrow. You'll be saving me the trouble. Do you want coffee?"

"No, thanks. I'm good." Dylan stopped to straighten a picture of Uncle Bill hanging in the foyer. After his mom died, this became his permanent home. Uncle Bill and Aunt Gerri took him and raised him. This house, with its creaky wide-planked wooden floors and thick crown molding, was his home. It was the one place that never really changed. The one thing he could always count on, especially when something significant happened in his life.

"Let's go to the sitting room, then. I want to show you my brand-new organ." Aunt Gerri headed into the large room to the left of the foyer.

"It's a Lowrey Holiday Classic…" Aunt Gerri stood proudly by her organ. "I just traded my old one in. This is my seventh organ and this'll probably be the last one I buy…"

Dylan sat down in his grandmother's rocking chair. "It's nice. I like it."

"I'll be sure to play it for you before you go." Aunt Gerri settled herself in another rocking chair. "So..." Her sharp blue eyes were curious. "What's the news?"

"Can't I visit you without being accused of having an ulterior motive?"

"Oh, I think I know you pretty well," Aunt Gerri said. "There's gotta be something real important going on to bring you all the way out here on a business day."

"You've always had my number ever since I was a kid." Dylan fiddled with the loose rocking-chair arm before he looked back at his aunt. "And you're right. There is something I need to tell you."

"Well, go on and tell me what it is so we can talk it out."

"I found out a couple of weeks ago that I have...a daughter." Dylan watched his aunt's face to gauge her reaction. "Her name is Hope. She's ten."

"Did you just say you've got a daughter?" Aunt Gerri stopped rocking. "Who's the mother?"

For the next half hour, Dylan talked and his aunt listened. He told his aunt about the first time he'd ever seen Hope at the barn and he recounted his recent conversation with Mackenzie. Like a confession, he didn't leave anything out. Not even the fact that he hadn't been sober the night Hope had been conceived or the fact that he had never dated Mackenzie. And when he was done, he felt as if a weight had been lifted. Now that Aunt Gerri knew about Hope, it was real. No matter what happened, no matter how tough it got, there was no going back.

When he had said his piece, Aunt Gerri thought a bit before she spoke. She rocked back and forth, mulling things over.

"Now that I think about it, I remember Mackenzie. She was a heavyset girl, wasn't she? But she had beautiful blue eyes."

Dylan nodded. "She still does."

Violet eyes.

"She was such a sweet little girl," his aunt said. "But so serious."

"She still is."

"Well…what does she want from you, Dylan? What does she expect?"

"She wants me to spend time with Hope. That's all. She doesn't want money…"

"Not even for the medical bills? Good gracious, cancer treatment can't be cheap." Aunt Gerri had always held the purse strings for the farm.

"I know," Dylan responded to his aunt's skeptical expression. "I thought it was strange, too. But she was adamant about the money. More than that, she doesn't want me to be a parent to Hope, either."

Aunt Gerri frowned. "But is that what *you* want? You're the child's father."

"Honestly, Aunt Gerri? I have no idea what I want."

"Well…I suppose that's where you need to start then, don't you? If you don't know what you want, how in the world can you figure out what you're going to do?"

Hope had picked Pegasus as their first father-and-daughter day. It seemed like a better idea than a restaurant, and he wanted Hope to feel comfortable, so he had agreed. Now that he was here, he started to doubt the soundness of that decision. Perhaps they should have met in private, at his house, *before* they went public. Dylan parked his car next to Mackenzie's Chevy and shut off the engine. Instead of getting out, he stayed in the car. He'd never felt capable of having a panic attack until today. His heart was racing, his mouth was dry and beads of sweat were trickling down the side of his face. He was a mess. The thought of spending the day with Hope made him feel panicked. He had absolutely no idea what to say to a ten-year-old girl; ten-year-old girls hadn't exactly been his target demographic.

"Quit being a coward," Dylan said to himself. "And get out of the stupid car."

After convincing himself to leave the car, Dylan headed to the office. Lucky for him, Aggie was the only one there.

She greeted him with a broad smile and a loud, booming voice. "I heard you were comin' out to lend us a hand today!"

Aggie stomped over to him in her crusty, knee-high black rubber boots and pumped his hand a couple of times. "Come on over here and take a load off. I've got your papers all ready to be filled out. Nothing fancy—but the long and short of it is, you're agreein' that if one of our horses kicks you in the privates or eats your pinkie for a snack, you're on your own. We volunteer at our own risk around here…so if you can live with that, I'll be more than happy to put you to work."

"I can live with it." Dylan sat down at the cluttered picnic table in the middle of the room and resisted the urge to start straightening it up. Instead, he forced himself to focus on reviewing the papers.

"I'll make you a badge so you'll feel official. We don't have riders today—just barn work. But anyone who wants to ride after the chores are done can saddle up."

Aggie handed Dylan a badge and Dylan handed her the filled-out forms. Dylan stood up and Aggie looked down at his pristine boots.

"If you're gonna hang with us, you're gonna have'ta get you some good old-fashioned muckers. Those fancy boots aren't gonna survive a fresh steamin' pile of manure, I guarantee *that*." When Aggie laughed, one eye stayed open and the other one shut completely. "I'm done with ya, so head to the barn. There's always plenty to be done and not enough hands to do it."

Dylan walked out of the office, around the corner, and bumped right into Mackenzie.

Their bodies hit together so hard that Mackenzie had the breath temporarily knocked out of her.

Concerned, Dylan held on to her arms to steady her. "Are you okay?"

"I wasn't expecting anyone to come around that corner," Mackenzie said, slightly annoyed. "But I'm okay now. You can let go."

Dylan released her arms quickly, as if he was pulling his hands away from hot coals. "Sorry. I did it again."

Dylan stared hard at Mackenzie. Something had just happened between them. When their bodies came together, they were a perfect fit. She was curvy and voluptuous and petite; not what he would normally gravitate toward. But he liked the way her body had felt against his. He had enjoyed the feeling of having Mackenzie in his arms. She felt like…home.

Mackenzie tugged on the front of her oversize, long-sleeve T-shirt. "I'm glad you came."

"I said I would," Dylan said defensively.

"I know." Mackenzie had worry etched into her forehead. "I know you did…but I was…"

"Worried that I wouldn't show?"

"Yes…I'm sorry. But, yes. Hope could hardly sleep last night. She's so excited to meet you." Mackenzie was speaking in a low, private voice. "But I think she's more scared than anything."

"Scared? Why is she scared of me?"

"She's not scared *of you*. I think that she's scared that you won't like her." Mackenzie pushed some wayward strands of hair away from her face.

"Well, then, that makes two of us, because I've been really worried that she won't like me, too." Dylan looked down at his outfit. "I changed my clothes three times before I finally put this together."

Mackenzie's eyebrows rose. Dylan was wearing a pressed Ralph Lauren button-down dress shirt, new dark-wash jeans and his spotless boots.

"I did mention that you were going to be doing barn work…didn't I?" Mackenzie asked.

"You mentioned it. I just wanted to look nice for Hope." Dylan frowned down at his outfit. "I look ridiculous, don't I?"

"No. You don't look ridiculous, Dylan. You just look… kind of dressy for the barn. That's all," Mackenzie tried to reassure him. "But stop worrying. Trust me. Hope doesn't care what you're wearing. So…are you ready?"

"Nope." Dylan's stomach started to feel a little queasy.

"What happened to the fearless Dylan Axel I used to know?" Mackenzie tried to tease his nerves away.

"He was too young to know better."

"Come on, Dylan." Mackenzie offered him her hand. "The best way to get something done is to start…"

Dylan took her hand, soft and warm, and let her gently tug him in the right direction. Their hands naturally slipped apart as they walked side by side through the barn's dusty center aisle. As they walked along, Mackenzie greeted the ragtag bunch of secondhand horses and the handful of volunteers working that day. With thirty geriatric horses to care for, Dylan understood why Aggie was so eager to sign him up. Organizations that relied entirely on donations, grants and volunteers were in a constant state of borderline panic and flux. Pegasus was no different.

"This way." Mackenzie tucked her fingers into the front

pocket of her jeans. "Hope's out back washing feed buckets."

Dylan could hear the water running from the hose and he stopped walking. "Wait."

"What's wrong?"

Dylan backed up a step. "Maybe this isn't the best place for this to happen."

"Oh, no, no, no, no, *no*. You're not backing out." Mackenzie's demeanor changed. She walked over to him and grabbed his hand. "This is happening *right now*."

Mackenzie pulled Dylan forward a couple of steps, into an open area with concrete slabs set up for washing the horses.

"Hey, kiddo!" Mackenzie slapped a bright smile on her face. "Look who I found…"

Under her breath, and only for Dylan's ears, Mackenzie said, "You're up."

Hope looked up from her task of washing out a large group of blue feed buckets. She looked at him directly and what he saw in her eyes was something he hadn't experienced with anyone other than his aunt Gerri: total acceptance. Hope's pretty face lit up with excitement as she smiled nervously at him. She dropped the hose and wiped her hands off on her jeans while she headed over to where they were standing. Hope wrapped her arm around her mom's waist for security. She looked up at Mackenzie, Mackenzie looked at Dylan, and Dylan looked at Hope.

"A*wwww*kward." Hope was the first to break the uncomfortable silence.

Dylan liked how Hope broke the ice. "You're right. It is."

Mackenzie ran her hand over the top of Hope's head. "Sometimes this one doesn't have a filter."

"That's okay." Dylan was immediately hooked by

Hope's shy, brief smile. "I have that same problem some-times."

"Do you know who I am?" Hope asked him.

"Hope…" Mackenzie started to correct her.

"No. That's okay," Dylan said to Mackenzie before he looked down at Hope. "Yes. I do know who you are. You're my Hope."

Chapter Six

"Here…" Hope slipped a blue-and-yellow rubber-band bracelet off her wrist and handed it to him. "I made this for you."

"Hey…thanks." Dylan slipped it over his hand onto his wrist. He held it out for Hope to see. "Does it look good on me?"

Hope nodded. "It's a friendship bracelet."

It took the child of the group to ease the tension, but it took the mom in the group to get things moving along.

"Come on…" Mackenzie squeezed Hope's shoulder. "Let's get back to work. Aggie would have a fit if she saw us all standing around getting nothing done."

The three of them put their nervous energy into finishing Hope's chore together. And it turned out that having a common goal to accomplish eased the tension between them. Of course, it wasn't perfect and there were some odd lulls in conversation. And Dylan caught Hope in the act of

studying him when she thought it was safe. Dylan understood her fascination, because he had to resist the urge to
stare at his daughter. Mackenzie, on the other hand, made
no bones about blatantly watching the two of them interact.
But by the time all of the feed buckets were washed and
drying in the sun, the tension between them had slowly
given way to a more relaxed, fun vibe.

"What next?" Dylan unbuttoned his cuffs and rolled up
his sleeves. His shirt was soaked, his boots were already
caked with mud, and it made him feel less out of place
than when he had arrived.

"Now we have to put all the feed buckets back into the
stalls." Hope grabbed some buckets. "Carry as many as you
can so we can get done quicker. Then, I get to ride Gypsy."

"Her favorite horse," Mackenzie explained.

Dylan grabbed as many buckets as his fingers could
hold. "Lead the way, boss."

His words made Hope laugh, spontaneously and loudly.
She smiled at him again, this time without the nervous-
ness. Hope's smile, Dylan decided, was a million-dollar
smile. It was addictive. He wanted to see it again and again.

"While you guys do this, I'm going to help Aggie in
the office," Mackenzie said. She looked at Hope specifi-
cally. "Is that okay?"

When Hope gave a small nod to her mom, Dylan felt
as if he had managed to accomplish something pretty
major: Hope felt comfortable enough with him to spend
time alone. One by one, Hope introduced Dylan formally
to the horses and it was obvious that Hope had a special
connection with each and every one of them. The horses,
some of whom pinned their ears back and gnashed their
teeth at him, all came to Hope for some love and attention.
It made him feel proud that, at such a young age, she had a
special way with these horses. They weren't pretty. They

weren't young. But she loved them just the same. In that, she took directly after kindhearted Mackenzie.

"This is Cinnamon." Hope rubbed her hand lovingly over the mare's face. "She's a sweet girl. Aren't you, Cinnamon? When you work with her, make sure you only approach her from her left side, because she's missing her right eye. See?"

Dylan nodded. There was a deep indent where the mare's eye should have been.

"If you walk up to her on her right side, she might get spooked and accidentally knock you over. But she wouldn't mean to hurt you."

After putting the feed bucket in her stall, Hope kissed Cinnamon affectionately on the nose.

"I've saved the best for last," Hope said excitedly. "This...is *Gypsy*."

The word *Gypsy* was said with flair, as if Hope were introducing the most amazing horse in the history of the equine. Dylan read the large plaque on Gypsy's stall: Warning! This horse will bite! Dylan then took a step back from the gate. Hope wrapped her arms around the mare's neck and hugged.

"What's with the sign?" Dylan asked.

"Oh," Hope said nonchalantly. "She's just looking for food, is all. That's why Aggie won't let us carry treats in our pockets. And we can only give them treats in their buckets, never by hand.

"Isn't she great?" Hope rubbed the space between Gypsy's sad brown eyes.

Gypsy was a spindly-legged barrel-bellied mare with giant, fuzzy donkey ears, a dull brown coat and an unusually long, bony face. Even in the best of times, Dylan knew that Gypsy had *never* been a prize.

Wanting to be diplomatic on his first day hanging out

with his daughter, Dylan said the only *noncommittal* thing he could say, "If you like her then I like her."

"I knew you'd like her, too." Hope nodded happily.

In between stuffing envelopes for the upcoming fundraiser, Mackenzie periodically checked on Hope and Dylan by poking her head around the corner. She didn't feel good about spying, but she *had to* check on Hope. And she was glad she did. If she hadn't spied on them, she would have missed a hallmark moment: the expression on her daughter's face when she introduced Dylan to Gypsy. Hope was beaming at him. She knew all of her daughter's many expressions by heart. That one? It was only reserved for those that Hope *really* liked. For Mackenzie, bearing witness to this moment confirmed for her that bringing Dylan into Hope's life was the right thing to do. It didn't nullify her fears for what a future with Dylan in it would mean for *her*, but for Hope? Her trepidation was erased just like words being wiped away on a whiteboard.

"Done!" Hope attached Gypsy's clean feed bucket to the hook in the stall and then exited the stall.

"Nice work." Dylan held up his hand.

Hope high-fived him. "Do you want to help me get Gypsy's tack?"

"Of course I do. I cleared my entire Sunday just for you."

"You did?"

Dylan nodded. He'd managed to win another smile from Hope. He was on a winning streak and felt like hugging her. But he didn't.

"That's cool," Hope said.

Hope grabbed the bridle, girth and saddle pad, while Dylan hoisted the heavy Western saddle onto his hip. With two of them working, they made quick work of grooming Gypsy before tacking her up. By the end of it, Dylan felt proud of the fact that he'd managed to get the job done without being on the losing end of Gypsy's teeth.

"You can ride, too, you know," his daughter said as she walked Gypsy down the breezeway.

"That's okay...I'd rather watch you," he said. He hadn't been on a horse since high school.

Mackenzie heard her daughter's voice in the breezeway and she met them at the barn entrance. There was a moment when she had a front-row seat to Hope and Dylan walking together, side by side, as if they had known each other all their lives. They had the same swing in their walk, these two. The same way of holding their shoulders, the same easygoing, couldn't-possibly-ignore-it kind of smile.

"Hey, Mom!" Hope greeted Mackenzie enthusiastically. "I was just telling Dylan all about the riding school I want to open up after college."

"I didn't even know they made ten-year-olds like this." Dylan smiled at them.

"Sometimes I don't believe that she's ten." Mackenzie handed Hope a bottle of water. "Hydration, sunscreen and helmet, please."

Mackenzie raised her eyebrows at Dylan over Hope's head. Dylan smiled at her and gave her the "okay" symbol.

"Sunscreen." Mackenzie exchanged the water bottle for the sunscreen bottle.

Hope put sunscreen on her arms and her face. She handed the sunscreen bottle back to Mackenzie along with Gypsy's reins.

"I'll be right back." Hope jogged over to the tack room to grab a helmet.

"How's it going?" Mackenzie asked quietly.

"Good," Dylan said. "Really good..."

"I was hoping that the two of you would...you know... figure each other out if I gave you some space."

"I think we did okay," Dylan said. "She's an incredible kid, Mackenzie. I mean…my God. So smart."

"Straight As," Mackenzie said with pride. "Even when she was at her worst with the chemo."

"I like her." Dylan's thoughts became words.

Mackenzie wasn't a crier. But when Dylan quietly said that he liked Hope, she felt like weeping with relief.

"Well…" Mackenzie turned her head away from him until she could put a halt to the waterworks. "I can tell that she's already crazy about you."

"Yeah? Do you think so?" Dylan was temporarily distracted by how the sunlight was reflecting on Mackenzie's face. It looked dewy and flushed and pretty. Her lips, lips that he'd never really noticed before, were naturally pink and plump. Kissable lips.

"I do." Mackenzie nodded. "I do."

Mackenzie liked how disheveled Dylan looked now. Gone was the catalog model posed in a barn. Part of his shirt was untucked, his jeans were dirty and the once-pristine boots were caked with mud and manure. He was sweaty and grimy and she liked him like that.

Irritated with her own musings about Dylan's masculine appeal, she decided to razz him the way she did when they were kids. "I bet your manicurist is going to have a heck of a time cleaning your nails."

Dylan checked his nails. "Yeah…you're probably right."

"I was just *kidding*! Don't tell me you really *do* have a manicurist, Dylan!"

"In my line of business, being well groomed is a matter of survival."

"Oh, dear Lord…" Mackenzie rolled her eyes. "I can't believe I've actually seen the day when Dylan Axel willingly submitted to a manicure. What happened to the guy who used to love to have grease up to his elbows?"

"Hey…there's nothing wrong with a guy taking care of himself. In fact…*ow!*" Dylan swung his head around quick. "She *bit* me!"

"What?"

Dylan glared at the mare accusingly. "You *bit* me!"

"Where'd she get you?" Mackenzie looked him over. "I don't see any teeth marks."

"That's because she didn't *bite* me on the arm." Dylan scowled at the mare. "Did you, you glue factory reject?"

Hope interrupted their conversation when she returned with a helmet. "What happened?"

"Nothing worth talking about. Here, kiddo." Mackenzie handed Hope the reins. "Why don't you get started and we'll be right behind you, okay."

"Okay. Come on, Gyps!" Hope led Gypsy to the riding arena.

When Hope was out of earshot, Mackenzie said, "She bit you on the butt, didn't she?"

"Let's put it this way…" Dylan said sourly. "It's going to be a long painful drive back to the city."

"Wait here." Mackenzie tried very hard to stifle her smile but failed. "I'll be right back"

Mackenzie returned with Aggie in tow.

"All right." Aggie held a first-aid kit in her hand. "Where'd she getcha? I swear that mare gets meaner every year…"

Mackenzie blurted out, "She bit him in the butt."

"Once a tattletale…" Dylan muttered.

"I'm not a bit surprised," Aggie said. "That's one of her favorite spots… She's gotten me on the fleshy part a couple of times. Do you want me to take a look? See if she broke the skin?"

"No, thank you!" Dylan stepped back.

"Oh, come on, Dylan…" Mackenzie teased him. "Don't be such a baby. Let Aggie take a look."

"Thank *you*," Dylan said to Aggie, then to Mackenzie, "But *no*."

"Suit yourself. But I suggest you grow eyeballs in the back of your head so you can see for yourself if she broke the skin." Aggie handed him the first-aid kit and headed back to the office. "And remember…you volunteered at your own risk."

"Which way to the bathroom?" Dylan asked Mackenzie.

"This way." Mackenzie smirked.

"I suppose you think this is funny…?"

"Not at all."

"Liar!" Dylan smiled at her. "What happened to the girl who used to have a little integrity, huh?"

"Here's the bathroom." Mackenzie pointed. "Light switch on the left."

Dylan went into the bathroom and examined his backside by turning his back to the mirror and straining his neck to look over his shoulder.

"Damn if she didn't break the skin." Dylan ripped open a packet containing an alcohol wipe. He dabbed the wound and then closed his eyes when the alcohol hit it. "And that smarts…"

"How's it going in there?" Mackenzie called through the door.

"She got me good." Dylan tossed the used wipe into the trash.

"Make sure you put some ointment on it and a Band-Aid."

"I'm not a contortionist, Mackenzie." Dylan pulled up his underwear carefully.

After a pause, Mackenzie asked, "Do you want me to do it?"

"It's fine."

"If you don't put something on it, won't it hurt worse when you drive home?"

"I'll manage." Dylan pulled up his jeans.

Mackenzie knocked on the door. "Why don't you let me help you?"

Not waiting for his response, Mackenzie turned the doorknob. "I'm coming in."

Dylan tried to lock the door but the lock failed.

"That lock's been broken for about a year now." Mackenzie leaned her hand against the doorjamb. "Will you stop pretending to be a prude and let me help you?"

"Really? You just open the door and waltz right in? What if I had been in the *middle* of something?"

"I could see your boots near the sink, okay? Now, quit whining and turn around."

"Mackenzie…" Dylan said. "The bite is on my *ass*."

"So? Do you think that I haven't seen your butt before? Give me a break! You and my brother and all of your stupid friends mooned everyone in the neighborhood! Remember?"

"Oh, yeah…I forgot about that."

"What did you idiots used to call yourselves again?"

"The Moonshine Gang."

"I'm sorry…" Mackenzie cupped her ear. "I didn't quite catch that?"

"The Moonshine Gang," Dylan said loudly.

"Thank you. I rest my case. Now, turn around, drop trou, then hand me the ointment. Please."

Grudgingly, Dylan turned around and dropped his jeans just enough to expose the wound.

"She got you, all right." Mackenzie squeezed some ointment onto the wound. "Hand me one of the big, square Band-Aids, will you?"

Mackenzie ripped open the package with her teeth.

"What's going on back there?" Dylan asked impatiently.

"I'm baking a cake...what do you think's going on?" Mackenzie pulled the Band-Aid out of the packet and tossed the empty wrapper into the trash.

"Voilà!" Mackenzie quickly applied the Band-Aid. "Done!"

Mackenzie left the bathroom while Dylan straightened his clothes.

"You're welcome," Mackenzie said when he joined her.

"*You* should be apologizing to *me* for barging into the bathroom like that," Dylan countered with feigned indignation.

"*You* should be apologizing for having a manicurist!" Mackenzie retorted.

Dylan stuck out his hand. "Call it even?"

"Fine. Even." Mackenzie shook Dylan's hand. "Come on...let's go watch Hope ride."

They walked out to the riding arena and both of them leaned up against the fence. Dylan watched Hope canter Gypsy. "She's got a great seat for riding."

"She definitely doesn't get that from me. I've always been a little afraid of horses."

"No. *That* she gets from me."

Mackenzie glanced at Dylan. They had known each other in another lifetime, when they were just kids. But there was something comfortable in their silences when it was just the two of them. That *something* was familiar, unrehearsed, effortless and impossible to fake. There was a shared history; they came from the same neighborhood. There was a common thread of values that transcended the years they had spent apart.

When Dylan spoke, it was in a lowered voice and for her ears only. "I know you told me that Hope has leukemia. But it doesn't seem possible. Just look at her. She's… perfect. She acts like a typical kid."

"She's been in remission for two years, so she's gained weight. And even though it's different and that bothers her, her hair finally grew back. But we aren't out of the woods yet. When she was diagnosed, she was put in the high-risk category, which means she has a greater risk of the cancer coming back."

"You know, when you told me about Hope, about her diagnosis, I've really tried to educate myself about her type of leukemia."

"ALL…"

"Right…" Dylan nodded. "But I still don't know what any of it means for Hope."

"What do you mean?"

Dylan turned his body toward her. "Is she going to be okay or not?"

Mackenzie looked at her daughter, so happy to be riding Gypsy again. "I don't know, Dylan. There's no guarantee. Her prognosis is good, but until we hit the three-year mark without a relapse, *I'm* not going to feel like we're out of the woods yet. She takes daily doses of medication, she goes in for regular testing and she still takes chemo. And let me tell you, when she does have chcmo, she's not the same kid. She can't get out bed, she's sick to her stomach, I can hardly get her to eat." Mackenzie watched her daughter. "That's why she pushes herself so hard in between…"

"Because she knows what she's in for…"

"Exactly." Mackenzie smiled and waved at Hope, who cantered in a circle directly in front of them.

"She never mentioned it to me." Dylan rested his foot on the bottom of the fence. "I sort of thought she would."

"She doesn't like to talk about it much anymore, and I

try to respect that. All she wants is to be a normal kid. Who can blame her? No kid should have to go through this..."

Dylan wasn't certain what had changed inside him. But something had. A switch had been flipped, an indelible mark had been made, and there wasn't any going back. When he had awakened this morning, he hadn't been a father...and perhaps he really wasn't still. But he *wanted* to be. He saw it now just as plainly as if it had been written across the cloudless blue sky...he had a chance to do better for Hope. He had a choice...he could reject the legacy left to him by his biological father and embrace the lessons he had learned from Uncle Bill. And it took Hope, sweet, honest, tenderhearted Hope, to make him see the light. Hope slowed Gypsy to a jog and then an animated walk. Gypsy's neck was drenched with sweat, her mouth dripping foam from engaging with the bit.

Cheeks flushed red, eyes bright with joy, Hope patted Gypsy enthusiastically on the neck. "Good girl, Gypsy! I'm going to take her for a walk to cool her down before I rinse her off." Hope dropped her feet out of the stirrups and let them dangle loose.

"I'll grab the gate for you," Mackenzie said.

Hope guided Gypsy through the arena gate and headed to an open field; Mackenzie and Dylan walked slowly back toward the barn.

"Have you told Jordan yet that I'm Hope's father?" Dylan asked in a low, private voice.

"No." She had led her family to believe that her college boyfriend was Hope's father. Only her father and brother knew the truth. It was hard to come clean on a lie, especially one as big as this one.

"I haven't told Ian yet, either." Dylan slipped his sunglasses back on. "I'll call him and see if we can get together with them tonight. We may as well tell them together."

Chapter Seven

Mackenzie and Dylan took the elevator up to Ian Sterling's penthouse. Dylan, Mackenzie noted, was impeccably dressed in pressed khaki slacks, a custom-tailored navy blazer and spotless shoes that had to have cost more than one month's rent. She, on the other hand, still had on her baking clothes: an oversize Nothin' But Cupcakes polo, new black Converse and an old pair of baggy chinos that were permanently stained with food dye.

Mackenzie took a small step away from Dylan. Whenever she was near him, she felt like a dumpy bag lady. She caught her reflection in the highly polished brass elevator fittings. Had she been having an odd Alfalfa moment this whole entire time? She quickly tried to smooth the out-of-control curls.

Mackenzie glanced over at Dylan, who was standing stiffly next to her. He looked as nervous as she felt. "So… how's your backside?"

Her attempt to get him to loosen up a little worked. He cracked a smile. "Sore. Thank you for asking."

"Well…you're not the first victim."

"And I won't be the last…" The elevator came to a slow stop, the light dinged. "This is us."

In front of the condo's ornate door, Mackenzie started to feel queasy from nerves. Telling your family that you've been lying to them for ten years didn't exactly seem like a fun time. When Dylan opened the unlocked door, she wished she were anyplace other than where she was.

"Anybody home?" Dylan announced their arrival.

"Dylan! Mackenzie!" Barefoot, dressed in faded low-slung boy jeans and a simple white tee, Jordan appeared at the top of the stairwell leading up to the main floor.

"Come on up! I apologize in advance for the renovation mess…"

At the top of the stairs, Jordan hugged Mackenzie first, and then Dylan.

"Jordan…this view…"

"I know, right? Crazy good. Once it's remodeled, it's going to be heaven on earth…"

"She's taking advantage of the fact that I can't see the invoices," Jordan's fiancé, Ian, commented as he walked into the room.

Mackenzie had seen pictures of Ian Sterling, world-renowned photographer and ex-model, but to see him in person was an entirely different experience. He was tall and built, high cheekbones, strong jawline. Sculpted lips. He was a perfect physical match for tall, athletic, naturally beautiful Jordan.

Jordan went immediately to Ian's side and linked arms with him. "Knock that off, *GQ*… Mackenzie doesn't know you're kidding. I'm just warning you guys. He's been cracking a lot of blind jokes lately…" Jordan confided to

Mackenzie as she nonchalantly guided Ian over to where Dylan and Mackenzie were standing.

"And Jordan is determined to suck all the fun out of this little adventure…" Ian said about his blindness.

Even though it was dusk, Ian wore dark sunglasses. Diagnosed with a rare form of macular degeneration called Stargardt disease, Ian was legally blind.

Jordan had a glow about her that Mackenzie envied. No man had ever made her all girlie and dewy and *flushed*.

Jordan introduced Mackenzie and Ian. They shook hands, and then Ian and Dylan gave each other a hug.

"Let's talk in the study…it's the only room Jordan hasn't torn apart…"

"Yet…" Jordan wrapped her arms around Ian's body and squeezed him tightly. "You know you love me."

Ian dropped a kiss on the top of Jordan's head. "Yes, I do…"

They all grabbed drinks and then headed to the study. There were two love seats on either side of the coffee table. Jordan curled up next to Ian on one love seat, which left the other one for Mackenzie and Dylan. Dylan waited for her to be seated before he joined her. No matter how she tried, she couldn't avoid touching Dylan's body. They were shoulder to shoulder and leg to leg on the tiny love seat.

"Okay…" Jordan got the conversation started. "I'm about to keel over with curiosity. What are the two of you doing here…*together*?"

Mackenzie and Dylan exchanged looks.

"Do you want to tell them?" Dylan asked her. "Or should I?"

"I'll do it. I'm the one who got us into this mess…"

"Well…I hardly think that's the case. It took both of us to—"

Exasperated, Jordan interrupted. "For the love of God

and all that is holy in the world…will you *please* tell us what's going on?"

Ian touched Jordan's leg to get her attention. "What?"

"Let them talk," Ian said gently.

Jordan frowned at Ian but gave Mackenzie and Dylan the floor.

"I have to set the record straight about something." Mackenzie wiped more sweat from her palms onto her pant legs. "Dylan is Hope's father."

Mackenzie's abrupt confession was followed by silence. Like a pretty kaleidoscope, Jordan's facial expression changed from confusion to shock to disbelief.

"I'm sorry…what did you just say?" Jordan leaned forward a bit.

"Hope is Dylan's child," Mackenzie repeated. It actually felt good to get this out in the open. She had never liked lying to her family. She had wanted to keep it from her father and Jett so they wouldn't tell Dylan, but the lie had metastasized to the rest of the family.

Jordan stared at the two of them, speechless in her contemplation, and Ian hadn't said a word. He was just listening, taking it all in.

"I'm Hope's father." That was the first time he had uttered those words aloud to anyone other than himself. "Hope is my daughter."

Jordan sat back. "Wait a minute…you mean…*Hope* Hope? As in, *your* daughter, Hope?"

Mackenzie nodded silently.

"But…I thought Hope's father was your boyfriend from college…the one with all the Star Wars toys…"

"Star Trek," Mackenzie corrected. "He was a Trekkie…"

Jordan rolled her eyes. "Whatever…same difference."

"Not to a Trekkie," Ian said. "They're completely different."

Jordan twisted around to look at Ian. "Really? Now you decide to chime in?"

"He's right," Dylan agreed. "Two completely different things."

"Can we get back to the important part of this conversation, please?" Jordan looked at everyone questioningly. "I mean…how do the two of you even *know* each other?"

The conversation that followed took longer than Mackenzie had originally anticipated. She was hoping for a more "drive-by" kind of deal that didn't require much emotional energy. That didn't happen. While Ian remained quiet for the entire conversation, he appeared to be listening intently to every word. Jordan, on the other hand, decided to earn her junior Perry Mason badge.

"Look…" Mackenzie finally said, exasperated. "I wasn't signing up for the Spanish Inquisition here, okay? I was young and I thought I was doing the right thing for all of us. Would I do it this way again?" Mackenzie caught Dylan's eye and held it. "No. I wouldn't." Mackenzie broke the gaze. To her cousin, she said, "But I can't go back. All I can do is say that I'm sorry for lying to you. I wasn't trying to hurt anyone. I was just trying to do the best I could for Hope. That's what I'm still trying to do…"

"Oh…hey…" Jordan crossed the short distance to Mackenzie's seat and wrapped her arms around her cousin's shoulders. "I didn't mean to upset you. I'm just surprised, that's all. I love you, Mackenzie. And I love Hope…no matter what. Okay?"

Jordan knelt down beside Mackenzie. "Hey…let me give you the five-cent tour of this place. I want to show you all the finishes I've picked…hand-scraped wide-plank hardwood…new custom cabinets throughout…"

"Hey—I *heard* that," Ian told his fiancée. "I still have excellent hearing."

Jordan laughed and returned to Ian's side. She leaned down, took his gorgeous face into her hands and kissed him on the lips. "I love you, my handsome man…"

"I love you more." Ian squeezed her hand, kissed it affectionately before letting it go.

Dylan watched Mackenzie and Jordan leave the room. He waited several seconds to make certain they were out of earshot before he said to Ian, "You haven't had much to say."

"Not much to say, I don't think." Ian pulled his wallet out of his pocket. He pulled a card out of the wallet, brought the card close to the side of his face so he could use his still-intact peripheral vision to read the name, then he held it out to Dylan. "Here. You might need this."

Ben Levine, Attorney-at-Law.

After looking at it, Dylan slipped the card into his wallet.

"You have a child." Ian twisted the cap off his bottle of water. "How do you feel about that?"

"Terrified." Dylan could be honest with Ian.

"You need to know your rights. We have the photography business to think of…we're launching the modeling agency in a couple of months…"

"I know. Mackenzie doesn't want child support, but…"

"People change their minds all the time. Call Ben."

"I will." Dylan nodded pensively. "You know…I spent the whole morning with her today. Hope. She's a great kid. Looks just like Aunt Gerri."

"Is that right?"

"Yeah…" Dylan smiled when an image of Hope's sweet, expectant face popped into his head. "Do you want to meet her?"

"Of course I do. She's your daughter." Ian finished off his water. "I'm not saying you shouldn't get involved...I'm just saying that you should cover your bases. That's all."

"Expect the best..." Dylan said.

Ian finished their motto. "But prepare for the worst."

After their visit with Jordan and Ian, Mackenzie and Dylan rode the elevator down to the ground floor together. Through the lobby of the building and out onto the city sidewalk, they paused for a moment just outside the front door. Noticing a large group of tourists heading their way, Dylan put his hand on the small of her back and guided her to the left. Then he put his body between hers and the group so she wouldn't get bumped.

Once the boisterous group passed them by, Mackenzie said, "You didn't have to leave when I did. You could have stayed."

Dylan had his hands in his front pockets, his blazer thrown over his arm. "It was time for me to head out, too. Did you walk here from the bakery?"

Mackenzie nodded.

"I'll walk you back," he said. Even though downtown San Diego was a pretty safe place, even at dusk, he didn't like the idea of her walking back to the bakery alone.

"It's not that far..." She looked over her shoulder toward the direction of her business.

But once she saw that Dylan was going to insist on seeing her safely back to Nothin' But Cupcakes, Mackenzie stopped protesting and started walking. At a crosswalk, waiting for the light to turn, she asked, "What does your girlfriend think of all this?"

The light turned and Dylan stepped into the crosswalk at her side. "Actually, Jenna and I had an amicable parting of the ways..."

"Not because of Hope?" She stepped up onto the curb.

"No. Not because of Hope." He reassured her. "She decided to finally make the move to LA, and I support her decision. It's what's best for her career. The breakup was inevitable."

"Well...I'm still sorry. She seemed really—" she searched her brain for a positive comment that she could say truthfully "—energetic."

Dylan shot her a quizzical look before he laughed. "Yes...you're right. She is very energetic."

They reached her storefront and Mackenzie pulled the keys out of her tote bag. "Well...this is me. Thanks for walking me back."

"Are you heading home or sticking around here?"

She slipped the key into the lock. "I have some work to do before I head home."

Mackenzie opened the door and walked quickly to the alarm keypad. She punched in the code and the beeping sound stopped. The only light in the front of the bakery was from the cases that had been emptied the night before by Molly.

"Thank you again for making sure I got here safely," she said to Dylan, who had followed her in and locked the door behind them. "But I'm sure you've got things to do. I'll be fine here by myself."

Sometimes she liked to come to the bakery after hours just to have some time alone—Ray and Charlie were always happy to watch Hope for her. She liked the bakery when it was quiet and dark the way it was now. She could be by herself with her thoughts while she baked. It was therapeutic, especially when she had something worrisome on her mind.

He knew she was politely trying to send him on his way, but he wasn't ready to leave just yet. He was enjoying her company. He felt relaxed around her; she made him laugh in a way that most women didn't.

"My schedule's pretty clear, actually. How about a quick tour?"

He heard her let out her breath and knew she was about to cave. "There's not much to see…and I really do have work that I've got to get done."

"I promise I'll stay out of your way…" He held up one hand as if he was taking an oath.

For the second time that night, Mackenzie gave in to Dylan's persistence. She was wasting time talking to him when she really needed to be working on the cupcakes. Molly had called to tell her that they were about to run out of one of their bestsellers, red velvet with cream cheese frosting. It was her mother's recipe, so she guarded it. She was the only one who made them; she needed to make several large batches and freeze some of them for later.

"I could help you," Dylan offered.

Mackenzie slipped into her white baking coat. "You can help me by sitting over there and not moving."

He smiled at her no-nonsense way of bossing him around her kitchen and obediently sat down on a stool out of the way. It was interesting to see Mackenzie in her element. Here, in the kitchen, she was absolutely sure of herself. She gathered the ingredients for the cupcakes first, and then measured each ingredient carefully before adding them, one by one, to an industrial mixer. While the batter mixed, she prepared the baking pans, deftly dropping specially designed Nothin' But Cupcakes cupcake cups into the pans. In the zone now, she didn't even seem to notice that he was sitting nearby.

Dylan had never really cared about watching someone cook before, but watching Mackenzie was different. He was fascinated by how easily she moved from one area of the kitchen to the next; it was like watching a well-choreographed dance.

"What kind of frosting are you going to make?" he asked.

Mackenzie glanced up at him, with a somewhat surprised expression in her pretty eyes. He had been so quiet, and she had been so focused, that she forgot for a moment that she wasn't alone.

"Cream cheese." She switched off the mixer and then set to the task of filling the cupcake pans.

Once the cupcakes were baking in the ovens, she made the frosting, which she could store in the refrigerator until morning. Now all she had to do was wait for the cupcakes to cook and cool. With a satisfied sigh, hands on hips, Mackenzie nodded to herself. Then she looked over at Dylan, who hadn't really bothered her at all.

"Do you like cream cheese frosting?"

Dylan had been leaning on one elbow. He sat upright. "Yes. I do."

Mackenzie took a large spoon out of a drawer, scooped up a large helping of freshly made frosting and handed it to him. Dylan ate all the frosting at one time; he closed his eyes happily and then licked the spoon before he handed it back to her.

"Good?" she asked, but she could tell by his smiling lips that he approved.

"Mackenzie…" he said seriously. "You are an artist."

His sincere praise for her baking made her entire body smile. When someone truly enjoyed her baking, it made the struggle to keep her business afloat worth it. Mackenzie felt herself relaxing with Dylan; after all, this wasn't the first time he had loitered in her kitchen. He was always hanging around with Jett when she had baked with her mother.

"Do you want to wait for the cupcakes to finish baking? I'll frost one just for you."

He looked more like the young boy she remembered when he asked, "Just one?"

The month after he first met his daughter sped by for Dylan. And even though he hadn't intended to become a regular fixture at Pegasus, that's exactly what had happened. It started out innocently. It was an opportunity for him to spend time with Hope on the weekends. Then something unexpected happened: the place got to him. The kids, the horses, the other volunteers…the parents… all of them had an impact. He discovered that he was surfing less and mucking out stalls more. He was handy with a hammer and Aggie had him on her radar. On the weekends, he traded his Testoni lace-ups for rubber muckers and his polo button-ups for Pegasus T-shirts. Instead of going out with his friends, he went to bed early on Friday night so he could be up early and fresh for the riders on Saturday morning.

And always, *always*, there was Hope. She was the main event. He found himself missing her during the week and regretting having to say goodbye on Sundays. He didn't mind the status quo for now, but this arrangement wouldn't work in the long term. He wanted to have a say in Hope's future; he wanted to be her *dad*.

"Hey…" Mackenzie appeared at the entrance of the feed room. As usual, she was dressed in oversize clothing, long sleeves, and her hair was haphazardly pulled up into a ponytail. Dylan wished she would fix herself up every once in a while.

"Hey…" Dylan pulled a bale of hay off the tall stack in the corner and dropped it on the ground.

"Where's Hope?"

Dylan used the bottom of his T-shirt to wipe the sweat that was dripping off his face, exposing his stomach. She was human. She looked. And her eyes latched on to the barely visible trail of hair leading from Dylan's belly button directly to his...

Dylan dropped his shirt; when she looked up at him, he was smiling at her. His expression told the story; he'd caught her red-handed.

"She's helping Aggie with Hank—he's got a pretty nasty gash on his fetlock and you know how he feels about anyone messing with his hooves." Dylan hoisted the bale of hay onto his shoulder. "Excuse me."

Mackenzie stepped to the side so Dylan could move through the door. She had watched Dylan closely over the past couple of weekends. She couldn't deny that he had a special way with all the kids, especially Hope. They all loved him. When they could, they trailed after him, and he was happy to let them. He had become the Pegasus Pied Piper. It was...endearing. And Aggie, who was pretty tough to impress, had come to rely on Dylan as part of her small circle of trusted volunteers.

"Do you feel like lending a hand?" Dylan cut the twine holding the bale of hay together.

"Sure."

Loaded down with armfuls of hay, Dylan tackled one side of the barn and Mackenzie tackled the other. When Mackenzie reached Hank's stall, she tossed the hay over the stall fence for the old gelding.

"Hey, Aggie. Time to wrap up, kiddo," Mackenzie said to Hope, who was watching Aggie treat Hank's wound. "You have school tomorrow."

"Okay, Mom...I'll be right there."

Mackenzie waited for Hope at the barn entrance and watched the sun set on the horizon. All day, every day, it seemed as if she was running around like a chicken with her head cut off—monitoring Hope's health, helping Hope with homework, working in the bakery, paying the bills, shopping for groceries, doing the laundry...one chore led into the next, one day bled into the other. She couldn't remember the last time she had actually allowed herself to just stop and enjoy a sunset.

"It's going to be a full moon." Dylan came up beside her.

Not wanting to expend her limited resource of energy on small talk, Mackenzie only nodded. She wanted to enjoy the view just a little bit longer before she had to rally the energy to cook dinner and do a load of laundry. She was having a perfectly lovely time until she felt something crawling on her neck. Startled, she slapped at the side of her neck and tried to spot the offending bug.

Dylan, looking sheepish, held a piece of hay in his fingertips. "You had a piece of hay stuck in your hair."

"Don't *do* that!" Mackenzie punched Dylan hard on the arm. "I thought it was a bug!"

Dylan rubbed his arm. "Man...you really know how to pack a punch..."

"Of course I do... You and Jett and the rest of your idiot friends thought it was hilarious to ambush me with dead bugs all the time! I *had* to learn how to defend myself."

"I never did that to you!"

"Yeah...you did."

"Well, I don't remember doing that, but if you said that I did, then I suppose I'm sorry."

"Your apology, however halfhearted, is accepted."

Dylan glanced over his shoulder; Aggie and Hope were coming out of Hank's stall and his window of opportunity was about to close.

"Mackenzie..." Dylan crossed his arms to give them

something to do. "I was wondering…do you want to come over for dinner Friday night?"

"Um…we can't. Hope's spending the weekend with one of her friends from Relay For Life. I don't normally let her spend an overnight, but this family knows the drill because their daughter has ALL as well, so…"

"I know. Hope told me. That's all she talked about today was her sleepover, which she *never* gets to do. What I meant was…do *you* want to come over Friday night for dinner…with me?"

Mackenzie lifted her brows questioningly. "Why?"

Dylan looked at her as if he couldn't quite figure her out. Perhaps he was used to automatic yeses to all his invitations.

"Because…" he said. "I think it'd be good for us to spend some time together. There are a lot of things we still need to figure out. Don't you agree?"

"I suppose." Up until now, she had been very good at dodging Dylan's attempts to sit down and discuss how they were going to move forward as coparents.

Dylan tucked his hands into his pockets and lifted his shoulders questioningly. "Oh, come on, Mackenzie… what's the worst that could happen? If nothing else, you'll get a free meal out of the deal. And, I really didn't want to brag…"

"Of course not…"

"But I *have* been told that I'm pretty amazing with my grill."

Chapter Eight

Mackenzie stood in front of her closet, staring at the sad collection of old clothing hanging askew on wire hangers. After several attempts at finding something even remotely fashionable to wear to Dylan's house for dinner, Mackenzie groaned dramatically and threw herself face down on her unmade bed. Dylan always looked so put together; she wanted at least to *try*, for her own sake, to look halfway decent for a change. But, in truth, she didn't really want to go at all. What she *really* wanted to do with her first kid-free weekend was to procure a bag of ranch-flavored Doritos and to watch the Food Network in bed. When her cell started to ring, she reached out with her hand and felt around on the nightstand for the phone. Not lifting her head up, she put the phone to her ear.

"Hello?"

"What are you doing?" It was Rayna calling.

"Slowly suffocating myself with my hypoallergenic pillow…"

"I take it the hunt for an outfit isn't going so well?"

Mackenzie rolled onto her back and wrapped herself in her comforter like a burrito. "I think I'm going to call him and tell him I'm too tired…"

"I'm coming over…"

"Is that gangsta rap?" Mackenzie took a time-out from her own crisis and tuned her ear to the loud music blasting through the phone.

"Yes. Charlie had a bad day at work. Max and I are coming over."

Moments later, Rayna and her rotund feline arrived in her bedroom. She peeled the comforter back and found Mackenzie inside. Max jumped up onto her bed with a grunt. He nudged her hand so she would pet him.

"Mackenzie…you can't back out. How long has it been since you've done anything remotely fun?"

Mackenzie tried to remember but couldn't.

"If you have to think about it for *that long*, then it's been *way too* long. And do you know what I think? I think that hidden beneath these rumpled, oversize clothes is a beautiful, curvy woman just dying to come out and play." Rayna tugged on Mackenzie's arm until she was upright. "Now… you go take a shower because you smell really sweaty. Max and I will try to find you something less…boxy to wear."

Needing to clean up anyway, Mackenzie took a quick shower and shrugged into her bathrobe. She wiped the moisture from the bathroom mirror and frowned at her own reflection. She looked tired. Dark circles, a little bit of stress acne on her chin.

Lovely.

When Mackenzie returned to her bedroom, her dirty

clothes had been collected and deposited in the hamper. And Max was happily lounging on her freshly made bed.

"What did you do in here?" Mackenzie asked.

"Oh…I just picked up a little so I could see what we're working with," Rayna said offhandedly. "You do know that *square* isn't a flattering shape for a woman's body, right?" Rayna had pulled several tops out of her closet. "Why are all your clothes two sizes too big?"

"I don't have time for shopping, Ray…you know what I *do* have time for?" She sounded defensive. "Payroll. And hospital visits. So, no offense, but having a fashion *moment* just isn't high up on my priority list."

"I know how busy you are." Rayna's hands stilled and she looked over her shoulder at Mackenzie. "But you're still buying clothes for your *old* body. And you may not believe me, but a good pair of jeans and a pretty blouse can change your whole outlook on life."

Mackenzie caught her reflection in the dresser mirror. Yes, she had lost a ton of weight. But when she looked in the mirror, all she saw was *fat*. And, with Hope's illness and always struggling to make ends meet, it was easier just to buy oversize, comfy clothes and avoid reflective surfaces. She couldn't remember the last time she had actually tried something on in a fitting room.

"Now, *this* is pretty!" Rayna spun around and held up a deep purple short-sleeved blouse that Hope had convinced her to buy. "What do you think? It still has the price tag on it."

Mackenzie shook her head. "No. I don't do short sleeves. My arms are too…" She wrinkled her nose distastefully. *"Jiggly."*

Disappointed, Rayna hung the blouse back in the closet. "You're your own worst enemy…you're hot and you don't even know it."

Mackenzie opened her dresser drawer and pulled out her favorite long-sleeved San Diego Padres shirt. "It's ridiculous that I've even been spending *one second* stressing about this…it's *Dylan*. Not a *date*. So I'm not gonna get all gussied up, when I *never* get all gussied up, and make Dylan feel all weirded out because *he* thinks that *I* think that this evening is something more than it is. Which it's not."

"It's a date." Rayna sat down on the bed next to Max. "Friday night. And he's cooking you dinner at his place? It's a date."

Refusing to indulge in Rayna's fantasy, Mackenzie stepped into the bathroom to slip into the Padres shirt and a pair of jeans. Mackenzie sighed. The jeans were tighter around the waist than they used to be. Why did it always have to be such a battle? If she didn't watch every bite, consider every carb or exercise several times a week, the scale would turn against her.

Whatever.

"Trust me, Ray…I'm not Dylan's type." Mackenzie grabbed her comb and began the chore of untangling her thick, wavy hair. "And he's not really mine."

"You actually have to *date* to have a type…and besides, you guys have a daughter…you must've been attracted to each other at some point. Right?"

"That was—" Mackenzie stopped combing her hair for a second to think. "I don't know what that was."

"A night of unforgettable passion?" Rayna raised her eyebrows suggestively several times.

Mackenzie scrunched up her face. "Uh-uh. Honestly… it was…really, really *awkward*."

"Oh…" Rayna wilted. "See…judging from pictures, I would've thought Dylan would be good in bed. For a man. He's got that sexy, squinty-eye thing going on."

"I don't know what you're talking about." Mackenzie had never noticed Dylan having a sexy, squinty anything. It was *Dylan*. Annoying, mooning, bug-throwing *Dylan*.

Rayna held up her pinkie and wiggled it. "Is he really... you know? Tiny?"

"What?" Mackenzie looked perplexed at Rayna's bouncing pinkie for a minute before she caught Rayna's meaning. "No...*no*. He's *fine* in that department. It's just that we had way too much to drink..."

"Which never works in a guy's favor..."

"And I didn't want him to touch me anywhere because I was *bulgy* all over...."

Rayna's brows lifted. "Now I'm actually kind of surprised the two of you managed to procreate."

"That's what I've been trying to tell you." Mackenzie twisted her hair up into a bun and secured it with a clip. "I can guarantee you that neither one of us wants a repeat of that night."

Deflated, Rayna said, "So...not a date."

"No. Definitely not a date."

Dylan met her at the door, stylish, freshly showered and shaved. Not a surprise; he even managed to make sweaty and dirty at the barn look good. What *was* a surprise was the table setting. Dylan had obviously put some thought into setting the table for two. There were two lit candles on the table that caught, and held, her attention.

"Now that you're here, I'm going to throw the salmon on the grill. You said you liked salmon, right?"

Mackenzie slipped her tote off her shoulder. "Yes..."

"Make yourself at home and I'll be right back. Unless you want to keep me company...?"

"No." Instead of putting the tote down, Mackenzie clutched it to her body. "I'll wait here."

I'm on a date.

Panic. Sheer unadulterated panic. Mackenzie quickly texted Ray: I'm on a DATE!

Ray shot a text back: Told U so! Yippee!

"Yippee? That's the sage advice I get?" Mackenzie turned the phone on Vibrate and tucked it into her pocket. *Now what?*

Should she leave or should she stay...*that* was the ultimate question.

"All right..." Dylan reappeared and headed for the fridge. "I hope you like sweet red wine...?"

Mackenzie nodded. She was still trying to figure out how to back out of this situation gracefully. Could she fake a stomachache? Menstrual cramps? It's not that she didn't want to be on a date with *Dylan* per se...she didn't want to be on a date with *anyone*. Relationships took time and energy and she had very little of both of those resources to spare.

Dylan poured the wine, handed her a glass and then held his glass up for a toast. "To Hope's continued health..."

Mackenzie touched her glass to his. "To Hope's continued health..."

"And to new beginnings," Dylan added.

Mackenzie hesitated before she took a sip of the sweet wine. She put her glass down on the counter. Dylan quickly pulled out a coaster and put it under her glass.

"How's the wine?" Dylan asked.

"Good..." Mackenzie stared at the coaster for a moment. "Good. Um..."

"I'm glad that you showed, Mackenzie...I was actually pretty sure you were going to cancel on me..."

Mackenzie blurted out, "I almost did."

"See..." Dylan laughed. "That's one of the things I really like about you…you're honest. Why don't we go sit down, get comfortable."

"No," Mackenzie said tentatively, then more strongly, "No."

"That's okay. We don't have to sit. I read somewhere that standing is actually better than sitting. Better for the circulation, I think."

"I need to clear something up between us, I think…"

"What's that?"

"I mean…there's the table and the wine and the candles…it's Friday night." Mackenzie had one hand resting on her tote. "This feels kind of like a…date."

Dylan put his glass down slowly on a coaster. "That's because I thought it *was* a date."

"Oh…"

"But you didn't." Dylan stared at her for a moment before he blew out the candles.

Crap! She had hurt him. And now Mackenzie was at a rare loss for words as she watched the two twin ribbons of smoke rise from the extinguished candles.

"This is embarrassing." Dylan gulped down his wine and put his glass in the sink.

Both hands clutching the tote, Mackenzie said, "If I'd known that you thought this was a…date…I would never have said yes."

This wasn't the first time he'd embarrassed himself in front of a pretty woman he liked, but in this case, with Mackenzie, it stung just a little bit more than usual.

"I need to check on the salmon," Dylan said.

How she had managed to land on the defensive in this scenario, Mackenzie couldn't figure out…but on the defensive, she was. She followed Dylan to the outdoor kitchen. She sat down on the very edge of a built-in bench; Dylan pushed open the lid of the grill a bit harder than he normally would.

"The salmon looks good," Mackenzie said for lack of anything more helpful to say.

Dylan flipped the salmon steaks over, seasoned them and then shut the lid tightly. Mackenzie felt like a grade-A heel; all she wanted to do now was to smooth things over with Dylan and to get the heck out of Dodge.

"Why would you think this was a date, Dylan?" Guilty, Mackenzie switched from contrite to accusatory.

"Just forget it, Mackenzie." Dylan started to walk back to the house. But then he stopped. "No. You know what? *Don't* forget it. Why *wouldn't* you think this was a date?"

"Because…you're *that*…" Mackenzie waved her hand up and down. "And I'm *this*…I'm not your type."

Dylan sat down on a bench across from her. "How do you know what my type is, Mackenzie?"

"Christa? Jenna? Tall, blonde, skinny." Mackenzie held up three fingers. "And, me? Short, chubby, brunette. Not exactly rocket science."

"You forgot pretty…"

Mackenzie held up a fourth finger. "Pretty goes without saying."

"No," Dylan clarified. "I meant *you*. I think *you're* pretty. And funny and sweet and a really great mom to Hope."

Mackenzie crossed her legs and crossed her arms protectively in front of her body.

Dylan continued, "You know…Jenna and I both loved to surf. And I managed to sustain a relationship built on a mutual love for surfing for nearly a year. You and I have a child together…"

Now Dylan had her full attention.

"And I look at you and I look at Hope…and I think…

maybe I have a chance at what Uncle Bill and Aunt Gerri had together."

"You can't force a family." Mackenzie pulled her sleeves down over her hands and recrossed her arms.

"No, you can't. But you can try to build one." Dylan leaned forward, forearms resting on his thighs. "This doesn't have anything to do with *my* type, does it? That's just an excuse. This has to do with the fact that I'm not *your* type, right?"

"My friend Rayna says that you actually *have* to date to have a type…and I don't. Date, I mean."

"I know. Hope told me. Your friend set you up with a socialist three years ago?"

"He was a *social* worker. A very nice *social* worker. You and Hope certainly cover a lot of subjects, don't you?"

"She likes to talk to me. I like to listen. But let's not get off topic here. I like you, Mackenzie. I want to spend more time with you. And I get that I'm not the obvious choice for you because I don't have a five-page *community service* section on my résumé…but you've gotta admit, I'm a changed man."

Mackenzie thought about Dylan at Pegasus, mucking out stalls, caring for the elderly horses and bonding with the kids. Mackenzie thought of Dylan with Hope; how sweet and kind and patient he was with her. Hope loved him.

Mackenzie held up her pointer finger and her thumb an inch apart. "You've got about this much community service street cred."

The timer next to the grill buzzed. Dylan checked the fish and then pulled them off the grill.

"Come on! Just look at these bad boys." Dylan showed her the steaks. "I can't believe you're really going to let them go to waste."

Mackenzie tugged at the front of her jersey; he had gone to some trouble to make her a healthy meal. "I didn't dress right…"

"Hey—" Dylan sensed that Mackenzie was caving "—if that's the only thing holding you back from hanging out with me tonight, then I'll change. And we can eat out here."

The salmon and broccoli did smell really good. And she *was* really hungry.

"And let's be honest." Dylan's dimples appeared. He was teasing her. "You think I'm sexy when I cook, right?"

"I'll admit…that I *like* a man who can cook."

"See there?" Dylan grinned at her triumphantly. "We can *build* on that!"

Good as his word, Dylan had changed into shorts and a short-sleeved polo, and they dined outside with the ocean as their view. Once Mackenzie stopped focusing on the "date" aspect of the evening and just focused on Dylan, she started to relax and have a good time. They laughed as much as they talked. And there was never a lull in the conversation. They reminisced about their childhood. They talked about Hope and her future aspirations. They talked baseball and surfing and cupcakes. Mackenzie couldn't believe it, but she was sad when the clock on her phone flipped over to nine.

"It's not too late…how about a short walk on the beach? Work off some of this dinner?" Dylan leaned against the island while Mackenzie loaded the last dish in the dishwasher.

"I wish I could…but I've got an early morning at the bakery." Then she surprised herself by adding, "Can I take a rain check?"

From the look on his face, she had surprised Dylan, as well. "Sure."

Mackenzie slipped her tote onto her shoulder and Dylan walked her to the door. They walked down to her car together; Mackenzie pulled her keys out and unlocked the car door. Not wanting to linger in that uncomfortable "end of the night, should I go for the kiss?" moment, Mackenzie wrapped her arms around Dylan's waist, hugged him quickly and then stepped back.

"Thank you…I'm glad that I decided not to go home early…"

Dylan rocked back on his heels. "That's very flattering, thank you."

Mackenzie felt an internal cringe. "That didn't come out right."

"That's okay, Mackenzie." Dylan reached out and opened her car door. "I was just teasing you."

Mackenzie climbed behind the wheel and Dylan closed the door firmly behind her. He tapped on the window so she would roll it down.

Hands resting on the door, Dylan asked, "How 'bout we fill that rain check tomorrow? Say, around seven? We can order in, watch a movie."

"Okay." Mackenzie nodded. She had just accepted a second date with Dylan without one millisecond of hesitation.

"Don't back out," Dylan said.

"I won't…" Mackenzie cranked the engine. "Good night, Dylan."

Dylan nodded his head goodbye as she rolled up the window, shifted into gear and pulled out slowly onto the darkened street. She felt odd driving away from his house—like something significant had just happened to her but she wasn't exactly sure *what*. And, even the next day, as she moved through normal business at the bakery, she still wasn't quite sure what had happened the night before. Dylan hadn't made his thought process a secret: he wanted to see if there was a chance for the two of them, along with Hope, to become a family. That thought had never crossed her mind. But now…was Dylan onto something? *Could* they be a family? If it worked, wouldn't that be the best thing for Hope?

"You're okay to close up, Molly?" Mackenzie untied her apron and lifted it over her head.

"In my sleep, little one." Molly continued to wipe down one of the café tables near the front of the small bakery.

Mackenzie boxed up two of the best-looking giant cupcakes in the case, and gave Molly a kiss on the cheek before she headed out. It was rare that she left the bakery early on a Saturday night, but for once she didn't feel guilty. She felt *anticipation*. She had caught herself thinking about Dylan off and on all day. That just didn't *happen* to her. She had never had a really big crush or even fallen in love, not the way she had seen her friends do—the head-over-heels, can't-sleep, can't-eat, can't-talk-about-anything-else kind of love. In fact, she couldn't remember ever feeling *lust* for anyone before. She had felt a very strong affection for her college boyfriend, but her inability to commit to *Star Trek* had ultimately ended their three-year relationship.

When Hope was born, her entire focus, and all of her love, was aimed at her. She didn't care about dating or romance or marriage. She had Hope. That was enough. It wasn't until Hope was in elementary school that Mackenzie started to think that there might be something missing in her life: intimacy. Romance. *Sex*. But then Hope was diagnosed with ALL and thoughts of a relationship disappeared.

"Wear your hair down this time…" Rayna was on speakerphone.

"You're right. My hair does look good down."

"Are you going to wear the purple shirt?"

"Uh-uh…no. We're walking on the beach, Ray. I can just dress like me."

"Okay…but promise me you'll wear something smaller than extra-extra large! Give the poor man *something* to look at…"

"Bye, Ray!"

"Call me later!"

Unlike the night before, Mackenzie took a little extra time getting ready. She made sure that her long-sleeved V-neck shirt didn't have any stains and she rummaged through her drawers to find a newer pair of jeans. She tried on several pairs and finally selected the jeans that made her J.Lo booty look the best. She let her hair air-dry, leaving it thick and long and falling down her back. She had to admit, she did have beautiful hair. She dug through her messy bathroom drawer and fished out an old tube of mascara from the back. The mascara looked crusty and the brush brittle, so she gave up on that idea. But she did find a tube of lip gloss. Teeth thoroughly brushed for an extra couple of minutes, followed by a long gargle of mouthwash, Mackenzie applied lip gloss and headed out the door. This time when she left the house, there wasn't any confusion about the night. She knew that this was a *date*, and she couldn't wait to see what the night would bring.

Chapter Nine

She actually felt nervous at the thought of seeing Dylan. She had called Hope to say good-night and now she was standing outside his door, holding her cupcake offering. At some point, a flip had been switched and *just Dylan* had suddenly become *Dylan*. When Dylan opened the door, she thrust the box at him.

"Here."

Dylan pulled one long-stem lavender rose from behind his back and held it out for her. "For you."

Pleased and surprised by the romantic gesture, Mackenzie exchanged the cupcakes for the rose. She lifted the rose up to her nose and breathed in the strong, sweet scent.

"Thank you," she said with a small smile.

"You must've read my mind." Dylan stepped back so she could come inside. "I was craving your cupcakes today."

When they reached the kitchen, Dylan immediately opened the box and grabbed a cupcake.

"Are they both for me, or do I need to share?" Dylan removed the wrapper from the first cupcake and took a large bite.

"They're for you…"

"Hmm…always incredible." Dylan started in on the second cupcake. "I just realized, I've never even bothered to ask you how you got into the cupcake business in the first place."

Mackenzie crossed her arms protectively in front of her, those old, never-forgotten feelings of defensiveness shooting to the surface. "A lot of people ask me that. I always think that there's a built-in insult in there…like they're really asking why a woman with a weight problem would own a bakery…"

Dylan looked at her as if she had lost her mind. "But… that's not what *I* meant."

Ill at ease, Mackenzie tightened her arms around her body. "I'm sorry. Sometimes that old stuff creeps up out of nowhere and flies out of my mouth before I can stop it. Do you ever wish you had a rewind button on your mouth?"

"All the time." Dylan finished the cupcake and put the box in the recycling bin. "And can we just clarify something right now? I happen to think that you're a beautiful woman. Okay?"

"Okay." Mackenzie nodded.

"And I really like it when you wear your hair down like that."

"Thank you." Mackenzie uncrossed her arms. "Do you still want to hear about the bakery?"

"Of course."

"You remember that my mom and I used to bake cupcakes together before she died."

Dylan nodded as she continued, "I remember her always talking about opening up a cupcake shop, but she never got the chance to do it. When I got older, making cupcakes always made me feel happy, and for some odd reason, when I work with sugar and butter, I don't want to *eat* it." Mackenzie smiled a self-effacing smile. "So, when Dad saw me floundering after high school, he offered to send me to school to get my associate's in baking and pastry arts, which then led to a bachelor's degree in bakery and pastry arts management."

"And the bakery?"

"Dad's idea. He made the initial investment, but I'm not gonna sugarcoat it…no pun intended…it's been really tough being a single parent and running a business. After Hope's diagnosis…" Mackenzie paused before she confessed something to Dylan that only Ray knew. "I seriously considered closing. But I have employees to think about…"

"I think you're a really strong woman, Mackenzie. I know how hard it is to run a business."

Mackenzie pulled a small photo album out of her tote. "I brought something for you to look at."

"What's that?" Dylan took the album, flipped to the first page.

Once Dylan realized it was a photo album full of Hope pictures, he slid onto a stool to get more comfortable while he looked at it.

"Look how tiny she was!" Dylan stared at Hope's first baby picture. "'Hope Virginia Brand, 6 pounds 4 ounces, born 3:13 a.m., August 20.'"

"She was an early-morning baby."

"How come there aren't any pictures of you pregnant?"

"Are you kidding me? I would have killed someone if they tried to take my picture when I was pregnant! But, you know, Hope is the reason why I finally lost the weight…"

"How so?" Dylan flipped to the next page.

"After she was born, I knew that I had to get healthy. I

worked really hard to lose the baby weight and then I just kept on losing. The fact that I was doing it for both of us made it easier somehow."

"I would have liked to see you pregnant," Dylan said. "I wish I had been able to be there when Hope was born."

The photo album chronicled Hope's childhood. A childhood he had missed. The little girl in these pictures was lost to him, and a feeling of loss and sadness hit him out of the blue. Dylan used his thumb and forefinger to rub unexpected tears out of his eyes and then he pinched the bridge of his nose to stop more tears from forming.

Wide-eyed, temporarily struck dumb, Mackenzie hadn't expected this reaction from Dylan. When she had played the "photo album scene" over in her mind, she had imagined them laughing and smiling and talking about Hope. Instead, she saw grief. Not knowing what else she could do for him, Mackenzie wrapped her arms around Dylan's shoulders. She hugged him so tightly that the muscles in her arms started to shake. He sat, like a rock, still pinching the bridge of his nose. The sorrow that Dylan felt over having missed his daughter's life was palpable and profound. And, ultimately, she was the one to blame.

"I'm sorry," Mackenzie repeated over and over again. "I'm so sorry."

Dylan turned to her, reached for her and enveloped her in his arms. They clutched each other tightly, their arms entangled, their chests pressed together, their thighs touching. Without warning, Mackenzie's own guilt, her own sorrow and her own feelings of regret overwhelmed her.

"I'm so sorry…" Her tears were absorbed by the material of his shirt.

Dylan pulled back, caught her face between his hands and shook his head.

"Mackenzie…" Dylan wiped her fresh tears away with his thumbs, still holding her face in his hands. "It's okay."

Their eyes locked. And Mackenzie couldn't have looked away if she had the will to do it. Dylan's eyes were naked, raw, unshielded windows into his soul. She continued to stare into his eyes as he moved his thumb sensually over her lower lip. Then his mouth was on hers, without pretense, without warning. Dylan's kiss was soft, tentative, gentle, at first. Then demanding, possessive, sensual. He tasted like sugar; he slipped his tongue past her lips, pulled her body more tightly into his body. Her leg muscles turned to Jell-O; her breathing was quick and shallow. Dylan's arm cradled her back, his fingers fanned out between her shoulders. He kissed her again and again, going a little bit further, taking a little bit more. And then it happened to her. From somewhere deep inside her, untapped and neglected, Mackenzie felt *desire*. Like tiny electrical shock waves sent tingling and pulsing to the core of her body. Intuitively, Mackenzie pressed her groin into Dylan's… seeking…

The noise Dylan made in the back of his throat struck a primitive chord. And the feel of his arousal, rock hard, thick, searching…made her feel crazy inside. Out of control. She wanted to rip off her jeans, right there in the kitchen, and demand that Dylan use his body to put her out of this new, foreign, *torturous* misery. Mackenzie pushed back against his arm, pushed her hands against his chest. She had to put some distance between them before she let her body's driving needs overrun her reason.

Dylan's arms opened and they both took a step back. Chests rising and falling, desire still sparking in both of their eyes, they were silent. Stunned by what had just happened and uncertain of their next move. Mackenzie touched her fingers to her lips. She had never been kissed like that before; she thought those kind of kisses were for other women. Not her.

"I need to go to the bathroom," Mackenzie blurted out.

Dylan resisted the urge to adjust himself. "Down the hall—second door on the right."

Mackenzie headed to the downstairs bathroom and Dylan chose to head upstairs to the third-floor master bedroom. He took the stairs two at a time; he waited until he had reached his bedroom before he gave in to the need to make the necessary adjustments.

What the hell just happened?

Mackenzie had made him nuts: the sensual curves of her womanly body. The full breasts, the roundness of her hips. The way her hair smelled, the feel of her soft lips… the taste of her…it all drove him wild. And he'd wanted to take her right there on the kitchen floor; *would have* taken her, if she had only given him the green light. Dylan sat down on the edge of his bed; he needed some time to cool off before he went back downstairs. If he didn't, he wouldn't put it past himself to try to talk Mackenzie out of her pants and into his bed.

Mackenzie darted into the bathroom and locked the door.

What just happened?

She was shaking, not from being cold, not from fear… from *lust…desire…passion.* The most sensitive part of her body, between her thighs, was *throbbing*, for God's sake! She was…*embarrassed.* And hornier than she'd been since she was pregnant with Hope. She couldn't remember the last time she had wanted a man; she had mentally shut down her sexuality years ago. Eventually, her body had followed. But now? Now her body was turned back on with a vengeance. And she was hot for Dylan Axel. With few good options available to her, Mackenzie sat down on the edge of the tub until she could think of a better plan. What does one do in a situation such as this?

Run for your life?

"Mackenzie?"

Dylan's knock on the door startled her, made her jump. "Are you okay?"

"I'm fine!"

An unconvinced pause and then Dylan said, "Are you sure? You've been in there a long time..."

"I'll be out in a minute!"

Mackenzie splashed cool water on her face, glad now that she hadn't put on mascara. Yes, her eyes were watery, red and puffy...but at least she didn't look like a drowned raccoon.

She pointed at her own reflection. "You are *not* a coward. Just go out there and deal with this head-on!"

Determined to exit stage left as soon as possible, she open the door, marched back into the kitchen and prepared to deliver her excuse.

"I hope you like zinfandel..." Dylan had uncorked a bottle of wine.

"I do." That didn't sound like much of an excuse.

Dylan grabbed the bottle, two glasses and a blanket.

"Let's head down to the beach," he said.

Dylan seemed to know exactly what she needed, exactly how she needed it. And instead of making an excuse, as per the plan, she found herself following Dylan down to the beach. When they reached a good spot on the sand, he spread out the blanket. After they were settled, Dylan poured them both a glass of wine and they touched glasses.

"To first kisses." Dylan made the toast.

"First kisses?" Mackenzie didn't take a drink.

"Yeah...tonight was our first real kiss. I don't remember much from the wedding, but I *do* remember that you wouldn't let me kiss you."

"Oh…I'd forgotten about that." Not sure she wanted to repeat that toast, she took a sip of the wine instead. "Good wine."

Night had fallen and they practically had the beach to themselves. There was a party just kicking in to high gear several houses down, but none of the partygoers had wandered down to their small stretch of beach.

It took a second full glass of wine, but Mackenzie no longer felt the least bit awkward or embarrassed.

"Killer view, Dylan…"

"I like it…" Dylan nodded, his eyes focused straight ahead.

By the third glass, Mackenzie had kicked off her shoes, dug her toes in the sand, and she felt all swirly and dreamy like buttercream frosting atop a cupcake. By the fourth glass, Mackenzie was flat on her back, loose as a goose, admiring the stars.

"You're not going to be able to drive home now," Dylan noted.

"That's true," Mackenzie agreed nonchalantly.

Dylan finished his fourth glass of wine. They had finished the bottle. "And I'm not going to be able to *drive* you home."

"That's also true…"

"So…you'll have to spend the night."

Mackenzie giggled. "And here I thought I was too old for a sleepover."

Mackenzie was obviously three sheets to the wind and he was buzzed. It was time to get off the beach. Dylan helped Mackenzie stand up, helped her get steady on her feet and walked up the stairs behind her just in case she tipped backward. Back in the kitchen, Mackenzie folded her arms and laid her head down on the island.

"Come on…" Dylan said kindly. "I'll get you set up in the spare room."

Dylan made sure she had everything she needed for a comfortable night: new toothbrush, toothpaste, a comfortable bed…privacy. He even brought her the top of his pajamas to wear so she wouldn't have to sleep in her clothes. Languid and carefree from the wine, Mackenzie finished in the bathroom, tossed the decorative pillows onto the floor and rolled herself into bed. She sighed happily and snuggled into the downy pillows. Alone, in the dark, her mind drifted back to Dylan's kisses. Her body undoubtedly wanted more and more and more. But did she?

The next morning, she had the answer to that self-imposed question. Slightly hungover, and a little bit headachy, Mackenzie brushed her teeth and then, still in Dylan's pajama top, she left the guest bedroom. The house was quiet as she headed up to Dylan's third-floor master suite. Other than the unmade, empty bed, the room was spotless. The man really was a total neat freak. Her chronic messiness would drive him nuts! Mackenzie stood in the doorway for a moment, rethinking the soundness of her plan. Perhaps she should just turn around, sprint back to her room and catapult herself back into bed.

And she almost did, but then she heard a toilet flush and Dylan appeared, wearing the bottom half of the pajama set, stripped bare above the waist, hair mussed, scratching his chest hair. He didn't notice her as he walked sleepily back to his bed and flopped backward. Mackenzie, frozen to the spot, had been trying, since she had awakened, to formulate her best pitch line, and she had decided on, *Dylan—would you make love to me?*

"Dylan…?"

Surprised by her voice, Dylan bolted upright. "Geez... you scared the crap out of me, Mackenzie." Dylan collapsed back into his fortress of pillows.

"Sorry..."

"Don't worry about it..." Dylan yawned and stretched.

It took him a minute to focus his eyes and really get a look at Mackenzie. Standing shyly in his doorway, hands in the fig-leaf position, she was filling out his pajama top in a way that made his body stand at attention. He pushed himself into a sitting position and casually pulled the covers over the lower half of his body. He had to force himself not to stare at her legs; Mackenzie had really sexy, curvy legs.

"Are you hungry?" Dylan asked after he cleared his throat.

He needed to get her out of his bedroom. The last thing he wanted to do was go too far too fast and run her off the way he almost did last night.

"No." Mackenzie tugged on the bottom of the pajama top to cover more of her legs. "I mean...yes. I am. But no."

Dylan half smiled, half laughed at her odd response. "Say what?"

Mackenzie twisted her fingers together, losing faith in the sanity of her plan. She had been trying to keep things simple and uncomplicated with Dylan back in her life; what she was about to propose was a first-class ticket to *complicated*.

"Yes, I *am* hungry...but *no*, that's not the reason I'm here. In your bedroom..."

"I'm listening..." Dylan was intrigued...and hopeful. Perhaps Mackenzie didn't need to leave his bedroom after all.

"I was wondering...how you would feel about—" she

shifted weight from one leg to the other "—actually, what I'm trying to ask is…do you want to…make love to me?"

"Yes." Dylan took her up on her offer in record time.

"Yes?" Her voice had jumped an octave.

"Yes." He nodded. "I would…like to make love to you."

The man had said yes, which is what she wanted, right? But now she wished she could press Rewind and take back the offer. This couldn't be a good idea, could it? Sex complicated everything. And this situation was already complicated *enough*.

"Come join me…" Dylan peeled back the covers on the empty side of the bed.

Instead of taking the sane and safe option, she walked slowly toward him.

"You look really good in my pajamas…" It was a genius idea to lend her the top of his favorite pair.

Dylan found Mackenzie's nervous smile endearing. He had been used to women who were sexually confident, even aggressive at times. This was a nice change. When Mackenzie reached the side of the bed, she quickly slid beneath the covers and pulled them up to her chin. The tips of her fingers were white from gripping the covers so tightly.

"Did you know—" Dylan turned on his side, kept his hands to himself "—that most men are really nervous about sleeping with a woman for the first time?"

"Is that true or are you just making that up to make me feel better…?"

"I'm not making it up…it's true."

Mackenzie loosened her death grip on the covers. "Are you nervous now?"

"Yeah," Dylan admitted. "Sure I am…"

"Why?"

"Because…there's a lot pressure on a guy to perform, women just don't get it. We're always worried about are we big enough, are we hard enough, are we going to last? Not to mention the pressure of trying to give a woman *multiple* orgasms when it's hard enough just to figure out how to give her one. And trust me, all guys know that our performance, good or bad, is going to be discussed, and dissected, at length with their friends. I'm telling you…it's a lot of pressure to be on the guy end of things."

His attempt to make Mackenzie feel more comfortable with him must have worked, because she put her arms on top of the covers. They were still pinned tightly to her sides, completely blocking him from her body, but it *was* progress.

Dylan reached over, tucked her hair behind her ear and then lightly rested his hand on her arm. "We don't have to do this, Mackenzie. It's okay to change your mind."

"No!" Mackenzie protested. "I *want* to do it. I'm rusty, okay? And I would think," Mackenzie snapped, "that with all your vast experience, you'd know how to get the ball rolling. Aren't you the one with the bachelor pad and models-slash-actresses prancing about half-naked? I made the first move, why can't you make the—"

Dylan's kiss cut off the rest of her words. She liked the minty taste of his tongue; she liked the masculine smell of his skin—no cologne, just Dylan's natural scent. By the time Dylan ended the kiss, Mackenzie no longer felt like complaining. She wanted less talking and more kissing.

"Here…" Dylan tugged on the covers that were still pinned down with her arms. "Let me get closer to you."

Once he managed to coax the covers out of her control, Dylan pressed his body into hers. She continued to lay on her back, stiff and unmoving, when he wrapped his arm around her and draped his leg over her thigh. Dylan made a pleasurable noise as he nuzzled her neck.

"Aren't we supposed to do this *after*…?"

"Relax…" Dylan whispered near her ear.

Relax. Relax. Just relax!

"Open your eyes, Mackenzie…" Dylan was admiring her pretty face.

She opened her eyes; it was embarrassing. She only made love in the dark with her eyes closed. And now Dylan wanted them open?

"You have the most amazing eyes… Have I ever told you that before?"

She shook her head. She liked his eyes, too. In the soft morning light, they looked mossy green with flecks of gold around the irises.

He ran his fingers lightly over her lips. "Soft lips."

Those two simple words were followed by a kiss. Once he started kissing her again, he didn't stop. He seemed to enjoy the taste and the feel of her mouth. And she found herself responding to this gentle seduction. He wasn't in a hurry; he wasn't just going through the motions to get to the end zone as fast as he could. Dylan was making her feel special, beautiful…cherished. At first, she was a passive partner, timid and unsure. But his kisses started to change that and she began to touch his body—the hair on his chest, his biceps.

Dylan forced himself to go slow, take his time. Her touch was so tentative and she was so unsure of her own sexuality that it felt as if he was in bed with a virgin. Her body was so voluptuous, so soft, that all he wanted to do was to get rid of that stupid pajama top so he could feel her breasts. He wanted to hold them, massage them…kiss them. The scent of her hair and the feel of her silky skin were aphrodisiacs to him.

Dylan pressed his hard-on against her body, and that's when she felt it again: that throbbing, yearning sensation between her thighs. The next pleasurable sound she heard was her own. Dylan had slipped his hand into her panties and nudged his fingers between her thighs. When he felt how aroused she was, Dylan whispered into her ear.

"I want to be inside of you, Mackenzie." Dylan's voice had a husky, sexy quality now. "Do you want that, too?"

"Yes." Why was he talking so much? "Why are you *talking*?"

Chapter Ten

Dylan gently guided her onto her back. Her pretty lavender-blue eyes were filled with uncertainty and desire, lips parted, cheeks flushed pink, chest rising and falling quickly. She was…stunning. A goddess. And he couldn't wait to see all of her…to love *all* of her. He reached for the top button of her shirt. But Mackenzie stopped him.

"No. I want to leave it on…"

Dylan was disappointed but respected her wishes. A woman as sexy and beautiful as Mackenzie should be proud of her body, not hide it. He shifted his focus, peeled the covers back, exposing her simple white cotton briefs. He caught her eye as he traced the edge of the panties, starting at the inner part of her thigh up to the outer curve of her hip.

"But we will need to take these off…"

This time Mackenzie nodded. Not in a hurry, Dylan gradually inched the covers down, revealing her thighs, knees, and finally her tightly crossed ankles. Dylan noticed a small white scar on her upper thigh; he ran his finger across it.

"I remember when you got this. You cut your leg on a piece of glass in your father's garage."

Mackenzie nodded. Dylan leaned down, kissed the scar before he began to inch her panties down. He was so methodical and deliberate, dropping sensual kisses on her stomach, on the soft fleshy inner part of her thighs. He wasn't in a rush. She wanted to tell him to *hurry up*, but bit her lip instead.

"Mackenzie...you're stunning." Dylan knelt beside her, her underwear now on the floor.

He was the stunning one. Dylan's body was ripped and lean from pounding the waves. There wasn't an ounce of fat on the man; he was a thing of beauty. Dylan stood up, stripped off his underwear and reached for a condom. Mackenzie pulled the covers up over her body and watched, fascinated, as Dylan rolled the condom on. It was bizarre. Dylan had given her a child, but this was the first time she was seeing *all* of his body. The night they conceived Hope, she had insisted on a completely dark room.

Dylan joined her under the blanket and she was relieved that he got right down to business, covered her body with his. His weight felt good, pressing her down into the mattress. His hard shaft felt good, pressed into her belly. Dylan held her face in his hands, but she kept her eyes squeezed tightly shut.

"Mackenzie..." He said her name so sensually. "I wish you'd open your eyes."

Mackenzie opened her eyes. Why was he so patient when she felt as if she was suffering from a serious case of sexual frustration?

"I care about you, Mackenzie. I always have. And...I don't take what we're about to do lightly..."

Aching, throbbing, frustrated, Mackenzie sunk her fingernails into his shoulders. "Dylan! Stop *talking*!"

Dylan smiled down at her but followed orders. He kissed her and eased himself into her body, slow and controlled until he was fully inside of her. Their bodies completely connected now, Dylan didn't move. He dropped his head down, took a minute to compose himself. He didn't want to disappoint Mackenzie with a super-short performance. Mackenzie squirmed beneath him, begging him with her body to *move*.

"Mackenzie," Dylan whispered roughly. "You're driving me crazy..."

His fingers in her hair, his lips on her lips, Dylan began to move. But, slowly, as if he wanted to savor the moment, as if he didn't want this moment to end too soon. His long, deep strokes were exactly what her body had been craving. She lifted her hips to meet him halfway, to take more of him in.

"Wrap your legs around me." Dylan gently bit down on her earlobe.

She wrapped her legs around him, held on to his biceps. Dylan locked his arms to hold himself above her; he closed his eyes and let her watch him. They were starting to learn each other's bodies. Dylan was less cautious now, less gentle, and more demanding and intense. And she *liked* it. Dylan wrapped his arms tightly around her shoulders, curled himself around her, and drove his body into hers. And then he drove her right off the edge of reason and straight into the arms of ecstasy. All of the tension, all of the anticipation and frustration and *building* gave way to orgasmic ripples pinging pleasure signals all over her body. Her loud, vocal orgasm triggered Dylan's.

He thrust into her one last time, deep and hard, and then groaned loudly.

Dylan's breathing was heavy, his body felt heavy atop hers. He was still between her thighs, where she felt raw and wet. Dylan kissed her on the neck; he kissed her on the lips. He pulled the covers up over their still-connected bodies and held her tightly in his arms as if he sensed that she needed that reassuring pressure. She felt emotions, out of nowhere, surge through her. Dylan had just given her an amazing gift—her first *real* orgasm. After his breathing returned to normal, Dylan propped himself up on one arm so he could look at her.

"Are you okay?"

She nodded, still feeling a bit scandalized by her own behavior. She had never been so...*vocal*...in bed before. But she had to admit, that it had been...*liberating*.

"I should take care of this..." He reached down between them, secured the condom between his fingers, and then slowly pulled out of her.

Dylan returned to the bed quickly, propped himself up on the pillows and opened his arms for her.

"Come here. Let me hold you."

Mackenzie wanted to be close to him; she wanted to be in his arms after the lovemaking they had just shared. Dylan wrapped his arms around her, held her tight and sighed like a satisfied, contented man.

"This is a great way to wake up..." Dylan slid his fingers into her hair, a smile in his voice. "You're a wildcat..."

Mackenzie ran her fingers through his chest hair, smiled but kept quiet.

"I don't think anyone has surprised me the way you just did..." Dylan kissed the top of her head and rubbed her arm. "Hey...what are you doing today?"

"No plans, really. The bakery's closed on Sundays and I don't pick up Hope from her friend's house until four."

"And I already called Pegasus and told them that I wouldn't be there today, so my day is free. Why don't we spend the day together."

"What did you have in mind?"

"Breakfast, for starters."

"Agreed…"

"Then, surfing?"

"Negative."

Dylan laughed. "Okay…the hot tub, then."

"Uh-uh…I don't have a swimsuit."

"Skinny-dipping is encouraged."

"I never negotiate on an empty stomach. Let's eat first and then we'll talk."

Dylan was an organized, clean cook. She would drive him nuts; her bakery was spotless, but when she baked, she was a whirlwind—a *messy* whirlwind.

"You really do have a little OCD thing happening, don't you?" Mackenzie observed Dylan cleaning the counter throughout the cooking process.

"I guess. I just like things to be clean, organized. What's wrong with that?" Dylan twisted the rag dry and then dropped it over the faucet.

"We could never get married," Mackenzie said without thinking.

Really? You just brought up marriage?

"Oh, yeah?" Dylan flipped over the pancakes. "Why not?"

"Not that I was suggesting that *I* think that we *should* get married. It was just an observation…"

"You still haven't told me why not…"

"In the hypothetical?"

"If you'd like..." Dylan leaned back against the counter, crossed his arms in front of him.

"You are obviously a neat freak. And I am...*not* a neat freak."

"I know." Dylan smiled at her, set her heart fluttering. "I've seen your office, remember?"

"That's right." Mackenzie nodded. "So...you see my point?"

"No. I don't." Dylan put a stack of pancakes on a plate for her. "I have a maid. Problem solved."

Mackenzie could never imagine her life with a maid, which was yet another difference between them, but she decided to move on to a different subject. Dylan saturated her pancakes in butter and syrup, piled crispy bacon onto her plate and served her hot coffee. He ignored her calorie concerns, citing that everyone should allow themselves to have at least *one* cheat day a week and this was it. His logic, and the fact that he seemed to like a woman with a good appetite, encouraged her to devour the pancakes along with a second helping of bacon.

"I really don't normally eat like this," Mackenzie said, looking guiltily at her near-empty plate.

"Do you want more?" Dylan asked. "There're a couple of pieces of bacon left."

Mackenzie pushed her plate away from her and cringed. "Uh-uh...no. I've eaten too much already."

Dylan had managed to charm her into complacency and all she could think of now was how many calories she had just consumed.

"Hey..." Dylan leaned on his forearm and stared at her face. "Mackenzie...please stop beating yourself up about the food. Okay? Give yourself permission to have a little fun."

After they cleaned up after breakfast, Dylan convinced

her that the next logical step was to step down into his hot tub.

Mackenzie went to the guest room to change into a pair of Dylan's boxer briefs and a T-shirt. She called to check on Hope and then quickly sent Ray an I'm OK text message before she emerged from the room wearing Dylan's makeshift bathing suit.

"I look ridiculous," she complained to Dylan.

Dylan was in his surf trunks, bare to the waist, and barefoot. "Not to me you don't."

Dylan circled behind her and pulled the extra material of the T-shirt toward the back. "Here…let me tie a knot back here or the shirt will float up when you get in the water."

Now standing in front of her, he eyed her appreciatively. "There. Perfect."

Mackenzie looked down. Dylan's adjustment to the outfit pulled the front of the shirt tight over her breasts.

"Was that for my sake or yours?" she asked, half-teasing, half-serious.

"Both…" Dylan wasn't shy about admiring her with his eyes. "Definitely both."

She felt self-conscious walking out to Dylan's hot tub, but once she slipped into the hot, bubbling water, Mackenzie forgot all about her silly outfit. Dylan was right—this was bliss.

"Aaaaah." Mackenzie sank down farther into the water.

"Uh-huh…didn't I tell you?" Dylan slid in beside her.

"You did."

Beneath the water, Dylan reached for her hand. Pleased, she intertwined her fingers with his, dropped her head back, closed her eyes and let her mind go blissfully blank. Time moved but they didn't. Not for a while. Not until the sun, beating down on her scalp, finally became too hot to bear. Mackenzie sighed deeply, opened her eyes and moved to the middle of the hot tub. Dylan's interested eyes followed her every move. She leaned back and dipped her hair back into the water so she could cool off her scalp, and to slick her hair back. When she stood up and turned around, Dylan was smiling at her.

"What?" Mackenzie asked. "Why are you grinning at me like a Cheshire cat?"

Dylan's eyes drifted down to her breasts. "Can't I admire you?"

Mackenzie followed his gaze. The wet T-shirt had molded itself to her breasts, leaving nothing to the imagination. Mackenzie immediately sunk down in the water to her neck.

"No…" Dylan shook his head. "You've got to stop doing that."

Dylan was at her side, his arm around her waist; he kissed her as their bodies floated backward toward the side of the hot tub. Dylan lifted her into his arms, spun around and pulled her onto his lap. Then he kissed her again, his tongue taking possession of her mouth, his hand taking possession of her breast. He was already aroused; she could feel it against her thigh.

"When I take you back upstairs, Mackenzie…" Dylan whispered sensually into her ear. "I don't want there to be anything between us this time."

Mackenzie knew that Dylan was referring to the fact that she hadn't let him take off her top when they had made love. Her body wanted Dylan again, and so did she.

"Dylan…" Mackenzie moaned pleasurably into the sun-warmed skin on his neck. "Take me back upstairs…"

After they made love for a third time, Mackenzie took a shower, alone, in the guest bathroom. Dylan offered to share his shower with her, but for some reason, even after all of the lovemaking, a shower seemed somehow too...*intimate*. Mackenzie hurried through her shower, got dressed and made the bed. She tried to arrange the decorative pillows exactly as she had found them but finally gave up.

Dylan was lounging in the den, flipping through TV channels, waiting for her. "What would you like to do with your free afternoon?"

Mackenzie smiled a mischievous smile. "There is something that I'd really like to do."

"What's that?"

Mackenzie's smile widened. "Drive the Corvette."

She thought that Dylan was going to shut her down immediately. To guys like her brother, Jett, and Dylan, their cars were their babies. And they didn't let *anyone* get behind the wheel.

He shocked her when he said, "I'll let you drive her. We can take her down to Ocean Beach Pier. Have you been to the restaurant on that pier?"

Mackenzie shook her head no.

"Have you ever tried fish tacos?"

She wrinkled her nose distastefully. "No..."

"Then today is your lucky day, Mackenzie!"

They gathered their things and then Dylan handed her the keys to his pride and joy. She slid into the driver's seat and wrapped her hands around the steering wheel. As she backed out of the garage, she was half expecting him to have a change of heart and scream for her to stop. It didn't happen. They rolled down the windows, turned on the radio to a classic-rock station and headed to the pier. She wanted to open her up and really test the horsepower under the hood, but she didn't. The last thing she wanted to do was leave even so much as a scratch on a car this valuable. They parked and walked down to the beach. Dylan's phone had been ringing and beeping with texts and emails. He finally just shut his phone off and left it in the car. She didn't ask about who was trying to contact him, but she knew his recent history. He was a single, good-looking guy with deep pockets and a party pad. She didn't doubt his friends, both male and female, were missing one of their regular spots to party at the beach.

They walked side by side, but Mackenzie wasn't ready to hold hands in public. They never stopped talking, that's what she liked about hanging out with Dylan. She wouldn't have thought that they'd have much to say to each other, but they did. He made her laugh; he was silly and goofy and liked to joke around. He'd never really taken life too seriously when they were kids, and he still didn't. He still liked to have fun, and he wanted to take her along for that ride.

"Okay…be honest…" Dylan had just demolished five fish tacos. "You shouldn't have judged, right?"

The Ocean Pier Restaurant was built on the side of the pier. They were sitting at a small table with an incredible view, and Dylan insisted that she, at the very least, take a bite of their famous fish tacos.

Mackenzie chewed the small bite of fish taco thoughtfully.

"Well?" Dylan demanded impatiently. "Awesome, right?"

"It's…pretty good…" Mackenzie said, glad that she had refused the tacos and stuck with an egg-salad sandwich and water. She was still pretty full from breakfast and she couldn't just stop worrying about calories because he had encouraged her to do it. Calorie watching was her normal. Dylan, on the other hand, had been happy to tell her during the car ride that making love to her had left him famished.

"Pretty good?" Dylan acted as if she had just stabbed him in the heart. "You're killing me! These are *legendary*. Try another bite…"

"No!" She pressed her lips together and shook her head. "I wouldn't dream of taking even one more bite away from you…"

"Okay…" He was perfectly happy to polish off the rest by himself. "Are you sure?"

The taco had left a bad taste in her mouth that couldn't be washed away with water alone. She nodded yes while she dug through her tote to find her mints.

They finished their lunch, cleared their table and stepped out onto the pier. Dylan looked around. "Are you up for a walk?"

"Sure," she agreed. They had walked a little ways, when he gave her a curious look. "I thought you liked me."

"I do…"

"Then how come you're so far away?" He offered her his arm.

She took his arm and they strolled together along the pier. When the sun felt a little too strong on her face, the salty mist from the water crashing against the pier seemed to come just at the right time when her skin felt too hot. She couldn't remember the last time she had been to the pier. She had certainly never been here on a date. In this moment, she was content; happy to be walking beside Dylan.

At the end of the pier, Dylan asked, "Do you want to head back or sit down on one of these benches and people watch?"

"People watch, of course."

Like an old comfortable couple, they sat together on the bench. Dylan put his arm behind her shoulder; she leaned in just a little bit closer.

"Do you have the photo album with you? The one from last night?"

Mackenzie put her hand on her tote. "Right here."

"I'd like to finish looking at it."

"Are you sure?"

"I want to know more about our daughter."

Our daughter.

Dylan had never used that term before.

Dylan started at the beginning while Mackenzie told him the story behind each picture. Halfway through the album, they came to the pictures that chronicled Hope's cancer journey.

"Her face is so swollen in this picture. She doesn't even look like the same kid," Dylan said. Hope's face was puffy and round, her head completely bald, her eyebrows gone.

"Steroids," Mackenzie explained. "She could never seem to get enough food." Mackenzie pointed to the next picture. "This is when she first got her port put in for chemo. That was a...really bad day."

Dylan flipped through the rest of the photographs and then went back to the first picture—the one taken the day Hope was born.

"You know that I love her now, Mackenzie."

Mackenzie nodded. She did know.

"And, I'm...really worried about her. What if she relapses?"

Mackenzie didn't like to think about that. She put the album in the tote. "Then we fight it. That's all we can do."

They stayed at the pier for another hour; before they headed back to the car, Dylan insisted that he take her to his favorite ice-cream shop, which was famous for its waffle ice-cream sandwich. After the ice cream, Dylan drove them back to his place. Climbing out of the low-slung Corvette, Mackenzie couldn't remember having a better time with a man.

"Do you want to come in for a while? Or do you have to go?"

"I have to go. I pick Hope up at four. School tomorrow."

On the way back to the car, Dylan made her promise to return the favor and let him drive her vintage Chevy the next time they saw each other.

"I had a really good time with you, Mackenzie. And I know this is going to sound kind of strange, because we have Hope, so I *will* be seeing you again...but I want to see you again."

Dylan was leaning against her driver's door. For the whole entire day, right up until this moment, Mackenzie had felt really good about her decision to deepen the connection with Dylan. But now that she was getting ready to return to reality, her life...doubt was starting to creep in fast and loud.

"Why do I get the feeling something just went wrong here?" Dylan asked suspiciously. Mackenzie's body language, the expression on her face, had changed. Her eyes, which had been open and willing, were guarded.

"There's nothing wrong, Dylan," she lied. "It's just time for me to get back to real life."

He hadn't believed the lie. "I think we should make a date right now. How about if the three of us drive out to Aunt Gerri's house next Sunday? She's been asking for both of you."

"Um...let me check my calendar, okay? And I'll get back to you."

"Now, see...I feel like I need to get a commitment out of you...pin you down." Dylan frowned. "It seems like you're already having second thoughts about this weekend. I can feel you backing away from me..."

Mackenzie took a small step back. "I don't think I'm backing away from you..."

"Actually, you just literally *did* back away from me."

Dylan reached out, slipped his fingers through her hair to the nape of her neck and brought her lips to his. He kissed her until he felt her take a step back toward him. And he didn't *stop* kissing her, until she melted into his arms.

"So…" His lips were still so very close to hers. "Do we have a date?"

"You don't play fair, do you?"

"Not when it comes to you." Dylan kissed her again. "Do we have a date?"

"Yes, Dylan." He was a very persuasive kisser. "We have a date."

Chapter Eleven

"What do you think?" Mackenzie stood in the doorway of her room feeling *naked* in the short-sleeved purple blouse. It was Sunday, and they were scheduled to meet up with Dylan in an hour so they could all go out to his aunt's farm together. She wanted to look presentable, and even though she had been having misgivings about her weekend with Dylan, she wanted to look nice for him, too.

"I picked that out." Hope was a stylish kid. She loved jewelry and accessories; she cut pictures out of fashion magazines and couldn't wait to wear makeup. "You look pretty, Mom."

Mackenzie checked her reflection in the mirror again, tugged on the front of the blouse. It was strange seeing so much of her arms, and they still looked too *round* for her liking, but lately she'd started to think that she needed to force herself out of her baggy-fashion box. There was no doubt in her mind that Dylan's regular compliments had boosted her body image. She still had work to do, but at least she was able to finally cut the tags off this blouse and put it on her body. Mackenzie pointed to her reflection in the mirror.

"You look good," she said, then shut off the bathroom light and headed to the kitchen. She took a quick sip of her strong black coffee before preparing Hope's morning medicine.

"Did you make your bed?" Mackenzie called out to Hope.

She knew that she was never going to be a complete neat freak like Dylan, but she was starting to think that a little more organization wouldn't hurt. In fact, she was very proud of the fact that all their dinner dishes had made it directly into the dishwasher without their typical pit stop to the sink.

"Yeah." Hope showed up looking cute as a bug in a sparkly butterfly T-shirt, cuffed jeans and lavender tennis shoes. "But why'd I have'ta start doing *that* now?"

Mackenzie held out the pills for Hope. "It wouldn't hurt us to be a little neater around here…I made mine, too."

Hope made a face at the pills.

"I know, kiddo. But you gotta take them. Down the hatch."

Mackenzie handed Hope a glass of grape juice, watched her take her pills. When she was done, Mackenzie rinsed out the glass and put it in the dishwasher.

"You feeling okay today?"

"Uh-huh…" Hope nodded.

Mackenzie and Hope loaded into her Chevy and headed toward the bakery. She had agreed to meet Dylan there and she didn't want to be late. During the short trip from their house to the bakery, Mackenzie couldn't seem to get comfortable. She fiddled with the radio, the AC, her seat belt, the neckline of her blouse. She was fidgety and uncomfortable. Anxious. This would be the first time Dylan and she would be seeing each other after their weekend alone. He'd called, but she had made excuses: she was tired, she was working...bad reception, low battery. She just didn't know what to say to him, so it was just easier to say nothing at all. The farther away she got from the weekend, the more she beat herself up for jumping into bed with him. Yes, her body had been deprived in that area for years, but her brain knew better.

And, as often happened with spur-of-the-moment libido-driven decisions, by Monday night, Mackenzie was marinating in full-blown regret. It had been a *terrible* idea to sleep with Dylan. Their focus, their only focus, should have been on Hope—not on each other. She needed to tell Dylan how she felt when they were face-to-face and, hopefully, the two of them could agree to refocus their attention on Hope. If the right moment materialized today, she knew that she needed to have a talk with Dylan.

Dylan arrived at the parking lot behind the bakery ahead of schedule. He was usually early. While he was waiting for Mackenzie and Hope, he decided to try his attorney's private number. He was surprised when Ben actually answered.

"Hey, Ben! I was planning on leaving you a message."

"Do you want me to hang up?" Ben asked.

"No." Dylan laughed. "This is better."

"What can I do for you, Dylan?"

"I had a chance to look over the papers you emailed. Everything looks good, exactly as we discussed."

"That's what I like to hear. Just send a signed copy to the office and we'll have them in the mail to the mother this week."

"Actually…that's what I was calling you about. I'd like to hold off on sending the papers. Just for a little bit."

"May I ask why?"

"I'm hoping that we can work some of this stuff out on our own. So far, things have been pretty cordial between us. But if Mackenzie gets these papers now, I think she'll go ballistic and turn this into World War Three."

"I see. Well, ultimately, it's your decision." Ben paused for a moment of thought. "Why don't we do this…send over a signed copy and we'll hang on to the papers until you're ready to pull the trigger. How does that sound?"

Dylan saw Mackenzie's Chevy pulling into the parking lot and wanted to get off the phone quickly. "That sounds like a plan, Ben. Thanks for picking up on a weekend."

"Billable hours, my friend," Ben said jokingly. "Billable hours."

Hope hugged him hello and Mackenzie greeted him by handing him the keys to her Chevy. He didn't have a car with a backseat, so Mackenzie volunteered her car. And since he had let her drive his Corvette, it was his turn to drive her Chevy. The vintage Chevy had a bench seat in front big enough to fit all three of them. He was behind the wheel, Mackenzie was in the seat by the passenger door and Hope was seated between them. Dylan had the distinct feeling that Mackenzie was glad to put some distance between them in the car, especially since she had been giving him the cold shoulder all week. He'd thought they'd had a great weekend together. *She* came to *his* room. Not the other way around. But he'd blown off enough women when he was in his twenties to know when it was happening to him. He just didn't understand *why*. Luckily, they had Hope to fill in the large gaps in conversation between them.

"See this fence right here, Hope? All of this land belongs to my aunt." Dylan slowed down so Hope could see the farm.

Hope leaned forward, her eyes large. "Whoa...I wish she had horses still!"

Dylan made the turn onto the main driveway. He braked and stared at the For Sale sign posted at the entrance.

"I didn't know the farm was for sale," Mackenzie said.

"Neither did I." Dylan's forehead wrinkled pensively before he slowly let off the brake and headed toward the farmhouse.

Mackenzie saw the empty pastures and the weathered farmhouse in the distance and felt the memories stir inside of her. She had been Hope's age the last time she had seen this farm. Her mother had died the year before; Dylan had just lost his mother. Dylan's birthday party that year, the first without his mother, was one of those memories that had always stuck out in her mind when she thought of her childhood. Aunt Gerri and Uncle Bill had gone out of their way to make sure Dylan had the best birthday that he could possibly have. There was cake and presents and horseback rides and games. She remembered having a really good time; she remembered that Dylan's aunt had let her help in the kitchen. She also remembered that Dylan's smile, the entire day, had always been forced. The smile had never reached his eyes.

Dylan honked the horn and then shut off the engine. A few minutes later, Aunt Gerri swung open the door and came out onto the porch.

"There she is," Dylan said proudly.

Aunt Gerri waved both hands in the air, her bright blue eyes shining with a welcoming smile on her round face.

"Oh, my goodness! Let me look at you!" His aunt held

out her arms to Hope. "You're just the prettiest little girl I've seen in my whole entire life."

Unlike when Hope had met him, she didn't hesitate to hug his aunt straight away.

"And Mackenzie! I'm so glad to see you again."

Even though he wanted immediately to start questioning his aunt about the For Sale sign, he forced himself to wait. Aunt Gerri was brimming with things to say while she gave Mackenzie and Hope the tour of the place. Dylan followed behind them, biding his time until he could ask her about the sign.

"Here's a picture of Bill and me at our fiftieth wedding anniversary." Aunt Gerri stopped in front of a large portrait hanging in the formal living room. "It wasn't too long after this picture was taken that we found out he was sick."

They finished the tour in the front room. The last time he was in this room, he had told his aunt about Hope. Now Hope was here, admiring his aunt's year-round Christmas tree. He waited while his aunt showed Hope and Mackenzie her favorite ornaments. While he waited, he straightened the stacks of sheet music on top of the organ. And, then he got tired of waiting.

"Aunt Gerri…?"

"Hmm?" His aunt was showing Hope her favorite Olive Oyl ornament.

"There's a For Sale sign at the gate. When did you decide to sell?"

His aunt hung Olive Oyl back in her place. "Oh, a couple of weeks ago, I suppose."

Dylan breathed in deeply and then sighed. He'd been feeling anxious ever since he'd seen the sign. His aunt had always owned this farm, for as long as he could remember. It was a touchstone for him. It had always been there if he needed it.

"I didn't even know you were thinking about it…"

Aunt Gerri gestured for Hope and Mackenzie to have a seat. To Dylan she said, "Why do you look so surprised, Dylan? You had to know this would happen eventually."

"I don't know…" Dylan sat down in his grandmother's rocking chair. "I suppose I didn't think it would ever happen. Not really. I thought Sarah or Mary would want the property…"

"No," Gerri said of her daughters. "They both have big-time careers back East. They've never wanted the responsibility of the farm. None of you did…" His aunt smiled a wistful smile. "It's just time, I suppose. It's been time, really. Once Bill was gone, the place was never the same. And I want to be closer to town so I can see my friends. I want to be closer to my church. And I try to think about what Bill would want me to do. You know, your uncle was a black-and-white person, not an in-between person. I don't think he'd like to see what we worked so hard to build together shrink bit by bit until there's nothing left but this house. Better to let it go now. And you've got to remember, Dylan, this land is my retirement."

Sometimes the truth did hurt, Dylan thought. To his aunt, he said, "I'm just sad to see it go."

"I know you are, hon. You never were one for change. But unless you're in the market for a farm, it's got to be sold."

"You should buy it, Dylan!" Hope exclaimed, her face very hopeful. Dylan could see the dreams of horses dancing in her blue-violet eyes.

Dylan shook his head with a laugh. "Sorry, Hope. That's not gonna happen."

Hope jumped up from her seat, brimming with enthusiasm. She talked with her hands and her mouth. "But we could fix up the barn and rent out the stalls. We could give riding lessons out here and clinics and I could have my own horse…"

"I knew that was coming," Mackenzie interjected.

"And when I become a hippo-therapist, I could have my business here!"

"Now what do you want to be when you grow up? A hippa-what?" Dylan knew his aunt and she was getting a kick out of Hope's heartfelt plea.

That question was all the encouragement Hope needed. She sat down in the rocking chair next to Aunt Gerri's and told her all about her future plans. Mackenzie and Dylan's eyes caught occasionally while Hope and his aunt engrossed themselves in a conversation built for two. It reminded Dylan of a Norman Rockwell picture, the two of them together, sitting in rocking chairs in a well-lived-in farmhouse. His aunt had two daughters, both professionals, both living in big cities; his cousins had favored Uncle Bill. But his Hope? She favored his aunt to a T. And, right from the word *go*, they had hit it off, just as one would expect two peas in a pod to do.

"Well…you've definitely got your dad's imagination, that's for sure," Aunt Gerri said. Aunt Gerri didn't notice it, but there was a moment of discomfort between the three of them. No one had called him Hope's dad yet. "Do you remember, Dylan? You tried to convince Bill to turn one of the pastures into a skateboard park. He tried and tried, bless his heart," she said to Mackenzie and Hope. "I remember Bill coming to bed one night so impressed by Dylan. He said that he actually came up with a plan to charge kids so the skateboard park would pay for itself."

"I'd forgotten about that…" Dylan said.

"How about a tour of the farm, Hope?" Aunt Gerri asked. Dylan had a feeling she was just looking for an excuse to get the old golf cart out of storage.

Hope was more than willing to take a tour with his aunt. Aunt Gerri grabbed her keys and they all headed outside. Mackenzie watched Hope load into his aunt's golf cart, while Dylan sat down on the front-porch swing.

"If I know my aunt, they're going to be gone for a while. Come over here and keep me company."

Mackenzie waited until the golf cart disappeared from view before she took him up on his offer. She had wanted to catch Dylan alone, have a chance to set things straight between them. But now that she *did* have him alone, she wasn't exactly sure what she wanted to say to him.

"I'm actually glad that we have a chance to talk to each other without an audience."

Mackenzie nodded, tugged on the short sleeves of her blouse.

"I like that color on you, Mackenzie." Dylan complimented her blouse. "It matches your eyes."

Mackenzie didn't look at Dylan when she said thank-you.

"I wanted to tell you when I first saw you, but I was afraid that you'd be upset with me for complimenting you in front of Hope…"

When Mackenzie didn't say anything, Dylan continued, "And I guess I'm kind of confused here, Mackenzie. I thought we had a good time together last weekend. I know *I* did. I had a better time just hanging out with you than I've had with anyone else in a really long time."

Mackenzie examined her hands instead of returning his gaze. "I had a really good time, too, Dylan."

"Then what's wrong? You haven't been returning my phone calls. When I can get you on the phone, you're always rushing me off. Do you regret what happened between us? Is that it? Do you wish that we hadn't—" Dylan lowered his voice even though there wasn't a soul in sight "—made love?"

Mackenzie glanced at him. "I've been beating myself up about that all week…"

"Well…" Dylan gave a small shake of his head, looked off into the distance. "I'm really sorry you feel that way."

"This isn't about you, Dylan. It's not even about me. It's about Hope. Don't you think I've been lonely? Don't you think I'd like to have someone in my life? I would. But I can't even think about that now. All my energy has to be focused on getting Hope permanently well and keeping my business open. That's it." Mackenzie shook her head. "What happened between us last weekend…I take full responsibility for how far things went."

"Jesus…don't confess to me like you committed a crime! I don't regret what happened between us, either. I actually have some pretty strong feelings for you, Mackenzie."

And he did. Right there, on his aunt's porch, swinging on the porch swing with Mackenzie felt right. She was that missing piece of the puzzle, the one that completed the picture of his life. And from her demeanor…from her body language…it wasn't hard to read that his feelings weren't exactly returned.

"You don't have to say that," she said in a small, tense voice.

"Why shouldn't I say it, Mackenzie? It's the truth. And, from where I sit, we've got nothing standing in our way. You're single. I'm single. We already have a child together. Give me one good reason why we shouldn't *try* to be a family."

Mackenzie didn't feel as if she had one good reason. She felt as if she had a hundred good reasons. But at the core of all her reasons was Hope. What would it do to Hope if they tried to be a family and failed? She was closer to Hope than she had ever been to any human being in her life. And she knew, without a doubt, that Hope couldn't handle that kind of disappointment. Not right now.

Mackenzie stood up and moved to the railing. Putting some distance between them seemed like a good idea.

"If you don't have feelings for me, Mackenzie...that's one thing. But if you're just shutting me down because you're afraid..."

"*Of course* I'm afraid," Mackenzie snapped at him. "It's taken me a long time to get traction after Hope was diagnosed, okay? But I still feel like I've built a matchstick house...like the slightest move could make the whole thing burst into flames. I'm always dreading the next test results, always dreading the next medical bill..."

"But I told you that I want to help you with that," Dylan said.

The comment about the medical bills had just slipped out. Dylan had offered since the beginning to pay child support. He'd offered to help her with medical expenses. But she had always refused. For her, taking money from Dylan was like opening up yet another can of worms. There were a lot of legal strings that could come with that money...visitation, joint custody...and she just couldn't bring herself to wade into those waters just yet. The minute they sat down to establish paternity and child support, Dylan would have rights and she couldn't guarantee what he would do with them. She would have to consult him about educational and medical decisions. She had always prided herself on being able to care for Hope on her own. She had always prided herself on being a strong, successful single parent. The fact that change was already fraying the edges of her life only made her want to cling to how things "were" even more.

"I know you did," Mackenzie said more calmly. "And maybe that's what will happen…eventually. But for now, why can't we just take everything one day at a time?"

"I don't have any problem with taking things slow. But you've gotta be straight with me, Mackenzie. Is the only thing you think about what happened between us last weekend is that it was a mistake?"

Mackenzie rejoined Dylan on the swing.

"No. That's not what I think. What I think is that I have a responsibility as Hope's mom to think before I move. I owe that to her. And last weekend I lost sight of that."

She didn't want to hurt Dylan. She didn't. In her heart, she knew that she had never felt for another man what she had been feeling for Dylan this last week apart. And it scared her. She hadn't allowed herself to become vulnerable to someone in a long time and she wasn't so sure she had it in her to do it now.

"I want to be in a relationship, Dylan," Mackenzie confessed. "Not just for me. But for Hope. When she was younger, it didn't matter as much…now that she's old enough to have friends with two parents, she knows what she's missing…and I think…she wants a family. I wasn't able to admit it to myself for a long time because I wanted to be enough. I didn't want to think that I had made a mistake for all of us all those years ago. But I think…I know… that's why she wanted to find you in the first place."

"I want to try for that, too…"

"But what if we can't make it work between us? What would that do to Hope?"

"What if we *can* make it work?" Dylan answered her question with a question.

"If you're not closing the door on us…"

"I'm not." Mackenzie put her hand on his.

"Then we'll take it real slow... You're both worth the wait."

When Mackenzie saw Aunt Gerri's golf cart in the distance, she pulled her hand back from his.

"I think that if we always put Hope's best interests first, everything else will fall into place..." Mackenzie stood up and waved to Hope. She didn't look at him when she asked, "So, we have a deal?"

"Yes." Dylan stood up and stood next to her. He was close, but not *too* close. "We have a deal."

Chapter Twelve

Mackenzie came home late Wednesday night feeling worn-out and tired from the day. Her main goal was to spend some time with Hope, make sure the little girl was caught up on her homework and then go to bed.

"Hey, Mackenzie." Charlie was sitting on her love seat. The TV was on, but the sound was on Mute.

"Hey…" Mackenzie pulled her key out of the door and closed it behind her. She dropped her bag on the floor next to the door and slumped into a chair.

"You look tired."

Mackenzie dropped her head into her hand. "I am… We've had a ton of responses from the ad we ran in the trade magazine. A lot of special orders. This entire week is going to be crazy and Hope has chemo this Friday—" Mackenzie sighed "—so this weekend is going to be tough." Mackenzie looked toward Hope's bedroom. "Is she still working on her homework?"

"No," Charlie said quietly, shaking her head. "She went to bed early."

Mackenzie pushed herself up, looked at her watch. Hope usually fought going to sleep. She always wanted to stay up later than her official bedtime. "Is she sick?"

"She said that she was really tired and wanted to go to bed." Charlie stood up. "I've got an early morning tomorrow, Mackenzie, so I'm going to head home, okay?"

Mackenzie stood up, her mind on her daughter. She hugged Charlie. "Thanks for watching her."

"You know I love to hang with Hope." Charlie opened the door. Offhandedly, she said, "Oh…I put your mail on the kitchen counter."

Mackenzie locked and dead-bolted the door behind Charlie, grabbed the mail off the counter and went to check on Hope. Lately she had been getting a sickening feeling in her gut. Hope just hadn't been herself for a couple of days. Mackenzie sat down on the side of Hope's bed, ran her hand gently over Hope's head. She felt her forehead with her wrist. It was cool. Hope cracked open her eyes.

"Hi, Mom," she said groggily.

"Hi, kiddo. Are you feeling okay?"

Hope reached out for her mom's hand. "I'm tired."

"Are you having any other symptoms? Are you achy? Do you have a sore throat?"

Hope shook her head, pressed her face into the pillow. "Not really. Just tired."

Concerned, Mackenzie gently rubbed her daughter's back. "I think we should take you to the doctor tomorrow…"

Hope's eyes opened, she turned slightly. "No…" she begged. "Mom…we're going to finish making our birdhouses tomorrow in art class and then we get to hang them up around school! I'm already going to the doctor on *Friday*!"

Mackenzie stared down into her daughter's pleading eyes; it broke her heart that Hope had already missed out on so much after she was first diagnosed. So, against her better judgment, she agreed to let Hope go to school and wait until Friday to see the doctor as planned.

Mackenzie kissed her daughter on the forehead, stood up. "Okay, kiddo. Get some rest. If anything changes, you come get me, okay? I'll see you in the morning."

Mackenzie paused in the doorway for a second or two, watching her daughter drift back to sleep, before she quietly closed the door. Hope's blood would be tested on Friday. Maybe this was nothing to worry about, but she had learned from terrible experience not to minimize symptoms anymore.

She kicked off her shoes and flopped backward onto her pillows. She rested the pile of mail on her stomach, wanting to delay contact, for just a little while longer, with the stack of envelopes that had to be at least fifty percent medical bills. With a long, tired sigh, Mackenzie sat up and started to sift slowly through the mail. The second envelope had bright red paper showing through the cellophane. She ripped open the envelope, looked at the dollar amount and then started a separate "delinquent" medical bill pile. One by one, she separated the mail. As the medical bill pile grew in size, so did her anxiety. It was a daily ritual, with only a brief respite on Sundays. The mail, with its constant stream of bad news, now regularly triggered the feeling that she was slowly being buried alive in quicksand.

Mackenzie was glad to reach the last envelope in the pile; there wasn't any angry red paper glaring at her from behind the cellophane. But once she looked closer at the return address, her psyche shifted.

"Levine, Ernest and Seeger, PA"

She ripped the thick envelope open and pulled out the papers within. She didn't have to read the papers to surmise who had sent them. The only person in her life with a reason to retain an attorney was Dylan. And during their lengthy, private, *supposedly* open and *honest* conversation on Sunday, Dylan had failed to mention that his *attorney* would be contacting her.

Mackenzie began to read quickly through the lengthy documents. With each new written "demand" set forth by Dylan and his attorney, her shaky fingers tightened on the pages, crumpling the edges of the crisp linen paper.

She sat on the edge of the bed, stunned and still. Her brain was on fire: *Why* hadn't she seen this freight train coming?

Mackenzie slammed the papers down on her bed and picked up her phone. She scrolled through her recent-call list and stared hard at Dylan's name. She was tempted to call him right now; verbally blast him *right now.* But she didn't. She closed her eyes and tried to calm her body down: her brain, her heartbeat, her blood pressure. They were all out of control. As much as she wanted to confront Dylan about these papers, she didn't want to give him the advantage by being the out-of-control emotional one on the phone.

Instead of calling Dylan, Mackenzie got herself ready for bed. She doubted that she was going to get much sleep, but she knew she had to try. *This week* was not the week to be ragged from sleep deprivation. Now more than ever, she needed to be on her A game. Once she was in bed, and the lights were off, her mind wouldn't stop racing with thoughts. But there was one thought that ate at her the most: *How am I ever going to afford a lawyer?*

* * *

Mackenzie did her best to get through her day. She had gotten Hope to school, and she had gotten to the bakery early so she could start tackling the special orders that were starting to pile up. It was the first time she had ever wished to be *less* busy at the bakery. She had dozed off a couple of times, but when her eyes popped wide-open at 3:00 a.m., that was it for sleep. For the next two hours, she had stared into the darkness, frustrated and growing increasingly angry as time crept along. And now, thanks to Dylan, her eyes were burning and puffy from lack of sleep and her head was pounding.

"This is the last of them." Mackenzie boxed up the specialty cupcakes she had just frosted. She tiredly stacked the box with the rest of the special orders to be picked up by customers, and then took off her apron.

"Do you mind closing up for me today, Molly?" Mackenzie asked her manager.

"I don't mind a bit, little one. I've got nothin' but dirty laundry and drama waiting for me at home. I come to work to get away from it." Molly belly laughed. "Go home and get some rest. You're working yourself too hard."

Sitting in her car, Mackenzie truly wished she could take that advice. But she couldn't. She had ignored her phone all day in order to get through the special orders. Now she needed to deal with Dylan. He had called and she hadn't trusted herself to answer when she still had orders to fill. When she listened to his message, she was puzzled by the fact that he hadn't mentioned the letter from his attorney. He wanted to know if she was attending the emergency meeting at Pegasus.

"*What* emergency meeting?" she asked herself aloud.

Instead of dialing Dylan's number first, Mackenzie called Aggie.

"Aggie, it's Mackenzie... What's this I hear about an emergency meeting?"

"The owners've sold the property right out from underneath us. Our lease runs out in a month, we've gotten a notice to vacate and we've got no place to go. And even if we *did* have a place to go, we don't have enough money to get there. The grants've dried up, the donations've dried up... I was countin' on our annual fundraiser to pull us through another six months. Now that's off. We're in real trouble here..."

Rayna and Charlie had already agreed to watch Hope after school so she could get caught up at work and deal with Dylan. From Dylan's message, she knew that he intended to attend the meeting at Pegasus. She hadn't planned to confront him in a public venue, but at this point she didn't care. She would see what she could do to help Aggie and then she would find a way to handle her business *discreetly* with Dylan.

By the time she arrived at Pegasus, a record number of volunteers had crammed themselves into the narrow, dusty office. Everyone was tightly packed in the hot space, and the air was already muggy and stale. The volunteers wore worried tense faces as they wiped sweat from their brows and the back of their necks.

Mackenzie wound her way through the crowd to get closer to where Aggie was stationed. At the front of the pack now, Mackenzie spotted Dylan standing to Aggie's right. He was still dressed in business attire, complete with tie, slacks, cuff links and polished wing tips. She didn't imagine it. She knew she didn't imagine it. His eyes had lit up when he saw her and he had smiled at her in greeting. It amazed her how *cavalier* he could be about turning his attorney loose on her.

Jerk!

After the initial eye contact, Mackenzie refused to look at him. She kept her eyes aimed directly on Aggie, and did her best to focus on the crisis at hand. She would get to Dylan soon enough.

For a moment, Dylan was distracted by the daggers in Mackenzie's eyes that seemed to be aimed directly at him. And he was really certain that he hadn't done anything wrong. Maybe she was having a rotten day. Maybe she was understandably concerned about the fate of Pegasus. But she had looked at him as if he was enemy number one and now she was refusing to make eye contact with him at all.

What the heck did I do?

"The bottom line here is that we've got to relocate the horses and we've got a month to do it. We're gonna have to call all our riders and cancel this month's sessions so we can give this situation our total attention. I hate to do it, but it's got to be done. I need volunteers to start shaking some of our donors' trees to see if anything'll fall out. And I need everyone to start looking for a place where we can stable thirty horses." Aggie's sharp voice ricocheted in the small space. Her face was beet red, her deep-set eyes blazing mad. "If we can't get this done…if we can't find a place for all of 'em, we're not gonna have any choice but to split 'em up. And that'll be the end of Pegasus until we can regroup. That's what we're lookin' at. That's how serious this is."

Murmurs of concern and distress rippled through the group, while Aggie took a moment to collect her emotions. Dylan was standing close enough to her to see that her eyes, for a split second, had teared up.

"So…I appreciate all of you comin' out here today on short notice. All I can say now is let's get to work and make this happen."

Aggie abruptly ended the meeting and went through

the side door that led to the barn. Dylan went directly to Mackenzie's side; he waited patiently for her to finish talking to one of the other volunteers.

"I don't want Hope to know about this." Mackenzie was firm when she said this. "She's got enough to deal with right now."

"That's fine." Dylan took a step closer to her so a volunteer could walk behind him. "Hey…are you mad at me for some reason?"

Mackenzie shook her head in disgust. "You're joking, right?"

Surprised and confused, Dylan glanced around at the crowd and decided that they needed to go somewhere with fewer ears listening.

"Let's go outside," Dylan leaned down and said closer to her ear.

Mackenzie acknowledged everyone she passed, hugging some, commiserating with others, until she found her way out of the humid office and into fresher early-evening air. Dylan was on her heels, keeping pace with her as she made her way back to her car. She unlocked the doors.

"Get in." All of the anger and hurt she had been suppressing during the day was rushing to the surface, making it difficult for her to maintain a civil tone.

Dylan closed the door behind him; he had no idea what had set Mackenzie off like this. He hadn't done anything wrong!

"This week just keeps on getting better and better," Mackenzie muttered. She dug through her bag and pulled out an envelope. She thrust it toward him. "I got your little list of demands, Dylan. You want regular, *scheduled* visitation? You want to legally mandate that you're the only man Hope can call Dad? Are you *insane*? I'm not going to *force* my daughter to call you *Dad* if she doesn't want to do it!"

Astonished and confused, Dylan took the envelope. He pulled out the papers and studied them.

"These weren't supposed to be sent to you yet," he said.

"*Yet*? Why would you send them to me *ever*?" Mackenzie snapped at him. "What made you go behind my back and get an attorney? I've *never* put any pressure on you, I've *never* made any demands! All I asked was that you spend time with her. Get to know her. *Love* her…"

"I do love her." Dylan tucked the papers back into the envelope. "And I'm sorry that you got these papers. It was a mistake and I'll handle it. But the fact is, Mackenzie, you're the one holding all the cards. I wanted to know my rights, so I went to a lawyer. You had to at least suspect that I would…"

"Did you—" Mackenzie stopped talking for a minute to smile and wave at the volunteers walking past the car "—hire this attorney before or after we slept together?"

There was a long pause, a guilty pause, before Dylan admitted, "Before."

"That's just great, Dylan." Mackenzie pulled the envelope out of his hand and stuffed it in her tote. "That's just *great*." Mackenzie leaned back, gripped the steering wheel with her hands. She refused to look at him. "The worst part is that I had actually started to allow myself to care about you. I'd actually let myself start to think that maybe we could give Hope what she's been missing for a long time…a mom *and* a dad."

"We still can…"

Mackenzie bit her lip hard to stop tears from forming. She refused to cry in front of him over this.

"You *slept* with me knowing that you were going to serve me with papers! Why would I ever trust you again after you did a snake-in-the-grass thing like that?"

"You came to my room, Mackenzie. Not the other way around."

"You didn't have to say *yes*."

"I wanted to say yes! You're a beautiful woman. You asked me to make love to you and I *did*. And I don't regret it!"

"I'm sure you don't…"

Dylan looked up at the roof of the car, shook his head and then said, "I'm sorry you got the papers. I am. But I'm *not* going to apologize for going to an attorney so I know my rights. I've tried to talk to you about this before and you've always shut me down. You shut me down all the time, Mackenzie. You know you do."

In response, Mackenzie grabbed her keys off the console and stuck them into the ignition.

"Just forget it, Dylan. We're not going to solve anything tonight. I have a ton to do to get the bakery ready for the weekend, Hope has chemo on Friday, Pegasus is falling apart, and now, thanks to you, I have to figure out how in the world I'm going to get the money for a lawyer. Can this week *get* any better?"

"You don't have to get a lawyer…"

"Oh yes, I do." Mackenzie cranked the engine. "Please get out of my car."

Dylan stood in the empty spot where her Chevy had been parked and watched Mackenzie's taillights disappear around the corner. He'd never in his life seen Mackenzie lose her temper like that. She was understandably furious and he knew he'd screwed up big-time with her. And so, apparently, did everyone else.

"What the hell did you do to Mackenzie?" This was Ian's greeting when he picked up the phone.

"I took your advice and went to see Ben."

Dylan could hear Jordan commenting loudly in the

background. "I didn't tell you to serve her with papers. And now Jordan's walking around all pissed off at me..."

"Mackenzie called Jordan...?"

"Of course she did. And Jordan knows Levine is one of my friends."

"Sorry, man..."

"Don't apologize. Fix it. I don't like it when Jordan's pissed off at me. And now she's determined for us to pay Mackenzie's legal fees."

"Oh...crap..."

"My sentiments exactly. I'm telling you, I do *not* want to be caught up in the middle of this. I love you, you're my best friend, but you need to straighten this crap out right now."

"She wasn't supposed to get the papers, okay? Ben told his paralegal not to file them and she made a mistake and mailed them instead."

"I hope he fired her," Ian snapped.

"What does it matter? The papers were sent. The damage is already done." Dylan rubbed his forehead. "Look... tell Jordan that I'll fix it, okay? But in the meantime, I need a favor..."

There was a long pause and in the background he could still hear Jordan blowing her top. "Can you *hear* what's going on behind me?"

"I hear it..."

"And you're still asking me for a favor?"

"Yes...I know my timing sucks...but, yeah."

Two days after Mackenzie had received the papers, she was still refusing to take his calls. He had intended to give her a couple more days to cool off. But he wasn't going to wait indefinitely. He knew Hope was scheduled to have chemo and he didn't want to be shut out of these critical

moments in his daughter's life anymore. And even though
he realized that Mackenzie had good reason to be mad at
him, he had actually started to think that maybe he had a
good reason to be upset with *her*. He wanted to be there
for Hope in all the ways that mattered. But as far as the
world was concerned, he wasn't her father and he didn't
have any rights where she was concerned. That was Mackenzie's doing and he was justified in wanting it to be *un*-
done. He had actually worked himself up pretty good, so
he sounded less than conciliatory when Mackenzie surprised him with a phone call. If she wanted to start round
number two, he was willing.

"Dylan?" There was a distinct waver in her voice.
Mackenzie didn't sound mad. She sounded upset, as if
she was fighting to hold herself together.

Dylan was on his way to meet Ian at their CPA's office
to discuss the tax implications of expanding their business. His fingers flexed on the steering wheel hard when
he heard the raw emotion in Mackenzie's voice. She wasn't
calling to pick a fight.

"Hold on a minute, Mackenzie. I'm driving. Let me pull
over so we can talk."

Dylan pulled into a parking lot, turned off the engine.

"What's wrong?" he asked.

"Hope was admitted into the hospital. She…relapsed."
Mackenzie's voice cracked. "She's scheduled to have a
lumbar puncture today…she wants to see you, Dylan. Will
you come?"

"I'm on my way."

Dylan turned around and headed toward the hospital.
He called Ian on the way and canceled their meeting. Never
in his life had he felt the way he was feeling now. He had
loved people before. He had loved friends, family…women.

Mackenzie. But what he felt for Hope…that was an entirely new type of love.

Dylan worked to look calm on the outside. He wanted to be an anchor for Hope. But on the inside he was panicked. Dylan had been walking quickly right up until he reached the wing that housed Hope's room. He slowed down, even stopped a couple of times, trying to collect himself before he went into her room.

Pull yourself together, man.

But it was a hard thing to do. He was scared out of his gourd, and completely out of his league. The antiseptic smell of the hospital made him feel sick to his stomach. The beeping of the blood pressure machines, the buzzing at the nurses' stations, the coldness of the hallways, all unearthed memories that he had tried to keep buried. His mom had died in a place like this. Would his daughter die in a place like this, too?

"Look who's here, Hope." Mackenzie's face was drawn and tight. Her eyes were bloodshot from stress and worry.

Hope looked so small, so fragile, in that hospital bed. She was hooked up to IVs and monitors. Dark circles ringed her dull eyes. Her sweet round face was pale; her freckles contrasted with the sallow coloring of her face. This was not the same girl he'd seen less than a week ago.

"Hey, Hope," Dylan said from the doorway.

Mackenzie pointed to the wall next to the door. "There's hand sanitizer right there."

Dylan sanitized his hands before he pulled a chair up to the side of Hope's bed.

"Are you going to go see Gypsy tomorrow?" Hope's lips were dry, her voice weaker than usual.

"Of course…" Dylan smiled at her. "Of course I am."

"Will you give her a carrot for me? I don't want her to think that I forgot about her."

Dylan swallowed hard several times, pushing his emotions down with each swallow. "I'll get some carrots on the way home tonight."

"But don't give them to her by hand. Put them in her bucket."

Dylan nodded, reached for her hand and squeezed it reassuringly. Hope looked at him in the eyes, and then her face crumpled. Tears streamed down his daughter's face, her eyes shut tightly. Paralyzed, Dylan didn't know what to do.

"I'm going to miss the field trip." Hope hid her face in the thin white hospital blanket that covered her bed. "And I'm going to lose all my hair again."

Hope collapsed into Mackenzie's arms. Above Hope's head, Dylan's and Mackenzie's eyes met. And a silent agreement passed between them. A truce. Their disagreement washed away by Hope's tears. They had to be on the same team. They both had to be on Hope's team.

Chapter Thirteen

Watching Mackenzie help get Hope ready for the spinal tap gave him a new perspective on the mother of his child. There was a moment when Mackenzie was able to rise above her emotions to help the medical team like a pro. She was calm, collected, a steady hand for their daughter. He was impressed…from a distance. In business meetings, he was usually the guy at the head of the table. The guy with all the answers. But here? He was useless. And it didn't feel good.

Hope was given medication to help her relax. The medication would help her stay motionless during the procedure but would also allow her rest afterward. Mackenzie helped the nurse gently guide Hope onto her side and curled her into the fetal position. Hope wasn't crying anymore; in fact, once the procedure began, she didn't move and she didn't make a sound. Mackenzie ran her hand soothingly over the top of Hope's head. Hope's bare skin was exposed for the nurse to sterilize the area and apply anesthetic cream to her lower spine.

"You're a champ, Hope. Just hang in there and we'll be done before you know it," the doctor said as she prepared to puncture Hope's skin with the long needle.

Dylan caught Mackenzie's eye right before he ducked out of the room. He'd chickened out; he couldn't handle it. He hadn't been prepared, mentally, for this part of Hope's life. Yes, he knew she had been diagnosed with leukemia. Yes, he knew that she had to take daily medicine and weekly medicine, that she had a permanent port just below her collarbone for chemotherapy and blood tests. But knowing about something and *seeing* something were two different things. He had never seen her port before today. And no one in his life had ever needed a spinal tap before.

Thankfully, the entire procedure, from start to finish, took less than forty-five minutes, but to Dylan, it seemed as if he had exiled himself to the hallway for a much longer time. He heard the doctor tell Mackenzie that they should have the results back from the lab in a few hours and then doctor and nurse walked hurriedly out of the room, one right after the other, and on to their next patient. Dylan poked his head into the room; Mackenzie was tucking the blanket tightly around Hope's body. Hope had her eyes closed when her mother kissed her on the forehead. Mackenzie turned off the light to Hope's room, left the door cracked open and joined him in the hall.

"Sorry…I couldn't watch…" Dylan hoped that she didn't think less of him because he had left the room.

"I know…it's hard. I never get used to it."

"It didn't seem that way to me. I didn't even see you flinch."

"Oh, well…I've learned how to fake stability." Mackenzie smiled weakly. "But don't be fooled. My legs shake every time."

"Every time? Has she had a lot of these?" Dylan asked, surprised.

Mackenzie nodded. "That's how they check to make sure that the cells haven't spread to the spinal fluid. All we can do now is pray that they haven't."

They fell silent, two pensive figures motionless in the midst of the bustling backdrop of the hospital. It wasn't fair, to be standing here with Mackenzie. Hope should be in school and looking forward to riding Gypsy. She shouldn't be in a hospital bed, preparing for an intense round of treatment.

"Have you eaten?" It was the only thing he could think to ask at the moment.

"Uh-uh. No. I haven't had a chance. But I don't want to leave in case Hope needs me."

"I'll stay with her. You've got to eat."

"Are you sure?"

"I want to help you." Dylan wasn't used to feeling as if he didn't have something important to contribute to a situation.

A break would be nice actually. She had skipped breakfast and her stomach was so empty that it hurt. And there were phone calls that still needed to be made. Hope could be in the hospital for a while so this was her new temporary home. Arrangements had to be made. She'd have to contact the school, maybe bring in extra help at the bakery so they didn't fall behind. There was so much to do.

Mackenzie quickly grabbed her phone and wallet out of her tote. "Just make sure that she stays on her back, okay? I won't be long."

"Mackenzie..." Dylan saying her name made her stop.

She turned, took a step toward him, and he took a step toward her.

"I wanted to say…" He started to apologize, but the expression on her face stopped him.

"Can we just…not…right now?" Mackenzie asked him. She was exhausted, and stressed, and even though she was hiding it well, he knew that she was terrified that the cancer had come back. If she wanted to table the apology, he would table the apology. No questions asked.

"Sure…" Dylan had to put his hands in his pockets to stop himself from reaching out to her. She looked as if she desperately needed a hug; he wanted to comfort her. Was she receptive to that kind of support from him? He doubted it.

"Take your time." Dylan watched her walk down the hall. Mackenzie turned her head to look back at him, saw him standing there and smiled fleetingly before she disappeared around the corner.

Dylan closed the door behind him to keep the bright hallway light from flooding into the room. Sitting next to her bed, he marveled at the fact that anyone managed to rest in a place that made so much noise. Doctors being paged, nurses checking on patients, carts rolling loudly by. And if the noise didn't disturb you, the regular "vital signs" visits would. That's what eventually awakened his daughter. After a chubby nurse's assistant with a Minnie Mouse voice took Hope's vital signs, she looked up at him groggily, her eyes barely open.

"Where's Mom?" she asked. Her voice was weak, her lips very dry.

Dylan poured her a glass of water from the pitcher, took the straw out of the wrapper and dropped it into the disposable cup.

"She went to go get something to eat. She'll be back

soon. Here…" Dylan held the straw up to Hope's lips. Hope took a couple of small sips and then turned her head away to signal that she'd had enough.

Dylan put the cup down on the rolling table and sat down in the chair. Hope's eyes were closed again; he thought, for a moment, that she had drifted back to sleep. He reached through the metal bed rails so he could slip his palm under hers. Hope squeezed his fingers.

"Dad?" Hope's voice was so quiet and raspy that Dylan wasn't sure he'd heard her right. Had she just called him Dad for the first time?

"Dad?" Hope said again, this time more loudly…more distinctly.

"I'm right here, Hope…" Dylan couldn't have predicted what hearing that one word would make him feel. He knew he was Hope's father, but this was the first time that he truly felt like her dad.

"I'm cold."

Finally, something he *could* fix. Dylan flagged down a passing nurse and requested extra blankets. Dylan hovered by the door until the heated blankets arrived. Dylan quickly covered her with the blankets. He tucked the edges tightly around Hope the way he had seen Mackenzie do for her.

"Better?" he asked.

Hope nodded her response, never opening her eyes.

A few minutes later, Mackenzie came through the door.

"Everything okay?" she whispered from Hope's bedside.

Dylan gave one quiet nod. He almost told her about what had just happened. He almost did. But then he thought better of it. Mackenzie might not be so excited about the news and she had enough on her plate right now to deal with.

Dylan stood up so Mackenzie could take the most comfortable chair closest to the bed. He checked his watch. They still had another couple of hours before they would hear the results of the lumbar puncture. He picked up the chair by the door, moved it closer to the bed, sat down and started to scroll through his emails on his phone. Now he knew to bring his computer. In between reading and answering email, Dylan would look up from the task and watch his daughter sleep. Before today, he'd never tucked her into bed. Before today, she had always called him Dylan.

Dad, Dylan thought in amazement. *I'm Dad.*

Two weeks into Hope's hospital stay, Dylan started to feel like a seasoned hospital patron. He knew where he could find good hot coffee at just about any hour of the day or night. He knew when to eat at the cafeteria and when to avoid it like the plague. He knew the nurses, and custodians, and volunteers by name. And, unfortunately, he now knew more about steroids, and chemotherapy, and flushing ports than he had ever *wanted* to know. It was gut-wrenching to watch when Hope was at her worst. And, because of the relapse, the treatment protocol was much more aggressive. But the leukemia cells hadn't reached the spinal cord and that gave them reason to believe that a second remission could be on the horizon.

"I thought I'd find you out here." Mackenzie was wise to his best hiding spots. Sometimes he just needed to get away. Sometimes he just needed to *escape* the reality of the hospital.

Dylan scooted over so she could join him on the wrought-iron bench. This small, secluded courtyard was his favorite of his hiding spots. He'd eaten a lot of bag lunches under the shade of this old blue oak tree.

Mackenzie's hair was pulled back in a loose ponytail

and she was wearing the same Padres jersey she had worn the night they had kissed for the first time. There were so many times over these last weeks that Dylan craved Mackenzie. He wanted that physical connection with her. He wanted to love her and *be* loved by her, particularly during some of the worst moments with Hope. But she always kept him just an arm's length away. Close, but not *too* close.

Dylan reached inside his computer bag and pulled out a stack of her medical bills. He had come to her a week ago and insisted that she let him help her with the expenses. In the end, she couldn't argue with his logic. The stress of unpaid medical bills hanging over her head and ruining her credit was only funneling her vital energy away from Hope.

"These are paid."

Mackenzie stared at the large stack of envelopes on the bench between them. These envelopes had dogged her for years. They had robbed her of sleep; they had caused her so much stress and worry. And then, just like that...with no real fanfare, they were gone.

"Thank you..." Mackenzie reached for them. "Thank you."

"Thank you for letting me help." Dylan closed the lid of his laptop. "Is she still working with the tutor?"

She nodded yes. Hope was an overachieving kind of student, which she came by honestly from her mom. Other than her hair falling out again, the two things that really upset Hope about the relapse were missing school and missing out on Pegasus.

"Any updates from Aggie?" Mackenzie hated that she couldn't be more involved with solving Pegasus's crisis. As long as Hope was in the hospital, everything had to be put on hold. Even Pegasus.

"I think we've nailed down a viable option."

"Are you serious?"

When Dylan confirmed what he had just said, Mackenzie closed her eyes, her face tilted upward for a moment.

"Oh, thank goodness…" Now she could break *good* news to Hope instead of heartbreaking news.

"Where in the world did Aggie find a place that could take that many horses on short notice?"

When Dylan wasn't with Hope, he spent his wait time at the hospital trying to run down leads to place the horses. But what they really needed was more time, more money and a miracle.

"We're moving them out to Aunt Gerri's," Dylan said.

Mackenzie stared at him, shocked into silence. After a second or two, she asked, "Aunt Gerri is donating the farm to *Pegasus*?"

Dylan shook his head. "No. I would never ask her to do that. That's her retirement."

Dylan answered the question in Mackenzie's eyes.

"We're going to buy it from her."

"Pegasus is going to buy your aunt's farm? How? That land has to be worth…*millions.*"

"It is…"

"They can't afford that! I've seen Aggie struggle to buy enough hay some months…."

Dylan rubbed the stubble on his chin and face. The stress in Mackenzie's voice matched the stress that he had been feeling for weeks. He had no real idea how to make the farm work in the long term for Pegasus; all he had was a short-term plan. He was the numbers guy and the numbers just didn't work. Not yet.

"My aunt's agreed to let us lease the land for now." Getting his kindhearted aunt to agree to lend a hand had been the easy part. It was the logistics of the move that were the problem. Yes, they had plenty of volunteers willing to help and they had enough trailers lined up to accommodate the horses. But the farm hadn't housed horses for years. The infrastructure had deteriorated, the two standing barns needed to be cleaned out and cleaned up. The fences needed to be mended so they could use the pastures. And all of that took money. They'd already raised a decent chunk of change, but they needed more to buy the land. Lots of it.

"And..." Dylan continued. "We've already raised right around two hundred thousand dollars, so we've got some capital to work with..."

"Wait a minute...did you just say...two hundred *thousand*?" When Dylan confirmed the number, Mackenzie said, "You did this..."

It was a statement, not a question.

Dylan stood up and held out his hand to her. "I really need something to drink. Walk with me?"

She put her hand into his but her eyes never left his face. This man had grown; he had matured. In just a short few months, he had begun to care more about the condition of the world around him. And he had been a tireless support these last weeks at the hospital. Everyone had noticed it: Rayna, Charlie...Jordan.

"How did you pull this off, Dylan?" Dry, brittle leaves crunched beneath their feet as they walked slowly across the courtyard.

"Trust me...I couldn't do that on my own. I'm just good at turning money into more money, not fundraising. Some of the money came from our regular donors, Ian's been contacting some of our previous clients looking for sponsors, and I think your cousin, Josephine, is it? Her boyfriend's parents have some pretty deep pockets..."

Mackenzie walked through the door Dylan held open for her. "How much did you donate?"

Dylan followed her through the door. "I donated some."

"How much?"

"Some…"

Mackenzie stopped walking. "Dylan…how much of that two hundred thousand came from you?"

Dylan sighed, stopped walking and made a small U-turn so he could stand directly in front of her.

"How much?" Her eyebrows lifted with the question.

Dylan glanced around before he said, "A hundred…"

"Dollars?"

"No…" Dylan lowered his voice. "Thousand…"

Mackenzie was dumbstruck. She studied Dylan's tired eyes and then it clicked in her brain.

"You sold your Corvette…" She said that and Dylan stopped meeting her gaze. "Oh, Dylan…you didn't…"

Dylan turned his head away from her. "Don't make a big deal out of it, Mackenzie."

"Don't make a big *deal* out of it? That car meant *everything* to you."

"No. It didn't." Dylan's eyes were back on her. "Hope means everything to me. Okay? *You* mean everything to me."

Mackenzie swallowed hard several times to keep her emotions in check. She refused to let herself cry in the middle of the hospital lobby. But she wanted to cry. Eyes watery with emotion, Mackenzie asked Dylan, "Can I hug you?"

The pain in his eyes when she asked that question made her feel like a genuine jerk. She knew that Dylan had wanted to be consoled by her for weeks. She knew it. And yet, she hadn't done the one thing for this man that he needed from her. It was such a simple thing and she had denied him.

Dylan didn't nod, he didn't say yes; he opened his arms to her instead. She was the one to close the distance between them. He had already taken nine figurative steps toward her over the past few months, and it was her turn finally to take that one *literal* step toward him. They embraced, right there in the middle of the busy hospital lobby. Dylan held on to her so tightly. And she held on to him. When they were face-to-face, body to body, arms intertwined, Mackenzie could feel that they were a perfect fit. A perfect match. Hugging Dylan…being hugged by Dylan… was the most comfortable, reassuring experience she could remember having. Everything but Dylan, and the feel of his body, faded far into the background.

"Thank you…" Mackenzie rested her head on his shoulder.

Dylan's arms tightened around her, she felt him kiss the top of her head. "I've missed you."

Mackenzie leaned back a bit so she could put her hand on Dylan's face. "You're such a good man, Dylan Axel."

Dylan reached up and captured her hand, pressed his lips to her palm and then held her hand next to his heart. "I've always wanted you to think so. Even when we were kids."

"I do think so…what you've done for Hope…what you've done for me." Even though she had called a truce with him that first day in the hospital, this was the moment when she was truly able to release her resentment over the attorney's letter.

Dylan took a chance. The way she was looking at him, he wanted to believe that there was an invitation in her eyes. He kissed her. Gently, sweetly, tenderly.

"People are staring…" Mackenzie said when the kiss ended.

Dylan glanced around for a second then grabbed her hand. Instead of heading toward the cafeteria, Dylan started walking back toward the courtyard. He led her through the door, across the courtyard and behind the large blue oak tree. Hidden behind the thick trunk of the tree, Dylan pulled Mackenzie back into his arms and kissed her. The first kiss had been a question. The second kiss was a lover's demand. He leaned back against the tree and brought her with him. He deepened the kiss, teasing her tongue with his.

Ultimately, it was Dylan who ended the kisses. He held her by the shoulders, pinning her with narrowed, intense eyes. "I have to stop."

Mackenzie agreed. They needed to stop. If only it hadn't felt so good. If only she didn't want to kiss him again… right now.

"You've never let me apologize for not telling you that I had gone to an attorney. I've tried…more than once."

"I know…" He had tried, but just as he had said to her during their disagreement at Pegasus, she always changed the subject.

"Do you forgive me, Mackenzie? Can we move on now?"

"I forgive you," she said, and meant it.

Mackenzie's phone chimed; she checked it.

"Hope's done with tutoring," she said. "I need to get back to her. Can we…talk more later?"

Dylan nodded his agreement.

"Are you coming?" Mackenzie paused when he didn't follow her.

"In a minute…" Dylan glanced down toward the bulge near his zipper.

She wasn't really a blusher, but she did then. "Oh…do you want me to wait, too?"

"No. You go ahead. I'll catch up in a minute." While he was waiting, he realized how much his reality had shifted since Mackenzie and Hope. A couple of months ago, he was a successful business owner with a lot of time for parties, surfing and hot blondes. Now? He hadn't thrown a party since Ian's birthday, he had become a philanthropist, a curvy brunette had replaced the blonde and the Corvette was gone.

But that was all superficial stuff and now he knew it. The biggest change was the change that had happened in his heart. He discovered that he liked having a daughter. He liked being a dad and he was pretty good at it so far. In fact, he had started to think that he'd like to have more children. This time he'd be there from conception to birth and beyond. And he wanted to have those children with Mackenzie. She was the one for him. He loved her and when the moment was right, he was going to propose marriage. She might not know it yet, but Dylan was determined to marry Mackenzie.

Chapter Fourteen

One week at the hospital could feel like a month. Dylan had passed exhaustion a while ago and was now operating in a zone teetering somewhere between comatose and hysteria. He had taken to sleeping on his favorite courtyard bench and didn't even care anymore that he must look like a homeless person sleeping off a bender. Mackenzie rarely left the hospital, and when she did leave, it was to get something done for the bakery or go to Hope's school for a meeting. She hadn't had a real break, or real sleep, in weeks. And they were both starting to fray around the edges. The littlest thing would make them snap at each other, and there was a bite in their tone that was a symptom of their extreme fatigue and chronic worry. Mackenzie had let Rayna or Charlie stay with Hope during the day, but she had refused to leave Hope overnight. Mackenzie needed to get some actual sleep in an actual bed, and he was going to force the issue today.

"Uh…*wow*! You look like total crap!" Jordan met up with him at the hospital entrance, carrying her motorcycle helmet under her arm.

He could tell by the look on her fact that Jordan was shocked by his appearance. He couldn't really blame her; he was usually the stylish guy in the group. Even on casual days, Dylan wore slacks, button-down shirts, his customary Rolex watch and expensive shoes. Today, he was in a T-shirt, jeans and sneakers. His hair was shaggy, as if he'd missed his bimonthly appointment with the barber, and she had never seen him with a five-o'clock shadow before.

"Thanks for coming." Dylan hugged Jordan, glad to see her.

"Of course. What else?" Jordan asked. "Is Mackenzie really going to let me take a shift? I've been offering for weeks."

Dylan opened the door for her. "I'm not going to give her a choice. If I have to, I'll throw her over my shoulder and carry her out of here."

"Well, all right, caveman." Jordan laughed at the thought. "That'll go over well. If I were you, when you put her down, run like hell. Mackenzie may be little, but she packs a punch."

"Trust me—" Dylan pushed the button for the elevator "—I know."

Just outside Hope's room, Dylan slipped on a paper hospital mask. "Wait here for a minute, okay?"

Jordan waited for Dylan while he went into the room. The room was dimly lit because Hope was resting. Mackenzie was doing her best to sleep curled up in the chair. He had tried to sleep in that chair himself, so he knew how uncomfortable it was. He knelt down beside Mackenzie and rested his hand on her thigh.

"Mackenzie…" he whispered.

"Hmm?" Mackenzie cracked her eyes open.

"Come outside with me for a minute…"

"Why?"

"Just come outside with me…"

Mackenzie pushed herself upright slowly, yawned behind her mask and rubbed her eyes. Finally, she stood up, stretched her arms above her head and followed him quietly out of the room.

Mackenzie slipped off her mask. "Jordan!"

The cousins hugged each other in greeting.

"I wish you'd let me know you were coming. Hope's asleep. She's going to be really upset that she missed you."

"She's not gonna miss me," Jordan said. "I'm spending the night."

Mackenzie looked between Dylan and her cousin. "You are?"

"You need to sleep in your own bed, Mackenzie. You haven't slept in weeks." Dylan put his hand on her shoulder.

"No…" Mackenzie shook her head. To Jordan she said, "Thank you, but no."

Jordan was a good match for Mackenzie. They didn't resemble each other, but they were cut from the same tough cloth. Jordan had a really good chance of winning this round.

"You're welcome, and *yes*. You're going home. I'm staying here," Jordan said in a no-nonsense tone. "Hope's my family. You're my family. I get to help."

Mackenzie wasn't a shrinking violet, but she was a *weary* violet. "All right."

Dylan was surprised at how quickly Mackenzie gave in to her cousin, but he wasn't about to wait around to let her change her mind. He hustled her back into the room to grab her tote and kiss a still-sleeping Hope goodbye. He handed Jordan a mask.

"You have to wear this all the time. No fruit, no flowers. I'm going to drive Mackenzie home. Call *me*, not her, if you need something."

"No…she needs to call me…" Mackenzie disagreed. Over her shoulder, she said to Jordan, "You need to call me."

"*Go*…both of you." Jordan had her mask on. "I've got this."

Jordan watched her cousin and Dylan walk away together. Mackenzie had her arm linked with his and Dylan had the look of a man in love. Dylan and Mackenzie? On paper, they seemed like a really odd match, but, when Jordan saw them together, they just *fit*. Sometimes opposites really did attract.

Dylan drove Mackenzie home in his car, leaving her car parked at the hospital. She twisted to the side in the bucket seat, facing him, and closed her eyes. He typed her address into the GPS. He knew that she lived near Balboa Park, but he'd never been to her house.

Mackenzie wasn't asleep on the way home; she was just too tired to keep her eyes open. She was so exhausted that she felt sick with it. When Jordan showed up, she knew that Dylan had arranged it and that he was right. It was time for her to get some rest. If she got sick, then she wouldn't even be able to go into Hope's room, much less stay with her overnight.

Mackenzie heard the robotic voice of the GPS say the name of her street. She sat up, yawned loudly and then pointed to her small Spanish-style bungalow.

"That's me right there on the left."

Dylan pulled up in front of her house and parked. He

walked quickly to her side of the car, opened the door and held out his hand to her.

"Nice place." Dylan walked beside her up to the front door.

"Thank you. Hope and I love it here." Mackenzie turned off the alarm remotely and then slipped the key into the door. "Do you want to come in?"

"Sure…" He had been hoping for an invitation but wasn't so sure he'd get one.

Mackenzie walked in first, and then stepped to the side so he could come in. "You may as well see what you're getting yourself into…"

The way Mackenzie had described her penchant for messiness, he had been worried about what he may find behind the door. He was relieved to find that the quaint, shabby-chic bungalow was a little cluttered—a little disorganized. But it was clean. He could work with that.

Mackenzie dropped her tote and keys on the kitchen counter. "I have to sit down for a minute."

Dylan looked at her small curio cabinet tucked in the corner. "What's this?"

"I collect hearts," Mackenzie said with a yawn. "My mom had a heart collection and I just kept it going. Do you want to sit down?"

She put all the recipe boxes off the love seat onto the floor so Dylan would have a spot to sit. He joined her on the love seat; they sat shoulder to shoulder, thigh to thigh in the quiet living room.

Mackenzie sighed. "This is what I'm going to do… I'm going to take a really hot shower and then get into bed."

"Sounds like a plan," Dylan agreed.

Mackenzie turned her head toward him. "You can either go home, or you can join me. It's up to you."

Her words were blunt, to the point and completely un-expected. But his decision was an easy one to make.

"I want to stay with you…"

Mackenzie stood under the steaming hot water for a long time, letting the heat beat down on her aching neck and back. Sleeping in a chair had taken its toll on her body. After the shower, she got Dylan a fresh towel and one of Hope's unopened One Direction toothbrushes from under the sink. Dylan showered, brushed his teeth and shaved his face with a razor Mackenzie had told him was dull from her shaving her legs. He didn't put his clothes back on; instead, he just wrapped the towel around his waist. It wasn't like Mackenzie hadn't seen the goods before.

He carried his clothes down the hall and found Mackenzie already in bed. "Can I throw these into the washing machine?"

Mackenzie had been dozing off. She nodded sleepily. "Behind the sliding doors right behind you. Detergent's on the shelf."

Dylan threw his socks, underwear and T-shirt in the washing machine. He had noticed that Mackenzie had left one side of her small bed open for him, and he was looking forward to occupying it. He'd been thinking about getting Mackenzie back into his arms for the longest time. And tonight…*finally*…was the night. Dylan dropped his towel by the side of the bed; if Mackenzie minded that he was getting into her bed in the buff, she didn't say. She watched him, eyes half-mast, while he got into her bed. He was the first man she'd ever had in this bed, and she was glad that she had invited him to stay.

"Do you want me to hold you?" Dylan asked.

Mackenzie turned over and scooted back into his awaiting arms. Dylan wrapped his arm around her body, buried his face in her sweet-smelling neck and closed his eyes.

It didn't take but a minute for his body to start getting worked up over having her in his arms. She was warm and soft and sexy, and even as tired as he was, his body still wanted to make love. Knowing how sleep deprived Mackenzie was, Dylan moved his hips back slightly away from Mackenzie's body. She needed sleep, and as much as he wanted to love her right now, he needed to let her rest.

"Good night," she murmured.

When she snuggled even more deeply into his arms, Dylan closed his eyes and sighed contentedly. Relaxed and at home lying next to her, Dylan fell asleep with the certain knowledge that wherever Mackenzie was, that's where he belonged. They slept for hours. It had been dusk when they arrived home, but it was late in the night when Mackenzie awakened. She heard Dylan snoring beside her in the narrow bed, and she could see in the faintly lit room that he had pushed all the covers over onto her side. Not wanting to wake him, Mackenzie carefully peeled the covers back and tried to get off the end of the bed without wiggling the mattress too much.

"Where're you going?" Dylan asked in the dark.

"Bathroom…" Mackenzie whispered.

She slipped into the bathroom, peed, rinsed out her mouth and then opened the door. The light to the bathroom was still on, so Mackenzie got a full-frontal view of a naked Dylan scratching his chest hair just outside the bathroom door. Dylan had been asleep, but the lower half of his body was wide awake.

"I'll meet you back there…" Dylan let out a long yawn before he changed places with her.

Mackenzie hid a smile as she hurried back to bed. She checked her phone. Jordan had sent her a text saying that Hope was doing well. It was 3:00 a.m., which meant she still had some more sleeping to do.

Dylan took care of business in the bathroom, dropped his clothes in the dryer and then came back to bed. He immediately pulled Mackenzie back into his arms. But this time, instead of letting her go back to sleep, he started to drop small butterfly kisses along the back of her neck.

"Mackenzie..." Dylan breathed in her scent.

"Hmm?"

"Do you know that I love you?"

Her eyes had been closed, but she opened them. She turned her head toward the sound of his voice. "No..."

His lips were next to her ear, the feel of his breath sending wonderful chills down her back. Mackenzie shifted her body so she was facing him in the dark.

"Do you know that I'm in love with you?" he asked.

"No." Mackenzie didn't flinch when Dylan's hand slipped under her T-shirt. He slid his hand behind her back and pulled her closer to him.

Dylan found her lips in the dark. Kissed her, long and slow.

"I do love you..." Dylan touched her face, his fingertips tracing the outline of the lips he had just kissed.

"Do you love me, Mackenzie?"

She gently bit the tip of his finger. Her body was already responding to his kisses, to the feel of his lean, muscular body next to hers.

"Yes..." she admitted to him, and to herself.

Over the past several weeks, her feelings had grown for Dylan. They had deepened. When she looked at him, her heart felt full. When he was gone, she missed him. Lately, she had caught herself waiting for his phone calls and texts, and staring at the hospital doorway, awaiting his return. The love that she now knew she felt for Dylan was different than the love she had for Hope, but it was just as strong. She was in love, for the very first time in her life.

"Thank God," he said before he kissed her again. He gathered her into his arms, holding her so tightly as he deepened the kiss.

Without words spoken between them, Dylan stripped off her shirt and panties. His mouth was on one breast, his hand massaging the other. He sucked on her nipple, drawing it into his mouth, teasing it with his tongue, until she couldn't stay quiet. She pressed his head tighter to her breast and moaned softly. She slipped her hand down between their bodies and wrapped her fingers around his long, hard shaft. He groaned and she smiled a lover's smile. Mackenzie pushed on his shoulder so he would lie down on his back.

"What are you doing?" he asked in the dark.

Intent on her mission, she ignored him. He would know her intentions soon enough. His shaft was thick and silky and warm; it felt so good in her hand. The head of his shaft was large, and tasted salty when she drew it into her mouth.

Dylan's next groan was even louder. His fingers were in her hair, his leg muscles tensed in anticipation; Mackenzie was emboldened. Right then and there, he was at her mercy, she was totally in control, while she loved him with her mouth.

"Mackenzie...I don't want you to stop..." Dylan's voice was strained. "But you've got to stop."

Dylan pulled her up on top of him, kissed her and then pushed her onto her back. He was down between her thighs before she could stop him. She hadn't let him do that when they had made love before; this part of lovemaking always embarrassed her. She could give, but it was harder for her to receive.

But the minute she felt his hot mouth on her flesh, she couldn't remember why she'd ever said no to him before. Dylan slid his hands beneath her hips, lifted her body up and loved her with his tongue until she was squirming and aching and crying out for him to put her out of her misery.

Like a stalking tiger, Dylan moved up her body until they were chest to chest. His shaft was pressed into her stomach; she needed it to be pressed inside of her.

"Where are your condoms?" Dylan's teeth grazed her shoulder.

"I don't have any..."

The moment she said those words, it occurred to her that he was asking because *he* didn't have a condom. Dylan's body became very still on top of her.

"You don't have one?" he asked, frustrated.

Mackenzie shook her head. "No."

Dylan dropped his head into her neck, tempted just to lift his hips and slide himself into her tight, wet, warm body, damn the consequences. After a moment of silent debating, Dylan rolled off her body and sat up on the edge of the bed. He hadn't had sex for a month and he'd been too stressed out to worry about masturbating. But now? His body *knew* it had been deprived and it wanted relief ASAP. He was so hard it felt as if the skin was going to split wide open. And even the thought of risking getting Mackenzie pregnant didn't soften it one bit. In fact, the thought of impregnating her again actually turned him on even more.

Cold without his body on top of her, Mackenzie pulled the blankets up over her body. She wanted to scream. Her body was so sexually charged that all she could think about was getting Dylan inside of her. She curled her legs up and tried to stop focusing on the throbbing he had started between her legs. Head in her pillow, she closed her eyes. She opened them when she felt Dylan lift the blanket.

He was on top of her again and he was still aroused;

the head of his shaft was poised just outside the opening of her body. He took her face between his hands.

"Mackenzie?"

A small stream of moonlight had wound its way through the window slats; she could see the strong planes of his face. More important, she could make out his eyes.

"Yes, Dylan?"

"I want you to be my wife. I want to have more children with you."

Mackenzie swallowed hard before she spoke. "Are you asking me to marry you?"

"Yes, I am." He hadn't expected to propose to her tonight. But the moment felt right. "Marry me, Mackenzie."

"Okay…" she said simply.

Dylan reached between their bodies and guided himself in. He slowly, carefully, slid deeper and deeper until he was as deep inside of her as he could be. He waited for her to protest, to be the voice of reason when they both knew the risk. But she didn't. He pulled back, teasing her with sensual, controlled strokes. Her frustrated sounds signaled that she wanted more from him. She wanted more passion, more intensity, more, more, more… So he stopped worrying and gave himself permission just to experience Mackenzie. He deliberately and methodically loved her longer, and with more passion, than he had ever loved anyone before. When he loved her slowly, she demanded that he go faster. When he gave her one orgasm, she pleaded for another. But it was her unbridled, uncensored cry at the peak of her second orgasm that destroyed his carefully manufactured control.

"I'm going to come…do you want me to pull out?" Dylan gritted the words out.

Mackenzie locked her legs around him and kept him right where he was. That simple gesture drove him crazy;

he braced himself above her, arms locked, head thrown back as he exploded inside of her.

Dylan didn't move; he dropped his head down and caught his breath. Then he lowered himself down on top of her.

"Holy Toledo, woman..." Dylan laughed into her neck.

Mackenzie hugged him and laughed, too. She felt satisfied and *sexy*. She didn't even bother to cover her body when Dylan rolled to the side. They both lay on their backs, holding hands, savoring the aftermath of their lovemaking. Each time with Dylan was just a little bit better than the last. She was more comfortable with her own body. She was more comfortable with him. He thought she was beautiful, and she'd only seen him date really gorgeous women. It had helped her to start owning the idea that she was an attractive, curvy woman.

"Do you think that I got you pregnant?" Dylan's question interrupted her own internal dialogue.

Her hand moved down to her abdomen. The timing in her cycle could be right. "I don't know. Maybe."

"And if I did?"

The thought of carrying Dylan's child filled her with an immediate rush of joy. She *wanted* to be pregnant with his child again.

"Then Hope won't be an only child anymore."

He squeezed her fingers. "Will you be happy?"

"Yes..." she reassured him. "I've always wanted another child."

Dylan lifted her hand and kissed it.

"What about you?" she asked. "Will you be happy?"

He propped himself up on his side, put his hand on top of hers. Now they both had their hands on her abdomen.

"I hope I did get you pregnant."

His words were the exact reassurance she needed. She

was the mother of Dylan's child, and now she was going
to be his wife. That hadn't always been her dream, but it
was now. Still tired from weeks at the hospital, they pulled
the covers over their bodies and knew that they should try
to get some rest. For now, they had had a temporary re-
prieve from the harsh reality of hospital life. Dylan held
on to her tightly; the warmth of his hairy chest felt so good
against her back. He brushed her hair back off her shoulder, tightened his arm around her and let his head sink
down into the pillow. He was a father and soon he would
be a husband. And, maybe, just maybe, their lovemaking
had created a new life tonight. If they hadn't succeeded
this time, Dylan was hopeful that Mackenzie would agree
to keep on trying until they *did*.

Chapter Fifteen

Dylan's days of wearing expensive clothes and nice shoes were temporarily on hold. Until Pegasus was moved to the farm, he was relegated to jeans, T-shirts, work boots and a baseball cap. His partner, Ian, was taking charge of the business expansion while he split his time between the hospital and the farm. The new owners of the land Pegasus was currently occupying, investors with a plan to develop, had given them a two-week extension to vacate. It didn't seem like much, but it was actually a donation of sorts. As far as the investors were concerned, every day they delayed their project cost them money. The extra two weeks helped, but there was still a long list of things that needed to be done at the farm in order to keep the horses comfortable. As far as getting Pegasus operational again for riders, that was an entirely different problem for a different day.

He had found his uncle's old tool belt in the shed, and

wearing it made him feel like maybe Bill was watching, guiding him with his steady hand. He was actually surprised at how quickly he had fallen back into life at the farm. He'd even crashed a couple of times in his old room instead of driving back to his place.

"The delivery guy just called!" Doug Silvernail shouted to him from the far end of the barn. "You want them to stack the lumber out front?"

Doug was a contractor at his aunt's church who had donated his time to Pegasus.

"That works, Doug. Thanks!" Dylan shouted back. He pulled off his ball cap, wiped the sweat off his brow and then put the hat back on. He stuffed the sweaty rag back into his pocket and got back to the business of fixing the broken hinge on the stall door. When his phone rang again, which it had been doing nonstop all morning, Dylan cursed under his breath and pulled the phone out of his front pocket.

It was Mackenzie this time. He picked up the call immediately.

"Hey, sweetheart…" He smiled. Talking to Mackenzie was always the best part of his day. Because of his work on behalf of Pegasus, they hadn't been able to spend much time together, but they were in constant contact by phone.

"Dylan…?" The sound of her voice was different. She sounded emotional, and elated. "We just got the test results back…"

Dylan rested his hand on the stall door so all his attention could hone in on Mackenzie's next words.

"She's in remission!"

Relieved, Dylan squeezed his eyes closed for a moment and then looked heavenward. "Oh, thank God!"

He straightened back up, looked upward in gratitude

before he shouted out to the people scattered around the barn. "Hope's in remission! Hope's in remission!"

The people in the barn erupted in cheers. He needed to tell Aunt Gerri right away. On his way out of the barn, some of the volunteers slapped him on the back, shook his hand…it was a day they had all been praying for.

"When can she come home?" Dylan stepped out from the shade of the barn into the bright, hot California sun.

"Tomorrow…" Mackenzie was understandably emotional. He wished he were there to hug her. He wished he could hug both of his girls. "Here…Hope wants to talk to her dad."

Dylan stopped in his tracks. Mackenzie had never called him that before, and she had said it so casually, as if it was no big deal. Hope only called him Dad when Mackenzie wasn't around, so he'd thought that Mackenzie didn't know about it yet. Dylan knew that the subject would have to be broached at some point, but the right moment hadn't presented itself. And, for him, it wasn't urgent. He was going to marry Mackenzie and he was Hope's natural father. That's what mattered. The rest of the stuff would work out eventually.

While he was celebrating with Hope on the phone, Dylan continued on his way to the house. He found his aunt in the kitchen, surrounded by ingredients and pots and pans.

"Hold on, Hope…Aunt Gerri wants to talk to you…"

Dylan held the phone out to his aunt. "She's in remission."

Aunt Gerri's face lit up and she tossed up her hands in the air in excitement.

Dylan sat down at the kitchen counter while his aunt chattered excitedly with his daughter. The two of them seemed never to run out of things to say.

"Well, I'm just as happy as I can be, honey…I can't wait to see you. I love you, too," his aunt said before she hung up the phone.

She came around to Dylan's side of the counter and hugged him. "I can't wait until church Wednesday night. The whole congregation's been praying for her!"

His aunt had been in rare form ever since the revolving door of volunteers had started to come to the farm. Her solitary life had vanished and she was thriving. She was energetic and talkative and her kitchen was always open for business. Dylan covered the expense of feeding the volunteer crew, and Gerri was happy to have a reason to cook every day. She fed them and then she played the organ for them. She had been intending to move to town so she could be around people, but for now, the people had come to her.

"Okay…you go do what you know how to do so I can keep doin' what I know how to do. I'll ring the bell when lunch is ready." Gerri had reinstated the practice of ringing the dinner bell Uncle Bill had installed at the back kitchen door.

Dylan opened the back door, but he paused. "Aunt Gerri…?"

"Yes, honey?" Gerri was back to peeling potatoes.

"I'd like to marry Mackenzie here, on the farm. If she likes the idea, would you be okay with it?"

"Well, of course it's okay…this is your home."

It had been a nearly impossible task, but they had managed to pull it off. The two standing barns on the property had been brought back to life. They weren't pretty or perfect, but they were functional for the horses and that's all that mattered at the moment. Uncle Bill had an office space in the main barn, so that's where Aggie would store all of her Pegasus papers, forms and files. The fence around one of the larger pastures had been repaired; some of the horses couldn't be out together; they'd have to rotate the horses until the other fences were fixed. There were still some plumbing issues at both barns, so it was portable restrooms for now. If Dylan thought about all the things left to do, it would drive him nuts. Instead, he tried to concentrate on all the things they had already accomplished.

Even now, riding in the passenger seat of Aggie's truck as she turned up the driveway to the farm, it was still hard for him to believe that this long-anticipated day had finally arrived. He could see Mackenzie and Hope sitting on the porch swing waiting for the horses to arrive at their new home. His aunt appeared from inside the house as the large caravan of trucks, horse trailers, cars filled with volunteers and several rented moving trucks.

"My Bill would be so proud of this day..." Aunt Gerri beamed at Mackenzie and Hope.

Mackenzie put her arm around Gerri's shoulder, and they stood arm and arm, watching the procession head up the winding driveway.

Hope, whose hair had already started to fall out at the hospital, was wearing a bright purple bandanna on her head. Her eyebrows and eyelashes were gone. And she was still pale, thinner than before and still weak from the chemo. There were dark rings around her eyes that made them appear to be sunken into her puffy face. But some of the light, the fire, had returned to her wide lavender-blue eyes.

"I don't see Gypsy. Do you see Gypsy?" Hope leaned over the porch railing. Gypsy was all Hope could talk about for weeks. Mackenzie had taken Hope to the feed store so she could buy a large tub of special treats for all the horses.

"She's in one of those trailers, kiddo... They wouldn't

leave her behind…" Mackenzie saw Dylan through the windshield of Aggie's truck and, as was usual nowadays, her pulse quickened. She was simply head over heels crazy for that man. She could finally relate to the lyrics of sappy love songs and the tortured words of poems. She just *loved* him. He was her special somebody.

Dylan hopped out of the truck. He lifted up his arms with a tired, happy smile. "We did it. We're here!"

Aggie was already barking orders, directing traffic and setting the second phase of the move into motion. She had already moved some of her items into the office and she had spent quite a bit of time on the farm, getting familiar with their new digs.

"What can we do to help?" Aunt Gerri's bright blue eyes were dancing with excitement. Dylan turned to look at the cars, and trucks, and trailers and people. The farm was *alive* again.

"Just sit back and watch the show…" Dylan kissed his aunt on the cheek. To Hope, he asked, "Ready to see Gypsy?"

Hope nodded and slipped her hand into his hand.

Mackenzie and Dylan caught each other's eyes and held. "I'm going to help Gerri with the food. I'm sure everyone's going to be starved…"

With one last smile, a loving smile meant just for Mackenzie, Dylan took his daughter to the last trailer in the line. Hope was like the rock star of the day; this was the first time many people from Pegasus had had an opportunity to see her since she'd been in the hospital. But, because Hope was fresh off chemotherapy, and her immune system was still weak, all the people who wanted to greet her and hug her had to keep their distance. Hope's recovery was still too fragile for her to be exposed to viruses right now. It was already a risk to have her around this many people, but neither Mackenzie nor he had the heart to tell her that she couldn't be a part of this day.

Hope ran up to the last trailer when she spotted Gypsy. She stood on tiptoe so she could touch the white star on the mare's forehead.

"Hi, there, Gyps…you've got a new home now. A better home, with really big pastures and lots of grass and your very own stall…"

Hope looked at him. "She looks okay, doesn't she?"

"Yeah…I think she looks great."

"Hey! Axel!" Wearing faded jeans, motorcycle boots, a plain white V-neck T-shirt and a black paisley bandanna on her head, Jordan appeared from behind one of the moving trucks.

"Jordan…I didn't know you were going to make it today," Dylan said.

"Are you kidding me? Do you think I'd miss a chance to hang with my favorite second cousin?" Jordan reached out, gave Hope's hand a quick squeeze before she moved back a couple of steps to keep a safe distance.

Hope smiled up at Jordan. "I like your bandanna."

"I like yours." Jordan returned the compliment and then looked around. "Man…this is quite a posse you've assembled."

"I know…I still can't believe it," he agreed. "Mackenzie's in the house with my aunt if you want to say hi."

"Yeah…let me do that before you put me to work." Jordan blew Hope a kiss before she headed toward the house.

Jordan followed the sound of voices and the smell of good food cooking back to the kitchen. Mackenzie and Gerri were laughing and talking when she showed up. Mackenzie greeted her with a warm hug and then she introduced her to Dylan's aunt.

"Did Ian come, too?"

Jordan propped her hip against the counter, crossed her arms casually in front of her. "No. He hates crowds."

"That's too bad." Mackenzie frowned.

"Ian has always been a bit of an introvert," Gerri said. "He actually got a little worse when all the girls started to chase him senior year…"

"Hey…that's right!" Jordan exclaimed. "You know Ian!"

"Like he was another one of my own…" Gerri nodded. "He didn't really start to come out of his shell until he went to college. Modeling helped. But, now, with his eyes, I'm afraid he's slipping back into his old ways…"

Jordan leaned down, elbow on the counter, chin propped up by her hand. "I'm actually thinking about getting him a service dog. He'd die before he used a cane…"

"A service dog's a good idea. Get him a man's dog, like a black Lab. That would suit him." Gerri slid a pan of cookies into the oven.

"I'm gonna do it." Jordan nodded. Then she changed the subject. "So…I hear you're *engaged* now?"

Lately, Mackenzie had been blushing. And, now she was at it again. Mackenzie smiled shyly. "Dylan asked me to marry him."

"My nephew knows a good thing when he sees it…" Gerri smiled warmly at Mackenzie.

"I'm really happy for you… He's a really great guy." Jordan straightened upright. "Is Hope over the moon?"

"Totally over the moon…" Mackenzie put a bowl in the sink and ran water into it. "We already got our marriage license."

Jordan's jaw dropped. "Uh…*wow*! Where's the fire?"

"Dylan doesn't want to wait," she said. "And I guess I don't want to wait either. Dylan wants to get married here, in front of the old oak tree behind the house."

"Well, more power to you. I'd love to do a quickie wedding, but Mom is pulling out all the stops back home. Luckily, all I have to do is sit back, let her do her thing and approve the stuff she emails me."

"Aunt Barb knows how to throw a party…"

"She does…but honestly, Ian'd love to just elope, but he promised me we'd get married in Montana and I'm gonna hold him to it…" Jordan popped a chocolate chip into her mouth. "You've got to let me and Jo take you shopping for a dress. Jo dies for that kind of stuff. She's still trying to manifest a proposal out of *Brice*. Yuck." Jordan shuddered. "You *are* going to invite the Brand clan to this shindig, right? If you don't, trust me, you'll be able to hear Mom's hissy fit all the way from Montana!"

After the horses were all settled, the feed was in the new feed room and the tack was put away in the new tack room, his aunt's house filled up with hungry folks who had been working all day. One of the front rooms was set up with long tables for an all-you-can-eat buffet. Some of the food was brought in, but most of the food was home-cooked by Gerri. With their paper plates and plastic cups in tow, it was standing room only in Gerri's organ room. For this special occasion, and particularly for Hope, Gerri turned on the Christmas-tree lights.

"I haven't seen her this happy in years," Dylan whispered to Mackenzie. Mackenzie was perched on the arm of a chair and he was standing next to her. Hope had taken the seat of honor next to his aunt on the organ bench.

"Now…" Aunt Gerri said to her audience while she looked through a songbook. "I like to start off playing 'Do Re Mi' to limber up my fingers. I usually play it two times 'cause it has all the notes in the scale, plus you've got sharps and flats and it's a gay little tune so it puts me in a real good cheerful mood." Hope looked happy; she had even agreed to wear the white, protective mask that she hated just so she wouldn't miss out on the fun.

"And—" Aunt Gerri smiled at Hope "—once I'm all warmed up, I'll play 'Count Your Blessings' just for you!"

"Come outside with me for a minute." Dylan reached for her hand.

Mackenzie linked her fingers with his as he led her to the kitchen and through the back door. They walked down the back steps, across the yard, to the beautiful three-hundred-year-old oak tree that was growing behind Gerri's house. Under the tree, Dylan kissed her, slow and sweet.

"I love it here." Mackenzie was wrapped up securely in Dylan's arms, his chin resting lightly on the top of her head.

"Me, too…"

"I can't wait to marry you under this tree.…" She rested her head on his shoulder, listened to his strong, steady heartbeat.

"Have I told you lately how much I love you?"

Mackenzie smiled. "Yes. You have. And I love you."

Dylan loosened his arms, took a small step back. Mackenzie looked so pretty in this soft, golden early-evening light.

"There's something I need to do…" Dylan knelt down at her feet, took her hand in his hand.

"What are you doing?" Mackenzie laughed nervously. "You already *asked* me to marry you!"

"You deserve a better proposal than that, Mackenzie." Dylan stared up into her eyes. "You're so beautiful to me, do you know that? I look at you and you take my breath away. I can't remember what my life was like before I met you…before I met Hope…and I don't want to remember, because none of that stuff matters anymore. You're everything to me, Mackenzie. Will you marry me?"

Dylan pulled a ring out of his front pocket and poised it at the tip of her ring finger.

"You know I will…" There was an emotional catch in Mackenzie's words.

Dylan slipped the heart-shaped diamond engagement ring onto her finger.

"It's a heart, Dylan!" Mackenzie admired the ring. "I collect hearts!"

"I remember." Dylan had her in his arms once again. He kissed her and she kissed him. They embraced in the spot where they would one day say their vows. They embraced in the soft dusky light with the sound of nickering horses drifting up from the barns. It was a perfect, stolen moment between two people who had fallen in love.

Night had fallen on the farm and there were only a few vehicles parked in the grassy area next to his aunt's house. The food had been packed up, the dishes cleaned, the tables broken down to be put back in storage and the trash had been removed. His aunt was taking requests on the organ for some of the folks who were too tired to get up and drive home. Dylan was sandwiched between Mackenzie and Hope on the porch swing. Hope was tuckered out from her day; she was leaning against him, eyes closed as they gently swung back and forth on the swing.

"I want to shave my head." Hope spoke after a long stretch of silence.

"What?" Mackenzie leaned forward to look at her daughter. "Why?"

"Because it's falling out anyway…" Hope said. "And, I'm tired of it falling in my food when I'm trying to eat."

"Are you sure?" Mackenzie asked.

Hope nodded. "Yeah…it's time."

Dylan hugged his daughter closer. "I feel like shaving my head, too. You can shave mine at the same time."

Hope perked up. "*Really*? I can?"

"No…" Mackenzie objected.

"Sure…why not?" Dylan ran his hand over his hair. "I need a haircut. That way we can both grow our hair out for the wedding."

Hope had been spending time with Dylan at his beach house. She loved the beach and she loved spending time with him. This switch was hard on Ray and Charlie because they were used to watching Hope, but their lives were changing. In fact—Mackenzie hadn't really discussed it with Ray yet—Dylan wanted them to live in his house after the wedding. She loved Balboa Park and didn't want to leave, but Hope was so happy at the beach. It was hard for her to say no.

"Where is everyone?" Mackenzie took the key out of the door. "Hello?"

She dropped her tote on the kitchen counter. There were two dirty plates on the island, not in the sink. There was a glass on the counter without a coaster. Mackenzie put the dishes and glass in the sink.

"Hello?" She checked in the den next. Maybe Dylan and Hope had gone down to the beach. But when she checked the French doors leading out to the deck, they were still locked. When she didn't find them on the lower floor, she headed up the stairs.

"Dylan! Hope!"

"We're up here!" Dylan shouted from his bathroom on the third floor.

Mackenzie heard her daughter laughing loudly. The higher she climbed, the louder a suspicious buzzing sound became.

"What are the two of you doing in here?" Mackenzie stood in the doorway, horrified.

Dylan was sitting cross-legged on the floor; Hope had a large electric clipper in her hand. Dylan's button-down shirt, his pants and his fancy marble floor were covered with his hair. Hope had used the clippers to buzz a thick, crooked line from his forehead to the back of his neck.

"I'm the barber and this is my client," Hope explained.

"Have you looked at yourself in the mirror?" Mackenzie asked him.

"I'm waiting to be surprised." Dylan winked at her.

"I have no doubt it will be a surprise," she said.

Dylan was blissfully unaware of how horrible his usually perfect hair looked. "Come join us... We've missed you."

"I've missed you..." Mackenzie leaned back against the doorjamb. "You do realize that you've come over to the dark side, right? Do you know how long it's going to take to get all of those little hairs up off the floor?"

"That's why he has a maid," Hope told her as if she said the word *maid* every day and twice on Sundays.

Mackenzie took a step inside the bathroom, arms crossed over her chest. She frowned severely at her fiancé and Hope. "Um...that would be a *no*. Dylan, we're not going to teach her that. When the two of you are done, the two of you are going to clean this up."

"Okay, Mom..."

"Okay, sweetheart..."

Hope proudly buzzed off the right side of Dylan's hair. Mackenzie covered her eyes. "I can't watch this."

Mackenzie left them to their little shaving party, grabbed a glass of wine and went out onto the deck. Her mind drifted back to their first date. She hadn't even considered Dylan date material at that point and now she was engaged to the man. Life had a way of surprising you all the time.

"It feels really cold up there now." Dylan walked out onto the deck, rubbing his shorn hair. "What do you think? Do you still want to marry me?"

Mackenzie stood up and then reached up so she could rub her hand across his shaved head. "It's like peach fuzz now…"

"Peach fuzz? And here I was thinking that I looked like a tough guy."

Mackenzie shook her head and smiled. She hugged him. The fact that he had let Hope shave his head to make their daughter feel more comfortable about shaving her own head touched her. She liked him better with his hair, but she loved him more with his head shaved.

Hope came out on the deck and the three of them went down to the beach for a walk. Mackenzie knew full well that neither of them had bothered to clean up the hair in the bathroom, but she didn't say so. The truth was, she didn't want to miss a moment with them tonight. They could always clean tomorrow.

Chapter Sixteen

Several months had passed since the Pegasus gang had moved to Aunt Gerri's farm. Hope was still in remission and her hair had grown back enough to be styled into a cute pixie cut like her cousin Jordan's. Mackenzie was busier than ever between the bakery and the wedding plans. Dylan was an involved groom, which made the planning more fun than a chore. The invitations had been sent and many of her Montana relatives had RSVP'd. Her dad and Jett were coming down from Paradise with her nieces. Hope, Jordan, Josephine, Rayna and Charlie had helped her pick out a beautiful lace fit-and-flare wedding dress with a sweetheart neckline, capped sleeves and crystal embellishments. She had worried that she wouldn't be able to find a gown that would work with her curves, but she had. This dress gave her a perfect hour-glass figure while smoothing out the bulges and bumps. In all of the weeks leading up to the wedding, Mackenzie had been stressed out about the details, but she was never nervous about marrying Dylan. And now that the big day had actually arrived, she was excited to see her family and for Dylan to see her in her dress, but she still wasn't nervous.

The two of them had spent the night at Aunt Gerri's house, while Hope stayed with Rayna and Charlie. Dylan, having an old-fashioned moment, insisted that they sleep in separate rooms so he wouldn't see her before the ceremony. The morning of the wedding, Mackenzie awakened missing him. They had agreed not to move in together until after the wedding, and with their work and Hope, it wasn't always easy to find time to be alone. Mackenzie slipped on her bathrobe and tiptoed down the hallway to Dylan's room. She quietly opened the door and sneaked in. Dylan, as usual, was on top of the sheets, flat on his back. He was bare-chested but had worn pajama bottoms to bed. He was snoring lightly; she wanted her visit to be a surprise and now it would be.

Smiling at her own stealth, Mackenzie sneaked over to the bed.

"Dylan…" she whispered.

Dylan grumbled, stretched and rolled over onto his side. She poked his shoulder.

"Dylan…" This time a little bit more loudly.

Caught off guard and groggy, Dylan opened his eyes. When he realized she was standing by the bed, he smiled at her.

"Hey, baby…" he said sleepily. "What're you doing?"

"Happy wedding day…" She smiled at him.

Dylan yawned loudly while he roughed up his short hair, grown back now from his buzz cut, trying to wake up. He rubbed the sleep out of his eyes, and when the fog started to lift, he realized that this was the morning of the day he was going to marry Mackenzie.

"Hey..." Dylan propped himself up on his elbow. "What are you doing in my room? It's bad luck for me to see you."

Mackenzie shook her head. "No...it's bad luck for you to see me in my wedding dress before the ceremony. I'm not *in* my wedding dress..."

There was a saucy glint in her eyes as she slowly untied the belt on her robe. She opened the robe and let it fall to the floor. The robe was the only thing she had put on to come to Dylan's room. And now she was standing before him, completely naked.

Dylan's eyes drank her in. She was such a sexy, beautiful woman. He loved her curvaceous Marilyn Monroe figure: the large natural breasts, the small waist, the flare of her voluptuous hips. He loved her inside and out and he wanted her all the time.

"How do you feel about your luck now?" she asked him seductively.

Dylan didn't hide the fact that he was admiring every inch of her naked body. "I think I'm the luckiest man alive."

Mackenzie laughed softly; he held out his hand to her. Her hand in his, and still standing, Dylan leaned over and pressed a kiss on her rounded belly.

"Your body's changing already." He rested his free hand on her stomach, over their growing child.

She smiled, nodded and placed her hand over his. "A little. We won't be able to keep the secret much longer."

"We'll tell everyone after the honeymoon." He swung his legs over the side of the bed, pulled her between his thighs and hugged her close.

His head nestled between her breasts and Mackenzie kissed the top of his head lovingly. They had discovered that she was pregnant soon after Hope was released from the hospital. Once she was past the first trimester, she would feel safe to share the news. But, for now, it was a sweet, private secret that she could share with her husband-to-be.

"How are you feeling?" Dylan knew that Mackenzie had started to have minor bouts with morning sickness.

"I feel great today." She pulled back a little. "I'm marrying you."

His hands began to explore her back, her hips, and the moment took a turn to the sensual. Dylan's mouth was on her breast, sending wonderful tingling to the most sensitive part of her body. She tilted her head back, raked her fingers through his hair and savored his attention unabashedly. This was her man, and there was everything right about their lovemaking.

"Do you want to go for a ride?" Dylan asked her suggestively.

Mackenzie laughed as she always did at his not-so-subtle sexual innuendos. She stripped off his underwear, knelt between his thighs and took him into her mouth. Dylan closed his eyes; he braced himself back on his arms and groaned, long and low. Dylan reached for her, hunger in his eyes.

"Come here…" Dylan lay on his back with a smile; hands behind his head and shaft hard and erect and ready for her pleasure.

Without any pretense, Mackenzie sunk down and took him as deep within her body as she could.

"Oh…" The inside of her body was tight, and wet, and so incredibly warm.

And, then she began to move. Dylan watched her ride him; she was a thing of beauty. Her head was tilted back, her lips parted as she moaned with pleasure. Her breasts, so round and full, with pink nipples moved sensually as she rotated her hips. He could feel her hair, long and loose, brushing his thighs. Dylan felt her start to tense, and he knew instinctively that she was starting to peak. He grabbed onto her hips, thrusting inside her faster and harder.

Mackenzie collapsed forward and tried to stifle the sound of her orgasm in his neck. Her orgasm triggered his and they held on to each other tightly as the waves of ecstasy crashed over their bodies. Dylan rolled her over onto her back and smiled down at her.

"God, I love you…"

She reached up to touch his face. "I love you, too, Dylan. More than I can say."

She had laid in his arms until she heard cars, *plural*, heading up the driveway. She had peeked out the blinds to discover a caravan of cars heading their way. It looked like the Montana Brands had arrived, along with the makeup artist, and *she* was still naked, post coitus, in her fiancé's bed! She quickly put her robe back on, and after a lengthy goodbye kiss, she sneaked back to her own bedroom.

"Hey, Mackenzie!" Jordan banged on her door. "We're here. Open up!"

Mackenzie had taken a shower to rinse off the evidence of their lovemaking and now she was back in her robe. She opened the door and Jordan reached out, grabbed her wrist and dragged her down the stairs.

"Come *on*!" Jordan wouldn't let go of her hand. "Dylan's aunt wants us to use the sitting room downstairs to get ready. We can close it off completely and that way the groom can't sneak a peek before you say *I do*!"

Laughing now, Mackenzie was whisked into the sitting room and the doors were closed behind her. Thanks to Ian's connections, a celebrity hairstylist and makeup artist would be on the scene later to do her hair. Her cousin

Josephine Brand was unzipping the garment bag holding her violet bridesmaid dress. Stylish, classic Josephine had helped her with every detail of the wedding, from dresses to tent rentals and everything in between.

Josephine stopped what she was doing and ran over to give her a hug. "Mackenzie! Have you seen the ceremony setup? It's gorgeous!"

Josephine was Jordan's twin, but when they stood side by side, it wasn't easy to know that. Jordan wore her hair short and switched colors every other month, while Josephine wore her hair long and wavy and naturally golden-brown.

Now that her relatives had arrived, the quiet of the farmhouse was shattered. In the hallway, Mackenzie could hear Aunt Gerri greeting her family in from Montana. She heard footsteps coming down the creaky wooden stairs, and then heard Dylan introducing himself to her family. The front door opened and the male voices disappeared. With flare, Barbara Brand slid the doors open wide and joined them in the sitting room.

"Oh, Mackenzie!" Her aunt Barb's arms were extended toward her for a hug. "I'm so happy that we're here to see you get married!"

She had always had a special connection with Jordan and Josephine's mom. Aunt Barb never forgot her on special holidays, sending her special little gifts. Many of the hearts in her heart collection had been sent to her by Aunt Barb.

Mackenzie hugged her aunt so tightly. She was the closest thing to a mom she had today, and she was so happy that they had made the trip all the way from their ranch in Montana to attend.

Barbara, very chic and trim, her platinum hair slicked back into her trademark chignon, smiled lovingly at her niece. She pulled a small box out of her Hermès bag. "Your uncle and I want you to have this... Your grandmother wore this on her wedding day..."

Mackenzie opened the aged, blue velvet box. Inside was a perfect string of antique pearls. She had seen these very pearls in a picture of her grandmother on her wedding day.

"Oh, Aunt Barb...they're beautiful. Thank you."

Her aunt helped her put on the pearls. "You're beautiful. They suit you."

Her cousins gathered around to admire the necklace, complimenting her and assuring her that it was going to go beautifully with her gown. Aunt Gerri came in with a plate of food, and then they started to prepare her for the wedding in earnest. She watched from her chair as trucks pulled up with chairs, tables and food. Her makeup was professionally applied; her hair was swept up away from her face with long, loose curls down her back. Dylan was going to love her hair this way.

She had never been fussed over so much before, but it wasn't half-bad. It was actually kind of fun and the end result would make Dylan a very happy man. Rayna, who was going to perform the ceremony, arrived with Charlie and Hope. Hope bounced into the room excitedly and hugged her mom right away.

"Look what Dad gave me!" Hope held out her hand and showed Mackenzie a ring with a small heart-shaped amethyst in the center.

"It's beautiful, just like you..." Mackenzie hugged her daughter hard. "Jordan's going to help you get ready, okay?"

There was so much commotion in the room, especially after Rayna and Charlie arrived, that no one noticed that she hadn't touched her champagne. They laughed and they talked and they reminisced and they all got gussied up in their beautiful dresses. Hope's flower-girl dress was lace with a satin sash and lavender flower embellishments; she was beaming because she was allowed to have a hint of makeup applied. When they were all dressed, Josephine, Jordan and Charlie looked gorgeous in tea-length lavender chiffon dresses, strapless with sweetheart necklines. The women in her life gathered around her and helped her put on her wedding dress.

She worried that her tiny baby bump would make the dress too tight around the waist, but it was a perfect fit.

"Oh, my goodness, you're so special..." Aunt Gerri admired her. "You're the best thing that happened to Dylan, Mackenzie, and I love you. I hope the two of you will have fifty years together like Bill and I did..."

The ceremony was set to start in less than thirty minutes. Mackenzie was filled with nervous excitement and she couldn't wait to see Dylan. She stood in front of the full-length mirror that had been brought especially for her, and she couldn't believe that the attractive woman in the reflection was actually *her*. Her dress, her hair, her makeup...the pearl necklace...made such a pretty picture. She was a bride. She was Dylan's bride.

Barbara slid open the pocket doors leading out to the foyer. Hank Brand, her uncle and her mother's older brother, was talking with Aunt Gerri in the foyer.

Uncle Hank was lanky and tall; he had thick silver hair and deep-set blue eyes. He owned and operated Bent Tree Cattle Ranch in Montana and had done for as long as she could remember. He was wearing a navy blue suit, and his cowboy hat was in his hand, cowboy boots on his feet.

"You look just like Hope did when you were her age..." Hank studied her face seriously. He was a hard man, a tough man, but there was always a kindness beneath his weathered exterior. Hank had been very close with her mother, and she could tell that it still stung, all these years later, that his baby sister had died.

As the time for the ceremony to start approached, and the majority of the guests had arrived and been seated by the old oak tree, Mackenzie went back into the drawing room so Dylan wouldn't see her before the ceremony. Alone in the room, Mackenzie put her hand on her stomach and closed her eyes. She needed to harness her roiling emotions; she could feel tears of joy and anticipation and relief gathering behind her eyes.

"You are not going to ruin your makeup!" Mackenzie whispered to herself sternly.

The door to the sitting room slid open and her father poked his head in. "I've been playing heck to find you! This place is like a maze."

"Dad!" Relieved to see him, Mackenzie threw herself into her father's big, burly arms. "Oh, my goodness! You *shaved*?"

Jim Bronson was a hefty, barrel-chested man who had worn a thick unruly beard since he had retired from the auto industry. She hadn't seen the lower half of her father's face for over a decade.

Jim smiled self-consciously as he touched his fleshy, freshly shaven face. "I have more chins now than I'd like to know about, but I wanted to look nice for your pictures."

"Thank you, Dad…"

"Now, I know I'm a handsome devil like this…" Jim said with a spark of humor in his deeply set brown eyes. "But don't go getting all attached. I start growing my beard back tonight."

Mackenzie laughed; she touched a couple of nicks on his chin. The lower half of his face was whiter than the part of his face that had always been exposed to the sunlight. "That's okay…I don't think you're all that good at shaving."

Jim captured her hand, kissed it, then stepped back and twirled her under his arm just the way he had when she was a little girl.

"You look like your mom on our wedding day." Jim's expression was more serious now, his eyes watery. Mackenzie hadn't seen her father this close to tears since her mother's funeral.

Mackenzie hugged her father again, careful not to get makeup on his white tuxedo shirt. Jim accepted the hug and then, as he always did, changed the mood from serious to joking. He stepped back and twisted from side to side.

"I'm hurt that you didn't even bother to mention my getup." Jim raised his arms to show off his black tuxedo. "Do you think it's easy to find a monkey suit in extra-big and not-so-tall?"

The door slid open and Josephine poked her head into the room. "Dylan's about to take his place and then you'll come out."

Jim looked down at his daughter proudly. He offered his arm to her and asked, "Ready?"

Mackenzie accepted her father's arm. "Absolutely."

Dylan looked out of his boyhood bedroom window at all the people taking their seats. He would be a married man soon, and he'd been looking forward to this day for months.

"Can you believe I'm taking the plunge before you?" Dylan asked Ian, his best friend and best man.

Ian was sitting in a chair next to the bed. "I didn't see this one coming…"

Dylan smiled. "Do you have the rings?"

"Right here in my pocket."

Mackenzie had wanted a small intimate ceremony and

she had wanted simple, classic gold bands. He would have preferred rings that were a little more ornate, but in the end, he just wanted her to be happy.

Dylan saw Rayna take her position beneath the oak tree, and heard his aunt start to play the organ. As they had rehearsed, that was his signal to come down for the ceremony.

"They're ready for us..."

"Showtime..." Dylan stood up, shrugged on his jacket and headed down the stairs.

Once outside, Dylan walked down the aisle and took his position next to Rayna, who smiled warmly at him. He was glad that he had Ian to stand with him. Most of the guests were Mackenzie's family from Montana. He, on the other hand, didn't have much family. He had half brothers and half sisters from his father's side that he'd never met. All he really had was Aunt Gerri and Ian. But, after today, he had a whole new family; and most important, he would have Mackenzie and Hope. The organ had been moved outside for the ceremony, and when his aunt began to play the classic wedding march, he knew his moment to finally marry Mackenzie had arrived. A hush fell over the guests, and Dylan actually felt his knees buckle.

First, he saw his beautiful Hope walking down the aisle toward him throwing petals. Over the last months, she had bounced back from her bout in the hospital. Her pixie-cut hairstyle fit her round, freckled face perfectly. And she looked so pretty in her lace dress and lavender sash. Down the aisle came Charlie, the matron of honor, and then Jordan and her twin sister, Josephine. And then finally, finally, he saw Mackenzie and her dad poised to come down the aisle toward him. He was awestruck by the beauty of his bride. He always thought she was pretty, but today, in that dress, she was an angel in white lace. The crystals on her veil sparkled in the late-morning sunlight as she walked slowly toward him carrying a bouquet of purple orchids. Through the delicate fabric of the veil, Dylan met her eyes. And, for a split second, they were the only two people in the world.

"Who gives this woman to this man?"

"I do," Jim Bronson bellowed. Mackenzie pressed her lips together for a moment so she wouldn't laugh out loud at the sound her father's booming voice disrupting the otherwise serene, tranquil setting.

Jim lifted the veil off his daughter's face and kissed her lightly on the cheek. To Dylan he said roughly, "Take good care of her."

"I will, sir. I love her." Dylan shook her father's hand and then reached out for hers.

"You are beautiful…" Dylan said to his bride.

Mackenzie's eyes were full of love for him. "I love you…"

Beneath that sprawling oak tree, and before a small group of their close family and friends, Dylan and Mackenzie exchanged their vows. The ceremony was simple and quiet and traditional, as were their vows to each other.

Rayna performed her duties admirably, but there were a couple of moments when she needed to calm her own emotions; she was so happy that her dear friend had finally met her match. Mackenzie handed her bouquet to Hope, and Ian handed the rings to Dylan. With their wedding bands securely in place, hands clasped together, Rayna said the words they had been waiting to hear.

"By the power vested in me, I now pronounce you man and wife. Dylan, you may kiss your beautiful bride…"

They leaned in to each other.

"I told them no lipstick so you can kiss me for real," his wife whispered to him.

And he did kiss her for real. He took her in his arms and kissed her on the lips, and then he hugged her so tightly that he let her know that he never wanted to let her go.

"Ladies and gentlemen, Dylan and Mackenzie Axel!"

Mackenzie took Hope's hand and the three of them walked up the aisle, as a family, while the crowd cheered for them. It had been a perfect ceremony, on a perfect California day, and Mackenzie believed to her core that this was the start of a long and successful marriage. They held the reception in a large tent beside the house. There was dancing and eating and drinking and pictures being taken. Mackenzie couldn't remember a day when she had laughed so much.

"Are you having a good time?" Dylan had just danced with Hope and now he was back in her arms.

"This is the best day of my life…" She laughed as he dipped her over his arm.

"It's almost time for us to leave for the honeymoon, you know…"

"I know." Mackenzie frowned at him playfully. "Why won't you tell me where we're going?"

"It's a surprise." Dylan twirled her around to make her laugh again. "But I'll give you a hint…it's warm, it's an island and we are taking the private company jet."

"Sounds like heaven…" Mackenzie said. "But anywhere is heaven when I'm with you."

Finally, Dylan had to pull her away from her friends and family. They did have a flight to catch. Mackenzie was having such a blast that she hated to leave, but she knew it was time. Her last duty as the bride was to throw the bouquet. All of the single women bunched together and Mackenzie counted, "one, two, three…" and tossed the bouquet over her shoulder.

Without trying very hard to catch it, the bouquet landed in Josephine's hands. Surprised, she looked over at her longtime boyfriend, Brice, whose expression didn't change when he saw her catch the bouquet.

"Josephine…you're next!" Mackenzie said.

"We'll see…" Josephine lifted the flowers up for Brice to see before she brought them to her nose to catch the sweet scent of the purple orchids.

After Josephine caught the bouquet, Mackenzie and Dylan hugged and kissed Hope goodbye with a promise to bring her something back from their honeymoon. They climbed into the backseat of Ian's chauffeured Bentley, rolled down the window and waved to their friends and family who had gathered in the driveway. Aunt Gerri came up to the car and kissed both of them.

"I love you both…" Her eyes were damp with unshed tears.

"Thank you, Aunt Gerri…for today…for everything," Dylan said.

To Dylan she said, "Bill always kissed me good-night and told me that he loved me. You do that for Mackenzie and you'll have fifty years like we did."

Gerri had the last word before the window was rolled up and the car drove away. Mackenzie waved through the tinted back window of the car until the house was out of sight. Dylan draped his arm around her shoulders and pulled her into his body.

"Are you happy?" he asked her.

"So happy…" She leaned her head back on his shoulder.

She was Dylan's wife now; he was her husband. They had a daughter and another child on the way. Mackenzie turned in his arms so she could kiss her husband. Dylan kissed her sweetly, gently, his hand on her face.

"Have I told you lately that I love you?" His eyes locked with hers.

"Yes…" she said. "But tell me again."

* * * * *

5_INSHIP1

0215_ST_8

MILLS & BOON®

Why not subscribe?

Never miss a title and save money too!

Here's what's available to you if you join the exclusive **Mills & Boon Book Club** today:

✦ *Titles up to a month ahead of the shops*
✦ *Amazing discounts*
✦ *Free P&P*
✦ *Earn Bonus Book points that can be redeemed against other titles and gifts*
✦ *Choose from monthly or pre-paid plans*

Still want more?

Well, if you join today we'll even give you
50% OFF your first parcel!

So visit **www.millsandboon.co.uk/subs**
or call **Customer Relations** on **020 8288 2888**
to be a part of this exclusive Book Club!

MILLS & BOON®

Cherish™

EXPERIENCE THE ULTIMATE RUSH OF FALLING IN LOVE